A Winters

Romance

— • —

A Regency Anthology

Jayne Davis
Christina Dudley
Judith Hale Everett
Penny Hampson
Audrey Harrison
GL Robinson

Evershire Publishing

(EP)

Margaret sent this, thanks
Dear · X
17ᵗʰ Dec 2024

To our readers:
The authors who contributed to this anthology
represent both US and UK nationalities. Spelling
and punctuation in each story may vary accordingly.

——— · ———

If you enjoy these stories, please leave a review!
We would be so grateful, and would love to
hear what you think.

A
Winter's Romance

From Margaret
how kind of you.
love Mum . xx
Many thanks
Dec 24th 2024
Xmas .

Contents

Advice to Young Ladies

by Jayne Davis

ADVICE

to

YOUNG LADIES

on the matter of

Hufband Hunting

Being a Source of Inftruction and
Guidance to help Young Ladies find a
Suitable Hufband.

by

A Lady

Printed Privately and Available Only via
Carefully Selected Perfons.

Chapter One

Consider first your personal attractions. Not all young
ladies can claim genuine beauty; if you are not so
fortunate, do recall that a skilled dressmaker can hide
various defects in the figure and, likewise, a lady's
maid can contrive a complexion that is not off-putting.
—*Advice to Young Ladies*

February 1814, London

Miss Katherine Ardley placed a ribbon between the pages
and closed her novel as her half-sister was ushered back
into the mantua-maker's salon. The soft pink of the new gown
set off Cecy's golden hair and delicate complexion to perfection.
"You look lovely, Cecy."

Cecy turned to the full-length mirror and blushed, one hand
rising to cover the expanse of bare skin above the gown.

Lady Ardley tilted her head to one side as she inspected the
new gown, then turned to Madame Garnier. "Very good, Madame,
but it needs to be higher around the neckline."

Madame frowned. "Young ladies should make the most of their assets, my lady. This gown will make an excellent first impression at the house party you mentioned."

"Indeed it will," Lady Ardley said. "But not the impression I, or Cecy, wish to make. Can you add some lace, or a frill?"

Madame gave the slightest of shrugs, then nodded and summoned her assistant to fetch pins and lace before turning to Kate. "Do you wish for a new gown as well, Miss Ardley?

"No, not at the moment."

"Are you sure, dear?" Lady Ardley asked.

"Quite sure, Mama." Papa had paid an enormous sum for new gowns of all kinds a year ago, at the beginning of her second season, and was perfectly willing to do so again. But those new gowns had failed to compensate for Kate's outspoken manner and disinclination for making meaningless small-talk. Being the same height as some of her suitors hadn't helped, either, nor had her inclination for spending time out of doors, which resulted in a complexion that often had more colour than was fashionable. Her popularity had changed when her maternal grandmother died and left Kate a moderate inheritance; she was suddenly sought after by many young bachelors. And some not so young.

"But you are going to this house party as well, *hein?*" Madame said. "You will want to make a good impression, too."

Kate paused, but although the woman was clearly in search of more business, there was a trace of sympathy in her gaze. Kate's nondescript brown hair and eyes, and her height, made it clear that Lady Ardley was not her mother; did Madame think Kate was a neglected step-child? That was far from the case. "New gowns made no difference last year, Madame. Why spend more money on a futile endeavour?" Besides, she had no wish to compete with Cecy—this year would be her half-sister's chance to shine.

Madame nodded, gave a small smile, then left Kate to read her book in peace while she supervised the modifications and final fitting of Cecy's gown. But when they were leaving, Madame put a hand on Kate's arm and thrust a small book into her hand. "This might be useful, Miss Ardley."

"But—"

"No, no—please take it, but do not let anyone know you have it."

Kate, with no idea what Madame meant, could only nod and tuck the book into her reticule as she hurried to catch up with the others.

———— · ————

Kate forgot about the book until she returned from a musical soirée that evening. It had been an informal affair, organised by the mother of one of Cecy's friends to give the young people a chance to sing or play in public to increase their confidence. Kate was past the stage of wishing to show off her talent at the keyboard—such as it was—but had been happy to accompany some of the singers.

Her maid emptied her reticule and set the little volume on the chest of drawers. When Jenny had brushed out her hair and left, Kate picked it up, her brows rising as she read the title on the spine: *Advice to Young Ladies on the matter of Husband Hunting.*

What use was that to her? She wasn't set against marriage, but she did want to marry for love. She didn't need a husband to support her now that she had Grandmama's money, so she could afford to wait until she found the right man. She wasn't wealthy, but she would be able to live comfortably enough in Bath or Weymouth, when Papa could be brought to permit it.

Amongst impecunious widows and invalids.

She shook her head. Rather that than be tied to someone who'd wed her only for the money she could bring to the marriage.

But Madame Garnier was an astute businesswoman, as well as having a good eye for colour and style. Why would she give Kate such a thing? Picking it up, she flicked through the first few pages, pausing as her attention was arrested by a phrase advising those with 'defects in the figure' to seek the advice of a skilled dressmaker.

That, then, was Madame's motive in giving her the book. 'Defects in the figure' indeed! But despite her pique, she was curious as to what advice the book might contain. Not quite curious enough to put her current novel aside, but she could take it to Paynton Hall next week.

The house party would be Cecy's first entry into society. Although Lady Ardley strongly suspected that the party had been arranged to give Viscount Paynton's heir the chance to choose a bride, that had not been her reason for accepting the invitation. Rather, she hoped that Cecy would make friends with the other young ladies present, and so assuage some of her shyness before she began to attend larger entertainments.

Kate wasn't sure if Lady Paynton considered her a potential candidate as well as Cecy. However, looking like more of a bluestocking than she was would help to deflect unwanted attention from any other young men there. There would be plenty of new subjects for her to sketch and paint.

She picked up the book again the next day, while waiting for

Mama and Cecy to finish preparing for a walk in the park. There might be some hints to ease Cecy's shyness.

Or not, she thought, having looked at the contents list. The chapter headings included *Selecting Your Target*, *Stratagems for Gaining Attention*, and *Adjusting Your Conduct to His Tastes*.

Kate threw the book onto her bed in disgust. She didn't want a husband obtained by such means. And she didn't want one who only courted her for her inheritance, but the book would have no advice on how to avoid that.

She'd had some practice at discouraging suitors last year. Perhaps she should write a booklet on how not to get married? She shrugged, and added the book to the satchel that held her sketchbook, charcoal, and pencils.

Chapter Two

It goes without saying that both rank and wealth are desirable, along with a pleasant personal appearance and an amicable nature. However, such men are in generally short supply, and tend to be snapped up very quickly.

—Advice to Young Ladies

Paynton Hall, Buckinghamshire, a week later

Benedict Paynton stood by the library window, gazing out over the park, bare trees stark against the grey sky. The windows gave onto the drive, along which a carriage approached the house.

"Another young Miss come to bid for your hand?" Ben's younger brother, Major Arthur Paynton, limped over to the window, leaning heavily upon his walking stick.

"It's not an auction," Ben said impatiently. "No matter how much it might feel like it."

Arthur grinned. "Well, if you weren't the heir to a title, wealthy, and still with all your teeth…"

Ben rolled his eyes, under no illusion that his appearance would make any difference to husband-hunting mamas. "I wish you would get married," he muttered, not for the first time. "Then Mother might leave me alone."

"Following the drum is no life for a decent woman," Arthur said. "You wouldn't want me to give up my profession just so you could avoid the parson's mousetrap, would you?"

Ben sighed. "No, of course not. I know my duty—but I've had my fill of young women who are more enamoured of my future title than my person." And he wanted to be out riding his favourite hunter, not long recovered from a sprained hock.

"Who was it?" Arthur asked.

"Who was who?"

"The woman who turned you into such a cynic. I could ask Mother," Arthur added when Ben did not reply.

"That's blackmail!" Ben protested. But it wasn't a secret, really. "A baron's daughter I was courting last year. I overheard her telling a friend that I was boring, but it was worth putting up with what happened in the bedroom to have a title when Papa dies."

Arthur grimaced. "At least you found out in time." He leaned closer to the window as the carriage drew up and a footman handed down three women. "Two more candidates with their mother, I think." He looked at Ben. "That's five young ladies so far, by my count, and only two fathers with them. I thought you'd invited some friends of yours to divert the attention of so many females."

"I did. But they're going to a boxing match in Harrow today and will come on tomorrow."

"Aren't you going to meet the new arrivals?" Arthur hobbled back to the fire and sank into a chair with a sigh of relief, rubbing his wounded leg. "You'll never remember all their names if you wait until dinner to show your face."

"Neither will you," Ben pointed out.

"They're not here to court me. Besides, I have an excuse—doctor's orders not to be on my feet too much."

Ben sighed, envying his brother a little—if *he* had been a second son, he would have been free to follow his own choice of career as Arthur had. He took one last glance out of the window, where the pale stone of his pavilion made a stark contrast with the dark water of the lake and the bare trees.

———— · ————

In the front parlour, Ben was confronted by what felt like dozens of pairs of eyes as he walked into the room. He blinked, and the crowd resolved into only three young ladies, with a handful of parents or guardians.

"Ben, I'm glad you've come." His mother crossed the room to him. "Let me introduce you. Lord and Lady Farrell, I think you know my elder son, do you not?"

Lord Farrell stood and nodded. "Pleased to see you again, Paynton. Nice place you have here." His approving gaze passed from the ornate Ormolu clock on the mantelpiece, to the equally elaborate gilded frame of the mirror above it, then on to the brightly coloured flocked wall-coverings. "Very nice, indeed."

"We have my mother to thank for all this," Ben said. The ornaments were not to his taste, but this was not his house yet and, God willing, would not be for many years to come.

"My daughter," Lord Farrell said.

"Miss Farrell." Ben bowed over the hand of a pretty maiden with glossy black hair and blue eyes; eyes that turned modestly downwards after a brief, assessing glance.

Mother moved on to the next group of people. "Sir James, Lady Gildthorpe, may I make my son known to you?" Miss Gildthorpe was a pretty brunette with a pleasant smile but had little to say in response to his remarks. Miss Neston, a serious young lady sitting next to her mother, Lady Neston, greeted him with a forced smile, but replied pleasantly enough to his attempts at conversation.

He suppressed a sigh of relief that there were only three young misses with whom he was expected to converse.

Then the door opened and Foster announced three more women. "Lady Ardley, Miss Ardley and Miss Cecilia Ardley."

Mother hurried over. "I'm so pleased you could come, Lady Ardley, and that you arrived before the snow. Foster has a feel for these things, you know. He is hardly ever wrong."

Snow?

"My husband sends his apologies," Mother went on. "He intended to be here, but has been unavoidably detained in Town by parliamentary business. He hopes to join us tomorrow."

"Thank you for inviting us, Lady Paynton." Lady Ardley said. "May I make known to you my daughters, Katherine and Cecelia?"

Katherine was the older of the two; her brown eyes regarded the room with the same assessing gaze as Lord Farrell, and he thought a faint smile of satisfaction curved her lips. The younger sister was a beauty, as her mother must have been in her day; golden curls framed a heart-shaped face with rosebud lips, and her figure was nicely rounded. Like Miss Farrell, she had modestly downcast eyes, but the blush that accompanied her quiet greeting hinted that she might really be shy. That was more appealing than Miss Farrell's pretence.

"I hope you had a pleasant journey, Miss Cecelia," he said, as Miss Ardley wandered off and Mother and Lady Ardley started to pass on news about mutual acquaintances.

Miss Cecelia raised her gaze to his neckcloth. "Yes, thank you."

"Have you come far?"

"Only from London."

"I hope you enjoy your stay here." His neckcloth still appeared to be the principal attraction, so he gave up and walked over to where her sister was inspecting the clock on the mantelpiece. "Miss Ardley. I hope you had a trouble-free journey?"

She turned. "We did, thank you. It is but thirty miles, and we stopped for sustenance at Uxbridge."

How refreshing to find that this sister could speak more than a few words at a time, as well as look him in the face. She was not as pretty as Miss Cecelia, but well enough, and her eyes held intelligence. "You are admiring the clock, I see." To his mind, it was an overwrought monstrosity, with an overabundance of cherubs, flowers, and foliage.

"It fits this room, but in general, I prefer simpler designs. And the natural beauty of marble or wood can often be more attractive than gilding." She hesitated a moment. "I hope you don't mind my plain speaking."

"Not at all; my opinion is similar." Something about her answer didn't quite ring true to him, but he couldn't work out what it was. "I trust your rooms are acceptable?" That was far from the most fascinating topic of conversation, but what else could one say to a stranger of whom one knew nothing?

"Very much so, thank you." She glanced beyond him. "Excuse me, Mr Paynton, but I see my sister needs me."

Ben inclined his head as she smiled and walked over to Miss Cecelia, sitting alone in the middle of a sofa. Such a contrast between the two sisters, in both appearance and personality.

Contrast—that was it! Miss Ardley's pleased expression when she had first surveyed the room did not fit with her stated preference for less ornamentation; Mother's taste in furnishings was nothing if not ostentatious. Perhaps she had been pleased with the room's indication that the family was not short of funds? It wasn't really fair for him to resent her assessment; a woman had to know that a husband could support her. He let out a breath and dutifully went to talk to one of the other husband hunters.

———— . ————

At dinner, Ben found himself seated between Miss Neston and Miss Cecelia. Mother was clearly doing her best to ensure he talked to the young ladies she had invited, but Ben thought she had made a misjudgement this evening. Miss Neston spent most of the meal talking to Arthur, on her other side—asking him about his experiences in the Peninsula, from the few snatches he heard—and Miss Cecelia answered most of his remarks with few words and an apparent fascination with the tablecloth. Miss Ardley, seated across the table, seemed amused by his dilemma; or was she just interested in what Arthur was saying? He couldn't be sure.

"You looked like a lamb to the slaughter when you walked in," Arthur said to him when the ladies had left. "How was your dinner?"

"Getting a full sentence from the younger Miss Ardley is like getting blood from a stone. You were monopolising Miss Neston."

"She was monopolising me, rather. Intelligent woman." Arthur rolled the stem of his glass between his fingers, his lips curving as he cast a sidelong glance at Ben. "You could do worse than choose her."

"If I want a wife who ignores me." Although that might be better than one who talked too much.

He had the next few days to get to know these young women better. Father had issued no ultimatum about the timing of Ben's marriage, only a request that he didn't delay too long, but Mother would be disappointed if he made no effort while her guests were here.

If Miss Neston really had decided against him already—the thought dented his self-esteem a little—then paying court to her would satisfy Mother without the risk of ending up leg-shackled.

Chapter Three

Some men are attracted to women who can make intelligent conversation, but unless you know this to be the case, it is advisable to suppress any such tendencies you may have. There is little more injurious to a court-ship than a man feeling that his intellect is challenged.
—Advice to Young Ladies

With many of the men invited to the party still absent, Kate found herself seated at dinner between Lady Neston and Sir James Gildthorpe. Once the usual polite enquires about journeys had been made, the conversation of both her dinner partners was aimed at finding out more about Kate and her family—subtly, by Lady Neston, less so by Sir James. Kate didn't mind; it was better than sitting in silence, and she said nothing in her answers that they could not have discovered elsewhere. And in the pauses when both were talking with their other dinner partners, she had time to observe the target of all this effort.

Both the Paynton brothers were tall, with a build that indicated a certain amount of outdoor activity. She'd noticed tiny creases beside Mr Paynton's eyes when he talked to her earlier, and supposed he must smile often—certainly more than he was doing at the moment.

Kate's lips twitched in amusement as she returned her attention to her plate. Cecy's position beside him at the table showed that Lady Paynton thought her sister was a better prospect than Kate for her future daughter-in-law.

When Lady Paynton rose to withdraw, Kate hung back a little so she could leave the room with Miss Neston.

"Miss Ardley, isn't it?" Miss Neston said.

Kate nodded. "I couldn't help overhearing some of what you said to Major Paynton. Do you have a brother in the Peninsula? You seem to have been following events there closely."

Miss Neston's face turned pink, and she shook her head. "My brother is at Oxford." She said no more until they were seated in the parlour and tea had been served. With a glance at Lady Neston at the other side of the room, she turned to Kate and murmured, "Mama wishes me to attract the attention of Mr Paynton, but my... my affections are otherwise engaged. Do not consider me as a rival, pray."

"An officer?" Kate asked, equally quietly.

Miss Neston nodded. "My parents wish me to look higher."

Kate smiled. "Do you read, Miss Neston? Other than novels?"

"Please, just call me Jane. Yes, a little. Why?"

"I have found that intelligent conversation can be most efficacious in repelling unwanted suitors." Something she could put in her booklet on avoiding fortune hunters. "It does not work on all, however."

18

"You have unwanted suitors, too?" Jane asked, then bit her lips. "I mean... That is, I am not surprised that you have suitors, but—"

Kate laughed. "I know what you meant." And by the time she had told Jane about her grandmother's legacy, and heard about Jane's captain, she felt they could become friends.

———— · ————

Mama came into Kate's room as Jenny was brushing out her hair. "Lady Paynton is proposing a tour of the house after breakfast tomorrow," she said.

"That will be interesting."

"Possibly. However I would like you to decline, if you don't mind. Mr Paynton is to give the tour, and if you are there asking intelligent questions, Cecy will not say a thing." She raised a brow. "Unless you wish to bring yourself to Mr Paynton's attention? It's obvious the family have no need of your inheritance."

Kate rolled her eyes and shook her head, then thanked Jenny and dismissed her. "I don't mind staying out of the way," she confirmed. "But I thought we were not here to find a husband for Cecy."

"We are not. But if she cannot even look a man in the face, she will get nowhere this season. If you're really interested in the architecture and decorations, the steward or housekeeper can probably give you a personal tour." Mama smiled. "Without you having to be wary of attracting Mr Paynton's admiration for your knowledge."

"He may have a distaste for bluestockings." But Mama had a point. "Very well. If the weather permits, I will have a strong urge to sketch the outside of the house, or the grounds. I noticed an elegant little pavilion near the lake."

"Thank you." Mama patted her shoulder. "Sleep well, my dear."

Kate crossed to the window, stepping behind the curtains so the reflections of the fire and lamps did not obscure her view, but all she saw were furiously swirling flakes of snow. She might need to find a different excuse in the morning.

——— . ———

When she awoke, the snow had reduced to only a few flakes drifting gently downwards. Beyond Kate's window, trees and bushes poked through the smooth white blanket covering the garden and parkland. The wind had dropped, and a bright line on the western horizon indicated that the skies might soon clear.

Over breakfast, Mama leaned towards her and spoke in a whisper. "I hope you are not feeling unwell, my dear?"

Kate suppressed a laugh. "No, Mama, that will not do as an excuse. I have no wish to be confined to my room for the rest of the day! If necessary, I will ask to inspect the library and cement my reputation as a bluestocking."

"Do not go too far to give Mr Paynton a poor impression of you, Kate, please. He could be a good match for you."

Kate shook her head. "I have no wish to put myself forward."

She sought out the butler when breakfast was over, asking if he thought the weather would improve.

"I believe so, Miss Ardley," Foster said. "We may get some sunshine, but it is likely to remain cold."

"I wondered if it would be possible to get some exercise out of doors."

"There will shortly be a path cleared to the stables, miss, if that would suffice. It is not far, but you will be safe walking there."

"Thank you." Kate couldn't help smiling as she went to her room for her pelisse and sketching satchel. Foster concealed his feelings well, but hadn't completely hidden his doubt about her sanity, wishing to brave the cold and snow underfoot when she had no need to.

Foster directed her out through the servants' back door. Paths had been cleared through the courtyard, almost feeling like walled lanes because of the snow piled to each side. Beyond the enclosed area, the path bent towards the front of the house and skirted part of the garden, heading for the stable block beyond. The snow here was piled to one side, leaving a gentle downwards incline to Kate's left—where a lawn sloped towards the main garden, she supposed.

She trod gingerly at first, wary of slipping on compacted snow. But sand had been spread and her footing was firm enough to allow her to appreciate the way the sky was turning blue above her, and the almost-blinding white of reflected sunlight from the snow. Trees in the distance were stark black, their branches limned with snow, and the golden stone pillars and domed roof of the pavilion added warmth to the scene. Turning at the stables, she paused to admire the proportions of the house. The rows of tall windows on the ground and first floors must give the interior a light and airy feel.

Kate walked back slowly, choosing a vantage point from which to make her sketch; the pavilion showed to better advantage from here than it did from the main house. She wouldn't have much time to draw before her fingers froze, but she relished the challenge of depicting this mostly white landscape. Her spot chosen, she took a step away from the cleared path and unfastened her satchel.

Absorbed in the drawing taking shape on her paper, Kate didn't hear the quiet crunching of approaching footsteps on the path.

"Good morning, Miss Ardley."

Startled, Kate turned to face Mr Paynton and took a step back. A step into snow that gave way beneath her foot. Her sketchbook, pencil, and the contents of the satchel all went flying as she waved her arms in an attempt to keep her balance, but to no avail. She fell, landing on her back in deep snow, seeing only sky above her. Snow found its way inside the neck of her pelisse and soaked through her stockings and boots, making her shiver. She struggled to sit up—not easy with her legs stuck in the snow.

"Are you hurt?" Mr Paynton gazed down at her.

"No." No thanks to him. She managed to roll over and pushed herself to her feet, soaking her hands and arms in the process.

"I'm sorry I startled you. Take my hand."

She reached up; his grip was firm, and she gasped as he hauled her effortlessly to his own level, then put a hand in the small of her back to steady her as she staggered towards the cleared path. "Thank you, sir."

He gingerly stepped down into the hole she had made in the snow, and handed her satchel up to her. "Allow me to escort you back to the house."

"No need, thank you, sir." She had no wish to prolong the embarrassing encounter. Looking on the bright side of things, by the time she had changed into dry clothing, she would have kept her promise to Mama to avoid the tour. And her undignified fall must have killed any interest he might have had in her, so she had no need to worry about that. Unfortunately, that thought did little to cheer her.

Chapter Four

*Some feign a stumble or fall to attract the attention
of their target. However, this may do little more than
make you look undignified and clumsy.*

—Advice to Young Ladies

Ben viewed the snow shrouding the landscape with dismay when he woke up. By the time it melted enough to allow travel, his friends would be expected back in Town; he was doomed to remain the sole focus of female attention for the next few days.

Arriving early in the breakfast parlour, as was his custom, he piled his plate with ham and eggs while a footman poured coffee, gloomily contemplating the prospect of having a gaggle of young misses trailing after him while he expounded on the history of the house.

"That bad, eh?" Arthur said, limping into the room as Ben scowled at his plate. "It's only for a few days, and Father isn't insisting you pick one of them. Just don't let yourself get trapped in a compromising situation."

"Mother said she'd chosen carefully—she knows the families reasonably well."

"Hmm. Miss Farrell had a predatory gleam, if I'm not mistaken." Arthur grinned. "If you hurry and eat your breakfast, we can go to the stables before the monstrous regiment arrives. You won't need to face them until you give your tour."

"Good idea." And it was. Athene was pleased to see him, and the groom confirmed that her injured hock had taken no harm from Ben's short ride two days ago.

Ben inspected the other horses, taking his time and talking to them and the grooms, until Arthur cleared his throat and pointedly took his watch from his waistcoat pocket. "Mother won't like you being late."

"Damn you," Ben muttered.

Arthur laughed. "You go ahead—don't use my slow pace as an excuse."

Ben slouched along the cleared path, until he realised that not only was he acting like a sulky schoolboy, but one of Mother's candidates was standing by the path and might witness his behaviour. It was difficult to tell who it was, so bundled was she in coat, bonnet, and scarf, but as he got closer, her height indicated that it must be the older of the Ardley sisters.

"Good morning, Miss Ardley," he said, as cheerfully as he could.

She turned and stepped backwards, her foot sinking into the snow. He reached to grab her arm, but missed, and she landed in a heap, affording him a momentary glimpse of shapely legs encased in thick woollen stockings. He kicked at the snow near his feet—somewhere here was a flat-topped wall that gave onto the garden several feet below. Once he found the stone edging, he leaned over.

"Are you hurt?"

Her denial was accompanied by a delightful view of her rear as she rolled over and pushed herself to her feet. He felt a momentary regret that her form was encased in so many layers of clothing, before reminding himself that he was a gentleman.

His footing was firm now; he reached down and hauled her up onto the path, then retrieved her satchel. She curtly declined his offer to accompany her and stalked off at a brisk pace towards the house.

"What have you done, Ben?" Arthur had come up behind him.

"I merely said 'good morning', and she stepped into the snow-drift." He shouldn't feel defensive, but Miss Ardley's demeanour had been an odd mix of embarrassment and annoyance. "Didn't hear me coming, I suppose." What had she been concentrating on so intently? He looked at the trampled snow—was that a sketchbook? He jumped down into the hole her fall had made and picked it up; the pages were damp around the edges, but her pencil drawing had not been affected.

"She was sketching your pavilion?" Arthur asked, peering over his shoulder.

Ben felt unreasonably pleased that she'd chosen his design as her subject. "I'll have Foster give this to her, and send someone to look for anything else she might have dropped."

———— · ————

Lord Farrell and Sir James had joined Arthur in the billiards room, so Ben had an exclusively female audience when the party gathered in the main hall. He had given this tour several times before, and the words came out with little thought. "Paynton Hall was built after the Restoration when the Paynton viscountcy was created. That portrait shows the first viscount."

The young ladies and their mothers dutifully examined the portrait of a particularly grumpy-looking old man in a huge wig.

"This portrait is the second viscount..." Ben continued around the hall and up the stairs, pausing at each new portrait and wishing that Mother's idea of a tour did not include such a detailed history of the family. By the time he'd reached the painting done the year before Arthur was breeched, only Miss Neston and Miss Farrell were still managing to look interested.

"You have already seen the parlour and dining rooms," he went on. "On this side of the house there are several rooms holding the collections started by the third viscount and added to over the generations."

The next half-hour confirmed his initial impressions of the young women. Miss Cecilia ventured only murmurs of approval now and then. Miss Farrell's assessing gaze passed over everything, with little smiles of satisfaction at some of the more valuable pieces, and she gave fulsome praise in every room. Miss Neston lingered by the cabinets of objects brought back from India, but said little, and the others merely listened politely and moved on when he did. He wondered how Miss Ardley might have responded to his not-terribly-interesting remarks; she had not been shy when they spoke before dinner yesterday, and if she had been rather short with him this morning, that was understandable under the circumstances. It was a pity her mishap had prevented her from joining them—a few questions from his audience would have enlivened the proceedings.

"And that is all I have to show you today," he said, when they arrived back at their starting point. "You can see the orangery and the garden follies when the snow melts. If you wish to know anything more about the collections, my mother will be happy to inform you."

He couldn't blame the young ladies for their lack of enthusiasm—if their positions had been reversed, he would have preferred to look around in his own time. But Mother had insisted that this was a good way to show her candidates what they would be getting if they were successful in gaining his hand. Not that she had put it so bluntly, but it was what she had meant.

"Is there anything planned for this afternoon?" Lady Farrell asked.

"Mother had charades or card games in mind, but as several guests have been delayed by the snow, she might have arranged something else. I believe refreshments are being set out in the front parlour."

Once they were all heading for the parlour, he turned in the opposite direction and slipped into the library, closing the door behind him; he needed a respite from attempting to converse with young ladies with whom he had nothing in common. He paused as he noted the tea things on a table near the fire, and a female head above the back of a chair facing the window. It could only be this morning's snow maiden. "Miss Ardley."

Her head jerked, then she stood and faced him. "You startled me, Mr Paynton."

He couldn't help smiling at the chagrin in her tone as he walked towards her. And at the memory of her upturned in the snow; those shapely legs would be clad in thinner stockings now, and her gown showed that while her figure was not as full as her sister's, it was of attractive proportions. Very attractive.

He blinked. Had he been staring at her? "My apologies. I trust you have recovered from your fall this morning?"

She gave a wry smile. "Now I am dry and warm again, the only damage is to my dignity. I'm glad no-one else saw."

"What was engrossing you so much that you did not hear me enter the room?"

"I was sketching." Her smile widened. "Again. Foster said there was a good view of the pavilion from here."

"It was placed to be so."

"Oh, is it a recent construction?"

"It was finished last summer. Why are you so intent on drawing it?"

She tilted her head a little, as if assessing him—or possibly wondering if he was really interested in her motivation. To his surprise, he found that he was.

"It's the challenge of depicting a scene with little colour in it," she explained. "And the building sits well in its surroundings. It must look lovely in summer." She picked up her sketch pad, looking at it doubtfully. "The real challenge would be painting the subtle shades in the snow, but I must content myself with pencil sketches for today." She glanced around the room. "I think this is your sanctuary? I will leave you in peace."

That was why he had come here, but sitting alone by the fire now held less attraction than it had five minutes ago. "There is no need, Miss Ardley. You missed the tour of the house; if there is anything you wish to know, please just ask me. And I have paints and brushes, if you would like to borrow them while you are here."

Chapter Five

*If your target has pastimes beyond the usual manly
sports and gambling, the ability to converse on these
topics, even if only to a limited degree, will stand
you well in maintaining his interest once you have
attracted his attention.*

—Advice to Young Ladies

Kate was taken aback for a moment at Mr Paynton's invitation to stay in the library, not having expected him to deliberately further their acquaintance. "That is very generous, thank you, but it would not be polite of me to hide away in here for too long. However, unless the snow melts soon, I suspect we may be staying here rather longer than we anticipated. If that is the case, I will happily accept your offer."

A brief frown creased his brow. "Should you dislike having to stay longer?"

"Not at all." It was refreshing to talk to someone who had no ulterior motive. "I supposed, rather, that you would not care for a house full of... suitoresses." She paused a moment. "Is there such a word?"

He was smiling now, with shared amusement, and it turned his face from fairly ordinary to attractive. "If there is not, there should be! But what makes you think I do not care for having you all here?"

"Your enthusiasm last night in conversing with the other young ladies Lady Paynton has invited." The words had come out without thought; she had used sarcasm as an effective deterrent to some of her fortune-hunting suitors last year, but that had not been her intention here.

He chuckled, to her relief. "It did feel rather overwhelming for a while."

"I don't imagine Cecy helped by staring at her plate for most of the meal. Mama hopes she will make some friends here and overcome her shyness, to ease her way this coming season."

"You are not very alike." It was not quite a question, but she answered it anyway.

"We are half-sisters. Lady Ardley is my father's second wife."

Nodding, he turned slightly and waved a hand at the book-shelves behind them. "Do borrow anything you wish."

There would be plenty of choice—the floor-to-ceiling book-cases were packed with leather-bound volumes. She would have no need to read the little book Madame Garnier had given her, or write her own version, to while away the time.

The bookcases were separated by panelling, which sported dozens of paintings and drawings. Kate had inspected them before settling to her own sketching; some were clearly old, the colours dimmed with time, but there were several watercolours of the house and grounds. He had mentioned having paints...

"Did you paint these?" she asked, regarding him with more interest. Watercolours were usually seen as suitable for ladies. Real artists used oils—or so everyone said.

"Yes." He seemed a little embarrassed. "Coloured sketches, merely."

They were more than that, although the buildings were delineated in more detail than the vegetation and skies. She leaned closer to a painting of the pavilion; it was not quite the same as the building visible beyond the window. Not badly drawn, but different in design. "Is this how you wish it could be?"

He looked really embarrassed this time. "No; this was one idea I considered when I was designing it."

That was even more unusual. "Actually designed?" she asked. "I mean, as opposed to telling an architect the sort of thing you wanted?"

"Is that so impossible to believe?"

She hadn't meant to put him on the defensive. "Not at all. It looks elegant, and well sited." Some imp of mischief prompted her to continue. "However, I will reserve final judgement until the snow has melted enough for me to see it close to." But she couldn't imagine she would find anything to criticise.

"Are you interested in architecture, Miss Ardley?"

"Papa is, and I enjoy looking through his books of drawings and trying to work out why some combinations of shapes are more pleasing than others. I cannot claim to know a great deal about it, though."

He waved at the bookshelves. "I have several such volumes, should you wish to peruse them while you are here." He hesitated, then walked over to what Kate had assumed was a map chest, with a set of wide, shallow drawers. He took out several large sheets of paper and spread them out. "These are the plans for the pavilion."

Kate examined them with interest, tracing some lines with a finger. "These are separate rooms inside, I think."

"Yes. I intended it to be useful all year round."

Kate listened, fascinated, as he pointed out places for serving food, the columned terrace that allowed for sitting in sun or shade, and the section enclosed by glazed doors for use in colder weather.

"There is a gravel path leading to it," he finished, "so you may be able to inspect it before you leave." His enthusiastic expression faded. "If that really interests you."

Kate was surprised at the sudden change in his manner. "Why should it not?"

He ran a hand through his hair. "My family finds my enthusiasm tedious."

"Interests differ, do they not? And I *did* ask you about it." As she spoke, he put the papers back in their drawer. Kate spotted other drawings beneath, but he slid the drawer shut, so her chance to ask about them was lost. "Thank you for explaining it to me." She glanced at the clock on the mantelpiece, surprised to see they had been talking for nearly half an hour. "I think I should leave you in peace now."

He bowed. "It has been a pleasure, Miss Ardley."

It had been for her, too. As she crossed the entrance hall, Jane Neston and Major Paynton emerged from the front parlour. "Kate," Jane said, "the major has agreed to show me some of the family collections that we didn't have time to inspect on the tour. There are all manner of things—from native beads to

Greek and Roman art, and even fossils and butterflies. Would you care to join us?"

"Thank you, yes."

Today was turning out to be far more enjoyable than she had anticipated.

————— . —————

When the door closed behind Miss Ardley, Ben crossed to the cabinet that held the drinks tray and poured himself a glass of brandy. He was not in the habit of drinking brandy in the afternoon, but he needed some now.

What had possessed him to prose on about his design at such length? Perhaps because Miss Ardley had appeared to be genuinely interested, without the glazed eyes that his parents didn't even try to hide whenever he explained his interest in designing buildings.

He had other plans, many more. For alterations to this house to make it more convenient; a more practical arrangement of service rooms; lifts that would avoid maids having to carry laden trays up the narrow servants' stairs. For a townhouse, a church, a building to house offices. If he hadn't been the heir, might Father have allowed him to study architecture and make a profession out of it? It was not a usual occupation for younger sons, but he felt it would be as respectable as becoming an attorney or physician.

His mind turned back to Miss Ardley. He had not yet given much thought to the qualities he wished for in a wife, but he knew that intelligence and mutual interests were two of them. As he'd finished explaining his design to her, he had recalled that it was not the done thing to be alone with a young lady in a closed room, and then that he had been talking to her—or possibly at her—for some time. Without that recollection, he would have shown her some of his other ideas.

He crossed to the window, gazing up at the blue sky. When he'd walked to the stables this morning, the cold breeze had been from the north. He didn't need Foster's weather sense to know that it was set to be cold for several days yet, but the idea of being confined to this houseful of women for longer than planned no longer seemed as daunting as it had at breakfast.

With that thought, he set his glass on a table and went to see what Mother's guests were doing. Getting to know Miss Ardley better might not be a bad idea, although he must not show too much partiality and raise hopes that might not be fulfilled; that meant paying attention to the other young women as well. But his resolve faltered at the open door to the front parlour as a high-pitched burst of laughter sounded.

Behind him, Foster cleared his throat. "Major Paynton has taken Miss Neston and Miss Ardley to look at the curios, sir." He gave the slightest of smiles.

"Thank you, Foster."

"One of the stable boys brought these for you." Foster held out a small canvas bag. "I believe they are items Miss Ardley dropped in the snow this morning."

"Leave them in the library, if you please." He would give them to her later—to do so now would involve mentioning her upset in front of people she might not wish to know about it.

Chapter Six

Men are often delighted to explain their own interests,
irrespective of whether they think you will compre-
hend the details.

—Advice to Young Ladies

Kate and Jane followed Major Paynton to the next cabinet, displaying marble and bronze statuettes.

"These items were brought back from Greece by the fourth viscount on his grand tour," he explained, unlocking the cabinet and removing a bronze statuette. "That was before he came into the title, of course. This is a genuinely old item, but these others are copies, as his funds didn't run to buying more antiques." He handed the statuette to Jane, and another to Kate.

Kate watched as the major turned to answer a question from Jane. Jane had said she wasn't looking for a husband, but did the major know that? If he had taken a liking to Jane, intelligent conversation seemed to be an attraction rather than a deterrent.

Might that be the case for his brother, too? Mr Paynton had

seemed to enjoy explaining his design to her, and she had been fascinated by the details. Perhaps there were other men like them, so finding a husband who had thoughts beyond gambling and sport—and who had no need of her inheritance—might not be impossible, after all.

The major reached for another object to show to Jane, recalling Kate to her surroundings. The goddess she was examining held something in her arms—did the lettering on its base give a clue? That was the letter pi, then epsilon... "Persephone?" The goddess of spring, and those must be flowers.

"You can read Greek?" asked a voice from behind her.

She started, to her irritation, and spun around to see Mr Paynton regarding her with an amused smile. Had he crept up on her deliberately? "Mr Paynton, I wish you would tread more heavily when you enter a room!"

The other two looked around at her sharp tone.

"You startle easily, Miss Ardley," Mr Paynton said.

No apology. It was *her* fault, then, was it, that he kept surprising her? He had not deliberately startled her when she fell in the snow, surely, but for this to happen for a third time in a single day could be no accident.

"You did approach quietly, Ben," the major noted.

Kate gave him a smile of thanks, then turned back to Mr Paynton. "To answer your question, I recognise the letters and can sound out names."

"You were spared the tedium of learning the language, then."

"Indeed." That was one way of describing a lack of opportunity. Not that she'd ever had a burning desire to learn Greek, but that wasn't the point. Papa had ensured she was taught French and Italian, as they were considered suitable accomplishments for young ladies. "As you were spared the tedium of learning... embroidery." She'd almost said painting.

He was still amused. "I had no wish to learn embroidery."

"How fortunate!" She put Persephone back in her place. "Major Paynton, I believe there is a cabinet of fossils. Are they from this country?"

"Oh, they are Ben's," the major said. "I'll let him explain them to you." He took a brooch from the Greek cabinet.

That wasn't what she'd intended by her request. Not at all.

"I will be happy to show you, Miss Ardley," Mr Paynton said. "I am sorry I startled you just now—it was unintentional. You have an admirable ability to concentrate closely on what interests you." Kate opened her mouth to reply, but he held up a hand. "I said 'admirable', Miss Ardley. The ability to focus so deeply is something I envy." He did look contrite.

"I accept your apology; thank you."

"The fossils are in the next room." He led the way. "Did you wish to learn Greek? I seem to have distressed you with my remarks on that as well."

"Irritated, rather." She glanced at his face, wondering how much to say. But it would do no harm to explain. "No—but Papa would not have engaged a tutor for that if I had wished to, as it is deemed more appropriate for women to learn Italian or French."

"And I congratulated you on your lack of opportunity." He gave a rueful smile. "My apologies—I can see how that could be annoying. Now, here are the cabinets—three of them, as you can see. You must stop me if I prate on too long about them."

Kate peered closely at the labels in the first cabinet. "Did you collect all of these yourself?"

"Most of them. My family used to spend part of every summer in Weymouth, and I pestered Father to be taken to Lyme Regis, which is well known as a source of fossils." He picked out what looked like a coiled stone shell. "This is an ammonite. It was fossils like this, and similar present-day shells, that led me into architecture." He turned it over, showing a flat, polished face that displayed the internal structure. "The way the creature expands its shell by growing these little cells gives it strength, and made me think about the way buildings are put together."

"I like the shapes," Kate said, tracing the curves with one finger. "The shape of buildings interests you, as well as the construction, I think?"

"Yes, indeed." He chuckled. "Between us we have an artist's eye, and an engineer's. Neither of us is a naturalist, I think?"

"I do love looking at flowers, and butterflies—even beetles— but I don't wish to study their habits."

"Colour as well as form, then?" He moved to the next cabinet and took out a hemispherical lump of rock. "This is a geode."

———— . ————

Ben kept the geode in the cabinet with its cut and polished face down because he enjoyed the gasps of astonishment when he showed the inside. Miss Ardley did not disappoint, gazing at the vivid blue banding and the crystal-lined central hollow with widened eyes.

"That's beautiful! Did you find it?"

"Unfortunately not. My father bought this as a present for me." He held it out.

Her fingers brushed his hand as she took it, turning it so the crystal facets caught the light. "I'd love to be able to paint this."

"Can you not? I would find it simpler to draw than buildings."

She lifted her gaze to his for a moment. "I can draw it, certainly, but to reproduce that deep blue accurately... I think that could not be achieved with watercolours."

"Hmm, yes, I think you would need oil paints." He saw a brief grimace, quickly gone. "I suppose your father thinks that painting in oils is not appropriate for women."

"Something like that, yes. What are these other fossils?"

Ben took the object she was pointing at from the cabinet and handed it to her, enjoying the brief contact as their fingers touched again. "Barnacles. They are similar to those found today on rocks by the shore; unlike the ammonite, which has no extant equivalent."

He realised he was in danger of giving her another lecture. And that wasn't the only reason he should cut this discussion short. "There are some books about fossils in the library, if you are interested. I'm afraid I must leave you; Mother will expect me to spend some time with her other guests."

"Thank you for showing me."

"You are most welcome, Miss Ardley. Do inspect anything that takes your interest. Foster can provide the keys to the cabinets, if they are locked." He bowed and left her examining the barnacles.

———— · ————

The hour he spent in the parlour was as awkward and tedious as Ben had expected, despite his best efforts. He asked Miss Cecelia Ardley about her home and her interests, thinking to set her at her ease, but only learned that she enjoyed embroidery and watercolours—as most young ladies professed to—and that the countryside around their home was very pleasant. And no, she didn't enjoy riding; horses were so... big. However, that was more conversation than he'd managed the previous evening at dinner. When Lady Ardley took pity on her daughter and drew her away, her place was taken by Miss Farrell. That experience was just the opposite; she was all too happy to describe her home, her gowns, her much-admired singing and painting. She even asked him about his interests and made a good attempt at appearing fascinated by his answers, although she couldn't quite hide the somewhat vacant expression that said she was no longer listening. Perhaps he wouldn't have noticed, or minded so much, if he didn't have Miss Ardley as a contrast. With relief, he escaped to the billiards room until it was time to dress for dinner.

That evening's meal went better than the first, from his point of view. Miss Neston was seated next to him once again, but without Arthur on her other side she had more to say to him. Mother had abandoned her usually strict rule about not talking across the table, and the discussion turned to passing the time until the snow melted.

"You must have planned for some bad weather, Lady Paynton," Lady Neston said, her tone coming very close to criticism.

"Indeed, but I intended to take you to visit Lord Challan, who has a magnificent orangery and loves to show it, and a trip to Amersham. I had not anticipated being confined to the estate."

"The weather is set to be sunny, though, is it not?" Miss Neston said, with a sideways glance at her mother. "So some outdoor activity should be possible."

"So Foster says," Mother replied, with a grateful nod at Miss Neston.

"We could skate on the lake," Miss Farrell suggested. "It must be safe enough."

"I'm afraid not," Ben said. "The surface would have to be swept clear, and the snow is likely to be frozen to the ice by now. It would be difficult to make the surface sufficiently smooth. However, the terrace could be cleared." He looked around the table. "Does anyone enjoy archery?"

"We cannot stand around in the cold, Ben," Mother said doubtfully.

"That's the advantage of doing it on the terrace," he said. "Only the person shooting needs to be outside. If we have the targets set up suitably, everyone else can watch from indoors." And if that went well, he had an idea for the following day.

The discussion after that was quite animated; it seemed he hadn't been the only one not looking forward to several more days cooped up indoors with the same few people. When the ladies retired to the parlour, they were busy discussing the best way to play croquet in the ballroom.

Chapter Seven

If your target shows or tells you something in which
he takes pride, be sure to admire it whether or not it
warrants such praise.

—*Advice to Young Ladies*

Mama came into Kate's room before breakfast the next morning and waited until Jenny had finished arranging her hair.

"You're not going to ask me to decline the archery, are you?" Kate asked, turning on the stool to face her mother as Jenny left the room.

Mama sighed as she sat down. "No, dear. It was painful to watch Cecy attempting to talk to Mr Paynton yesterday in the parlour. Rather, him trying to converse with her—it was no better than at dinner on our first evening. The poor man did his best, but Cecy seems to be tongue-tied in his presence. I don't know what I am to do with her."

"You did tell her you aren't expecting her to attach him, didn't you?" Kate asked, her step-mother's suddenly arrested expression making her smile. "Even if you did, it might still bear repeating. That expectation may be what is making her so inarticulate."

"Yes, indeed. I certainly *meant* to tell her and thought I had done so. However, at the moment, I will be happy if she can leave here able to talk to the other young ladies. Miss Gildthorpe seems a pleasant girl, and is nearly as shy as Cecy. Her mother is congenial, and not over-ambitious, and that connection will help Cecy when she enters society." Mama fiddled with the fringe on her shawl. "You seem to enjoy Mr Paynton's company, dear. Is there some hope in that direction? Your papa would be pleased if your fancy settled on such a man."

Kate felt her cheeks getting warm. "He is pleasant to talk to, Mama. That is all."

Mama smiled as she stood up. "That is sufficient for two days' acquaintance."

Had it really been only two days? Less than that, really, for they had hardly spoken on the day they arrived. But despite her inauspicious beginning—on her back in the snow—she had enjoyed their discussion in the library and his explanations of the collections.

The morning's archery was enjoyable, as was the indoor croquet in the afternoon, despite neither activity giving Kate the opportunity to talk to Mr Paynton again. But his idea for the following day caught her fancy when he explained after dinner. He accepted his cup of tea and came to sit beside her.

"You must have been frozen after spending all that time outside during the archery, Mr Paynton."

"It was not too bad. I had the exercise of retrieving the arrows. Were you warm enough while you were outside?"

"Yes, thank you."

"Excellent. I am planning another *al fresco* entertainment for tomorrow."

Kate nodded, curious as to what it could be.

"I thought to have a fire warming the pavilion from first light, and provide hot soup, roasted chestnuts, and pies."

"Like the frost fair?"

"I suppose so. I wasn't in Town at the time, but I read about it in the newspaper. Did you go?"

"Indeed, yes. It was interesting—a novelty—but rather cold to do anything but walk about for a while. Having a warm building to shelter in has much more appeal. I look forward to having a closer look at your design."

He gave a warm smile that reached his eyes. "I look forward to showing you."

———— . ————

Ben went down to the stables early the next morning, before anyone else had even come down to breakfast. The path to the pavilion was still covered in snow, but the head gardener assured him that it was hard-packed, and the small pony cart had already taken wood for the fire and two maids to sweep and dust the rooms.

"Housekeeper says she's makin' gingerbread, sir," he added. "And the food's to be sent down at noon."

"Plenty of time, then," Ben said, relieved that his plans appeared to be going smoothly. He headed for the servants' quarters to check the housekeeper had also gathered cushions and blankets and had made enough food so the servants who had to work in the cold would have something to warm their insides.

By the time the party had breakfasted and donned warm clothing, the gardeners had spread grit on the path. Ben walked down with Miss Farrell on one arm and Miss Ardley on the other. Arthur was not far behind, with Miss Neston, having decided to risk a possible slip despite his still-mending leg injury.

Ben did his best to ignore Miss Farrell's chatter, being more interested in Miss Ardley's opinion. "It doesn't show to best advantage in this weather," he said as they approached the building. The heaps of snow cleared from the raised terrace distorted the clean lines of his design.

"It must make a lovely contrast against the trees in summer," Miss Ardley said. "Does it reflect in the lake when viewed from the house?"

"It does," he said, pleased with her comment. "Take care on the steps," he added, stopping a few yards from the entrance. Miss Farrell dropped his arm and continued towards the open door and warmth, but Miss Ardley did not move, her gaze following the columns upwards to the base of the domed roof.

"It has a delicate, airy feel," she said. "We toured Stowe last summer. This has a look of the two pavilions there, but is more practical, I think?"

She liked it! "Yes, the ones at Stowe are little more than a shady place to sit. Shall we go inside?"

The fire had taken the chill off the air in the room, although it could not really be described as warm. Arthur and Miss Neston followed him inside and looked around the interior. Arthur had been in Spain when the pavilion was built, and his injured leg had not permitted him to venture this far from the house until today. Ben awaited his opinion with some trepidation.

"It does look well, Ben," Arthur said, clapping him on the shoulder. "What is Father's opinion?"

"Grudging acceptance," Ben said.

"Well, I think it is splendid," Arthur responded. "Don't you think so, Miss Neston?"

"Indeed. Do I take it this was your project, Mr Paynton?"

—— · ——

Kate watched Mr Paynton's face as he answered Jane. The twist of his lips when he mentioned his father's opinion of the pavilion soon gave way to a happier expression as Jane admired its appearance. While they talked, Kate moved over to the glass doors that opened onto the terrace, trying to imagine this view in summer. Sunlight would shimmer on the water, and the curve of the shoreline would no longer be concealed by snow. A few swans would glide across the still water beneath a sky of a deeper blue, with puffy white clouds drifting lazily above. It would be cool in here, even on the hottest day.

The pony cart carrying the older ladies arrived, with the other young women, Lord Farrell, and Sir James walking behind it. Kate stepped aside to give them room to enter the building.

"What is your verdict, Miss Ardley?"

Kate managed not to jump this time, even though she hadn't heard Mr Paynton approach amidst the chatter of the arriving guests. "I like it very well. It is an ideal place for entertaining in summer, but also sitting quietly admiring the lake, or reading."

He shook his head, although his lips curved in a warm smile.

"Have I misspoken, sir?"

"No, not at all. I was surprised that your taste for tranquillity matches my own. It has another feature, outside, that I did not tell you about, although it is of little use at this time of year."

"Oh? Will you show me?"

He hesitated, glancing at the other guests.

"It is too bad of you, Mr Paynton, to raise my curiosity by telling me there is something to be seen, but not to show it! You could at least tell me what it is." She raised a brow.

"Hmm, now I think about it, it might be a trifle... indelicate." He tried to keep a straight face, but Kate could see the corners of his mouth twitching. He was teasing her.

"Ah, well," she said, trying not to laugh herself. "Never mind then. If you prefer talking to your suitoresses..." She shrugged and turned towards the table. "I shall console myself with a cup of chocolate."

"Touché, Miss Ardley." He offered his arm and they stepped outside, walking around the curve of the building to the side hidden from the main house. Although this part of the terrace had not been cleared of snow, Kate's half-boots sank into it far enough to give her confidence that she would not slip. They came to a door in the wall with a set of steps opposite that led down into an expanse of snow. A very flat expanse of snow.

"Is that an extension of the lake?" Kate asked.

"Yes, and hidden from view from most directions."

"Is there a jetty?"

He smiled. "A good guess, but no. This is a pool for ladies to bathe, should they wish to. They may remove their outer garments indoors and go straight into the water without being... That is..."

"Without becoming a spectacle for the curious?" Kate hid a smile; that men—*some* men—would ogle women in a state of undress wasn't a surprise to her. "Was that the indelicate matter?"

"One does not normally discuss members of the fairer sex removing their garments, Miss Ardley."

"Not in front of females, at least." Kate closed her eyes for a moment. She really should take more care what she said to him. But he was so easy to talk to.

He laughed. "Indeed. But I would never admit to a young lady that such a thing was discussed over the port. Or anywhere else."

"Hmm. So I'm not young, or not a lady?" She tapped a finger on her chin in pretended thought.

He gazed at her with an unreadable expression, until she began to think she'd offended him. But he spoke before she could apologise.

"You are—" He stopped and cleared his throat. "I meant neither of those things." His eyes narrowed as she laughed. "As you very well know!"

"The teaser teased," was all she said. "I do like your design, Mr Paynton." She recalled the other drawings she had glimpsed in the library. "Do you have the inclination to do more? I think the park here is big enough for several more buildings of this nature."

He turned away to look out over the bathing pool, but not before she saw his frown. "Not if my father can help it. It took me some time to persuade him to allow this. He finally said I could— and I quote—'build the damned thing, as long as I don't have to hear any more about it'."

"Oh. Would you... would you wish to design buildings for others, if your father permitted?"

"I should have liked the opportunity to try. It's not a matter of Father's permission, although I would not like to cause a family upset. But everyone who knows that this is my design regards it as a mere hobby. And in my position, it isn't really possible to become an apprentice to learn—or to show that I have learned and can be trusted with a commission."

"I can see how that would be awkward."

"Miss Ardley, I do understand your frustration with the restrictions you face because you are female." He returned his gaze to her. "Shall we go back inside?"

"Something hot to drink would be welcome." She set off, walking again in the undisturbed snow. She had not gone far when her foot encountered something solid beneath the surface. Her weight was on it before she realised, and her foot slid, tumbling her into the snow but, thankfully, not off the edge of the terrace.

She could almost have cried with mortification; this was the second time she'd been so clumsy. He wasn't laughing at her this time, but when he helped her up, a pain shot through her ankle and her breath hissed between her teeth.

Chapter Eight

A feigned fall carries the risk of real injury, which could
have you confined to a sofa for some days. It would be
a rare single man who is content to dance attendance
on an invalid for more than a short time.

—Advice to Young Ladies

B en determinedly kept his eyes above Miss Ardley's gently swaying hips as she set off back through the snow on the terrace. What had come over him? As she'd stood gazing at the bathing pool, his mind had conjured up an image of her clad in only a shift, stepping down into warm summer water. Her wet garment would cling to her figure...

He'd managed to ignore the effect those thoughts had on him and answered her normally—he hoped. Now was not the time to try to work out why a woman he'd initially thought merely passable now looked so attractive, not while he had guests to face.

Then she slipped; he reached to grab her arm, but he was too late to prevent her falling. She landed heavily, lying still for one horrible moment before she pushed herself up on an elbow. He took her hand to raise her to a sitting position, then offered his arm so she could get to her feet.

"Are you injured?"

"My ankle. I think I have sprained it."

"Let me get you back into the warm, so it can be attended to." He felt an impulse to pick her up, hold her close, and have her arms wound about his neck while he carried her, but sense prevailed. If he slipped, she could be hurt again. "Can you walk if you lean on me?"

She nodded, biting her lip as she leaned heavily on his arm and put a little weight on her ankle. Small, slow steps eventually got them to the cleared and gritted part of the terrace, and a footman hurried out to assist.

Her mother and sister hastened to the door. "Don't worry, Mama, it is only my ankle," Miss Ardley said as she limped across the room towards the fire. A chair was set for her and she sank into it.

"I'll send someone for the doctor," Ben said.

"No." Miss Ardley's voice was firm. "It is only a sprain, Mr Paynton. If you can get me a cold cloth and a stool to raise my leg, it will be well enough."

He frowned. "Nevertheless, Miss Ardley, I think—"

"No—I've sprained an ankle before. It is not worth risking someone else's safety to send for the doctor, nor to drag the poor man out in the snow for something that will mend itself if I rest it."

"Kate," Lady Ardley said, a hint of admonishment in her voice. "Mr Paynton only wants what is best for you."

Miss Ardley sighed. "I know." She met his eyes with a rueful smile. "Thank you, sir. If it does not improve within a couple of days, I will be glad for a doctor to be sent for."

"Very well. I will have the pony cart readied to take you back."

"There is no need," she said, before he could instruct a footman.

He met her gaze, to see amusement there. "Miss Ardley, I am doing my best to help you!" He pretended impatience; she knew it and smiled.

"Truly, sir, I would prefer to sit here for a while and warm myself before venturing into the cold again. I have plenty of company here." She gestured to her sister, now sitting beside her, then tilted her head to one side a little. "Or would you banish me to languish on a sofa alone in the house?"

He bowed. "By no means."

Arthur hobbled over and sat in a nearby chair. "I will keep you company, Miss Ardley, if you permit." He grinned at Ben. "You cannot abandon the other guests."

He was right, curse him. Ben just had time to send a footman to wait on Miss Ardley before being waylaid by Miss Farrell, eager to praise the pavilion and speculating how lovely it would be in summer.

He nodded and agreed at the appropriate times, but wondered why her comments grated on his feelings. Miss Ardley had said much the same, and he had not found it irritating—perhaps because she had not given the impression that she expected to be here later in the year to see it.

He kept an eye on her while he talked, happy to see Lady Ardley checking she was well, and Arthur keeping her entertained.

But half an hour later, as the food was almost gone and he was beginning to think it was time the party returned to the house, he saw Arthur summon a footman. The pony cart was brought round, and the footman gave Miss Ardley his arm.

Excusing himself from his current conversation, he hurried to the door as Miss Ardley settled herself in the cart. "Are you feeling worse? Shall I send for the doctor?"

To his surprise, Arthur laughed and Miss Ardley bit her lip, although he still detected a smile. "Thank you for your concern, sir, but it was a surfeit of sympathy and concern that has driven me away."

"And I added to it." He smiled, relieved that she was in such good spirits. "Please, make free of the library, if you wish."

"Thank you."

Then Arthur gave the order to drive on, and Ben had to return to the other guests. Some started to walk back, others awaited the return of the cart, but all seemed to have enjoyed the little excursion.

Clouds were gathering in the western sky as he walked back to the house. Only two days ago, he would have been pleased to see them heralding the likely end to the cold spell and the departure of Mama's guests. Now, it meant that Miss Ardley would be departing soon, just when he wanted to find out if their friendship could develop into something more.

——— . ———

Kate accepted Mr Paynton's suggestion to use the library, and was soon settled by the fire with a fresh cold cloth wrapped around her ankle, a pot of tea in easy reach, and several novels to choose from. She enjoyed the peace for an hour, but once the other guests returned she was beset with enquiries about her ankle again. She retreated to her room, reluctantly agreeing to Mama's suggestion that she have her dinner sent up on a tray.

Perhaps that was just as well. She was getting rather too fond of Mr Paynton's company—even finding herself looking round when someone entered a room to see if it was him. That wouldn't matter if the attraction was mutual. She thought it might be, to some degree, at least. He had certainly confided in her about his ambitions, and she doubted he had done so to many others. But being a favoured companion—if she was—in such a confined company was not necessarily a sign of the regard she wanted in a life's partner. No, the test would be whether he sought her out during the upcoming season. She hoped he would.

——— · ———

Kate awoke the following morning to find her ankle still painful if she put weight on it, although the swelling had largely gone. No doctor, then, but she must rest it as much as she could. Outside, the snow was melting; tree branches were no longer limned with it, and the hedges and shrubs in the garden showed dark beneath a grey sky. Most of the road from London had been well-maintained turnpike, so they would be on their way as soon as the local lanes were passable.

She breakfasted in bed before Jenny helped her downstairs and into a parlour with a view of the gardens, then went to fetch her drawing materials and the book she'd been reading. She was gazing out of the window, wondering if she felt like sketching, when Mr Paynton came into the room.

"Good morning, Miss Ardley. At the risk of annoying you, may I ask how you are feeling this morning?"

The little quirk of his lips that showed he was teasing was one of the things she found attractive about him. "Well enough, thank you, although I think it will be some days before I can walk about without assistance."

"You may well be at home by then," he said, the smile vanishing. He walked over to the window and stood looking out. "I sent a groom out on horseback this morning—he thinks mud in the lanes will make them difficult for a couple of days, but they might be passable now if anyone cared to try." He turned back, and gestured to her sketch pad. "My offer of paints and more paper still stands, if you wish to spend your time sketching. Mother has arranged games in the ballroom, and I'm afraid I am expected to participate."

That he wished to stay with her instead warmed Kate inside. "Thank you, but the gloomy weather does not inspire me."

"I can have the geode, or other specimens brought in, if you wish to attempt those. Or there is a case of butterflies and moths."

Why not? It would be a challenge, and she didn't wish to spend all her time reading. "Thank you. The butterflies, I think. It is very kind of you."

He gave a small bow. "It is my pleasure, Miss Ardley."

That was all he said, but the words did not sound like mere platitudes. She spent an enjoyable day painting butterflies as specimens, then some fanciful scenes of what the pavilion and lake might look like in summer, still warmed by the thoughtfulness of her host. It wasn't until she retired that evening that she recalled her idea of writing a guide on how to avoid fortune hunters, and asked Jenny to look for the little book that Madame Garnier had given her.

"Can't find it nowhere, miss," the maid said, after rummaging through all the drawers and cupboards in the room, and even looking under the bed. "Are you sure you brought it with you?"

"I thought I did," Kate said, trying to remember when she had seen it last. She hadn't looked at it since she arrived at Paynton Hall. It wasn't in the satchel that held the remains of her sketching equipment—had she only intended to put it in there rather than actually doing so? "Never mind, Jenny. That is all for tonight. I will have breakfast in bed again tomorrow."

Chapter Nine

It is of the utmost import that the target of your ambi-
tion does not discover this book of hints. Allowing him
to discover that you have used any arts at all to further
your enterprise will be detrimental to your chances of
success—may, indeed be fatal.

—Advice to Young Ladies

B en rose early on the day the guests were due to leave,
half-wishing that there had been an overnight downpour
that would keep them here another day. He had spent most
of the intervening time with the other young ladies Mother
had invited, or playing billiards with the two fathers who had
accompanied them. Miss Ardley seemed happy enough installed
in the library reading books about fossils or travel, and doing
a little more painting. Although he missed her company, he
found it strangely comforting to walk into the library and find
her there, as if she belonged in this house.

Perhaps she did. He would go to Town with Mother in a few

weeks, and he could further their acquaintance. The idea gave him a pleasant feeling of anticipation.

He was first down to breakfast—even before Arthur—and once he had eaten, he took a cup of coffee to the library and stood by the window, as he often did. He looked at the path to the stables that had caused her first mishap, spilling her and her sketches into the snow.

Sketches and other things. Foster had given him a small bag that same day, and Ben had told him to leave it in the library. And then forgotten about it.

Setting his cup down, he crossed to the desk. Foster had not left it anywhere visible, or he would have found it before now, so he looked in the drawers. There it was, in the drawer he opened every time he had business matters to deal with, but Mother's guests had put paid to that these last few days.

The bag rattled as he lifted it out and, as he expected, he found a selection of pencils and broken sticks of charcoal. But there was also a small book, bound in cheap brown cloth. He flicked it open, assuming it might be a sketchbook, but the pages inside were printed. Curious, he turned to the title page.

Advice to Young Ladies on the matter of Husband Hunting

Someone had written a book about how to get a husband? Good heavens.

Well, there were plenty of books of advice to be had on all sorts of matters, and young ladies did need husbands. But 'hunting'? That was a very direct way of putting it. What he found more surprising was the book's owner. He could imagine Miss Farrell, with her calculating glances, having one, but not Miss Ardley.

He rubbed a hand over his face. Thinking back, one of the reasons he'd first been attracted to Miss Ardley was because he thought she wasn't intent on securing him as a husband. But there had been that initial, assessing glance around the parlour when he first met her; he'd assumed at the time that she was like Miss Farrell, wanting to get an idea of his wealth.

He flicked through the pages, reading snippets here and there.

> *It goes without saying that both rank and wealth are desirable...*

Of course she had been assessing his wealth.

> *Some feign a stumble or fall to attract the attention of their target.*

Had her fall into the snow that first morning really been an accident?

> *If your target has interests beyond the usual manly sports and gambling, the ability to converse on these topics, even if only to a limited degree, will stand you well in maintaining his interest once you have attracted his attention.*

She had managed a sensible conversation about architecture, and hidden her boredom well. How had he let himself think she'd *really* been interested in such things? She was no better than the woman he'd almost married last year. And just as careless—letting him find this book was as fatal to her ambitions as the baron's daughter confiding her true feelings where she could be overheard.

> *Most people enjoy talking about themselves, so be sure to allow your target the chance to do so, and sympathise with what he perceives as his own troubles.*

Ben flung the book down and put one hand over his face, recalling their conversation about his architectural ambitions. What a fool she must have thought him, even while she was pretending to commiserate with him.

Someone knocked on the door, and entered without waiting for a reply. Ben spun around, about to berate whoever it was, but held his tongue as his brother limped in. "What do you want?"

Arthur's brows rose. "Good morning to you, too, brother. I came only to let you know the Ardleys are about to leave. I thought you might wish to bid them farewell."

"So early?"

Arthur shrugged. "Lady Ardley said something about an appointment this afternoon that she wanted to keep."

Ben was tempted to ignore their departure, but Arthur and Mother would want an explanation of such discourtesy. He picked up the book and put it into his pocket. He would say his goodbyes politely, if he could.

In the entrance hall, Lady Ardley and Miss Cecelia were already standing by the door with Mother. Arthur went to join them. Miss Ardley was slowly descending the stairs, leaning heavily on the banister. Ben didn't trust himself to pretend nothing was wrong in front of other people, so he went to meet her at the foot of the stairs.

"Goodbye, Miss Ardley," he said, bowing over her hand. He couldn't manage a smile.

"I hope it is farewell, rather." A small crease formed between her brows. "You will be in Town for part of the season, will you not?"

It would be best to make things clear now, rather than risk a confrontation in public. "I will be, but our association ends here."

The crease deepened, and he saw her swallow hard before she replied. "Have I done something to displease you, Mr Paynton?"

He took the book from his pocket and held it out. "It is time I returned this to you. I have never liked deceit, although I have to say these last few days have been entertaining." More than entertaining—he thought he'd found a friend.

—— · ——

With a dawning sense of horror, Kate recognised the little book she thought she'd left at home.

"You have done your best to follow its precepts," he went on, his voice hard and eyes narrowed. "Apart from the one about not letting your quarry discover you have the book. That was your crucial mistake, Miss Ardley. You may be pleased to know that your techniques were working very well until I read this. One of the grooms found it where you fell in the snow." He thrust it towards her. "I want a wife who wishes to marry *me*, not my future title or estates."

Kate took the book, blinking as she felt tears pricking her eyes. *I won't cry, I won't let him make me cry.*

If he really thought that of her, why wait until now to say so? Her dismay began to turn to anger. He'd had it for days, but instead of just giving it back, he'd assumed she had set out to entrap him and then led her on and... and been *entertained*. He'd been laughing at her behind her back the whole time.

"Perhaps I should write a similar thing for gentlemen," he went on, the sneer in his voice becoming more apparent. "On how to defend oneself from such machinations."

She had been judged without a chance to explain. How idiotic of her to think he'd been sincere in his attentions.

Kate drew a deep breath—she didn't want her voice to wobble now. "Goodbye, then, Mr Paynton. Please *do* avoid me should we encounter each other during the season." Then she turned on her heel and hobbled towards the door. Just in time, she recalled that her anger was only towards Mr Paynton, not the rest of his family, and attempted to smooth her expression. She managed to smile and say her thanks without making it too obvious to Lady Paynton and the major that she was distressed, and took her seat in the coach. Mama and Cecy climbed in and they set off down the drive.

To think she had been seriously considering Mr Paynton as a potential husband! She still had the book in her hand. Horrid thing.

Would he have paid her the same attention if he had not been entertaining himself at her expense? Possibly it had led to a lucky escape—who would wish to be tied to a man who leapt to conclusions like that?

With a muttered imprecation, she let down the window and flung the book out onto the drive. Madame Garnier's gift had been a curse, not a blessing.

"Kate, what are you doing?"

Throwing away foolish dreams. Kate took a deep breath. "Nothing."

Mama gave her a searching look, but asked no further questions. Kate kept her gaze on the passing bare hedges and grey skies, gloomily contemplating the forthcoming season. She could have kept the book and done the opposite of what it suggested in every case—used it as advice for repelling a man.

But that would be deceitful, too. There might be some men who would like her for herself, if only she could find them.

Chapter Ten

*Attracting the attention of your target is but the first
step in your marriage campaign. Misunderstandings
often arise in conversation or through circumstance.
Do not let such troubles linger, and be prepared to
apologise if the fault is yours.*

—Advice to Young Ladies

B en retreated into the library as Miss Ardley hobbled towards
the front door, and headed straight for the brandy. Somehow, confronting the scheming minx with evidence of her plotting had not felt nearly as satisfying as he'd anticipated.

It hadn't felt satisfying at all.

He took a large mouthful of brandy, almost choking on it,
and sank into a chair by the fire. She was an excellent actress,
he'd give her that. She'd looked genuinely puzzled when he
mentioned deceit, but hadn't been able to hide her dismay when
she realised what he was handing to her. He'd even wondered if
she had been about to cry.

He should be pleased to have rid himself of a scheming hussy.

The door opened as he was finishing his second glass of brandy, and Arthur came in. He stopped in front of Ben, leaning on his stick. "What did you say to Miss Ardley to distress her?"

"I suppose finding that she had failed to secure my interest might have done so."

Arthur's brows rose, and he held something out. "Has this anything to do with it?"

Ben frowned—it was that damned book again.

Arthur sat down. "Is this what you handed to Miss Ardley this morning?"

"It is. She has been following its advice. How did you get it?"

"One of the footmen saw it fly out of the Ardleys' coach window and went to fetch it. An interesting volume. How did *you* come by it?"

Ben felt his face getting warm. "She dropped it when she fell in the snow that first morning."

"I see. Ben, you're my brother, and I want the best for you. I like Miss Ardley, and was beginning to think that she might be the wife you need. A woman I would have been pleased to call 'sister'." He stood and dropped the book on the table beside Ben. "If you knew she had this, why did you wait until this morning before giving it back to her? It looks very much like you've been leading her on."

"A groom brought a bag with the things she dropped. I only looked in the bag this morning," Ben said.

Arthur shrugged. "Even if she has been following the advice in here, it's little different from what most young women would do."

And his brother became the second person today to walk

away from him in disdain.

Could he have made a mistake?

He picked the thing up. No—there was even a chapter on 'Compromising Situations', for heaven's sake.

> *It has been known for some young ladies to force a*
> *gentleman's hand by arranging to be caught with*
> *him in a compromising position... being discovered*
> *together in a closed room could be sufficient.*

That was why she'd been happy to spend so long with him in the library that first day. His lip curled. That had failed.

What else had she tried? Falling... He turned to that part again.

> *A feigned fall also carries the risk of real injury, which*
> *could have you confined to a sofa for some days. It*
> *would be a rare single man who is content to dance*
> *attendance on an invalid for very long.*

That made him rare—he'd been fool enough to wish to dance attendance on her.

But... wasn't that paragraph warning the reader *against* feigning a fall? And why would she pretend to sprain her ankle at the pavilion? She already had his attention at that point.

Shame washed over him. He wasn't quite ready to admit he'd been wrong, but he *had* judged her based on reading only a few sentences. He turned back to the compromise chapter.

> *I should caution you, however, against using such*
> *means at all. If you have to go to such lengths to obtain*
> *a proposal, you will have set yourself up for a life of*
> *misery tied to a man who did not want you.*

He'd also judged the book itself without reading it properly. Not that he approved of most of the suggestions it gave, but it did include some sound advice as well. And there was something Arthur had said...

His brother was in the entrance hall, but so were the remaining guests, about to take their departure. He managed to get through the farewells and thanks, then dragged Arthur back into the library with him and shut the door.

"What, exactly, did you say to me earlier?" he demanded.

"That you might well have been a complete fool?" Now Arthur looked amused, curse him.

"No, your exact words. Something about when I found the book."

Arthur thought for a moment. "If you found it before today, you've been leading her on. That bit?"

Ben sank into a chair and put his head in his hands. If he'd had more time to think about it, he might not have said what he had. "When I gave it to her, I said she lost it when she fell in the snow that first morning." But there was worse. "And that the past few days had been entertaining—she must have thought I'd had it all along." He didn't look up, and there was a long, uncomfortable silence.

When he eventually spoke, Arthur's voice had lost the sarcastic tone. "Two things."

"Go on," Ben said reluctantly.

"Why was she so distressed? I don't think thwarted mercenary plans would have had her looking as she did."

That made him feel more guilty. Even more of a blockheaded halfwit—and an unpleasant one, at that. "But why would she even have such a book if she was not husband hunting?"

Arthur shrugged. "How would I know? You could try asking her."

If she would even speak to him again. "What's the other thing?"

"Why are you so troubled by it?"

Because he'd just destroyed something good. Something with the potential... no, something that was lovely, and important to him.

Footsteps crossed the library floor, then the door opened and closed.

What could he do now?

——— · ———

Mama came to Kate's room that evening as she was preparing for bed, and dismissed Jenny. She didn't say anything, but sat in the chair by the fire and waited.

Kate sighed. She had tried not to think about Mr Paynton at all, and managed fairly well during the journey. Later, when Mama went out to the charity meeting that had caused them to set off so early from Paynton Hall, she had given an account of their visit to Papa which hardly mentioned Mr Paynton, and then spent a couple of unhappy hours wondering how she could have been so taken in. But her step-mother deserved an explanation at some point; it might as well be now. "Madame Garnier gave me a book," she started. The tale didn't take long, and Mama listened without interrupting. "And I hope to never see him again," Kate finished, vehemently.

Mama nodded, looking thoughtful. "Well, you need not receive him if he calls, but please do not give him the cut direct if you see him elsewhere."

"So as not to cause gossip that might harm Cecy's chances?" That was fair—none of this was Cecy's fault. "Mama, I will be polite if we happen to meet in company. You can't ask more of me than that."

Mama stood and patted her shoulder. "No, that is reasonable. There will be someone for you, Kate, and you know your father does not mind if you don't choose for another year or so."

That thought did little to cheer her.

"Goodnight, dear." Mama paused as she reached the door. "Kate, are you sure there was no misunderstanding between you this morning? Because if he was toying with you, he is a talented actor. I really thought he liked you well enough to seek you out when he comes to Town." And she closed the door gently behind her.

Liking wasn't enough. Not without trust.

It was good that Papa wasn't pushing her to marry, but another season or two wasn't very long to find a husband she wanted. Not after she'd already had two seasons and failed. Although her friendship with Mr Paynton had been made from whole cloth, it had felt real to her; could she find another gentleman who would arouse such feelings?

She would have to forget Mr Paynton first; his intention to ignore her should help.

———— . ————

But forgetting Mr Paynton would not be as easy as she hoped. The following afternoon, she returned from making calls with Mama and Cecy to be presented with a bunch of flowers and a salver on which lay a note.

"These came for you, miss," the butler said.

Recognising the writing, her heart began to race uncomfortably as she took the note. If he despised her for husband hunting, why would he write to her? *Had* there been some misunderstanding, as Mama suggested? She swallowed hard, and managed to speak normally as she asked the butler to have the flowers put in water.

"Who is it from, dear?" Mama asked as they removed bonnets and pelisses.

"Mr Paynton," Kate said. "We are dining with the Westons tonight, are we not? I will rest in my room until it is time to dress for that. Excuse me."

Ignoring Mama's concerned expression, Kate retreated to her bedroom and sat on the bed, turning the note over in her hands. If she was determined to forget Mr Paynton, she should ignore this. And he might still be entertaining himself at her expense.

But she had not thought him vindictive, and surely she was not such a bad judge of character? Hope won over caution, and she opened the note.

> *Dear Miss Ardley*
>
> *I am writing to apologise for berating you as I did on your departure from Paynton Hall. I may have misjudged events; however, that is no excuse for my hostility. Please, will you allow me to call on you to apologise in person?*
>
> *Ever your humble servant*
>
> *B. Paynton*

The wretched book had been hers, so there was some excuse for him thinking she had set out to hunt him. And it was possible that she had misunderstood what he'd said.

She needed to find out, but perhaps she should write to him. A letter would allow careful consideration of her words, ensuring there could be no further confusion.

Finding paper and pencil, for she knew the right wording would not come easily, she began work. But she still had only a rough draft written when Jenny came to help her dress for the evening. It was easy enough to explain how she'd come by the book, but far more difficult to explain that she hadn't been husband hunting while still conveying that she might, in fact, like to have him as a husband without being so forward as to say so directly. If, of course, he had not been laughing at her for most of their visit.

———— . ————

Jenny knocked on Kate's bedroom door late the following morning as she was making a fair copy of the letter. "Miss, there's a box come for you. It's in the parlour."

Kate set her pen in its stand, happy for a distraction from the words she was still not quite satisfied with. Downstairs, she found that the box was a polished wood affair with a hinged lid, and that Mama and Cecy were waiting with avid curiosity to find out what it contained.

"It's from Mr Paynton," Mama said, and Kate's heart began to race. "It must be a reply to your letter, dear. You did ask me if you might write to him, did you not?"

"Yes, but I haven't finished it yet. Was there a note with the box?" Why would he send this before she'd even replied to yesterday's note?

"No, but perhaps there is something inside. Do open it, Kate!"

Could it be a farewell gift? She hoped not, but still her hand trembled slightly as she lifted the lid, to see numerous wrapped objects of different shapes and sizes. Taking out a long package, she pulled off the paper to reveal a set of paint brushes with thicker, stiffer bristles than the ones she normally used. A larger muslin-wrapped object turned out to be a wide-mouthed glass jar with a cork stopper, containing a set of small bladders sealed with string.

Oil paints! He had remembered something she had wished for.

With growing excitement, more for what the gift might mean than for the objects themselves, Kate unpacked another, smaller bottle full of an oily liquid, three small canvases on frames, and some folded papers. She opened them warily, but the first paper wasn't a message at all—it was covered in labelled dabs of different colours.

"What is that?" Cecy asked.

"A chart to show me what colours are in here." Kate pointed to the jar. The other papers weren't in Mr Paynton's hand, and appeared to be instructions of some kind.

"An unusual gift," Mama said.

Not only thoughtful, but an acceptance that women need not be restricted to watercolours. That she might choose how to paint. "Will Papa allow me to accept this, Mama? He never wanted me to paint with oils."

"I'll see if I can persuade him, dear. Have you found a note?"

She looked in the box once more, removing the last object. It was heavy; pulling off the paper revealed the geode she'd admired at Paynton Hall, and wished to paint. There was writing on the wrapping paper.

> *Please will you give me a chance to apologise in person? BP*

Now, her notion of sending a letter seemed far too impersonal. She would meet him, but not here, where servants might be listening at the door.

Chapter Eleven

*If his interest is so fickle that you fear losing him if you
do not hurry into matrimony, your life together will
be fraught with difficulty. Courtship is a time to get to
know each other before you are irrevocably committed.*
—*Advice to Young Ladies*

B en took the note from the salver and waited until the butler
had closed the door before breaking the seal with shaking
fingers. What if it was from her father? Or she said no?

But it wasn't, and she hadn't.

You could take me to drive in the Park if you call at 3
o'clock this afternoon. KA

The relief he felt was soon swamped with nervousness. This
might be his only chance to apologise, to explain, and to ask
if she would forgive him. He still wondered why she'd felt the
need to consult such a book, but was it so wrong for her to have
followed some of its advice if they had come to have genuine
affection for each other?

He almost drove his valet to distraction by changing his mind several times about what to wear, but finally arrived outside the Ardleys' house little more than ten minutes early and left his groom to walk the horses. Before he could ply the knocker, the door opened and the Ardleys' butler gestured him to step inside.

"Miss Ardley will be but a moment, sir."

Peering past him, Ben saw Miss Ardley's halting progress down the stairs. She met his eyes, and his trepidation eased a little at her small smile of acknowledgement. She was well wrapped up against the cold, in a thick, high-necked pelisse and close bonnet.

He offered his arm to help her down the steps. She hesitated for a moment before resting her hand on it, and did make use of his support as she made her way to the pavement. He wondered whether he should lift her into the curricle, or if she would take offence at his presumption, but she decided for him, placing her good foot on the step and swinging herself up.

She must have caught his look of surprise. "My ankle is much improved, sir, and pains me little apart from when descending stairs."

"I am pleased to hear it." He climbed in beside her and took the reins from the groom. He was conscious of her closeness as he set the horses in motion, even through the many layers of clothing separating them. A curricle was not the best place to hold a personal conversation, particularly one that might decide his future happiness; he couldn't afford to be distracted by other traffic, so he kept his remarks to comments about the weather until they passed through the gates. Then he had no further excuse to delay facing his fate.

"Miss Ardley, I..." He cleared his throat, trying to remember what he'd planned to say.

"When did you find the book, Mr Paynton?"

That wasn't quite how he'd intended to start the conversation, but it did at least get to the point quickly—and was the crux of the matter. "A groom found it in the snow the same day that you dropped it. It was given to me later that day." He glanced sideways at her sudden movement; she was staring straight ahead, her shoulders stiff, but he ploughed on. "It was in a bag with pencils and so on, and was put into a drawer in my desk. I didn't open the bag until the morning you left, and then put the worst possible interpretation on your possession of the book. There is probably little in it that many mothers do not say to their daughters."

Some of the tension left her body, and she looked towards him, twisting in the seat to face him properly, her knee pressing on the side of his thigh. "The book was given to me, and I had read only the first page or so before I lost it. However, I can guess the nature of its contents from the title." She looked away. "I cannot remember your exact words, but I took what you said to mean you had had the book all the time and were toying with me. You are not the only one to make instant, and incorrect, assumptions."

"Why did you bring the book with you if you were not husband hunting?" Ben wished the words back as soon as he said them; it sounded as if he was accusing her.

"Most single women are husband hunting, Mr Paynton, but not in the way you mean. I find the idea of scheming and plotting to obtain a spouse as abhorrent as you. I put the book with my drawing things only because I thought I might have some time on my hands and contemplated amusing myself by writing a pamphlet to advise young ladies on how to avoid fortune-hunting men. You are not alone in wishing to be courted only for your personal qualities."

"Have you been... er, hunted?"

"I am an heiress, Mr Paynton. Of sorts. My grandmother died a little while ago and left me some money invested in the funds. That, with whatever Papa settles on me, would be sufficient to live on comfortably, but not extravagantly. Despite the amount being small by many people's standards, once my inheritance was known, I was suddenly much more in demand at balls and other events."

———— . ————

Mr Paynton didn't immediately respond to Kate's explanation, then his shoulders began to shake.

"I didn't find it amusing, sir!" Just as she was thinking they could put the misunderstanding behind them, he had to laugh at her!

"No, no, Miss Ardley. I am laughing at myself, not you."

"Really?"

He stopped the curricle and looked into her face. "Really, Miss Ardley. One of the things that led me to my half-witted conclusion that morning was the memory of you appearing to assess the furnishings and ornaments on the day you arrived."

Kate felt her cheeks warm. "I did," she admitted. "And concluded that you were unlikely to need my inheritance."

"You say you did not read the book?" He waited for her nod before setting the horses in motion again. "Then let me relate some of the advice in it. It suggests taking an interest in the target's pastimes, and allowing him to talk about them."

"Your fossils, and your architecture?"

He nodded. "Allowing your target to talk about himself—as I did at length several times."

"That is common politeness!" she protested.

"Indeed it is. And, if I had had a little more time between finding the book and your departure, I hope I would have come to my senses and at least asked you about the thing before jumping to conclusions. That is an excuse of sorts, but doesn't excuse me. If you see what I mean."

Kate couldn't help but smile. "I *think* so."

"Then there was feigning a fall to attract attention."

Of course there was. "And I fell twice. I can see why you might have entertained the thought that I was doing as it says."

"A few moments' rational thought would have told me you had not, for it warned that such a fall might merely make you look undignified, and—"

"On my back in the snow with my legs in the air?" She couldn't help laughing.

"I'm loath to agree with you, Miss Ardley."

"But I must have—"

"I would not wish to offend you by agreeing that your posture was somewhat undignified." His face was serious, but she wasn't fooled—the curl of his lips was small, but it was there. "The book also warned against the risk of real injury," he added.

"The prospect of dancing attendance on an invalid not normally being something that entices the male sex?"

"Exactly! Are you sure you did not read it?"

She wondered for a moment if he was accusing her again, but no—as he glanced at her, there was laughter in his eyes. The shared amusement that formed part of the connection between them warmed her inside even while a gust of cold wind made her clutch at her bonnet.

"That was one thing you did not try, to be sure." His smile widened. "Having played your trump card early by upending yourself in the snow and thereby attracted my attention, you had no need of more... dignified tactics such as having me retrieve a lost bonnet."

"I am not going to be allowed to forget that, am I?"

"Perhaps, in a decade or so, I might stop referring to the incident."

He was presuming a lot, but she found she didn't mind. Quite the opposite.

"In truth, Miss Ardley, I did my best to keep you entertained after you were injured, given my obligations to Mother's other guests."

"I have no complaints, sir."

"Ben. My friends call me Ben."

Male friends. But was it not a sign of more than friendship for a female acquaintance to use a man's given name?

He stopped the horses, turning to face her fully. "I hope we may be friends, Miss Ardley? If I am forgiven?"

"Yes, of course."

"May I call you Katherine?"

"Only if you wish to sound like a strict governess I once had. My family and friends call me Kate."

"Thank you."

"And I must thank you for your gift. I had almost finished writing an explanation to you when it was delivered, but speaking in person is much better." She looked down at her hands. "Papa was not pleased, but did not insist I return it. However, he will not engage a tutor, and I'm not sure how well I can teach myself."

"What you need is a husband who does not presume to limit your activities."

"Do you know anyone like that?" She managed to speak normally despite her sudden breathlessness.

"I think so." This time his smile went beyond mere friendship, and warmed her to her core. Another gust of wind carried the hint of moisture with it, and he looked at the sky. "Reluctant though I am to return, I think we must, or risk a soaking."

"Will you come in for tea?" Kate asked.

"It would be my pleasure. And may we choose some places to visit together that will not tax your ankle too much?"

"I'd like that."

When they arrived back, she waited for him to help her into the house, liking his strength when he lifted her down. Liking even more the easy conversation with her family, and the plans they made for the next few days. But best of all was the feel of his hand in hers when he bade her farewell, the brief press of his lips on her skin, and the look in his eyes that said he wished it wasn't just her hand he was kissing. She almost floated upstairs to her room, wondering how she could persuade Mama to leave them alone for a little while during his next visit so she could find out how it felt to kiss him properly.

She was going to enjoy this season.

Epilogue

Paynton Hall, July 1814

B en looked across the park as their carriage approached the Hall, pleased to be home with his new wife. Kate peered out of the same window, her head enticingly close to his, and her scent mingling with the aroma of cut grass drying in the sun. He reached for his coat and put it on; he envied women their light muslin gowns on warm days like this.

"Oh, we can see your pavilion from here!"

Kate's delight pleased him; he hoped his plan for the afternoon would please her. Then he groaned as the front of the Hall came into view. "Mother has all the staff lined up to greet us." His fault for sending a note from last night's inn, letting his parents know when to expect them.

"Is that bad?" Kate asked. "Mama said it is usually done."

"Only that I'm longing to stretch my legs." The carriage drew to a stop. Ben didn't wait for the door to be opened, but jumped out and let down the step. He looked up to where his valet sat beside Kate's maid on the roof, and the man gave a quick nod.

Good—he recalled his instructions.

Ben handed Kate down. "Welcome to your new home, my love. For now, at least. I will show you the Dower House tomorrow."

"And what you plan to have done to it?"

"Indeed, if I can persuade Father to give me a free hand." He offered his elbow, and she laid her fingers lightly on his arm as they walked up the front steps together.

"Welcome, my dear." Mother kissed Kate's cheek, and Father bowed over her hand.

Behind them, the carriage went on to the stables for their luggage to be unloaded. While Kate was being introduced to the staff, Ben had a quiet word with Foster. "You received my note?"

The butler nodded. "Yes, sir. All is arranged."

Finally, the introductions were over, and Mother led the way into a parlour where tea had been set out. "You must have a proper tour of the house, Kate, dear."

"But not until tomorrow, Mother," Ben stated firmly.

"Of course, Ben. Kate will want to rest after your journey. Did you enjoy your wedding tour?"

"Very much." Very much indeed. He looked at Kate, and her blush showed she understood exactly which parts of their trip he had enjoyed the most. But she kept a straight face as she gave her own answer.

"I particularly enjoyed seeing all the houses we visited. My father is interested in architecture, but never took us to see examples. It was most educational."

Mother frowned briefly before smiling. "Oh, I see you are joking, Kate." She stood. "Well, I will leave you to refresh your-selves. Water has been sent up to your rooms."

———— . ————

"I haven't offended her, have I?" Kate asked as Lady Paynton left the room.

"Not at all. She is sensible enough to know that we still appreciate time alone together. And will do for many years, I hope. Now, shall we retire?"

She felt her cheeks heating again as she took his arm. But he led her out into the garden, not upstairs. "Where are we going, Ben? I would like to have a wash and change my gown."

"Can't you guess?"

Ahead, the pale stone of the pavilion made a shimmering reflection on the lake, and there was even a pair of swans gliding serenely across the water just as she had imagined... was it only five months ago?

He glanced down at her, with what she thought of as his bedroom look. "All the gardeners are busy on the other side of the Hall."

"Oh." But there was no bed in the pavilion.

He grinned. "I can guess what you're thinking, but you're wrong."

When they reached the pavilion, she found that there was a bed—upstairs, in a room she hadn't seen last time. The window looked to the back, along an avenue in the woodland.

"We can use this as our own private place while the Dower House is renovated for us," Ben suggested, putting his arm around her. That would be lovely. But, to her surprise, he led her back down the stairs and into a side chamber—a small room lit only by a single window high in the wall. Benches lined two sides, with hooks above. Ben crossed the room and opened a cupboard. One shelf was filled with folded towels, the other with...

"Are those some of my chemises?"

"And a couple of my shirts, yes. My valet brought them down."

Towels. Spare clothing. Another door that must lead to the lake outside...

"I can't swim!"

He laughed. "I can teach you, if you wish, but the part of the lake nearest the pavilion is only waist deep." His smile faded. "We don't have to bathe if you don't wish to, but I thought in this warm weather, it would..."

His words trailed off as she stepped towards him and turned her back; she felt the gentle tugs as he undid her gown's ties at neck and waist. By the time she had stepped out of her gown, he had shed his coat, waistcoat, and breeches.

The water was cold at first, then only blissfully cool on her skin. She enjoyed the sensation until Ben splashed her and she pretended to try to escape, laughing as he caught her. And kissed her.

"Shall we go inside?" he whispered in her ear.

She nodded, smiling in anticipation as he took her hand. There would be many happy times here with Ben and, God willing, with their children.

The End

Jayne Davis was hooked on Georgette Heyer and Jane Austen from her teens, and always wanted to be a writer, but it was several decades and several careers before she self-published her first Regency Romance. Now she has 14 romances published, all set in the Regency or Georgian Eras, and has also co-authored *Writing Regency England* to help other authors with their own writing.

Find her on Facebook and Pinterest, or scan the QR code to go to her website at www.jaynedavisromance.co.uk where you can read a free short story, sign up to her mailing list, and stay up to date on her new releases.

Acknowledgements:

Editing: Sue Davison

My thanks to alpha readers Georgianna, Kristen, Melissa and Tina, and beta readers Anu, Barbara, Cilla, Corinne, Dawn, Diane, Doris, Julie, Karen, Leigh, Margaret, Mary M, Mary R, Melanie, Nicky, Patricia, Safina, Sarah D, Sarah M, and Sue.

A Christmas Wish

by Penny Hampson

Chapter One

'I'm warning you, Miss Mortimer. You spend far too much time teaching pupils whose fees are in arrears. I won't stand for it. Concentrate on the girls who have wealthy parents and are prepared to pay, not the ones I have on sufferance.'

It was late afternoon on a damp and dreary October day and this was the second warning that Miss Pugh had issued that week.

Jane bit her lip and gave a slight inclination of her head. The headmistress's threat had unnerved her, but she wasn't going to give the older woman the satisfaction of knowing that.

'You may go.' With a peremptory wave of her hand, Miss Pugh went back to the paperwork on her desk.

Jane left the headmistress's study on legs that barely held her up. Once outside, she slumped onto a chair in the vestibule. Her interviews with Miss Pugh always had that effect.

The maid who was dusting the bannisters sent her a sympathetic look. Jane smiled back and shrugged. Now was not the time to worry. Her girls would be getting restless and goodness knows what mischief they'd be getting into. And it would be her fault.

Her nerves now steadier, Jane stood up, smoothed her faded skirts, and patted her hair into place. Miss Pugh might intimidate her, but while she could, she would give every girl in her charge an education. For where would she be, if not for the one person who'd spent time educating her?

———— · ————

Early the following morning, Jane cracked open an eye and blinked up at the frost-laden skylight above her bed. Yes, it was still dark outside. Was it really time to get up?

'Thank you, Molly. I'm awake,' she called, and the gentle tapping on her door ceased.

She pulled the coarse blanket around her shivering shoulders and cast her eyes round the poorly furnished room. A plain washstand stood against one wall with a battered chest of drawers next to it. A rough wooden chair was placed at the side of her bed. Jane sighed. It was nothing like her comfortable bedchamber at home. But that was gone.

She gazed longingly at the empty fireplace. To have a fire in her room would be nice, but Miss Pugh had ruled that fires were not meant for the comfort of the staff. Coal was far too expensive.

Bracing herself to face the frigid air, Jane sat up and swung her legs over the edge of the bed. The cold floorboards sent icy shivers through her feet as she tiptoed across the room. After lighting the leftover stub of last night's candle, she quickly washed, gasping as the cold water met her bare skin. At least it had the merit of ensuring that she was fully awake. Dressing just as swiftly in a plain blue gown – one of the few that she'd deemed suitable for her new position in life – she pinned up her unruly chestnut locks, wrapped a paisley shawl round her shoulders, and headed for the girls' dormitory.

Not all of the pupils slept in the dormitory, only those who couldn't afford to pay for what Miss Pugh euphemistically termed 'luxuries'.

'Wake up, girls,' Jane called from the doorway towards the three rumpled beds lining the far wall. There was a rustling of bedclothes and then more than one groan.

'I'm up, Miss,' yawned Lucy from her bed.

'Can't we have a few more minutes, Miss Mortimer? It can't be morning already.'

Jane smiled at the sound of little Harriet's sleepy voice. The poor child was always the last one to rise. Blonde haired and with an impish smile, seven-year-old Harriet was one of the youngest pupils.

Jane lit the candle in the wall sconce using the small tinder box nearby. Shadows flickered round the room. It was as meagrely furnished as her own.

'I'm afraid it is. And you don't want to miss breakfast, do you? You know that Miss Pugh is particular about punctuality.'

'But I'm tired,' the little girl whined.

'Come on, Harry. I'll wager I can get dressed before you.' The challenge came from the bed at the far side of the room. A small figure untangled itself from the bedclothes and rushed over to the washstand.

Jane smiled at Meg and mouthed a thank you. Meg was ten years old. She had been a pupil there for two years and had been relegated to the dormitory when the payments for her upkeep had ceased. Her father, Major Wilson, had been killed on the Peninsula trying to keep Bonaparte's troops from conquering Portugal. Jane felt a pang of sympathy. The poor girl was all alone in the world. Meg's future prospects were bleak, much like her own. Despite this, the child had not lost her cheerful disposition.

At last, the three girls were ready to go downstairs and as Jane herded the two youngest towards the stairs, Meg clutched her arm.

'May I speak with you, Miss?'

Jane nodded. 'Harriet and Lucy, walk down with a bit of decorum, please. I'll be with you in a minute.' She turned with a smile to Meg. 'What is it you wish to discuss and will it take long? You know the rules about being late to the breakfast parlour.'

Meg's eyes were bright with excitement, a huge smile almost splitting her face.

'Oh, Miss. Wonderful news. Miss Pugh told me last night that a letter has arrived from Papa's solicitor. He apologised for not contacting me sooner.'

Jane tutted. 'I should think so. Did he not think that the news of your father's demise might affect your situation here?' Then not wishing to dampen the young girl's spirits, Meg's face was glowing with happiness still, she said, 'Has he discovered relatives that will offer you a home?'

Meg's smile dropped momentarily. 'No. Not family. But Papa did appoint a guardian, one of his fellow officers. Mr Simpson – that's the solicitor's name – has had trouble tracking him down.'

Jane patted Meg's shoulder. 'That is indeed good news. Did Mr Simpson indicate in his letter whether your guardian is still campaigning with Viscount Wellington or will he be returning?'

If Meg's guardian was still in Portugal, there was every

chance that he too, would perish like Meg's father. A prospect that Jane didn't want to raise in the young girl's mind.

Meg hopped from foot to foot. 'Yes, he is on his way back to England. Ooh, Miss. If only he would visit me here at the school.'

The little girl tugged on Jane's sleeve, gesturing her to lean closer. 'Last night I made a wish that he might come before Christmas and take me away from here. Perhaps if you wished too, Miss.'

Jane blinked away a tear and nodded. 'Of course I will.' She'd wished so many times that things would turn out all right, but none of her wishes had been granted. But it wouldn't do any harm to make a wish for Meg. That might be one wish that would come true.

The little girl was still babbling on as she started to skip towards the stairs. 'He can tell me all about Papa. I can't wait to hear about all his adventures. I'm sure Papa was very brave.'

Jane sighed as she followed her pupil downstairs to the breakfast parlour. It would be far better if the fellow paid Meg's school fees and ensured his new ward's prospects improved, rather than filling her head with stories.

Jane gave herself a mental shake. Oh dear, she was being unfair. It was possible that he'd only just been advised of his new responsibilities and was even now on his way to see Meg.

Jane tapped her fingers on the table as she waited for all the girls to assemble for breakfast; despite the rules, some of the older ones were dawdling. Distractedly, she shooed them in, her mind still on Meg's news.

Was Meg's new guardian really returning to England to care for his ward as he should, or merely taking advantage of the lull in campaigning to return home and enjoy life? All the papers had been full of praise for Viscount Wellington's successful strategy in preventing the French from taking Lisbon. Who would have thought that a line of fortifications stretching from one coast to another could be built in such secrecy? It was confidently reported that there would be no more action until spring. Yes, that was ample time for an officer to return home and sort out his affairs. And not a day too soon. Two whole years Meg had been neglected.

Jane looked over at the little girl, who was still beaming from ear to ear, and prayed that Meg's excited anticipation was not in vain. If only the child's wish could be granted. But life could be unfair; she didn't want to see one of her favourite pupils condemned to a life of loneliness and poverty like her own.

Chapter Two

Lieutenant Colonel Nicholas Anstruther gripped the ship's rail as another wave broke against the side, the cold, salty water soaking his greatcoat. Still it was better than being below decks. He was not a natural sailor and the pitching and tossing was far worse when confined to a crowded cabin. But what had he expected? The voyage from Lisbon was never the smoothest at this time of year. If he'd had the option, he'd have delayed his journey home until spring and calmer weather. But General Hill had insisted.

Nicholas chuckled. No wonder the general was nicknamed 'Daddy Hill'; he took the welfare of his men very seriously.

'Get home and sort out your estate, Colonel. You've barely recovered from your injuries at Bussaco.'

There wasn't only his estate to deal with. When his solicitor had written to inform him that he was now guardian to a child he'd never met, his shock had been greater than when he'd been informed of his father's death. At least, that had been expected, for his sire was well on in years. But guardian to a child?

Nicholas shook his head.

What had Major Richard Wilson been thinking to put his daughter in the care of his one unmarried friend? There was only one conclusion – he must have been delirious when he'd added that stipulation to his will. To make matters worse, two years had passed since Richard had died at Vimeiro and this new responsibility had only just been brought to his attention. Nicholas grimaced. What had happened to the child? Was someone caring for her?

Nicholas groaned as the ship pitched to one side, but not solely because of the rough sea. What did he know about children? Nothing. His mouth twisted into a wry smile. Well, he was shortly about to find out.

Through the sheets of rain obscuring the view ahead, a welcome coastline gradually emerged. Steep green hillsides dotted with sheep gave way to dense stark woodland, whose bare branches indicated the advance of winter. In between, rugged rocky outcrops were interspersed with small sandy beaches.

This was England.

The opening of a large estuary appeared, filled with craft of all sizes, some at anchor and others preparing to set sail. A fortified castle loomed into view on a promontory guarding the entrance of the estuary. Nicholas heaved a sigh. Pendennis Castle, a sign his journey was near its end.

The ship's rudder turned and the Lisbon packet's prow veered towards the Carrick Roads, the name given to the busy estuary. The bustling quays of Falmouth Harbour were crowded with fishermen, traders, and sailors, their noise carrying over the choppy water. Nicholas watched as the ship's crew skilfully lowered the sails and made ready to drop anchor. Soon he would be on dry land.

'Colonel, I've got your things all ready to be taken off.' The familiar voice of Penrose, his batman, broke Nicholas' concentration and he turned to see his servant saluting. A seasoned campaigner, Penrose had readily agreed to escort Nicholas, his commanding officer, on his final journey home.

'Thank you, Penrose, but there's no need to salute any more. I'm almost a civilian now, or will be as soon as I resign my commission.' He pointed to the nearing coastline. 'You must be pleased to be back in the county of your birth.'

Penrose shrugged and scratched his chin. 'Sorry, sir. I forgot. Old habits. Yes, might get a chance to visit my cousin. He lives hereabouts.' The older man's eyes squinted into the distance. 'I see we're docking at the King's Arms Quay. You'll need to get over to Green Bank, sir. The Royal Hotel there has a name for good accommodation and the mail coach leaves from there. I 'xpect you'll be wanting to head for London or your estate pretty soon.'

'Hmm, I might stay here a few days. I'm in no hurry to get back to Oxfordshire.'

Penrose cocked his head and sent his master a knowing look. 'Don't want 'em to see your face?'

Nicholas' hand automatically flew to the patch covering what had been his left eye.

'I rather think that I need to accustom myself to dealing with the world with only one eye before I go hurling myself into estate business. Besides, there's no family to speak of, so no-one to upset.'

'You'll manage, sir, I'm sure.' The older man's face lit up. 'I know, sir. You should call on the governor of Pendennis Castle.'

Nicholas frowned. 'Now why should I do that?'

The last thing he wanted was to mix with military men boasting about their exploits now his own army career had been so abruptly cut short.

'Governor Melvill was badly wounded out in India. Nearly died. Now he's lieutenant general of Pendennis Castle. According to my cousin, he's done a lot for soldiers who've been invalided out. He might be worth talking to … if you're struggling like.'

Nicholas bit back the retort on the tip of his tongue. The fellow meant well. It would be unfair to reprimand him, especially as Penrose had stoically put up with his short temper ever since they'd departed Lisbon.

Nicholas' fists curled and uncurled at his sides. Why, oh why had the French musket ball found only his eye and not killed him outright? How he hated his lack of sight, the scars, the pain, and the unwanted attention they brought. Yes, death would have been preferable to maiming. He was not good company.

Taking a deep breath, Nicholas replied, 'Governor Melvill, you say? I'll think on it. He sounds like an interesting man.'

After the mail packets were unloaded – the first items off the ship – the passengers and the rest of the cargo were taken ashore. It wasn't long before Nicholas was ensconced in a cosy private parlour with a tankard of ale to hand and the promise of a tasty dinner to come. He gazed into the glowing coals of the fire, nursing his drink. It was good to be back on dry land. He should be rejoicing, not feeling morose. But he'd give anything to be on the next packet back to Lisbon.

How was he going to deal with the rest of his days? Already he was missing the camaraderie of army life, the excitement, and the danger. How could running an estate and looking after a child compete with that?

Absent-mindedly stroking his chin, rough with a day's stubble – the sea had been too choppy for Penrose to attempt a shave that morning – Nicholas remembered that Penrose had recommended his nephew as a potential valet. It would be good to test the young man's shaving skills when he turned up for an interview in the morning ... that's if he hadn't been pressed into service on one of His Majesty's ships in the meantime. According to the landlord, the press-gangs were always on the lookout for likely fellows in these parts.

Nicholas' fingers wandered from his chin to the eye patch and the puckered skin surrounding it. The surgeon had reassured him that its appearance would improve given time.

Nicholas snorted. He hadn't believed it then and he didn't believe it now. His face, or at least half of it, was a mess. Still, he could have lost both eyes and been rendered totally blind. Now that would have been a disaster.

He slammed his tankard down on the table. There must be more to life than the army. If only he knew what it was.

He should have had a family of his own by now, but here he was, at the age of six and thirty still single and not a hope of attracting a wife. He'd left it too late.

Joining the army had been his way of dealing with rejection from the one female he'd plucked up courage to propose to. What had happened to Phoebe Travis? Probably married to a dull man and mother to lots of dull children. And she wouldn't give him a second glance now, despite his honours and prize money. Looks had meant everything to her.

Nicholas took another appreciative swig from his tankard. The ale was rather good. His mind went back to Phoebe. It had merely been a youthful infatuation. His heart had not been injured, just his pride. He should have rejoiced at escaping parson's noose. Instead, he'd rushed off in a fit of pique to join the army.

Purchasing a commission at the age of two and twenty was the best thing he'd done. He'd travelled to India, Germany, Denmark, and finally Portugal, his career mirroring that of his commander, Lieutenant General Viscount Wellington. Pity he didn't have the influential familial connections that his commander had or perhaps he too would have been promoted to the same dizzy heights. Also a pity that he hadn't followed Wellington's lead in returning home and securing himself a wife. But he had achieved the rank of lieutenant colonel and had been looking forward to chasing Napoleon's forces back into Spain.

Now, his army career was over. And no wife was waiting for him.

Nicholas gripped the tankard, his knuckles showing white, and drank until he'd drained the contents.

—— · ——

'Miss Mortimer, I want a word with you in my office.'

A shiver of apprehension slithered down Jane's spine. What had she done wrong now? Her stomach lurched. Had it been discovered that she was still teaching little Harriet, Meg, and Lucy?

No matter how hard she tried, she always seemed to upset Miss Pugh. It had been like that ever since she'd started working as a teacher at the Academy two years previously. Miss Fenwick, the deputy headmistress, had appointed her in Miss Pugh's absence and, as far as Jane could tell, Miss Pugh had barely forgiven her deputy. Luckily for Jane, parents who wished for their daughters to be taught Latin and French were sufficient in number for her to keep her position … at least for now.

Jane's skill in these languages was one of the few benefits of being a scholar's daughter; if only her father had spent as much time on his accounts and remaining solvent.

'Yes, Miss Pugh?' Jane stood in front of Miss Pugh's desk, feeling very much like a pupil herself.

'Take a seat.' Miss Pugh gestured to a chair without looking up.

Jane sat down.

Surely if this was her dismissal, she wouldn't have been told to sit.

After a few minutes, Miss Pugh set her pen down, removed her glasses, and looked over the desk at Jane. Her lips parted, revealing prominent teeth. Jane was reminded of a malevolent rabbit. Shockingly, Miss Pugh was smiling.

'You have no doubt heard that the child, Meg Wilson, has been notified by her late father's solicitor that her guardian has been found?'

Jane nodded. Where was this leading?

'I'm very keen to keep the child here,' said Miss Pugh.

Jane forced a smile and nodded again. So that was what the wily termagant was worried about.

'I thought perhaps that, as you seem to be close to the child, you would be able to explain to her guardian how well she is doing, and how she would benefit by remaining here.'

'Surely, that would be better coming from you, Miss Pugh. After all, you are the headmistress.'

Jane held her breath. It wasn't often that she stood up to Miss Pugh.

A sound came out of Miss Pugh's mouth. A strangled form of laughter.

'But you know her rather better. Yes, I think when the gentleman arrives I will greet him, of course, but I will leave it to you to show him the school and let him know the comfort as well as the learning that his ward enjoys here.'

Jane frowned. Show him the attic dormitory where Meg was housed? That would impress no-one.

Before she could reply, Miss Pugh spoke again.

'Of course, I've arranged for little Meg to be moved to one of the bedchambers on the first floor. The one with the fireplace and the rather pleasant view.' Her steely eyes narrowed. 'I'm determined to recoup, at the very least, all the charges she has incurred in the interim since her father's death. And I needn't point out that if Meg is removed from our care, I will hold you personally responsible.' She paused. 'Do we understand each other, Miss Mortimer?'

Jane swallowed. 'Yes.'

Once outside the office, Jane's shoulders slumped. What should she do? It wasn't in her nature to lie. But if she told the truth about the conditions that Meg had really enjoyed, her guardian, if he was a decent man, would have no option but to remove his ward. And it would mean dismissal for her.

Jane walked blindly towards her classroom, her thoughts tangled by the predicament that Miss Pugh had placed her in. It was unlikely that she'd find another position as a teacher in Bath. She didn't have funds to travel far in search of employment. And on top of everything, it was getting close to Christmas. If he should arrive before then, Meg's prayers would be answered. But would hers?

Christmas had always been one of her favourite times of the year, but not anymore. The last two Christmases spent at the Academy had been grim affairs, despite her best efforts. She had done her utmost to make things pleasant for those girls who were forced to remain there over the festive period. There were always one or two pupils whose families did not want them, or who had no family at all, and Miss Pugh was happy to let them stay, on condition that they earned their keep by cleaning or sewing.

Jane shuddered. Without a home or a position, her Christmas would be even worse.

She pulled a handkerchief from her sleeve and halted before the classroom door. Wiping her eyes, she took a deep breath, squared her shoulders, and pasted a cheery smile on her face before greeting her pupils.

'Now, girls, I thought we might decline some verbs, then afterwards, if the weather holds, we can go out for a walk.'

Chapter Three

Nicholas remained in Falmouth for several days, finding that the bustling pace of the town suited him. He followed his batman's advice and visited Pendennis Castle, where Governor Melvill and his wife, Elizabeth, made him very welcome. Melvill took Nicholas on a tour of the fortifications, showing him the men's barracks and the original castle structure, built in the time of King Henry VIII. With windows on three sides, the main tower had a commanding view of the Carrick Roads estuary, the open sea, and the adjacent coastline.

'Very impressive,' acknowledged Nicholas. 'If the French ever proceed with their invasion plans, they'll not get far if they pick this location to commence their campaign.'

Melvill chuckled. 'Yes, my men will be ready for them. They may be an Invalid company of soldiers, but my troops are as keen to defeat the enemy as any of His Majesty's soldiers.'

'My man told me that you were out in India. I was there too, for a time. Is that where...?' Nicholas gestured to Melvill's left arm, which was in a sling. The man's right arm wasn't much better, hanging limply at his side.

Melvill, a man looking older than his almost fifty years, sent him a rueful smile. 'Yes, I was there for six years all told. Four of them in captivity.'

Nicholas' good eye widened. 'You were one of those held by Hyder Ally?' He'd heard the stories of what had happened to the men. Out of one hundred and twenty-six soldiers only thirty stayed alive long enough to be released.

'Yes, the good Lord decided that he had a purpose for me.' Melvill smiled then nodded towards Nicholas' face. 'I daresay He has a purpose for you, else that shot that robbed you of one of your eyes might have done far more damage.'

Nicholas shrugged. 'Possibly. Though I'll have my hands full sorting out my estate and I've now got a ward, thanks to one of my fellow officers.'

'There you are.' An enigmatic smile appeared on Melvill's face.

As Nicholas strode back down the hill towards the town there was a spring in his step. It was time to move on and not dwell on what might have been. Tomorrow, he'd pack his bags and plan his journey to Bath. He would make a go of things. He might not find himself a wife, but he would ensure that his estate and tenants would prosper, and the child he was now guardian to would have every opportunity that her father's death had denied her.

———— · ————

Travelling was not the nicest of experiences in the colder months. Nicholas stared gloomily out of the coach window. How had he forgotten the rutted and muddy roads that made winter travelling in England hellish? There'd been several stops at post inns where the food was not the best and the rooms uncomfortable, something else he had not missed about his home country. Still, it was an improvement on sleeping under the stars in driving rain, foraging for food, and being a target for a French sniper. What he hated most was the rocking and swaying of the coach, which was almost as bad as the crossing of the Bay of Biscay.

As he stepped from the coach in front of the fine building that was the York Hotel, Nicholas heaved a sigh of relief. He surveyed the impressive frontage. So this was the place recommended by his fellow officers. Well, he'd soon discover if it lived up to its reputation of being one of the largest and best inns outside of London, patronised by those of the highest rank.

Nicholas' stomach rumbled. He checked his pocket watch. Disappointingly, the time for dinner was some way off. So, after approving the excellently appointed bedchamber and parlour that the manager, a Mr Lucas, had shown him to, he decided that a stroll was called for. Surely he would find something to satisfy his hunger pangs until dinnertime. There was no need to call on his ward until tomorrow.

Nicholas smiled to himself. He hadn't informed the headmistress of the exact day of his arrival in Bath. The element of surprise was a tactic that had proved useful when tackling the enemy; it might well be as effective when dealing with Miss Pugh and her establishment. He hadn't a clue whether the school was good or bad, but he would find out.

Waving away the attentions of a waiting chairman – he might be half blind but he wasn't a cripple and spending one shilling and sixpence to travel a mile was an unnecessary expense – Nicholas set off, leaving the young Penrose to unpack.

For the first time in many days, the tension left Nicholas' shoulders and neck. The surrounding buildings, constructed in a pleasing honey-coloured stone, reflected the rays of the winter sun. It was even dry underfoot, a pleasant change after days of rain. How nice it was to stroll aimlessly, without worrying about his men or the next encounter with the enemy.

He tipped his hat to a gentleman and his lady. The lady's mouth opened in shock and was that fear in her eyes? Nicholas' mouth twisted as he strode past the couple.

What was he thinking? It wouldn't do to upset ladies with his disfigured face. He hurried on, pulling the brim of his hat down low.

He'd not gone far before he arrived at a broad thoroughfare declaring itself to be Milsom Street. He paused to inspect the vista before him. Lined with private residences and shops of the expensive variety, it was crowded with well-dressed people. Perhaps down here there was also an establishment selling something to eat.

Nicholas' nose twitched. An enticing smell filled the air. A confectioner's sign rocking in the breeze caught his attention. A pastry or two would be just the thing.

Striding into the pastry shop, he kept his head low, glancing this way and that. Good, there was an empty table in the corner, out of sight. No need to upset anyone by showing his scarred face.

Mrs Molland's pastries were indeed excellent. It didn't take him long to polish off several. Patting his stomach, he reached into his waistcoat pocket for his watch. Plenty of time left still to explore and perhaps visit one of the bookshops he'd spotted. Ah, yes, he mustn't forget to call in at a haberdasher's to purchase ribbons.

Little girls liked ribbons, didn't they? He couldn't call on his ward empty-handed. Goodness, he wasn't even sure how old she was.

As luck would have it, across the road was the very shop he needed. Earls' Emporium seemed to sell items that might appeal to a young lady: hats, gloves, all sorts of fancy goods. They were sure to stock ribbons. Nicholas marched purposefully across the street towards the haberdasher's door and in his haste collided with a diminutive figure who was walking on the pavement.

'I'm terribly sorry, I didn't see you.'

He held out a hand to steady the female he'd sent spinning. Her hat was all askew and her glossy chestnut tresses had escaped their pins and were covering her face.

Nicholas held his breath. At least he hadn't cannoned into an old dowager. Wellesley was known for his short temper, but some dowagers Nicholas had met were far more formidable than his old commander.

'Oh dear. N-no, I must apologise. I wasn't looking...' The lady's voice trailed off as she turned to face him.

He braced himself for the coming hysterics.

'Would you mind, terribly?' Her voice was hesitant, but with a gentle, melodious tone. She thrust a package towards him. 'If you could kindly hold this for a moment, I can tidy my hair and adjust my hat.'

'Yes, of course.' Nicholas swallowed, unable to take his gaze off her.

He watched as, with deft fingers, she tucked her hair back under her hat. Such lovely hair, the colour of shiny horse chestnuts.

The young woman gave her hat a final pat, her lips curving into a smile as she looked up at him and took back her parcel.

Nicholas braced himself again. Perhaps his scars hadn't registered with her the first time she'd looked at him.

'It must be quite difficult in your situation to navigate crowded streets,' she said, pointing to his missing eye. 'I take all the blame for my misstep.'

Her reply took him off-balance.

'No, really, it was entirely down to me.'

It was impossible to drag his gaze away from her pretty, open face. She wasn't in the first flush of youth, but not in her dotage. No more than five and twenty and decidedly attractive.

Her eyes, their colour midway between dark blue and grey, sparkled with amusement. 'Then let us agree to differ.' She gestured to the shop door behind her. 'Was that your destination?'

Nicholas nodded. How could he delay her? Her smile was sending his pulse racing. It had been so long since an attractive woman had smiled at him, openly and without fear. *The ribbons, that's it!*

'Perhaps you can assist me,' he ventured.

She arched an eyebrow.

'Help me to choose a colour,' he said in explanation. 'There's someone I wish to purchase ribbons for. She's quite young, a child in fact, and I have no idea what she would like. Do you think you could?' He sent her a pleading look.

This was something different. He was accustomed to issuing orders, not begging favours, but to spend more time in her company he'd happily beg.

'What luck. I know exactly the sorts of ribbons that would appeal to young girls. I would be pleased to help you.'

Nicholas held out his elbow and she laid her hand on it. Even though she wore gloves, tingles of electricity shot up his arm.

They entered the shop. Unable to wipe the smile from his face, Nicholas headed for the counter.

How wonderful to have a woman on his arm.

'How may I help you, Sir and Madam?'

He heard a stifled chuckle from his companion. At least she was amused at the shop assistant's error and not scandalised.

'I would like to purchase some ribbons and this lady - a friend - has kindly agreed to assist me.'

'Yes, this gentleman would like to see ribbons in pastel hues, colours suitable for a very young lady, to be used, I daresay, for decorating her bonnet or a dress.' The young woman turned her eyes towards him. There was a becoming flush to her cheeks. 'Have I got that right?'

Nicholas chuckled. 'Exactly right, thank you.'

The assistant brought out trays of ribbons in all different shades of pinks, yellows, creams, and blues. The young lady picked one or two of each, feeling the quality. As she leaned over, scrutinising them, the blue ribbons decorating her own hat came into Nicholas' view. He blinked. They seemed rather worn - a faded version of their original hue, no doubt. Perhaps when she'd bought them they'd matched the colour of her eyes. The rest of her garb was rather plain and somewhat severe. Her velvet pelisse was faded and worn in places. Nevertheless, she exuded grace and elegance.

After several minutes' perusal, she sighed. 'I think I'd recommend any of these. But if you are really unsure about which colour the young lady would prefer, I'd suggest the cream ones. That shade will go with many different colours.' Tucking her parcel firmly under her arm, she bobbed a curtsey. 'Well, I must be going now. I do hope that I've been of some help.'

Stunned, it was some moments before Nicholas could speak. He spun round. She was already at the door.

'But I don't know…'

The door closed behind her.

Nicholas exhaled. There was no point in making a fool of himself by chasing her. She didn't want to further their acquaintance. Shoulders slumped, he turned back to the counter.

'I'll take two yards of each of these.' He pointed to ribbons of each different shade. On a shelf, behind the assistant, he spotted yet another colour. 'And a yard of that, if you please.'

The assistant's eyebrows rose as he measured out the new dark blue ribbon. Nicholas didn't care. At least he'd have something in memory of his encounter with a lady who hadn't flinched at his appearance.

Chapter Four

A warm glow filled Jane's chest despite the cold weather as she walked briskly up Milsom Street. It was uphill all the way to Camden Crescent and she'd get another lecture from Miss Pugh if she was late. She really shouldn't have agreed to help that gentleman in choosing ribbons but there was something about him that had made it difficult to refuse. He'd almost knocked her over, but the reason for that had been obvious once she'd caught sight of his face. Initially, he'd looked forbidding with his black eye patch and scarred cheeks, but then a smile had lit up his face, making his scars and eye patch disappear.

At first, she'd formed the impression that he was unsure of himself, which seemed strange. Everything about him spoke of a military background – his firm step when he'd walked her into the shop with his head held high, as if on parade. His clothes too, spoke of quality and good taste.

She sighed. How nice it would be to have a suitor like that, but very unlikely at her advanced age. She had nothing to recommend her. She swiped at her eyes with a gloved hand. Goodness, the cold air was making her eyes water.

Lansdowne Road was steep but less crowded. Jane slowed her pace. The shadows were getting longer. A cloud of misery descended on her. If only she had somewhere other than the Academy to spend Christmas, which was fast approaching. Advent and Christmas used to be her favourite times of the year. As a small child, she'd enjoyed helping her mother to stir the pudding and always hoped that she would be the lucky one to find the coin hidden in it.

Jane's mouth tightened. Miss Pugh considered Christmas pudding an indulgence. The most any pupils who were unlucky enough to be at the Academy for Christmas could hope for was a handful of raisins and nuts.

Jane's heart suddenly skipped a beat.

If she didn't convince Meg's new guardian to keep his ward at the school, Miss Pugh would carry out her threat and she would be homeless this Christmas.

Breathing heavily now, Jane continued her trek back. The Academy was situated on Camden Crescent, an elegant, curved terrace that had some of the most beautiful views over the city. Jane smiled ruefully; the price paid for the incredible view was the steep climb. A climb that she might not need to undertake much longer if she didn't carry out Miss Pugh's instructions.

———— · ————

After a breakfast of bread, butter, a slice of plum cake, and an excellent cup of tea – a life on the march had accustomed Nicholas to a rather abstemious meal in the early hours of the day – he donned his greatcoat and beaver hat and set off for Miss Pugh's

Academy. Mr Lucas, the manager, kindly accompanied him to the entrance of the hotel and gave him very clear instructions on the location of Camden Crescent, pointing out its elevated position above the town.

'It's quite a climb, I'm afraid, Colonel, and it's starting to rain. You might be better summoning a chair.'

Nicholas roared with laughter. 'I'm not quite in my dotage. If you saw some of the terrain my men and I were forced to cross in Portugal – and, I might add, in much worse weather – you wouldn't suggest it.'

Mr Lucas gave an embarrassed smile as Nicholas clapped him on the shoulder. 'I meant no offence, Colonel.'

'None taken,' grinned Nicholas. 'It's a good thing I've brought my umbrella. Thought the clouds were gathering when I looked out of the window this morning.'

With a cheery wave to Mr Lucas, Nicholas set off on his journey. The manager had indicated that the road he needed was the one across the street. A crossing boy stood on the corner, his eyes watchful. The boy scampered up to Nicholas, then hesitated as he caught sight of Nicholas' face.

'C-c-clear your way, Mister?'

Nicholas sighed and touched his hat. 'Indeed, thank you.'

There was a momentary lull in the stream of carts and carriages coming along the road and the young lad darted out, sweeping away the muck and droppings. Nicholas followed closely. It wouldn't do to turn up at the school smelling of the stables. Safely on the other side, he tossed a coin to the lad. Grabbing it mid-flight, the young boy sent him a curious look.

'How'd your face get like that, Mister? Wos you in a fire?'

Nicholas paused. Might as well let the inquisitive little chap know. 'No, not a fire. It was a Frenchman who took my eye. Debris from a cannon explosion caused the rest of the damage.'

The boy's eyes widened like saucers. 'You're one of those wot's fighting old Boney?'

'I was.'

'Blimey, wait till I tell my pals I've seen a hero.' The boy leaned on his brush, a broad grin on his face.

'Not a hero,' Nicholas muttered under his breath.

Walking at his usual punishing pace, it didn't take Nicholas long to reach Camden Crescent. Since setting off, the wind had picked up and the rain had begun to lash down. He stood for a moment peering at the Bath stone frontages of the terrace, both hands clutching on to his umbrella. He squinted at the polished brass plaque near the front door of the first building; the words Pugh's Academy were just about discernible.

With brisk determined steps, Nicholas marched up and hammered a loud tattoo with the door knocker.

———— . ————

With one leg crossed over the other, Nicholas leaned back in his seat and let his gaze roam about the room. Miss Pugh's brief absence was the perfect opportunity to examine his surroundings. At his feet was what looked like an expensive Turkey rug; the polished oak desk was at least as large as the one in his late father's study. And was that an extravagant ormolu clock on the mantel-piece? Nicholas stood up to examine it. Above the porcelain clock face adorned with cupids, a gold eagle was attacking a serpent.

Nicholas tutted. It might be the fashion, but in his opinion, it was hideous.

He rubbed his newly shaven chin thoughtfully – Penrose had done a good job that morning – what a twittering, encroaching woman Miss Pugh was! His lip curled in disgust. She'd started fawning over him as soon as he'd declared his business there. According to her, his ward, Meg, was a 'wonderful, darling, and apt pupil', who'd made so many friends at the school that it would be a disaster to the poor child if he should remove her. Nicholas smiled sardonically as he continued to examine the clock.

But at the time, he'd nodded to Miss Pugh and given a non-committal grunt.

No need to let the enemy know your intentions. And yes, he was definitely regarding Miss Pugh in the light of an adversary.

Were all her staff as bad? She'd sent for a Miss Mortimer, his ward's main teacher, and when the woman hadn't arrived, Miss Pugh had gone off in search of her, muttering what he was sure were curses under her breath. He chuckled. Miss Pugh was no paragon.

Would the absent Miss Mortimer be as frosty-faced and unpleasant as her employer? Undoubtedly.

Poor little Meg Wilson, to be compelled to live in a household with two such ogres.

He held out his hands to the fire blazing in the grate. Well, Miss Pugh didn't stint on the coals. If her pupils enjoyed the same luxury, he just might forgive her a little for being a Friday-faced harridan. There was nothing worse than being cold and no reason for little girls to suffer that hardship, especially when the headmistress's well-furnished study was so cosy.

'Ah, I see you are admiring my clock.' Miss Pugh's voice caught him unawares.

'I've not seen one as … intricately worked as that before.' He kept his tone neutral.

'It was a gift from a parent,' she trilled. 'A family heirloom that they had no use for. Such good taste, don't you think?'

Nicholas smiled and ignored her question. 'Miss Mortimer?' He raised his eyebrow.

Miss Pugh's mouth thinned. 'I'm afraid she has taken the girls for an outing. So inconvenient, when I wished particularly for her to speak with you about your ward.'

'And I take it that my ward is also absent?'

Miss Pugh sniffed. 'Yes. It seems you have had a wasted journey.' Her face brightened. 'Well, perhaps now you've satisfied yourself that she is being well looked-after, you can continue to leave her here.'

Nicholas pursed his lips. 'I couldn't possibly depart Bath without seeing my ward. As I'm sure you'll agree, that would be most remiss of me.'

Miss Pugh's eyes narrowed. Her reply came through gritted teeth. 'Of course.'

Nicholas turned as he got to the door. 'I'll call back tomorrow. Please ensure that my ward is present.'

Bolstered by this easy success at outmanoeuvring an enemy, Nicholas couldn't prevent himself grinning all the way back down into town.

———— . ————

It was Jane's second time in a week to be summoned to Miss Pugh's room. The maid had told her that the headmistress wished to see her as soon as she returned that afternoon.

Jane frowned as she removed her hat and pelisse and handed them to the maid. What did she want now?

She patted her hair back into place and called to the giggling girls, who were heading up the stairs. 'Go and tidy up, girls. It will soon be dinnertime.'

She tapped on the headmistress's study door and stepped inside.

'There you are, Miss Mortimer, at last,' snapped Miss Pugh. 'Where have you been?'

'I thought I'd take a few of the girls out for a walk. Some of them were keen to make purchases, you know, as it is getting near to Christmas. Small gifts to take back for their families, that sort of thing.'

'I hope you did not encourage them to make frivolous choices.' Miss Pugh's face was stern.

Jane sucked in a breath. Why did the woman have to be so disapproving? Had she not heard of Christmas?

'Of course not. Mostly they were improving books for their younger brothers and sisters.'

'Hmm.' Miss Pugh was still eyeing Jane with displeasure. 'Miss Wilson's guardian called and he was most disappointed that both you and she were not here to receive him. He was quite angry in fact and, I have to say, your absence put me in a most awkward position. He was not the best tempered of men and so forbidding-looking.'

Jane's stomach coiled. Oh dear, how awful for Meg if she should have an ill-tempered guardian.

'Is he returning?' she asked nervously. Perhaps Meg would be better off staying at the school.

'Yes. Tomorrow.' Miss Pugh scowled.

'Very well.' Jane turned and with leaden steps went to inform Meg of her guardian's imminent arrival.

Chapter Five

The following day was crisp and clear, and a hard frost lay on the skylight window of Jane's room. She shivered as she scuttled over to the washstand. At least there would be a fire lit in the parlour where she and Meg were to meet her guardian.

At breakfast, Jane could barely eat. Meg too, picked at her food. Jane gazed at her sympathetically. Poor child, her lack of appetite was down to excitement at the expectation of meeting a kind man like her father, not the forbidding horror that Miss Pugh had described.

The minutes went slowly in the classroom as Jane took her pupils through the Commentarii de Bello Gallico. Caesar's account of the Gallic Wars was written in straightforward, simple Latin sentences, not too difficult for novices of the language to understand.

Jane rested her chin on her hands with only one ear taking in the hesitant translation Mary, one of the older girls, was attempting. If only real life was as simple, Jane thought, not the nuanced mess that it often was. She glanced out of the window to the frost-tinged rooftops of Bath. When would the odious gentleman come? Was he even now making his way puffing and panting up Lansdowne Road?

——— . ———

There was a tap on the classroom door, making the heads of her pupils turn. The maid poked her face into the room. 'Miss Pugh wants Miss Wilson, if you please, Miss Mortimer.'

Jane swallowed, then smiled convincingly at Meg. 'Off you go, my dear.'

The clock in the hall chimed the quarter hour. Meg had been gone for at least half an hour. Knots formed in Jane's stomach. She wanted her ordeal to be over.

Without warning, Miss Pugh swept into the room.

'I'll take over here, Miss Mortimer.' An audible groan came from the girls. Miss Pugh silenced them with a glare. 'Hurry along to the parlour. Don't keep the colonel waiting,'

Jane put down her book and sped off, closing the door with a click as she left. Pulse racing, she dashed down the stairs. Better to get it over with. Her hand was shaking as she raised it to tap on the parlour door.

A male voice barked, 'Enter.'

Jane cleared her throat, squared her shoulders, and went in.

The broad-shouldered figure at the fireside had his back to her; he was loading more coals onto the fire.

Jane grimaced. Miss Pugh would not approve.

Meg looked up and smiled brightly from her seat near the fire.

'Colonel Anstruther said he didn't see the need to let the fire go out, just because Miss Pugh is not here.'

'Quite right,' said the gentleman at the fireplace. 'No point in being cold for the sake of adding a few lumps of coal.'

His task completed, he put the coal tongs down, straightened up, and turned around.

Jane gasped. 'It's you.'

The gentleman's expression, which at first had been harsh and unyielding, softened and his lips curved upwards.

Her pulse quickened. This was not the horror that Miss Pugh had described.

'We meet again.' His deep voice sent warm shivers up Jane's spine.

Meg looked puzzled. 'Do you know Colonel Anstruther, Miss?'

'Er....'

'We met quite by accident a couple of days ago,' interrupted Colonel Anstruther. 'It is Miss Mortimer you have to thank for your ribbons, Meg.' He gestured Jane to a chair. 'I'm very pleased to make your acquaintance, finally.' There was a gruff, masculine chuckle. 'I must say, I was expecting someone quite different.'

Meg giggled. 'You mean someone like Miss Pugh, don't you? Miss Mortimer is not like her, she's lovely.'

'Shhh, Meg. Remember your manners.' Jane blushed. This was all so embarrassing.

'But it's true,' protested Meg.

'Now, now,' said the colonel, patting Meg on the shoulder. 'It may well be true. In fact, I'm pretty certain it is, but you are putting Miss Mortimer to the blush.' He smiled at Jane. 'According to Miss Pugh, you are to tell me about Meg and how much she is enjoying her life at the school.'

He cocked his head expectantly, ignoring the look of disgust apparent on Meg's face.

Jane trembled. Just tell him the truth.

'Yes, Meg is doing very well at her lessons. She is an excellent reader and is studying Latin, French, and history, as well as the usual feminine subjects of needlework, music, and singing.'

'Latin, eh?' He sent an amused glance at Meg. 'Do you enjoy it? I never did.'

Meg bristled. 'Yes, Miss Mortimer makes the lessons interesting. She makes all her subjects interesting.'

The colonel's face swivelled back to Jane. 'You teach Latin? An unusual subject for a female teacher. I daresay I'd have paid more attention if my tutor...' His voice trailed off. There was a mischievous glint in his eye.

Jane's cheeks started to burn. Was he flirting? Surely not.

'My father was a scholar,' she said briskly. 'I was his only child, so he felt that I should benefit from his learning in the absence of a son. Perhaps I should show you round the school.'

Meg leapt out of her seat. 'Yes, I'll show you my new room. It has a fireplace.'

The colonel's brow furrowed. 'New room?'

Meg looked at him guilelessly. 'Yes, I was put in a dormitory in the attic with two other girls when Papa died, then this week Miss Pugh said I should have a room of my own again.'

'This week, eh?' The colonel looked questioningly at Jane.

Jane sucked in her cheeks, not knowing how to answer. She so wanted Meg to have a good home and this gentleman would look after her. But if Meg went away, she would lose her position.

But this was no time to be selfish. She must tell the truth.

As Meg skipped to the door, Jane moved closer to the colonel so that only he could hear. She breathed in his scent of clean linen and cologne with a subtle hint of orange.

'I believe Miss Pugh wants Meg to stay at the Academy, because of the fees.'

The colonel frowned for a moment. 'I understand. Thank you.'

After showing the colonel the classrooms, the parlour, and Meg's new bedchamber, Jane walked back with him to the office, where Miss Pugh was now seated at her desk.

Jane drew a breath. It was most peculiar; walking round the school had never made her breathless before. But she'd never had such a compellingly masculine companion before.

'Thank you, Miss Mortimer. You may return to your classroom, and you too, Miss Wilson.' Miss Pugh sent an ingratiating smile to Colonel Anstruther. 'I'm sure you wouldn't want your ward to miss too much. Young girls need structure to their days.'

Jane took Meg's hand, closed the door, and headed to her class, every nerve in her body tingling. Her future lay in the conversation that would shortly be taking place.

———— · ————

Nicholas walked back to the York Hotel deep in thought. What an enlightening morning it had been. His ward was a delightful child and it wouldn't be a hardship to take her back with him to the estate and engage a governess. He could rely on his house-keeper, Mrs Sloan, to look after her needs in the meantime.

No, Miss Mortimer was the problem. Ever since that first meeting on Milsom Street when she hadn't reacted with horror to his face, he'd prayed that he'd see her again. His prayers had been answered that morning. When he'd turned round from the fireplace to see her looking as shocked as he, his heart had leapt in his chest. It had been difficult to breathe. Then she'd smiled.

In that instant he knew.

But how to win her? One misstep and all his hopes could be dashed.

Good grief, he'd even tried flirting with her! She'd coloured up so charmingly, but something told him that if he wanted matters to work out with Miss Mortimer, flirting was not the way to go about it.

A proper courtship was needed.

There was something else that bothered him. Miss Mortimer seemed nervous and guarded in her speech, unlike his refreshingly honest ward. He'd quickly guessed that Meg's new accommodation at the Academy was all about charging him higher fees. Miss Mortimer had confirmed that with her whispered words. What an awkward position she must have found herself in.

He smiled, remembering how Miss Mortimer had leaned into him. She'd smelt of lavender.

Nicholas pursed his lips. He needed to plan a campaign. And it wasn't too difficult to consider Miss Pugh as the enemy. If he removed Meg from the school, he would have no excuse to see Miss Mortimer again. As much as he wanted to rescue the little girl from the headmistress's clutches as soon as possible, he wasn't going to risk his chance of happiness.

An hour later, a satisfied smile settled on Nicholas' face. His missive to Miss Pugh was on its way. He knew her weak spot and he was going to exploit it.

Chapter Six

Jane hadn't slept a wink since the colonel's visit. Convinced that her honesty left him with only one option, she'd been dreading the next summons to see Miss Pugh.

It came after breakfast.

'You wished to see me?' Jane's heart pounded as she stood before Miss Pugh's desk.

Miss Pugh waved a paper at her. 'Colonel Anstruther requests more time to consider whether his ward remains here or not.' She gave an unladylike snort. 'What does a man like him know about a school for young ladies? He has no children of his own.'

'But it shows he is a considerate guardian. He is not rushing to make his mind up,' Jane ventured.

She could afford to be brave. Thanks to the colonel, her position was safe for a while longer.

'Bah! He has requested that you and the child join him tomorrow for an excursion into Bath.'

Jane stifled a gasp. He wanted to see her? No, he was merely ensuring that Meg had a suitable companion. Most gentlemen of her limited acquaintance were not entirely comfortable in the company of children.

Miss Pugh turned gimlet eyes on Jane. 'Make sure that you persuade the colonel of the difficulties for a single man in raising a child and the benefits of leaving her here.'

Jane swallowed. 'Of course.'

The next day, Jane and Meg set off to meet with Colonel Anstruther at his hotel. He was waiting for them at the entrance, a broad smile on his face. In his caped coat and tall beaver hat pulled low, partly masking his scars and eye patch, he was the epitome of a well-dressed gentleman.

Jane's pulse began to race. This was silly; he was pleased to see Meg, not her. But how nice it would be to have a gentleman like the colonel to greet her with such a beaming smile.

'Good day to you, Colonel.' She bobbed a curtsey. 'It is very kind of you to invite me to accompany you and Meg.'

He twinkled at her. 'I thought it would be nice to have a charming lady on each arm for my first proper excursion into Bath.'

Meg giggled. 'But I am not quite a lady yet. I'm only ten years old.'

He leaned down to her. 'But you are very charming, and if you follow Miss Mortimer's example, I'm sure you will grow to be a perfect lady.' He sent a speaking look to Jane.

She blushed. Did he really think she was perfect? *Don't be silly, Jane. He is just being kind to put Meg at her ease.*

He held out an elbow for each of them. 'Now, I thought we'd start by visiting the Pump Room. I'm told it's the place to be seen.'

'I won't have to drink the water, will I?' Meg pouted. 'I've been told it has a nasty taste.'

'My dear, you don't have to,' he answered. 'But I've learned to try things for myself before accepting someone else's opinion. I will certainly take a glass.' He winked at the little girl. 'Though I may not drink it all.'

Meg's nose wrinkled. 'In that case, perhaps I'll have a sip.'

'Good girl. Best not to dismiss things before you've given them a chance.' His head bent towards Jane. 'Have you tried the water, Miss Mortimer?'

'I confess I haven't. My school duties mean that I do not get to visit Bath's attractions very often.' The truth was, she very rarely was free and certainly did not have the funds to enjoy the delights of Bath.

He patted Jane on the arm, sending warm shivers through her. 'Well, it will be a novel experience for all three of us.'

The Pump Room was not too crowded. Ladies and gentlemen were perambulating round the room, while others stood in groups near the tall windows conversing. Jane sighed inwardly. The ladies were all dressed in their finery, their clothes of the first stare. Her worn blue velvet pelisse and matching hat with its faded ribbons were drab by comparison. Still, the colonel didn't seem to mind. He'd done nothing but smile at her.

The colonel led Jane and Meg over to some seats near one of the fireplaces.

'Wait here. I will fetch us some water.' At the dismayed expression on Meg's face, he added, 'Just a sip.'

As he walked away, Meg leaned in to Jane. 'He's nice, isn't he, Miss?'

Jane, gazing at his retreating back, nodded and smiled. Yes, the colonel was very nice.

After nearly an hour in the Pump Room with the colonel telling a bright-eyed Meg about her father's adventures – where did the time go? – the colonel decided it was time for some sustenance.

'I thought we might try a pastry shop I discovered the other day.' He grinned at Meg. 'I think you'll enjoy their wares much more than Bath water.'

'And will you tell me more about Papa? I'd like that very much.' Meg's eyes lit up as she spoke of her father.

Jane had enjoyed listening to the colonel too, though she was sure that life on campaign was rather more brutal and bloody than the version he was giving to his ward. But how kind of him to take the time to talk to the girl. Most men, even those who were fathers, did not expend as much effort on their offspring. She had been lucky with her own father; what he'd taught her had enabled her to earn her living.

As they walked through Abbey Square to their destination, Meg skipped ahead to look at the shop windows and their enticing displays.

Jane spoke. 'You must have been very good friends with Major Wilson. I think it's very kind of you to spend so much time with Meg. She is enthralled by your stories.' Yes, Meg was as besotted as she.

The colonel turned his head. 'Yes, we were friends, but, as you know, I lost touch with him. It took some time for news of his death to reach me ... and as for making me guardian to his daughter ... well, it came as a complete shock.' He leaned in closer, using his hand to mask his words as he spoke. 'Miss Pugh has probably already informed you that I am unmarried, and I have no experience with children at all.''

Jane caught the familiar scent of his cologne. It was intoxicating. If she wasn't careful she'd be doing something foolish. He mustn't know how much she was attracted to him.

He paused for a moment. 'I had almost given up hope of marrying ... my face, you see?

Jane's eyes widened. 'You think that we females only have regard for gentlemen with perfect features? What shallow creatures you must think us. I'm sure you will find someone who'll regard your injuries as a badge of honour and who would be proud to call you husband.'

She bit her lip. She'd spoken of her own feelings. Goodness, he surely wouldn't guess. He was too far above her touch and could never consider a lowly teacher as a marriage prospect.

'Oh, there is someone,' he said softly. 'I just need to ensure that she will marry me for love and not out of pity.' There was the same enigmatic smile on his face again.

Jane's insides melted. Did he realise the effect he had on her? No, it wasn't possible. He was talking about somebody else.

'I hope you are successful in your courtship, Colonel.'

A block of ice formed in her stomach. This was torture to spend time with a kind and perfect gentleman, when all the time he was thinking about another. *Pull yourself together, Jane. No more indulging in impossible fantasies.*

'So do I,' he answered.

———— · ————

Nicholas regarded his two companions over the rim of his teacup. They were both charming and good company. His ward was a spirited young girl but with good manners, no doubt instilled in her by her teacher, whom she seemed to adore. Yes,

Miss Mortimer was adorable, though she didn't know it. It was far too soon to reveal his feelings for her.

'Now tell me a little about yourself, Miss Mortimer. I've spoken so much about my life in the army and of course about Major Wilson. It's only fair that we learn something about you. Wouldn't you agree, Meg?'

'Yes, please, Miss.' Meg put down the bun she'd been nibbling. 'I'd love to know about when you were a girl.'

Nicholas congratulated himself. His tactic of enlisting the little girl's support was bound to persuade Miss Mortimer to open up about herself. How could she refuse a plea from her pupil? There was so much he wanted to learn about this intriguing woman. Good grief, he didn't even know her first name!

Jane's eyelashes fluttered, her cheeks flushing a becoming pink.

'I'm not interesting at all, I'm afraid. I'll bore you.'

Nicholas was not giving up. 'Well, I'll help by asking some questions.' He tapped a finger on the table. 'No excuses.'

Jane smiled at him shyly. 'I suppose, if you insist.'

Nicholas gazed at her. If she looked at him like that all the time, he'd be in heaven.

'Where were you born, Miss?' Meg started.

'In a small village in Hampshire. I was an only child. We lived very quietly there.'

'I remember you told me that it was your father who taught you Latin,' said Nicholas.

Jane nodded. 'That's right. He was a very scholarly gentleman. He taught me Latin and French so that I could assist him with his correspondence, for he corresponded with many other academically minded gentlemen.'

Nicholas watched Jane as she spoke. Her eyes had turned misty when speaking of her father.

'Was your mother as versed in academic subjects too?' he asked.

Jane giggled, a girlish sound. 'Not at all. She was much more practical, taking care of the accounts and running the household.' She took a sip from her teacup.

Nicholas was sure there was more. 'How did you come to be a teacher here in Bath?'

Yes, what was she doing employed at that awful place? A young woman as attractive and intelligent as her should have been snapped up into matrimony by any fellow with sense. Lucky for him she hadn't.

Her eyes avoided his gaze. Instead she glanced at Meg, who had resumed nibbling her bun and was now engrossed in watching the passers-by through the window. 'That is simple,' Jane said in an undertone. 'When Father died nearly three years ago – my mother had died some time previously – I discovered that he had neglected his financial affairs. A loan he had taken out needed repaying, other debts had accrued, and in short, I was forced to sell up.'

Her hand shook as she set her cup back onto the saucer. From the set of her mouth it was clear that she wasn't going to add any more.

'So, you are all alone in the world?'

Nicholas restrained himself from taking her hand. If only he could tell her that she needn't worry.

'Yes, I've no family at all.'

'That's very sad, Miss.' Meg, her bun now consumed, broke the silence left by Jane's words.

'No, it isn't,' declared Miss Mortimer brightly. 'For you see, I have the pleasure of teaching you and all the other pupils at Miss Pugh's Academy.'

Meg leaned into Miss Mortimer's side and there was a look of admiration in the little girl's eyes.

'I'll miss you when I leave.'

Jane put her arm round the young girl's shoulder. 'I'll miss you too, dear.'

Chapter Seven

After they finished their tea and cakes, Nicholas stood up and declared that further exploration of Bath was required. He'd march for miles if it meant spending more time with Miss Mortimer. Happily, his two companions agreed.

Even though it was winter, not a cloud marred the vivid blue sky, and the brisk pace he set ensured that they did not feel the cold. They went past the abbey to Pulteney Bridge, where they paused for a while to allow an excited Meg to marvel at the weir below, then they strolled down Great Pulteney Street and reached the entrance to Sydney Gardens.

Nicholas checked his pocket watch and frowned. 'It is getting rather late, so we do not have time for the gardens today. Perhaps we can visit them tomorrow, if you'd like that.'

'Yes, please.' There was no doubt about Meg's feelings on the matter.

Nicholas cocked his head and sent Miss Mortimer a crooked smile. 'And you?'

A look of concern crossed Miss Mortimer's face. 'Although

Meg would love another excursion with you, I'm afraid that I must decline.' She smiled apologetically. 'I have classes to teach.'

Drat! This was not in his plan. Masking his disappointment, Nicholas replied, 'What a pity. I will miss your company.'

They retraced their steps and headed back to the York Hotel. Nicholas had arranged for dinner to be served in one of the private parlours. It was another chance to convince Miss Mortimer of his desire for her happiness.

The smell of the delicious dishes brought smiles to everyone's faces. Little Meg's eyes grew wide at the sight of the food laid out on the table.

'Look, Miss, isn't it wonderful? A whole chicken, a ham, and a salmon. Ooh and puddings too!'

Nicholas chuckled. 'What? Don't you enjoy this sort of fare every day at the Academy? Miss Pugh told me that no expense was spared when it came to meals for her pupils.'

Miss Mortimer gave an audible sniff. 'Miss Pugh believes that too much food dulls a girl's mind.'

Nicholas didn't think his dislike of Miss Pugh could grow any more, but he was mistaken. What a penny-pinching woman.

Nicholas enjoyed the meal, not because of the food, which was excellent, but on account of the company. Meg kept him amused with her stories about her friends at school, while Miss Mortimer's interest in his life on the Peninsula and India made him think that perhaps his time there had not been wasted.

All too soon it was time for them to depart. Penrose brought in their outdoor clothes.

As Nicholas waited for Meg to put on her bonnet and pelisse for the walk back to the Academy, he drew Miss Mortimer to one side. Her fresh lavender smell reminded him of an English garden.

'I have a proposition for you,' he said in an undertone.

To his alarm, her gentle expression turned frosty and he saw her body stiffen.

He inwardly cursed himself for using the wrong words.

'Let me explain,' he added hastily. 'I wonder if you would accept the position of governess to my ward. I can see that she has the utmost regard for you, and if I'm any judge, I think that feeling is mutual.' This was one way to get to know her better. Best not to frighten her off with talk of marriage. Not yet, anyway.

To his relief, her face softened, but there was a troubling hint of anxiety in her eyes.

'I'm honoured, Colonel, indeed I am, but I'm afraid that I must refuse your kind offer.'

A shaft of ice pierced Nicholas' chest. 'Why, may I ask?' His words came out croaky, his throat dry with disappointment.

'I have other pupils who require my tuition here in Bath, and I couldn't leave just like that. It would not be fair.'

Numb with shock he nodded. 'Very well. I'll escort you back. It's getting rather late and I must apologise to Miss Pugh for delaying you.'

——— · ———

Jane lay in bed looking sightlessly at the blackness of the night through the skylight window above her bed.

What had she done? Burned her bridges. After Colonel Anstruther had departed, she had been summoned to Miss Pugh's office and been given her notice.

'You have until the end of this term and then I want you gone.' Miss Pugh's tone was venomous. 'You should have convinced him to leave the girl here, but you didn't. You have only yourself to blame for your situation.'

Jane's mind was in a haze as she left the office. Could she find a new situation in the few weeks left before term finished? It was unlikely, but she'd try. There must be other schools who required a teacher with her skills.

Now in the middle of the night her situation seemed even worse. Why had she turned him down?

Deep inside she knew the answer. How could she live in the same household with the man who had stolen her heart?

The colonel had told her that he was planning marriage and it would be unbearable to see him happy with someone else. Of course, she wanted him to find happiness, but it would be better for her not to witness it. It was difficult enough to hide her feelings; it would tear her apart to see him every day and keep them secret.

Jane rolled over and thumped her pillow. Hot tears ran down her cheeks. It was nearly Christmas and soon she would be home-less. And the only man who'd ever made her feel wonderful would be leaving her life forever. She rubbed her eyes. They'd be red in the morning for everyone to see, but it didn't matter. She'd be leaving soon.

The next morning Jane rose early, even before the maid's awakening knock rattled on her door. She washed and dressed in a trance and made her way to the attic dormitory. There were only two little girls there now. After the usual grumbles, she shepherded them down to the breakfast parlour.

A few minutes later, Meg bounced in.

Jane looked up from her seat and smiled at the little girl. At least some good had come of the colonel's visit. She patted the chair beside her. 'Come and sit next to me, Meg. Soon you will be going to your new home. Isn't that wonderful?'

Meg's face turned solemn. 'I know I will be happy with the colonel. He has told me to call him Uncle Nicholas, by the way.' The little girl bit her lip. 'But ... I'll miss you. If only you could come with me, Miss Mortimer.'

Jane swallowed. 'I'm sure your new governess will be nice. The colonel, your Uncle Nicholas, will make sure of that.'

Jane picked up her coffee cup with a trembling hand. Nicholas. His name was Nicholas. How apt. He was rather like a Saint Nicholas, coming in and rescuing little Meg just before Christmas. If only someone would come and rescue her.

———— · ————

Nicholas woke up with a headache. He only had himself to blame. After he'd returned from escorting Meg and Miss Mortimer back to the Academy, he'd ordered a bottle of port. But it was never a good idea to drink alone. It only took two glasses before he gave up and retired to bed.

Alas, sleep wouldn't come. The noises of carriages and carts going by on the road below his window carried into his room. It was odd, because out in Portugal he'd slept in the open air through thunderstorms and the noise of distant cannon.

No, it was Miss Mortimer who had kept him awake. Every time he closed his eye he'd seen the image of her smiling face.

How had he got it all wrong? He'd offered her the position of governess to his ward, convinced that she would accept. The child obviously loved her teacher. And from what he'd gleaned, that feeling was reciprocated, with Miss Mortimer protecting Meg from the worst of Miss Pugh's rules.

But she had turned him down.

It would have been a subtle way to get to know each other better. Now he would never know if she had any feelings for him.

He called for Penrose, who hurried in. 'I've got your hot water ready, sir.'

'Thank you. Yes, I'm ready for my shave.'

Putting on his banyan, Nicholas sat listless on the chair near the dressing table and looked at his reflection in the mirror. His good eye was bloodshot, his hair disordered, and there was dark beard growth across the lower part of his face. He'd never been a vain man, but this morning, the sight of his face disgusted him.

'Is everything all right, sir? You seem a little...' Penrose lathered the brush and started to apply it to his master's face.

'Never mind me, Penrose. Just a bit blue-devilled today.'

'Why is that, sir, if you don't mind me asking? I saw you last evening with your ward – a nice young girl – and the lovely lady. Her teacher, wasn't she? Wish I had someone who looked at me like that.'

Nicholas jerked upright, his gaze sharp on his valet. 'What did you say?'

Penrose, a sheepish expression on his face, took a quick step back. Fortunately, he had not started with the razor. 'Don't mind me, sir. Talking out of turn.'

Nicholas softened his tone, but not by much. Army habits were hard to break. 'Nonsense. Repeat what you just said. That is an order.'

Penrose's Adam's apple bobbed in his throat. 'I was saying that the teacher was looking at you all dreamy-like. Like you were her hero.'

'Are you sure?' Nicholas barked.

'Yes, sir. Though you probably didn't notice. I think you were listening to the little girl chatter on. It was when I brought their outdoor things in, sir. Definitely, sir, I'd say she likes you.'

Nicholas drummed his fingers on the arms of the chair.

'Better get a move on with my shave, Penrose. I'm going out.'

'What about breakfast, sir?'

'Breakfast? There's more important things than breakfast.'

Chapter Eight

Jane was shepherding the girls out of the breakfast parlour when a hammering on the front door startled her. Whoever was making the noise sounded desperate to gain entry. Had Miss Pugh not paid one of her outstanding bills?

'Hurry along, girls. This doesn't concern you,' Jane called as she shooed her charges across the hallway, down the corridor, and into the classroom. Mr Rowland, the elderly butler Miss Pugh employed, hurried past her wheezing noisily. His rotund figure made speedy movements difficult. The banging on the door became more insistent.

Jane closed the classroom door behind her and sighed with relief. She'd had enough upheaval in the past few days to last her some time, she didn't need any more today. And she certainly didn't want her girls to hear a bad-tempered tradesman hurling abuse.

'Right, girls. Where did you get to in your lessons yesterday? Did you finish the work I set you?'

Before long, the girls were busy with heads bent over their books. All seemed to have quietened outside too.

From her desk at the front, Jane looked over sadly at the empty place that was normally Meg's. She would miss the little girl. Meg had been excused lessons that morning because she was leaving and needed to pack her belongings. Jane smiled, thinking of the better life in store for her favourite pupil.

A tap on the door interrupted Jane's reverie.

The maid bobbed her head in. 'Miss Pugh wants you, Miss Mortimer.'

Jane's insides tensed. What else was that woman about to threaten her with?

Jane stood up and tapped her ruler on the desk to get her pupils' attention. 'Girls, I won't be long. No talking now.' As soon as the door closed behind her the giggles and chatter started, but she was in no mood to sort it out. She had Miss Pugh to deal with.

As she got closer to Miss Pugh's study, she heard voices. Jane slowed her steps. One of the voices belonged to Miss Pugh, the other ... no, it couldn't be.

Jane tapped on the door and went in, just in time to hear Miss Pugh declare in strident tones, 'This is most irregular, Colonel.'

The colonel, for it was he who answered in a voice used to command, 'I'll be the judge of that. Now are you going to give me some privacy or not?'

Miss Pugh, who was not a small woman, seemed to shrink a little. Then she saw Jane and smirked. 'Well, here you are. What a sly one.'

'Get out.' The colonel's quietly spoken order sent the older woman scuttling out of the door.

Jane frowned. 'I don't understand. What is going on? I thought you were collecting Meg this afternoon.' Her heart sank. 'Have you changed your mind about taking her away?' Seeing Meg's disappointment would be heartbreaking.

He held out his hand. 'Come here, Miss Mortimer. I have something to say.'

He smiled and with a puzzled look she placed her hand in his. She was not wearing gloves and the touch of his skin against hers sent delicious tingles through her. If this was his way of saying goodbye, she would treasure this moment forever.

'I'm afraid I misspoke yesterday when I offered you the post of governess.'

'No need to apologise. I turned it down after all. I'm sorry too, but I'm sure you'll find another suitable governess.'

Was that why he'd sent for her? To apologise? Goodness, her heart was beating so fast, her words were tumbling out. Better get this over with. 'Shall I send for Meg?' Jane turned back towards the door, but his grip on her hand didn't loosen.

'I want to make you another offer, if you'll only listen for a minute.'

It was as if she'd been doused in cold water. So that was what he wanted. No wonder Miss Pugh had been outraged. She spun round, her eyes flashing. 'I'll not be your mistress.'

'My dear, only listen, that's not what I'm asking. I wouldn't insult you in that way.' He let out a deep breath. 'Goodness, I don't even know your first name.'

Her pulse was racing so fast she could barely think. He'd called her 'dear'.

'It's J-Jane.' Her eyes widened. Why was he kneeling?

'Jane Mortimer, will you do me the honour of accepting my proposal of marriage?'

Dumbstruck, Jane stared at him as he looked up at her. She'd heard people speak of a lover's look, but she'd never seen one ... until now. She must be dreaming.

'Say something, my darling Jane.'

'I can't,' she answered.

'You can't marry me?'

'I can't speak. I don't know what to say.'

'Say yes, that's all. We can leave here today. You can stay with Meg. I'll rent some rooms for you both and arrange for the banns to be called. We can be married before Christmas.'

The room was spinning. She closed her eyes. Had he just asked her to marry him? The gentleman she'd fallen in love with at first sight? That only happened in fairy tales.

Jane opened her eyes. Colonel Anstruther was standing before her, hope and anxiety playing across his face. His scars and missing eye didn't matter to her. All she saw was a man in love.

'Yes, I will be honoured to marry you ... Nicholas.'

His eyebrow arched. 'You know my name. I like it even better when you say it.' He wrapped an arm round her and tipping her chin upwards, he kissed her gently on the lips.

'I've wanted to do that ever since we first met.' His voice had gone husky.

'Really?' She smiled up at the man who had stolen her heart.

'Yes, really. You didn't flinch at the state of my face. And spending time with you has taught me that you are not only beautiful on the outside but your character is beautiful too.'

Jane giggled. 'Why would I flinch? I don't see your scars or missing eye. I see a brave man who has fought for his country. A man who is prepared to look after an orphaned child ... a kind and considerate man who thinks of what might please a little girl he has never met.'

He held a finger across her lips. 'Stop. You will make my head swell. Who would think that the purchase of ribbons would lead to this?' He put a hand in his greatcoat pocket and pulled out a stream of dark blue ribbons.

Jane looked at him questioningly. 'When did you buy those?'

'The same day that I met you. In addition to the ones I purchased for Meg, I bought these. I thought that if I never saw you again, they would be a reminder of the charming lady with the kind blue eyes who wasn't afraid to smile at me.'

A little over three weeks later Lieutenant Colonel Nicholas Anstruther and Miss Jane Mortimer were married at St Swithin's church in Walcot. It was reported that the bride and groom both looked very happy as they, together with the groom's young ward, departed the church to journey to the groom's estate in the county of Oxfordshire ... just in time for Christmas.

The End

Penny Hampson writes mysteries, and because she has a passion for history, you'll find her stories also reflect that. *A Gentleman's Promise*, a traditional Regency romance, was Penny's debut novel and the first of her Gentlemen Series. There are now three novels in the series, with the fourth, *An Adventurer's Contract*, due to be released by the end of 2024. Penny lives with her family in Oxfordshire, and when she is not writing, she enjoys reading, walk-ing, swimming, and the odd gin and tonic (not all at the same time).

Visit her on Twitter, Facebook, and Instagram, or on her website at pennyhampson.co.uk. Scan the QR code to learn more.

A Worthy Alteration

by Judith Hale Everett

Let me not to the marriage of true minds
Admit impediments; love is not love
Which alters when it alteration finds,
Or bends with the remover to remove.

—William Shakespeare

Chapter One

When the carriage belonging to Peter Holydale, Viscount Windon, drew up in front of the Black Bull Inn at Wolsingham, county Durham, the snowy yard was a hive of activity. The stage had just arrived, having immediately disgorged its passengers, and trunks and parcels were being unloaded and carried about, passengers stamped in the cold and hallooed for their baggage, and grooms dashed here and there, their breath a fog in their faces, as the sweating horses were led away and six fresh ones put to.

Gazing distastefully through the window at this hubbub, Lord Windon knocked the head of his cane against the roof of the carriage and his coachman hurriedly descended from the box, tugging respectfully at the brim of his hat.

"Where the devil are we, Pratt?" inquired his lordship. "Oughtn't we to be at Randley by now?"

"Beggin' yer pardon, m'lord," said the grizzled retainer, rubbing his mittened hands together for warmth. "We arter be there—howsomever there's no Ballam Road what I can find. Gripson's gone to inquire the way."

Unable to share his precise feelings on the matter to so staid and venerable a retainer as Pratt, Windon merely sighed and nodded, pulling the rug off his shapely legs—which were encased in spotless buckskins and gleaming Hessians—to thrust open the door. He descended from the coach, exhaling as he rose to his full six-foot height to survey his surroundings, his many-caped greatcoat furling about him.

It was a respectable inn, with enough grooms to keep the business efficient—indeed, the stage was already preparing to depart—and an ostler that only now had glimpsed his lordship. The man hastened over on bandy legs, bowing as he halted before this latest estimable guest.

"Afternoon, yer honor! Might yer honor wish to step into the taproom? It's as cold as hell froze over—"

Windon produced a shilling and waved him away. "No, no, thank you. Only stopped for directions. Won't be a minute."

The ostler thanked him and bowed himself away as his honorable guest took a few paces from the carriage to stretch his legs. They'd made good time today, but it was dashed tedious going. The cold hadn't affected Windon much, thanks to a warm brick at his feet and the plush fur rug for his legs, but he'd still be devilish glad to arrive at his destination. He'd never been to Randley, and if he'd not the promise of Miss Tyndall's lovely blue eyes at his arrival he would never have come to this godforsaken place, for it would not have taken his mother's disapproval to keep him away.

"I do not know what I can have done," Lady Dewsbury had declared upon hearing of his intended expedition, "to have been saddled with so addle-pated a son! You simply must go chasing after every pretty face that offers. When will you learn, I wonder?"

"Suppose you'd have me make up to some hatchet-faced female," he had muttered, grimacing.

"That is not my meaning, and you well know it," rejoined his mother. "It is nothing to do with the young lady at all, but with you, Windon! Until you learn that young ladies are not mere adornments to one's consequence, you will never desire to attach one."

"Have attached her!" he had said indignantly. "Miss Tyndall's fairly smitten, and assures me Lady Tyndall particularly wishes me to come to them at Christmas."

His mother had favored him with her blandest gaze. "Certainly she does. I am only amazed her ladyship did not follow her daughter to Bath directly she learned of your appearance there. Althea Tyndall was ever a grasping female—but then, she did snare Lord Tyndall. But all that doesn't signify in the least, for Miss Tyndall's being smitten is nothing to the point. Anyone can be smitten, but few are able to excite a lasting passion—"

"Now there you're out! Never felt for any other lady as I do for Miss Tyndall!"

"Oh?" she had inquired, brows rising. "What of Lady Veronica, or Miss Treanor? And need I mention Lady Serena?"

He had huffed and turned away, but she went on inexorably, "You said exactly the same thing of every one of them, and yet they have all gone on to marry someone else. Protestations are useless—you will never desire nor have the power to secure a lady's true affections until you look for more than a pretty face."

Lord Windon kicked at a stone as he recollected this very disagreeable dialog, resolving again that he would show his mother. Indeed, perhaps he would offer for Miss Tyndall—if not during the house party, sometime in the near future—for besides being angelically pretty, she was the most darling, the sweetest, most captivating—

His mental image of this paragon vanished away as his gaze fell upon one in the flesh, just emerging from the door to the inn. She wore a heavy, fur-lined cape over a blue woolen pelisse, but the countenance framed by the hood testified to the perfections hidden beneath the layers of her clothing. Her face had an elfin quality, the lips a cupid's bow, the eyes a deep and trusting brown. Dusky curls peeped from the recesses of the hood, and the gloved hands that held a portmanteau before her were small and elegant.

Lord Windon's view was obscured a moment as the stage lumbered out of the yard, but when it had passed, he saw that she was speaking with the ostler, who shook his head in answer to her inquiry. The lovely eyes were downcast a moment as the lips frowned, and when she again raised her eyes, her distress was evident, even from across the inn yard. Another inquiry was productive of still more consternation, and Windon knew his moment had come.

Closing the distance in a few strides, he swept off his hat and bowed. "Beg pardon, madam, but I perceive you're in distress of some kind." He returned the hat to his head and gazed fully upon the upturned face, his own a careful mix of concern and admiration. "Might I be of assistance?"

"Oh!" The lady colored deeply, one hand coming up to cover her sweet mouth. She dropped her gaze, stammering a little, "I did not perceive—forgive me—you are very kind, my lord—I am so very obliged—however, I cannot accept—"

Windon's view of her charms being impaired by her refusal to look at him, he felt it imperative that he put her at ease. "Assure you, ma'am, I've nothing to do that cannot wait. Merely on the way to a house party, but plenty of daylight left to offer a trifling service."

She at last rewarded him with a peep from her brown eyes, though they showed not trust but something else—embarrassment? He smiled reassuringly, angling to get a better view of that elusive countenance.

"Most humble servant, ma'am. Pray, allow me to know what's distressed you."

Another peep from those enchanting eyes, this time less anxious. "Do you not—that is, do you really mean to help me, sir?"

"Anything in my power," was his immediate reply.

She inhaled, glancing about as though in search of confirmation. But as the ostler had returned to his duties and the grooms had all disappeared into the stables to see after the horses from the stage, there was no one else to whom she could turn. Letting out a breath that puffed in the cold air, she lifted her chin, gazing for the first time directly at Lord Windon.

"I thank you, sir. It is only that I was to have been met here by my aunt's carriage, but it seems she has—" She hesitated, dropping her gaze again for a moment. "She has mistaken the day, to be sure. I might walk to the house, for it is only a matter of a few miles—"

"A few miles!" exclaimed Windon, who never walked when he could ride. "I'll not hear of it! Pray allow me to take you up in my carriage. Catch your death walking all of a few miles in this weather."

She colored becomingly again, looking away. "It is very cold. But I do not wish to take you out of your way."

"Don't know the way, so can't take me out of it," he said blithely, tipping his head forward and smiling again in a coaxing manner.

"But surely you know where you are going," she said, opening her eyes wide.

"Coachman assured me he did—however, seems he was mistaken. And not having been to this particular locality, I'm quite as lost as he. So, you see, I am at your disposal." He gave another sweeping bow.

"But sir, you are being nonsensical!" chided his companion, a twinkle coming into her brown eyes. "You would not have me believe that you do not intend to inquire the direction!"

In his element, Windon replied airily, "Never fear, my man's gone into the inn to do just that, but even should it prove to be opposite your own, I'll still not allow you to walk, ma'am, depend upon it!"

She bit her lips, but could not keep them from turning up enchantingly, a dimple appearing in her cheek. "You are too kind. Very well, I shall accept your offer, with many thanks."

Windon brushed away her gratitude with a wave of his hand, taking her portmanteau and handing it to Gripson, who had just at that moment exited the inn. The valet took it without comment, being inured to his master's ways, and awaited his instructions.

His lordship turned again to the young lady and inquired, "Now where might we deliver you, ma'am?"

"As you are strangers here," she said, raising an ironical eyebrow, "I am persuaded it will be best that I give my directions to the coachman."

This she did, while the valet strapped the portmanteau onto the back with the other luggage. Then Windon handed her into the carriage, settling himself on the back-facing seat and tapping the roof with his cane to signal his readiness to depart. The coachman gave his horses the office and the carriage set into motion.

She seemed disinclined to look at him, as though her maidenly modesty precluded such forwardness, but after a moment she favored him with a shy glance and inquired, "What was your destination, sir—if it is not impertinent to inquire?"

"Place called Randley," he supplied readily. "Never been there—gracious, are you quite well?"

The young lady was staring wide-eyed at him, her face drained of color. At his inquiry, she blinked several times, swallowed, and looked away, stammering, "I—I am very—well, sir, thank you. A—a momentary dizziness—the movement of the coach, you understand. I am much better now. You—you have never been there?"

"Never. Met Miss Tyndall in the autumn in Bath, but not Lord and Lady Tyndall—weren't with her. Know 'em yourself?"

She cleared her throat. "I—I do. Quite well, in fact. Particularly Miss Tyndall."

"Friend of yours? Well!" He blinked, recalling his undying love for Miss Tyndall. "Yes, incomparable, Miss Tyndall."

"Quite incomparable, to be sure."

Windon's gaze flitted away, his mind attempting to reassert his now hopelessly fuzzy image of Miss Tyndall as the pinnacle of perfection. This was not terribly successful, as it somehow always resolved into the image of the lady sitting before him.

"Perhaps you've been invited to the house party?" he asked hopefully.

"No—that is, I had not heard. I have been away, you see."

"Might be an invitation awaiting you at—your aunt's?"

She looked out the window, her hands twisting together in her lap. "I do not anticipate it." She flashed a smile at him. "It is a Christmas party, I collect?"

He nodded, his interest in the party gravely impaired by the likelihood of his enchanting companion's not being there. "Do you remain in the neighborhood?"

"I—I do. I am—that is, I live with my aunt," she said, her smile a trifle stiff.

"Perhaps I might see you, then—about the neighborhood."

She turned her head away again, humming in a noncommittal way. "I expect you will be kept busy at Randley. How—how long do you anticipate your stay to be?"

Windon shrugged. "Invitation was for two weeks. Bound to be a boring moment I could sneak away."

"Oh, it will not be a bore, sir—you may depend upon that!" she said with a wry little smile. "Lady Tyndall is nothing if not resourceful. She will have provided for every detail. Wait and see."

He agreed politely with her, but inwardly cringed at the notion of every detail being provided for. Nothing was so tedious as the minute plans of an over-zealous hostess—except, perhaps, a party that did not include the most enchanting lady in the neighborhood. The divine Miss Tyndall's memory was rapidly deteriorating, and he sighed contentedly as his gaze drank in the lovely countenance of the lady seated across from him, admiring the alabaster skin and the gentle curve of the cheek as she contemplated the passing landscape.

He cleared his throat to try if he could discover her name, but the carriage swung onto a lane and his companion jerked her head, bending closer to the window as though she had not seen anything through it all this time. She turned suddenly to him.

"Pray, stop the coach."

"Why? Are you ill?"

"No, no—only I fear we have come too far."

He peered out the window, glimpsing a stately Georgian mansion at the end of the drive. "Is not that your aunt's house?"

"Yes—only—oh, pray, stop the coach! You may put me down here."

He frowned at her. "But it's twenty yards away. Couldn't do so shabby a thing as set you down before we've reached the house."

She bit her lip, wringing her hands, but did not pursue the matter. In minutes, they had reached the top of the drive and stopped at the foot of the steps. The door of the house opened instantly, emitting a butler and two footmen, who came quickly to open the door of the carriage.

The young lady practically leapt out, turning back only to say, "Thank you, sir!" before hastening up the steps and into the house. Windon, bewildered, bent forward to look after her, and saw her exchanging agitated words with a handsome but grim-faced woman in puce satin, who cast scandalized looks toward the coach.

His lordship drew back, wondering what the young lady could have said of him to induce such disapprobation, and thinking it might behoove him to get along to his house party. Cravenly, he pulled the door shut and knocked his cane on the roof, only to have his valet come up to the window. He let it down impatiently, seeing over Gripson's shoulder that the grim-faced woman was descending the steps of the house with all the grandeur of a queen coming to pass a sentence of death.

"Dash it, man, let's be off!" he hissed, watching the lady's progress with growing anxiety.

"But sir, we are arrived."

"What? Devil take you, Gripson! Of course we've arrived, and best be off before that gorgon comes to take off my head for some dashed silly scruple!"

His valet regarded him with patience. "You do not wish to stay, sir?"

"No!"

"Very well, sir. Allow me to make your excuses to Lady Tyndall—though, as she is just here, perhaps you should like to do so yourself."

Chapter Two

L ord Windon stared at his valet. "What—Lady Tyndall? Here?" With a bow of his head, Gripson stood aside, allowing the grim-faced woman to come up to the coach to address his master.

"My dear Lord Windon!" she said, an ingratiating smile relieving the hard lines of her face. "You must forgive the familiarity—I feel as though we know one another, so much have I heard of you from Honoria. I am so glad you have come! It is a great kindness in you to travel all this way, and leave behind your family at Christmas—how is dear Lord Dewsbury? The gout is not to be trifled with, to be sure. I am certain he is comfortable at home where dear Lady Dewsbury can take good care of him. Will you not come in, sir? I trust my niece has not frightened you away with her forwardness?"

"F-forwardness?" managed Lord Windon, gazing in stupefaction at his hostess. "Your niece—that was your niece?"

The smile became a little sour. "She did not even tell you that, eh? Good heaven, what an ill-mannered girl. Yes, sir, my niece, Miss Stowe. She is come to be a governess to my younger children and a companion to Honoria." The smile once again brightened. "You will see Honoria presently—she is as lovely as ever, and so looking forward to your visit."

The carriage door opened and Lord Windon stepped down, still rather bemused. "Miss Stowe is a governess? Here?"

"Yes, though not a very good one," Lady Tyndall said, ill-disguising her displeasure at his interest in the wrong young lady. "If it were not for her dreadful circumstances, I should never have employed her. But a near relation—" She sighed. "One does what one must for those beneath one."

"Your niece."

Lady Tyndall fluttered a hand as she guided his lordship up the steps and into the house. "Lord Tyndall's sister's child. A marriage quite below her station, though he was a gentleman. But poor Letitia is dead, and so is Mr. Stowe—rest his soul. One does not like to speak ill of the dead, but there was some shocking mismanagement, and their child was left destitute. Such impecuniousness gives one a disgust for such persons—for one only imagines they have earnt it with profligacy. I fear they have passed their taint on to their progeny, as is so often the case—but I saw it as my duty to take Prudence in. I trust that, in giving her a respectable home and occupation, a change might be effected, and her character saved. After today, however, I begin to doubt my good will."

Lord Windon, now being divested of his greatcoat, blinked. "Character—saved? Not a bit of it—merely brought her here in my coach." He blinked again, the bemusement clearing from his brain, and certain facts coming to the fore. "No carriage sent for her, you know! Had to do the gallant thing, or she'd have froze."

Lady Tyndall tittered a bit consciously. "Oh! Well, it has been such a day, with guests expected and entertainments to prepare. Her coming entirely slipped my mind! It is what comes of making her arrangements at the last minute. She was to stay all of Christmas with that old governess of hers, you see, but there was an ill relation or some such and the woman was obliged to go attend. At any rate, I would have been pleased for Prudence to stay where she was, but Honoria insisted that she return. Honoria is always so generous to her cousin—and, indeed, to anyone! Just one of her many excellent qualities, you know."

"Indeed," said Windon, beginning to grasp that he was in no trouble at all, and that Lady Tyndall's dislike was directed entirely at her niece. "Look forward to furthering her acquaintance, ma'am. And Miss Stowe's."

"Oh, I daresay you have seen all there is to see of my niece, my lord," simpered her ladyship. "A governess, you know."

Windon cocked his head. "But Miss Stowe is your niece. Surely she'll be joining the party."

Her ladyship's smile became something of a grimace. "Oh, dear me, no. Did she claim to do so? How odiously coming of her!"

"Not a bit of it, ma'am!" Windon said, firing up over this traducing of a lovely girl's character. "Said she hadn't known at all of a party—didn't even say she was your niece. Dashed well would have refused my offer of the carriage and walked three miles, or four miles, or whatever it is from the Black Bull, but that I wouldn't take her nay. Wouldn't have been gentlemanly— devilish cold weather for a walk."

Lady Tyndall had the grace to look somewhat abashed, but recovered quickly, saying, "My wretched memory! How providential that you happened upon her, sir. She did, I trust, express her gratitude properly."

"Very, ma'am, so properly that I hope to see more of her—at the house party."

Her ladyship looked acutely uncomfortable as she led him toward the drawing room. "I fear it is impossible," she said in a wheedling tone. "What would people say? A governess! My dear Lord Windon, my—nor even Honoria's—generosity cannot extend so far."

"But ain't she Miss Tyndall's companion?" pressed Windon, not so easily put off.

"Certainly, but with so many guests at the party, Honoria shall not want her. No, my niece will be far too occupied with little Henry and Anne. They are sweet children, the best in the world, but so high-spirited. She will have no time to join in a party, even were it proper for her to do so. Now here is Honoria and some other of our guests. Honoria, dearest, here is Lord Windon!"

His lordship was instantly distracted from his campaign to assure himself of Miss Stowe's amiable company, for his admiration of Miss Tyndall was miraculously revived upon seeing her. Indeed, he could not help but see the resemblance to her cousin, only with light coloring—celestial blue eyes and honey-gold curls. She was perhaps a bit plumper than Miss Stowe, but the low-cut white muslin gown she wore attested to this being entirely in her favor.

She smiled delightedly up at him. "My lord, how lovely that you have come."

Windon bent low over her proffered hand and murmured what was proper, the tragedy of Miss Stowe's not being allowed to be of the party fast receding from his mind.

——— · ———

When Honoria retired to her bedchamber to dress for dinner, she was pounced upon by her cousin, who had been pacing the room for nearly a half-hour awaiting her.

"Oh, Nora! I do not know what to do!" she cried. "I am utterly undone!"

"Goodness me, Prue. Whatever can you mean? Has Henry climbed the drainspout again?"

"No, no, he and Anne are with Nurse today, and I cannot be more grateful!" She allowed her cousin to lead her to a chair, where she sat with a gusty sigh. "Nora, did you see Lord Windon?"

Honoria regarded her bemusedly. "Certainly. But what has Lord Windon to do with Henry?"

"Nothing—forget Henry! Did his lordship say anything about—about me?" Prudence inquired, her brown eyes anxious.

Her cousin blinked back. "No, how could he? He does not know you, Prue. Did you perhaps get a touch of the sun at Dimstock?" She reached to lay a cool hand on Prudence's forehead, but it was pushed impatiently away.

"Nora, he does know me—that is, we have met before. However, it is of no consequence, for he did not even recognize me."

"You are not making sense, Prue. How can he have recognized you? He only just arrived and you have been upstairs."

"He took me up in his carriage this afternoon, when I arrived on the stage! Oh, how could I have been so idiotish? He told me he was at Wolsingham to attend a house party—who else could he have been visiting but Aunt Tyndall? Oh, I wish I were dead!"

"Do not say so, Prue!" Utterly bewildered, yet deeply concerned,

Honoria drew up the footstool and sat beside her cousin, patting her hand where it lay limply on the arm rest. "But I do not follow—you say you met his lordship? It can only have been in London, then, for since your mama—that is, since you were obliged to—"

Prudence had closed her eyes, a pained expression flitting across her features. "It was at the Dowager Marchioness of Foxham's ball."

"Oh." Honoria sat back on the stool. "I had forgotten about that. You were in Town only a few weeks, after all."

"He took me down to dinner," continued Prudence in a resigned tone, "and was so charming! I could tell he greatly admired me, and I hoped—well, it was not much of a chance, for I was only there out of Lady Strickland's kindness, but one cannot be blamed for hoping."

"No." Honoria patted her hand again, then her expression changed, her brow furrowing. "How did it fall out that he took you up with him today? Did not Mama send the carriage for you?"

Prudence rolled her head on the headrest to regard her cousin. "No. I daresay she forgot—again. If it had not been so cold, I should gladly have walked, but he was there, and insisted he was at leisure and could take me wherever I wished. I know I ought not to have accepted, but it was bitter cold, Nora. And he was very persuasive."

"And rightly so," said Honoria approvingly. "He is excessively amiable, though a sad rattle—but you must know that. It is of no consequence, however, for he is every bit as eligible as ever he was," she added forlornly, and sighed. "Mama is very pleased."

"Is she very vexed with me?" asked Prudence.

Honoria looked up from her unhappy reflections. "Who?"

"Aunt Tyndall. She was horridly displeased when she saw that I had come with his lordship. I swear I did not imagine he was to come here, and to a house party—Nora, why did not you tell me of the party when you begged me to come home?"

Her cousin averted her eyes, color coming into her cheeks. "I did not wish to disappoint you. I had hoped to persuade Mama to include you, but—" She sighed again. "As I feared, she remains unmoved. It is monstrous of her to deny you—it is not as though you were born a governess."

Prudence could not help but chuckle. "No one is born a governess, silly! But I have fallen sadly in the estimation of the world, and cannot but be grateful there is a roof over my head. Things could be much worse, you know. Oh, poor Mama! Poor Papa!"

"They would be mortified to see what has become of you, Prue!" declared Honoria, a mulish look on her pretty face. "And all because Mama is jealous!"

"Oh, Nora, how could she be? I have never believed it, for you are as beautiful as an angel."

"As are you, and she insists upon setting you up as competition to me. As though you would attempt to cast me into the shade."

"I could not, even if I were so mean-spirited as to try."

"Be that as it may, Mama refuses to see it."

They sighed in united discontent with the injustices of their world, clasping hands with fierce loyalty.

Prudence smiled wanly. "At least you are good to me, Nora. I cannot be unhappy with you always taking my part. I might not have been allowed to visit poor Miss Dickerson at all if you had not championed my case to my aunt. Thank you again for lending me your cape and pelisse. It was so lovely not to fear for my appearance."

"It is a shame you had to sell all your pretty things." Honoria slumped, resting her chin in her hand. "I only wish I could persuade Mama to give you another Season—your first was so unhappily curtailed. The injustice of it vexes me infinitely! If you were to get a husband, Mama could be easy, but she will not agree to it."

"It would be shockingly expensive, Nora."

"Pooh! We have the house in Town, and you could have my old gowns—they are perfectly good. I declare I wore them no more than twice each, and Mama intends to buy me all new next Season."

Prudence shook her head at this extravagance, but patted her cousin's hand. "It is better to put all talk of that behind us, my dear. I must accept my new station and do my best to fit into it."

Honoria pursed her lips, a twinkle coming into her eye as she looked at her cousin askance. "You will have to do better than that, Prue. You are a deplorable governess."

Prudence smiled, but looked downcast. "I cannot deny it. I simply cannot seem to teach your brother and sister anything. I do try, but Henry is so very wild, and Anne has taken me in dislike. I fear she is much like my aunt."

"It is too true. If only Papa would take Henry in hand, but dear Papa is so very insensible, for all he is a perfect dear."

"When he can be got to leave off hunting and riding. I fear it irritates my aunt that he is forever in the stables or gone off to visit one of his cronies."

The two cousins exchanged a rueful look and were once more thoughtful.

After a moment, Prudence said, "I must not annoy her during the house party. If I keep out of sight, perhaps she will forget that I made Lord Windon's acquaintance. Indeed, she will not know that we are otherwise acquainted, for he shall not have mentioned it, having forgotten all about me."

"It is very likely, for he did not speak of your meeting to me," agreed Honoria optimistically. "Perhaps Mama will not give it another thought."

But such was not the case. As Prudence readied herself for bed that night in her tiny attic bedroom, the door opened and Lady Tyndall entered, her handsome countenance every bit as grim as it had been upon perceiving the mode of her niece's arrival that afternoon.

"Well, Prudence," she said, eying her niece with dislike. "You have had a very great honor this day. It has, no doubt, gone to your head."

"Indeed not, Aunt!" cried Prudence, her eyes averted in what she hoped would be construed as abject humility.

Her aunt humphed. "I trust not, for it will only lead to sorrow if you do. His lordship was quite adamant in his motives for taking you up, and they were entirely altruistic. Do not begin to imagine that he meant anything more than to ease the suffering of a poor dependent, as is his duty as a peer of the realm."

"Certainly, ma'am." She felt Lady Tyndall's gaze rake over her.

Her ladyship sniffed. "Anne reports you were impertinent at dinner. I shall remind you that while you are in my employ you will treat the children with the respect their station deserves, or you shall find yourself at the employment office without a reference."

"But ma'am," cried Prudence, looking up quickly. "She called Nurse a gargoyle! You would not have me let her do so without—"

"Nurse may defend herself as she sees fit. She has been our faithful retainer since Honoria was born and has earned that right—unlike yourself." She picked up a small ornament on the dressing table and looked it over, replacing it with a look of distaste. "I trust there is no need for a warning to you, Prudence, that you will behave properly during my house party. Honoria shall dispense with your services as a companion during the next fortnight, and you shall devote yourself to the children. You will not descend from the upper rooms except by the servant's staircase, and you will endeavor to be unheard and unseen by my guests. Do you understand?"

Prudence sighed, but it was only as she had expected. "Yes, Aunt."

Chapter Three

L ady Tyndall's other guests arrived over the following two days, and the ladies in the party being of merely tolerable aspect, Lord Windon's loyalty to Miss Tyndall's beauty was not to be challenged by them. He was only mildly troubled by the memory of Miss Stowe's face, as well, for he did not catch even a glimpse of her during that time, as she conscientiously adhered to her aunt's commands.

But a chance remark by Miss Tyndall regarding her cousin having attended the Dowager Marchioness of Foxham's ball during the Season brought a memory fluttering into his head of a lovely brunette with smiling brown eyes, who had captivated him at that ball. His mind was not a quick one, nor was it tenacious, but perhaps because Miss Tyndall's face was continually before him, he could easily trace the lines of her cousin's, and he began to be possessed of a conviction that Miss Stowe and the brunette were one and the same.

By the third day, Lord Windon had received enough reminders—between his own admiration of Miss Tyndall and Lady

Tyndall's admiration of her for him—to wonder if he might contrive another meeting with Miss Stowe. It had occurred to him that he was guilty of a solecism, for a gentleman ought not to forget an acquaintance made, especially if that acquaintance was a lovely young woman with rosebud lips. As a gentleman, he could not allow such a lapse to be perpetuated—even were she a governess—and he envisioned a romantic apology, followed by a few stolen moments together, wherein he could drink his fill of her beauty.

The following morning, Lord Tyndall took the gentlemen out to bring in the yule log, and Lord Windon's bay mare had the misfortune to step in a rabbit hole and strain a hock. Rather than simply allow a groom to take his mount to the stables, Windon elected to go along, for he really had better things to do than wander about in the cold searching out a dashed big tree.

As they came across the paddock toward the stables, however, an unholy racket sounded from within. The mare, already troubled, tossed her head and shuffled, and the groom hastened to soothe her lest she worsen her injury. Affronted at the indignity being perpetrated in his horse's sanctum, Windon strode to the door to put an end to it, and stopped short. There, in the middle of the floor, was a young boy, kicking and screaming while a drably-dressed female attempted, without success, to restrain him.

"Good gracious, Henry!" cried the lady, her back to Windon as she danced around the boy to avoid his kicking feet. "Stop this at once! You will ruin your coat! Whatever can be the matter?"

"They're all gone away!" the boy wailed, flailing about in his tantrum. "They're getting the yule log with Papa, and all the horses are gone!"

The lady ceased her fruitless attempts at restraining her charge and put hands on hips, regarding him in annoyance. "Certainly they are, you ridiculous boy. You could not expect that they should walk so far in the dirt and snow!"

"But I wanted to see the high-bred-uns! Papa promised, but it's been three days already, and I've not seen none of them!"

Windon's mare tossed her head again, backing and whinnying as she put undue strain upon her injured hock. This was enough for his lordship.

"Now see here, my boy," he said sternly, making his presence known. "Can't go on caterwauling in the stables like a fishwife! Not a wife! Not a fish! Besides, Calliope needs peace and quiet. Better do as your nurse says and go away. Back to your books!"

Henry sat up with a start, his legs splayed out before him, and regarded this impressive gentleman with wide eyes. "I wasn't at my books, sir!" he squeaked. "I was playing at tin soldiers, but I wanted to play with real horses!"

"It don't signify what you were at! No excuse for making a racket and troubling decent folk. Not gentlemanly, you know! Daresay your nurse don't like it above half!"

With this, Windon gave a nod to the nurse, who had only half-turned and did not raise her eyes. He pitied her, poor creature, to have the charge of this brat. Her shapeless grey pelisse was covered in dust and straw from the floor, and her hair was wisping about her face where it had come loose from the severe bun at the back of her head. A plain, poor creature, to be sure, who did not deserve to be served so.

"Do you, ma'am?" he inquired kindly, with a bow.

"No, I do not, sir," she said without turning to him, but

crouching low to pat at the red, tear-streaked face of her charge with her handkerchief. "As you say, it is unseemly and unbecoming a young gentleman."

The timbre of her voice gave Windon pause, but it was not until she helped the boy to his feet and turned to guide him out of the stable that his eyes narrowed, gazing intently upon the face now fully in his view. He inhaled sharply.

"What the devil—Miss Stowe!"

Her eyes flew to his, her cheeks pink, but she lowered her gaze once more and said only, "My lord, I hope that you will forgive Henry for disturbing the peace of your morning. Henry, beg his lordship's pardon."

Henry drew himself to his full four feet and said manfully, "I beg your pardon, sir, for cat—cater—making a racket. May I meet Calliope?"

Miss Stowe remonstrated with him, but Lord Windon, recovering from his stupefaction, gestured him toward the mare, if only to have a moment alone with the governess.

"Mind you don't startle her again, young man," he said over his shoulder. "I'll not have her injury made worse!"

"I'll be as quiet as a mouse, sir," whispered Henry, and tiptoed up to the groom holding the mare's halter.

Miss Stowe attempted to slip past his lordship, but he put out a hand to stop her.

"What's all this, then?" he inquired, his brows lowered as he gazed anew at her face. It certainly was Miss Stowe, but the enchantment of her elfin countenance was marred by the severity of her hairstyle and the Quakerish cut of her gown. In all his imaginings of this meeting, she was fashionably dressed and ravishingly coiffed, for that is how he had seen her before. But this romantic vision was shattered by the dowdily-dressed scarecrow of a female before him.

The color deepened in her cheeks as she sought to look anywhere but at him. "I—I am a governess, my lord. I know I ought to have told you—only I did not think—I did not know what I should do. I hoped that I should never see you again—that is, I—I beg your pardon."

"I know you're a dashed governess, but that don't give you cause to dress like an ape leader!" He was overcome by a crashing sense of ill-use, as the connoisseur in him revolted. "Where's that enchanting pelisse you had on, and the curls? What can you be about? You never wore something this hideous to Lady Foxham's ball. It's beyond anything! This 'do is devilish ugly, too, and you ought to know it! It won't do at all—won't do at all! I tell you, ma'am, if you ain't careful, you'll frighten away all the gentlemen in the party!"

Miss Stowe, whose pink cheeks had been thus far one of her redeeming features, paled alarmingly, and her eyes, which could not meet his an instant before, were now fixed on his face and sparking dangerously.

"Then it is providential that I will not be of the party, sir," she snapped, "for whatever either of us could wish, I am yet a governess, and grateful to be! You may not like it, but it is not my place to try to improve my looks, much less to attempt to attract gentlemen meant to partner my cousin and her friends. I have borne many trials since my aborted Season, and I'll thank you not to throw them up in my teeth! I did not desire it, but I know my place, and I hope I am wise enough to take pains to look as though I do, for if I do not, I will not even be a governess anymore—I will be nothing! Good day, sir!"

And she sailed away, plucking Henry away from the mare and leading him, protesting in whispers that gradually grew louder the farther they were from Calliope, back into the house. Windon gazed after her in shock until the sidelong glances of the groom standing stock-still beside the mare brought him to himself.

"Go on, man, take her inside. Cold compresses—you know what to do. I'll be down after dinner to see how she goes on."

With all the dignity he could muster, he turned and marched back up to the house. Nursing his own hurt pride, he went to his bedchamber, called Gripson, and ruminated on his injuries while his boots were removed and his raiment changed suitably for a morning indoors.

Miss Stowe hadn't cause to fly at him like that. It had been almost more than he could bear to see her so altered—after such satisfying visions, too. He'd only given her a piece of advice, and very good advice it was! What did she think she was about, to skin her hair back and put on such horridly drab clothes—it was a crying shame, that's what it was! A pretty girl like her—no, an Incomparable! She had captivated him at the ball and again at the inn, only to hide away behind those weeds—for that was what they were, practically widow's weeds, and as attractive! How could she mock his admiration with that get-up? It was an affront to discerning eyes everywhere.

His valet finished and Windon dismissed him, going down to the drawing room where he found Miss Tyndall ensconced with the other ladies, engaged in tying ribbons for decoration. There was a general twitter of welcome at his entrance, and Lady

Tyndall rose to learn what had brought him back betimes.

"I see," she said when he had told of his horse's injury, a sly smile in her eyes as she led him over to Honoria's side. "A strained hock. Well, one can only be grateful our good Hamley has charge of the stables, for he is a magician with such things, depend upon it. You must not worry about a thing! Well, my lord, you must make do with us, now! Honoria, dear, Lord Windon will not wish to sit about while the ladies are employed with the ribbons. Do take him up to see the long gallery."

Amid the disgruntled whispers of the other ladies, Miss Tyndall rose obediently and led Windon out into the hall and back up the stairs to the first floor. Down the corridor to the left, they entered the long gallery, where centuries of Tyndall ancestors gazed down in various states of dissatisfaction upon their visitors. Windon, whose conscience had become restless, shuddered under their scrutiny.

"Now, really, Miss Tyndall, must we? Ain't there a parlor or—or a library—dash it! They make one's skin crawl!"

Miss Tyndall giggled. "You are being nonsensical. They are only paintings. However, I will take your arm and bear you up as we pass through, for the library is on the far side. But I must not quiz you, for I will own that I did not like to come here as a girl, fancying as I did all these people knew my very thoughts! Oh, what shivers it sent down my spine, especially when my thoughts were not precisely what they ought to have been!"

Distracted momentarily with curiosity as to what sort of improper thoughts the angelic Miss Tyndall might ever have entertained, Windon allowed himself to be led further into the hall. But the succession of her revered ancestors all gazing sternly down at him—ancestors she shared with Miss Stowe, no less—soon renewed his discomfort.

"Nothing fanciful about it, Miss Tyndall!" he declared, planting his feet and refusing to go farther. "I can feel 'em piercing my soul!"

Her laughter echoed through the lofty gallery. "But you have nothing to fear, I am persuaded, Lord Windon! Whatever could you be ashamed of?"

"Not a thing! That is, not the sort of thing I'd like to tell. Not that I'm some sort of rum touch—" Windon grimaced, thinking he had better make a clean breast of it. "Only, I seem to have vexed your cousin."

Miss Tyndall blinked. "My cousin? You've seen Prudence?"

"In the stables."

"The stables! Whyever was she there, I wonder?"

Windon coughed. "Brother of yours—Henry, is it? Having a tantrum on the stable floor, dust and straw everywhere. Miss Stowe trying to talk sense into him."

"Oh dear," said Miss Tyndall, dismayed. "How unpleasant."

"I'll say! Boy caterwauling to beat the band! Nearly spooked my horse!"

"Oh, certainly, but I did not mean for you. I meant for poor Prudence." She sighed. "Henry can be frightfully horrid when he does not get his way. I hope your presence calmed him. He holds sporting gentlemen in the greatest esteem."

Windon frowned. "Seemed more taken with Calliope. Not that I blame him—fine animal, complete to a shade."

"Oh, famous!" cried Miss Tyndall, smiling warmly at him. "He does love horses. That must be why he was in the stables. I'm sure Prudence was excessively grateful to you for distracting him."

He snorted. "Not in the least! Nearly bit my head off!"

"No! I cannot credit it! Prudence is the most charming creature, and could not act so improperly." She lowered her brows, her pretty lips pursing in disapproval. "You must have done something odious, Windon. Did not you say you had vexed her?"

"But it ain't my fault!" He put up his hands in defense. "She took a pet when I told her she ought to dress up and curl her hair. Looked frightful, like some old scarecrow! No accounting for it! Couldn't have been the same young lady I met at Lady Foxham's ball."

"Then you recollected that," said Miss Tyndall, her mouth pursed.

Windon looked hard at her. "Told me yourself, didn't you? Though I wouldn't credit it after today if I hadn't seen her myself looking ravishing at the Black Bull. Dashed waste of a pretty face in that fusty old gown, if you ask me."

"I must agree with you, sir," said Miss Tyndall, turning away. "But it simply would not do, you know. She is now a governess, after all. Mama would send her packing in a trice if she was so coming as to dress herself up. Prudence is quite lovely, and Mama could not bear to have her outshine me."

She sighed, plumping down on a settee beneath the likeness of a particularly somber ancestor. Windon, non-plussed, sat beside her.

"Don't see why she would," he said loyally. "Incomparable yourself, you know. Hold your own, to be sure."

She smiled sadly but shook her head. "Thank you, Windon, but Mama is terribly jealous. And she is anxious that I make a splendid match. She says that I was not born so lovely for nothing and has been throwing me in the way of every titled gentleman we meet."

Windon could not miss the note of wistfulness in her voice. "Sure to make a good match! Taken with you myself! That is, think you're the loveliest—"

"Oh, pray do not continue, sir!" she cried, cringing away from him, then bowing her head. "Forgive me, I beg. You cannot know, and I would not have led you on for the world."

Hovering between relief and injury, Windon murmured, "Nothing to forgive, ma'am. Had the notion you were amenable—title and all that. Quite a splendid match, if I say so myself."

"But I do not wish to make a splendid match!" she said mournfully, blinking back a tear. "I—there is—I beg your pardon, sir, but I can no longer dissemble. There is a certain gentleman—"

He turned toward her, intrigued. "Attached already? If that don't beat the Dutch! Had no notion—told my mama you were smitten, and all the while, she was right! Well, suppose it's all for the best. Who is the lucky fellow?"

She had been anxiously watching him throughout this odd speech, but perceiving that he was not about to rant and rave about his love for her, she exhaled and said, "You do not know him, I am sure. He is a mere Mr. Benchley of Pattendon Hall. His fortune is only a competence, and his consequence non-existent. Mama will not allow me to think of him—not with you showing so flattering an interest."

Windon's brows shot up. "Dashed awkward business."

Miss Tyndall sniffled noisily and he automatically handed her his handkerchief, lost in his own thoughts. He was not a powerful thinker, but he had enough experience with the machinations of match-making mamas to comprehend Miss Tyndall's despair. He was a viscount, after all, and the promise of an earldom far outweighed a competence, no matter how well the gentleman loved the lady. It did not bode well for Miss Tyndall's chances at happiness. But Lord Windon, if not prone to thoughtfulness, was a romantic, and the lady's plight touched him deeply, sufficient to overcome any affront he might have taken over her rejection.

Sitting up, he declared, "I will help you, ma'am, though I don't quite fathom how at the moment."

Miss Tyndall turned to him, the handkerchief suspended at her cheek and hope alive in her glistening eyes. "Will you help me, sir? Oh, do you mean it?"

"Said I would, didn't I? Well, man of my word. Never one to stand in the way of true love. Will help you if only I can fix upon something. Can't leave the party—not good ton. Besides, don't wish to."

"Oh, but you needn't, sir! Indeed—" A strange look came over her countenance, and she stared into the distance. "Indeed, it would be better that you stay, I am persuaded."

She leapt up and began pacing back and forth and murmuring to herself, unconscious of the disapproving stares of her forebears. "It is perfect—only too perfect! And Mama will be obliged to put a good face on it."

Windon had jumped to his feet as well, his curious gaze following her. After a full minute, he inquired politely, "Got an idea, ma'am?"

She stopped, clapping her hands. "To be sure! Oh, forgive me, but this is beyond anything!" Rapturously, she clasped her hands before her chest. "Lord Windon, will you pretend to be a friend to my dear Mr. Benchley? He is our neighbor, you know, and you may ride over to his estate tomorrow, and take a letter to him for me. But before you go you will let it be known that you know him—oh, from school or something—and that you have a deep regard for him."

Windon blinked, considering this. "Suppose I could. All sorts at school. Possible I did know him. Always did have a lamentable memory."

"Certainly! Gentlemen are always forgetting such things. Mama will never suspect you, depend upon it! But my letter will tell Fred all about my plan, and why he must pretend that you are old schoolmates, and then he will return with you, and Mama will be obliged to invite him to the ball Thursday next!"

Windon nodded gamely, though not quite following.

"You must mention the ball, you see," she said, gazing intently into his eyes to make sure he understood. "If you mention it to him in her presence, she will be forced to be civil and invite him, for she has invited all the other neighbors."

"Ah! Certainly, ma'am."

"And then, he will tell you—again in Mama's hearing—that he intends to make me his wife, and you will be so encouraging and congratulatory that she must give up all hope of your offering for me. And if you can manage to tell Papa what a fine fellow Mr. Benchley is, and that he would make me an excellent husband, then Fred's way will be made safe!"

Again, Windon nodded, a trifle overwhelmed at the part he was to play but spurred on by the gallantry to which he always fell victim in the company of a lovely woman.

Observing his rather dubious look, however, she suddenly blanched, taking her lower lip between her teeth. "Dear me, is it too much? I beg your pardon. I suppose it is excessively impertinent to ask you to practice such gross deception. What must you think of me? I can only imagine that I have overexcited myself and am somewhat frenzied in my mind." She plumped back down on the settee.

"No, no, ma'am!" he said quickly, dismissing the immense impropriety of her request with an airy hand. "Nothing to it! Nothing at all, assure you! Friendly fellow, I'm told. Can make a friend of anyone. If—Fred—will abet us, then all's right and tight. Good cause, you know!"

She beamed upon him once more. "Oh, thank you, my lord! I knew I could depend upon you. It is a good cause—it is my only hope for happiness, after all. And I shall be forever grateful—Fred too! We shall never forget your kindness!"

He brushed aside her thanks with many murmured protestations, relieved when at last she stood and linked arms with him, leading him back out of the gloomy hall and away from the accusatory gazes of her—thankfully—deceased relations.

Chapter Four

Prudence was not to witness how Lord Windon played his part two days later to perfection, for she was consigned to the schoolroom as usual, endeavoring to impress upon Anne the necessity of learning her French verbs, while Nurse kept Henry occupied with a puzzle near the window. The schoolroom, located on the third floor at the back of the house, overlooked the stables, and it was when Prudence was again explaining to her recalcitrant charge that a lady must not only speak French but read it as well that Henry let out a little shout. All eyes turned to him as he leapt from his chair and pressed his nose to the window.

"He's come back! Look at that sorry nag Papa's given him— nothing like his Calliope, but she's got a strained hock. She's a prime goer—his lordship let me meet her. He's a right one!"

Prudence came to stand beside him, her dignity still smarting over Lord Windon's attack on her looks two days before. Seeing his lordship astride her uncle's chestnut, magnificent in his greatcoat and shining hessian boots, she sniffed and turned away.

"Really, Henry, you ought not to use such vulgar phrases. I am persuaded you hardly know what you are saying."

"'Course, I do!" he cried, turning with a pout. "What do you know? You're only a female."

"Now, Master Henry," remonstrated Nurse, "that's no way to speak to Miss Stowe. She knows enough to be a governess, I'll remind you, and that's enough for you!"

Smiling her thanks, Prudence looked again to Henry, who was craning to watch the horseman dismount and hand his mount off to a groom. "You must mind your manners and come back to the table, Henry."

He merely clung to the glass. "There's another gentleman—that's Mr. Benchley! What's he doing here? Devilish irregular!"

"Henry!" cried Nurse and Prudence in unison, as the latter hastened once more to the window.

Henry hunched a shoulder, blushing. "Papa says it—why can't I? Besides, it's not as though it's a proper curse."

Not heeding this, Prudence looked out to see Honoria's Fred, who had been inflexibly denied the house only last month, swinging down from his horse as easy as you please. She inhaled sharply, wondering what Aunt Tyndall would do now, and what Lord Windon had to do with it. From the apparent camaraderie between them, his lordship had brought Mr. Benchley back with him from his ride. Was he aware of the mischief he was making?

Shaking her head in consternation, she turned back to the table where Anne had been reluctantly conjugating, only to find the chair empty and the door to the corridor open.

"Oh, dear me!" she cried, hastening to the door. "Where has she gone?"

Nurse wrung her hands. "Right down to see the ladies, unless I'm mighty mistaken, Miss Stowe."

Prudence sagged, sure she was right. Only this morning at breakfast, Anne had been lamenting that she would never learn to be a lady without a proper one to be an example to her, and how unjust that there were several fine ladies in residence but she was never to be in company with them.

"Watch Henry," she adjured Nurse before hurrying down the corridor to the back stairs, wondering anxiously what her aunt would do to her for allowing Anne out of her sight. When she reached the door of the drawing room, she stopped, too anxious to do more than peek in.

There were several ladies and some gentlemen, arranged in groups of two or three about the room, working at tying balls of mistletoe and arranging pine boughs. The interest of these employments had been supplanted, however, by the young girl who stood simpering in the middle of the room, clinging to her mother's skirts and using all her wiles to encourage an invitation to stay.

"You are very pretty, ma'am," Anne said to one of the ladies, who tittered appreciatively and glanced sidelong at a gentleman near her. "I should like to be as handsome as you someday. May I sit beside you?"

Lady Tyndall chided her in a carefully indulgent tone, "Oh, you are a naughty, naughty girl, Anne. It is not time for you to come away from the schoolroom. What will the ladies think of you? I declare, they will imagine you are allowed to run wild like a hoyden, when it is only that your governess is horridly remiss."

Prompted to action by this declaration of her incompetence, Miss Stowe stepped forward. "There you are, Anne! Forgive me, Lady Tyndall. I will take her back to the schoolroom instantly."

Lady Tyndall's syrupy smile became rigid and she murmured in a low voice, "Yes, you will, Prudence. I wonder only that she was allowed to leave it in the first place. You know my wishes concerning the children during this house party. I am seriously displeased."

"Forgive me, ma'am," said Prudence again, bowing her head. "I fear Anne slipped out while I was attending to Henry. It will not happen again."

"If you value your position, it had better not," was the acid reply.

Then Lady Tyndall's eyes widened, her gaze over Prudence's shoulder. "Lord Windon! Dear me, you are back so soon from your ride. You find us a trifle out of order, and no doubt are wondering why the nursery seems to have come to be in the drawing room! Miss Stowe was just collecting my sweet little Anne, who was curious about the ladies."

"Quite," said his lordship, his gaze lingering only a moment upon the governess as he took in the scene before him. "Very tempting, all this loveliness."

Prudence closed her eyes tight against the wave of mortification that rose up to color her cheeks. All this loveliness did not, she was sure, include herself, dowdy scarecrow that she was.

"Yes, sir," said Anne, turning her wide blue eyes innocently upon this new potential ally. "I so wanted to sit and admire them, only Miss Stowe insists I must conjugate French verbs."

There was a titter of sympathy from the ladies, and good-natured laughter from the men. Lord Windon glanced to Lady Tyndall and seemed to make a decision, returning his gaze to Anne.

"Lived by two rules as a boy," he said solemnly. "Always obey Mama, and always attend to your lessons."

"Oh, that's too bad, Windon!" cried a lady, but she was drowned out by calls of, "Hear, hear!" from the gentlemen.

Lady Tyndall, taking courage at this, said with smiling firmness to Anne, "You may come down after your dinner, my dear, and sit with us while the gentlemen are at port. But French is exceedingly important for a young lady to master, and so I cannot allow you to miss your lessons, even as a treat. Miss Stowe knows my sentiments well, and ought to have taken them more to heart."

Another titter echoed around and Prudence, unable to lift her eyes, murmured, "Certainly, ma'am," and took her charge's hand to lead her from the room.

At that moment, however, another gentleman appeared in the doorway. Lady Tyndall, her indulgent gaze rising from her daughter to wither into indignation at sight of him, turned an alarming shade of red, and Prudence trembled for Fred's well-being. Before her ladyship could do herself or anyone else an injury, however, Honoria leapt up from where she had been sitting on a sofa and ran to greet the newcomer.

"Mr. Benchley! Oh, Lord Windon has brought you back to sit with us! How charming! It has been an age since I have talked with you. How is your mother? Still recovering from her bad chill?"

She led him back to the sofa and chattered away, to the endless consternation of her mama. Lord Windon, apparently feeling himself obliged to explain, said smoothly, "Ought to have informed you, ma'am, beg pardon. Had such a fine time with old Benchley that I couldn't leave him behind. Thought he could come back and continue the visit here. Friend of the family, I'm persuaded. Known Miss Tyndall since the cradle, or some such. Knew you couldn't object."

This was true enough, as Prudence observed from sideways glances at her aunt and Lord Windon. Lady Tyndall did not dare to gainsay the viscount, who was her most honored guest, even though he had so easily and innocently overturned her cherished ultimatum that the odious nobody Benchley should never darken her doorstep again.

After some moments of inward struggle, Lady Tyndall produced a smile. "Certainly, my lord! Certainly. Mr. Benchley is a near neighbor, to be sure. Had I even an inkling that he was known to you, I should have invited him to be of the party, but I had not, you know, naughty boy! A pity you made no mention of it before, for I have already made up the numbers at table, and cannot think of fitting another gentleman in. Poor Benchley cannot stay to dinner, and it is too bad, for he must ride home in the dark. But there really is nothing to be done. You apprehend, I am sure."

Looking as though he did not in the least apprehend, Windon nevertheless smiled and said, "To be sure, Lady Tyndall. Never ask it of you—Benchley had no idea of staying to dinner. But I would take it as a personal favor to me if he was invited for the ball. Tells me he knew nothing of it. Told him I was sure it was a mistake.

Made sure he'd be on the list—near neighbor, you know. Miss Tyndall informs me all the neighborhood is invited."

Lady Tyndall stood as though frozen into a statue—all but the muscles in her jaw, which seemed unable to calm themselves. At last, she said, "An unfortunate mishap, I assure you. Mr. Benchley was always to be invited—how odd that his invitation did not reach him! What a fortuitous thing that you went to visit—that you are acquainted with him at all, my lord—so that we would not be deprived of his company, and perhaps have been made to understand something entirely erroneous by his neglecting to attend."

"Glad to have been of service, ma'am," said Windon, bowing with ineffable grace and advancing into the room.

As he passed toward the sofa where Honoria happily sat with her lover, Lady Tyndall's countenance—which only Prudence was privileged to perceive—transformed to one of thunder. Her gaze snapping to the hapless governess, she growled in an undertone, "Why are you not gone? I believe it was not Anne's curiosity but yours, Prudence, that led her here. Do you so miss being in respectable company that you will inflict your degrading presence upon us? It will not answer, for you have fallen too far! Do not be getting ideas above your station, I warn you. Now get out of my sight!"

Prudence scurried from the room, Anne protesting all the way down the corridor, but the scene in the drawing room had been too mortifying for the governess even to think to remonstrate with her.

———— . ————

As Gripson divested him of his boots and socks, Windon sat in the wing chair and gazed into space, ruminating on the dashed uncomfortable mess he had been thrown into. The Tyndall

household seemed all in a muddle, and he could hardly congratulate himself on promising to assist in sorting it out. Indeed,
his part today had scarcely seemed to help matters at all. Lady
Tyndall, if he didn't miss his mark, was likely to burst a blood
vessel if anything more untoward happened at her party, and
Windon feared there might be a scene or two yet to come.

To a gentleman steeped in his own habits and cares, altruism
did not come naturally. Certainly, he did the civil at all times,
and performed gentlemanly feats of gallantry with alacrity, but
Miss Tyndall's situation was unique in his experience. As was
Miss Stowe's, and it was to her that his thoughts had turned
more and more as the days went on, much to his discomfiture.
Indeed, the trials and travails of a governess had never much
entered his head before now. It was somewhat discomposing,
therefore, to find that he could not keep this particular governess
from his thoughts.

He certainly hadn't liked how she had been treated this afternoon by her aunt. He had overheard the horrid insinuations the
woman had made as he had come into the room, and had caught
some of the scathing words that had sent Miss Stowe flying from
it. The governess's discomfort had been a great strain on his
sangfroid—it had taken all his breeding not to rake down Lady
Tyndall on the spot, for he wouldn't treat a dog with such disdain,
much less a beautiful woman. But Miss Stowe, he reminded
himself, was no longer to be regarded as a beautiful woman—she
was a governess, and according to Society, this prohibited her
being anything but a dowd.

He stood to allow his valet to remove his coat and waistcoat,
then dismissed him and pulled at his neckcloth, endeavoring

to recollect some details of his own governess, and those of his friends. What he remembered corroborated what he had lately been told: all of them plain, drab, resigned things, if he wasn't mistaken. Miss Dooley—was that his governess's name? He had been so young when he went off to school, scarcely older than Henry, to be sure. Miss Dooley, he thought it was, was beak-nosed and thin, with steel-grey hair and fierce black eyes. Try as he might, he couldn't recall what she had worn—her memory was swathed in grey and black, with only a trace of a white lace collar he thought she must have worn to church.

Every other governess he'd ever seen was the same—he hadn't paid enough attention to notice much of what they looked like, only that they were plain, drab, spare females, and nothing to trouble himself over after he had left his own schoolroom behind. How odd that he should be troubling himself over Miss Stowe.

But Miss Stowe was nothing like any other governess he had known. His memory of her at Lady Foxham's ball was fuzzy at best, but he could still envision her as he had seen her at the inn—rosebud lips, brown eyes glowing, chestnut curls peeping from her hood. And her pelisse, while it covered her from neck to toe, was cut fashionably enough of fine wool to be quite alluring. It ought not to be forbidden that she wear such things, if she had them. But perhaps she had borrowed them from her cousin, which meant she had none of her own. It didn't much signify, for Miss Tyndall had assured him it was out of the question for Miss Stowe to even attempt good looks, and after Lady Tyndall's derisiveness today, Windon was inclined to agree, more's the pity. Dashed waste of good looks only to give them an airing on holidays.

As he removed his breeches and climbed into bed, several snippets of conversation regarding Miss Stowe's situation swam in his mind. She was a poor relation—it was not her place to attempt to attract gentlemen meant for her cousin—she must not be a burden—she was grateful to be a governess. Now that was a travesty if there ever was one—so incomparable a beauty, grateful to make herself plain as a doorpost and to hide every charm, only to please a cat of a woman who didn't even have her best interests at heart!

The connoisseur in him was pained, much as an art lover would be pained to find a masterpiece cut from its frame and hidden in a dusty old attic. But more than that, his sense of honor smarted at having added to her distress. She scarcely dared look at him now, for fear of raising her aunt's jealousy. What could he do? The art lover would rescue the painting, but Windon could hardly rescue Miss Stowe—could he?

Chapter Five

As Honoria lay her head upon her pillow, her bedroom door creaked open and her cousin, clothed in her nightrail and a worn dressing gown, slipped in. Pressing a finger to her lips, Prudence crossed to the bed and jumped under the covers.

Honoria squealed. "Your feet are frozen, Prue!"

"I'm sorry, Nora. The maid neglected to lay a fire in my room. I am in disgrace after Anne's escapade this afternoon, you know."

Honoria promptly popped out of bed and retrieved the warming pan. "I'm sorry I did not make the case better—but I was in such a state!" she said, adding a few coals to the pan.

"But why? You did not even try to speak to me in the drawing room."

Honoria passed the copper pan under the sheets at Prudence's feet. "No, for I was on pins and needles for when Fred would appear."

Prudence cocked her head. "Then you knew he would come? Nora, did you know Lord Windon was acquainted with Fred?"

"Indeed, I orchestrated their acquaintance," Honoria said, giggling as she set the pan on the hearth and jumped back in bed.

Prudence demanded to know all and her cousin was happy to oblige her, speaking in such glowing terms of Lord Windon's kindness that Prudence's irritation at him diminished to almost nothing.

"I hope it all turns out for you and Fred, Honoria." She smiled in real conviction then turned on her back, gazing up into the darkness of the canopy. "I wish I were not obliged to be a governess. Lord Windon admired me, Nora. I know he did—at the ball last Season he hung about me all the evening. And though he forgot about that, he was excessively eager to ensure he would see me again after he drove me here from the inn. But when he saw me dressed as a governess, he was so shocked he took me to task—can you believe it?"

Honoria nodded. "He told me, Prue. But you must forgive him—he is a gentleman, after all, and has no notion of how it is with young ladies who must become governesses. It is my belief he hasn't given a governess a thought in his life—until now."

"Only to dismiss it. He hardly looked at me in the drawing room today—and I cannot blame him. I was a wren among peacocks. Miss Duerden's gown nearly had me green with envy—did you see the rouching? Oh! I would die to have a gown like it—if only for one day!"

She sighed, her breath puffing into the cold air. "I try to be content, Nora, truly I do, but it is so very hard! We had such hopes for my Season! Mama planned everything, down to the last slipper, even though she was ill. And then that odious man cheated Papa and we had to flee London, then Mama died, and then Papa—" She swallowed down her emotion and said haltingly, "I—I know I ought not to—to complain, but it seems so—so horridly unjust!"

A warm hand came to clasp hers under the bedclothes and she turned to find her cousin's eyes bright with intent.

"And so it is!" Honoria whispered fiercely. "But it needn't be all bad. Why should you not have a beautiful gown—if only for one day? Perhaps I cannot restore you to your old life, but I can grant you that wish."

"What do you mean?" inquired Prudence, dashing the tears from her cheeks.

Honoria's eyes narrowed conspiratorially, a dimple appearing as she smiled. "The ball on Thursday. We will dress you in one of my gowns and you will come, like a princess from a faerie tale. Once you are in the ballroom, there is nothing Mama may do about it, for she will not like to make a scene, and you may dance to your heart's content, and be admired as is your right!"

Prudence's heart fluttered at the enticing vision, but she said, "She will sack me, sure as anything, Nora. It ought not to be attempted."

"Pooh! Faint heart." Honoria nudged her with a toe, pursing her lips in a mischievous smile. "I will contrive to make it all right. I will talk to Papa, and make him think it was all his idea to give you a treat. He has a tender spot for you, Prue—he simply is too careless to do anything about it of his own accord."

Prudence bit her lips, but her dimples peeped, too. Did she dare? It all sounded too delightful, and the thought of wearing a lovely gown, of being again in a position to be admired, of putting off her lowly status for one wondrous night, was difficult to dismiss.

"Do you really think Uncle will speak for me?" she whispered. "I do not know what I shall do if Aunt Tyndall sends me packing. There is Miss Dickerson, but—"

Honoria placed a finger against her lips. "I forbid you to worry about that. It will all turn out right, depend up on it! I have it all worked out. Now, you'd better go back to bed, but take the warming pan and make yourself a fire, or your feet will be too frozen to walk, much less dance at the ball!"

Giggling, Prudence slid out of bed and, collecting the warm-ing pan and some wood from the basket beside the fender, blew her cousin a kiss goodnight and slipped from the room.

———— . ————

Lord Windon considered he must be running mad. He had never been a man of much depth, but he knew himself well, and it was only with astonishment that he acknowledged, while he had not been privileged to even glimpse Miss Stowe for three days, she had been foremost in his thoughts, and her beauty had scarcely anything to do with it. On the contrary, since he had watched her scurry from the drawing room, his chief concerns had been the injustice of her situation and what he dared do about it.

Never before had a lovely woman—and definitely not a dowdy one—inspired such anxiety. Even at his most romantic, it was unlike him to concern himself with anything so sordid as the consequences of social exile—such things were beneath his notice. He had been, until now, content to move from one fashionable event to the next, collecting beauty as he might a posy of flowers. But now he had no use for a posy, for how could he admire it when he was haunted by the thought of Miss Stowe consigned to the dreary life she had been obliged to take up?

His mama had been right, after all, and Windon found it dashed disturbing. His deeper feelings, so long immature, had blossomed through the forced acknowledgment that Miss Stowe was more than a pretty face. The circumstance was not as distasteful as he had imagined, however—indeed, he felt rejuvenated, vitalized, and determined. If this was a "lasting passion," he could comprehend why so many gentlemen gave up their liberty to pursue it, and he only hoped his mama, upon discovering he had at last formed such an attachment to a lady, would be so delighted she would overlook the fact that the lady was a governess.

Yearning to see the object of his musings again, but without an idea of how to effect a meeting that would not antagonize his hostess and further distress the governess, Windon was not displeased to see little Henry come running from the shadow of the stable door to greet him as he dismounted from his Monday morning ride.

"Good day, sir! I'm glad to see Calliope is well. May I say hello?"

"Daresay you should be in the schoolroom," replied Windon, dismounting and glancing toward the house in the hopes of seeing Miss Stowe, in all her drab glory, come running out.

"Yes, but I don't give a fig for that," said Henry ingenuously, already patting the mare's neck. "Horses—especially Calliope, here—are far more interesting, don't you think?"

"Infinitely," said Windon, nodding to the groom who had come up to take the reins, a signal that he approved the boy's visit. "But it's bound to make your mama angry."

"She don't know. The drawing room's at the front of the house."

Windon's brows went up as his pulse quickened expectantly. "Ain't the schoolroom at the back? I'll be bound Miss Stowe can see the stables."

Henry shrugged, producing an apple. "Does Calliope like apples? I snabbled one from the kitchen."

Calliope gave her own answer, nibbling at the purloined fruit without a care for its provenance. Windon exchanged an amused look with the groom and settled against the stable doorframe in preparation for Miss Stowe's imminent arrival. He had not long to wait. Before the mare had got rid of the evidence of Henry's misdemeanor, the governess came flying from the kitchen door and down to the stables.

She skidded to a halt, her chest heaving and tendrils of her hair escaping from the tight bun at the back of her head to wisp softly around her face. She did not notice Windon, who had drawn a little into the shadows so he could more easily admire her rosy complexion and fine eyes, which were accentuated by vexation and exercise.

"Oh, Henry, you served me such a trick!" she cried, trying to catch her breath. "You cannot continue running off like this! Your mama will be so angry if she finds you here and not at your lessons!"

"I hate my lessons!" declared Henry, intent upon the fast-dis-appearing apple.

"I know, Henry, but I cannot let you be forever pestering the gentlemen's horses!" returned Miss Stowe in pleading accents.

"Not to worry, Miss Stowe," said Windon, emerging from the shadows of the doorframe. "If Lady Tyndall gets the wind up, I'll say it was my idea. Got a knack for telling fibs, I've discovered."

The governess blinked, gazing at him a few startled moments before putting a hand to her hair and lowering her eyes as she endeavored to pat the stray tendrils back into place. "You are too kind, my lord. But Henry ought not to be a bother to his mother's guests. Come along, Henry."

"No!" Henry stamped his foot, wiping his slobbered hand on his nankeens. "His lordship said I could talk to Calliope, and I shall!"

Before Miss Stowe could remonstrate with him, Lord Windon said sternly, "It's not gentlemanly to speak so, Henry. Never good form to take a pet. Besides, not the thing to contradict a lady."

"But she's no lady—she's a governess," pouted Henry.

Miss Stowe's cheeks became even rosier, and Windon said quickly, "A governess is a lady, Henry—the sooner one learns that, the better! No more arguments. Calliope needs her rest. Go on now, and I'll ask Miss Stowe to bring you again tomorrow morning."

Appeased, Henry said goodbye to Calliope and trotted obediently back to the kitchen, not even waiting for Miss Stowe.

She dipped a quick curtsy. "Thank you, my lord. You are very kind."

"Least I could do," he replied, feeling oddly conscious. He sent off the groom with a nod of his head and said to her, "Might I escort you into the house, Miss Stowe?"

"Oh! Oh, dear me, no, sir. It really is not necessary."

"Believe it is necessary," he said brusquely. "A lady wants protection."

She stared at him, a faint blush rising in her cheeks. "Oh! But it is only a step to the house. I—I cannot imagine there is much danger."

"Don't signify. Gentlemanly thing to do." And he offered his arm.

Miss Stowe gazed at him in stupefaction for some moments, then slowly placed her arm within his own. He sighed and smiled, relieved she had allowed him the honor of protecting her—and grateful she could not possibly hear the thumping of his heart as it tried to beat out of his chest.

———— . ————

The following three days passed as though something out of a dream for Prudence. Everywhere she went, a benign influence seemed to have penetrated. Anne was sent for during each afternoon to sit with the ladies, relieving the strain on governess and nurse alike. The second day, both Prudence and Anne found a small posy at her dinner plate, so that one could simper and the other could wonder and blush in peace. The evening of the third there was a box of bon bons on Prudence's pillow when she went up to bed, and Honoria smilingly vowed it was not from her.

Two mornings Lord Windon himself arrived in the schoolroom to invite Henry to visit Calliope, and Nurse insisted Prudence go along with them to supervise her charge. If her lips pursed against a smile as she shooed Prudence out the door, only one person blushed at it. And as the groom drew Henry into talk about the mare's finer points, Windon spoke so charmingly to her that she could have imagined herself to be just another guest at the house party.

The night of the ball, Prudence waited as arranged until the first stately dances were finished and she was certain her aunt was safely amid her guests in the ballroom. Then she flitted along the corridor and into the throng where Honoria, waiting by the door, grasped her by the hand.

"I'll introduce you like a regular guest, and then everyone will believe you are, and Mama will not be able to do a thing about it!" Honoria whispered exultantly, drawing her cousin into the crowd. "Lord Windon! Good, you are not dancing." She spoke loudly, so that several persons near them could hear. "You are acquainted with my cousin?"

"To be sure," murmured Windon, his eyes wide as he gazed at Prudence.

She felt her cheeks heat. She knew she looked well—how could she not? Honoria had lent her the most ravishing dress of silver thread-net over a pale blue skirt, with deep blue and white rosettes along the hem. She had further insisted upon Prudence wearing her second-best pearls, and had clasped two silver bangles on her wrists.

"Windon!" hissed Honoria, looking significantly at his lordship.

He blinked, coughed, and bowed, raising his voice to speak quite as loud as Honoria. "Miss Stowe! Could never forget. Met at the Dowager Marchioness of Foxham's ball last Season."

"My lord." Prudence hoped her color was not so high as to give the wrong impression, for she was truly grateful to him for what she could only guess was more deception. Whatever it was, it was doing its work, for there were approving murmurs and interested stares from all around the room.

Windon took her hand and carried it to his lips. "Care to dance?"

Delight bubbled up in Prudence's chest and she smiled brilliantly. "Yes, thank you, my lord."

He led her into the set and for the next quarter hour she floated on air. Windon was an excellent partner, light on his feet and solicitous, and she thought she could ask for nothing more.

But then, just as the second set struck up, Lady Tyndall caught sight of her, and favored her with such a malevolent look that Prudence stumbled as she found her place, colliding into Lord Windon.

He caught her by the elbow, assisting her to remain upright. "Anything the matter?" He glanced about, and by the set of his mouth, she guessed he had seen her aunt.

"Perhaps, I ought to sit out," she suggested faintly.

"No, by Jupiter," Windon said firmly, leading her into position. "Take it as an affront if you went away." He bent to say in her ear, "Been hankering to dance with you for days. Mean to make the most of it."

Her pleasure at this gallantry precluded speech, and she went about the next dance in nearly the same state of contentment as she had the first. But she knew it could not last. As soon as the music ended and Lord Windon led her to the side of the room, Lady Tyndall pushed toward her through the crowd. Prudence trembled, anxious whether Honoria had succeeded in winning over Lord Tyndall to her cause and fearing she had not. But then she felt a steadying hand on her arm, and she glanced up to see Lord Windon still beside her.

Lady Tyndall reached her and, seeing his lordship by her side, quickly schooled the thunder in her expression to a false smile. "Prudence! I wonder at your coming down tonight. Are not Henry and Anne in need of you?"

"N-no, Aunt," Prudence stammered. "They are both asleep, and—and if you recollect, Nurse has charge of them at night."

Before her aunt could reply, Lord Windon smiled widely and said, "Pleased you changed your mind, ma'am, and included your niece. Very wise. Always good to have as many pretty women as possible at a do like this, in my opinion. Miss Tyndall can't be the only handsome one."

Lady Tyndall's simper looked suspiciously like a grimace. "Honoria does look lovely tonight, does she not? You made a handsome pair, the two of you, opening the ball. I declare, I have never seen a couple better suited."

Windon seemed to consider this, then shook his head. "Can't agree. Better pair over there." He gestured to the other side of the room, where Mr. Benchley stood speaking animatedly with Honoria. Lady Tyndall gasped, but he went on blithely, "Look as though they were made for one another. Wouldn't be surprised if they made a match of it."

Her ladyship, who had visibly been struggling against outrage, looked quickly at him and said, "But my lord, you were to—that is, your attentions to Honoria have been very particular! Indeed, she expected an offer from you and would feel shockingly used if it came about you had a change of heart."

Windon cocked an eyebrow and said smoothly, "Beg your pardon, but nothing of the sort. Came only to forward my friend Benchley's suit. Miss Tyndall knows it well enough—seems she's quite content, too."

Lady Tyndall blustered a bit, but at last clamped her lips together and got hold of herself. "You will pardon me, my lord, but it is only a case of long friendship turned to calf-love. I'm afraid it simply would not do. Poor Mr. Benchley is not what we could wish for our Honoria."

"Nonsense!" boomed a new voice, and Prudence and Windon turned to find that Lord Tyndall had joined them. "Fred's a capital fellow, excellent seat. Never seen such a hard goer—neck or nothing! My kind of sportsman. He'll do very well for Honoria, Althea, mark my words. They'll make a famous match."

"George!" cried Lady Tyndall, growing as pale as she had been red a moment earlier. "We agreed that it was not our wish—such meager expectations! And so nearby!"

Lord Tyndall humphed. "Not a bit of it. Neat little property, Pattendon. Good hunting, fine grounds. Besides, so near to Randley, won't require half the land of a gentleman farther off. Honoria will do fine with him. Already gave him my consent."

"Well done!" said Windon, shaking his lordship's hand. "Felicitate you, sir! As I said, you couldn't ask for a finer son-in-law."

"Thank you, thank you. And you, puss," he said, chucking Prudence under the chin. "You look as fine as five-pence. Glad I thought to give you a treat. Every girl should have a ball once in a while."

"But George," objected Lady Tyndall weakly, "a governess."

"Humph. All work and no play made Jill a dull girl. Can't have a dull governess for my son and heir, can I?"

With that, he went away, and Windon, taking Prudence's hand and pulling it through his arm, followed his example, leaving Lady Tyndall gasping like a landed fish.

"Good heaven, Lord Windon!" cried Prudence when they had passed out of earshot. "I could never have foreseen such a turn of events! Only last month poor Fred was turned off the place, and here he is engaged to Honoria! And all due to your kindness in helping them!" She gazed up at him with shining eyes. "You seem to be a miracle worker! I am so happy for them that I declare my aunt may banish me forever and I should not give it a thought."

Windon's eyes widened in alarm. "*I'd* give it a thought, however! Mustn't allow her near you. Have just the thing for it—introduce you all around. Have you dancing all night! Can't banish you then."

He was as good as his word. Prudence was soon dancing with an amiable young man from the neighborhood, with two others promised in their turn. Windon bespoke the supper dance, and took her safely down to the dining room, never leaving her side or allowing Lady Tyndall an opportunity to whisk her away. He talked and laughed, listened and inquired after her history, and altogether made her feel as though she were not an interloper at all, but an interesting and desirable companion.

Prudence had not been so well-entertained in months, and her only discomfort was a strong yearning at the close of the ball that Lord Windon be forever in her company. It could never be, and even she was not so bird-witted as to imagine it could. She was a governess, and much as she had enjoyed her one evening of playing at being a gentlewoman again, she knew she must return to her real life.

But as she laid her head upon her pillow that night, she resolved to treasure up this night in her memories, there to be recalled during those moments she knew would come when she dearly wanted the comfort of a dream come true.

Chapter Six

L ord Windon arose the following morning in the best of moods, having enjoyed the sleep of the virtuous and victorious. His generous spirit had won the day, both for Miss Tyndall and Mr. Benchley and, if he was not mistaken, for himself. Miss Stowe had shown a marked preference for his company, and he had never been so bewitched in his life. Not even halfway through the night he had come to a blinding conviction that no matter what she looked like, Miss Stowe was his ideal, and the only thing for it was to make her his wife.

No more did he wish for a pretty face to adorn his arm—he had found a lady to cherish and protect, and if she would consent to make him the happiest of men, she could dashed well wear whatever she pleased. He did enjoy when she dressed up, but he had to admit that the skinned-back hairstyle had grown on him, at least when tendrils of hair escaped to wisp enticingly about her face. If this was madness, then he had to admit he was quite content to be mad.

"A pleasant evening, sir?" inquired Gripson as he settled his lordship's coat over his broad shoulders.

"The best yet, by Jupiter," replied Windon, his hands busily tying his neckcloth.

"Am I to wish you joy, sir?"

"Not today, but soon. Must go home and tell Mama, then return to sweep her off her feet." Windon dusted his hands together, envisioning Miss Stowe's warm brown eyes widening and filling with delight at his offer.

"Miss Tyndall is a lucky young lady, if I may be so bold, sir."

Windon's eyes flicked to Gripson's in the mirror. He was not a quick thinker, but he noted the ironical set of his valet's lips and said, "She is, Gripson. Set to marry her neighbor. Love match—been attached for years. Practically arranged it myself."

The brows rose a fraction and Gripson said, "Then it is a different lady, sir?"

"Certainly, jackanapes! Can't marry an engaged lady! Girl for me is Miss Stowe, the lady we brought from the inn. Turns out she's Miss Tyndall's cousin. Governess here."

The valet blinked, slowly. "The governess? I beg your pardon, my lord—I fear I do not comprehend the matter. You came in pursuit of the young lady of the house, but now you intend to make an offer for the governess?"

Windon gazed blandly at him in the mirror, a little tight about the mouth, and then his lips widened into a grin. "Precisely, Gripson. Seems to me you are up to all the rigs." He stood and tugged down his cuffs. "I shall depend upon you to prepare Mama for me. Don't want her to have an attack of the vapors."

Then he strode to the door and opened it, whistling as he went down the hall. He found Miss Tyndall alone in the breakfast parlor, but he had scarcely assimilated that she had an air of despair about her when she jumped up and grasped his hand.

"Oh, Lord Windon, thank goodness you are here! I have just had the most horrid shock."

"Lady Tyndall's not nixed the engagement!" he exclaimed, indignant.

She shook her head. "No, no! It is worse! She has sacked Prudence!"

"Sacked—" In utter astonishment, Windon sank into the nearest chair. "Beg pardon, can't stand."

Miss Tyndall obligingly sat as well and poured him a cup of tea, spooning sugar into it as she hastened to explain. "Mama has just told me. Oh, it is too vexing! She insists it is because Prudence is a terrible governess, but it is plain as day it is all over her having attended the ball—which was my idea! Prue worried she would be sacked, but I convinced her, and now I wish I had held my tongue! I was certain I could keep her from losing her position, and I spoke to my papa particularly about it yesterday, but Mama must not have consulted him, because she packed Prudence off this morning and she is gone!"

"Gone." Windon was having difficulty seeing straight. Was this another symptom of insanity? He felt as though the walls were closing in on him.

"It was to be the faerie-tale ending, too! Fred and I, and you and Prue! It was all worked out to a T. Drat Mama's prejudice! I am not even on the marriage mart anymore, and yet she could not stand to see Prudence make a better match! My sweet, kind, good Prue, who deserves the world! Oh, it is too vexing."

"Vexing."

Miss Tyndall paused, staring at him, her brow furrowing. All at once, she remembered the sugar and saw that she had spooned half the sugar bowl into his tea. With an impatient huff, she pushed away the dish and snapped her fingers at him.

"Windon! Are you going to simply sit there and repeat all I say? I tell you, Prudence is gone this hour and more! You must be on your way if you are to catch her!"

"Catch her—" At last he blinked and looked into her eyes. "Catch her? You know where she's gone?"

"Certainly I know! She has only one other friend in the world— her old governess, Miss Dickerson at Dimstock. Mama put her on the stage from the Black Bull at eight this morning. It must be halfway to York by now!"

"Good God!" Windon jumped up. "Must go after her! Call my carriage—no, take my horse—no, must have some way to bring her back."

"For heaven's sake, take the horse and go after her. It will be faster than a carriage, and you may hire a vehicle after you've got her. Besides," Honoria said, smiling rapturously, "it's far more romantic to ride after her *ventre à terre*!"

"Assuredly!" he said, much struck, then turned and ran out of the room. But after a thought, he returned, swooping upon the basket of rolls and grabbing out two. Putting one in his mouth, he took Miss Tyndall's hand and pumped it, then ran out again.

He was mounted and riding Calliope down the lane in five minutes. The miles to the Black Bull were accomplished in no time, and he swung down to assure himself that Miss Stowe had boarded the stage heading toward York. This was corroborated by the innkeeper, who watched him leap up into his saddle and tear off down the road with great interest, and the cause of this flight was the subject of much speculation the rest of the day.

As he rode, Windon had leisure to consider what he was about, and it occurred to him more than once that he was being foolish beyond permission. What gentleman in his right mind would ride *ventre à terre* after a governess? But he comforted himself that he was not in his right mind—he had resolved some days ago that he was indubitably insane, and could not be held to the same reasonable expectations as the ordinary gentleman.

The miles flew by, therefore, in rapt contemplation of his true love, and after a few false hopes raised by the sight of antique carriages with unusually large bodies ahead of him, he came at last to a hill, up which was lumbering what could only be the stage. On his sweating horse, he cantered by, peering into the stage windows for a glimpse of his quarry, but he could not be sure she was within. Nevertheless, he reined in at the top of the hill, leaving room for the stage to stop on level ground, and positioned Calliope so she was blocking the road.

The coach soon topped the hill, and the coachman drew up and, with many curses at him, demanded to know his business.

"Beg pardon, must speak with one of your passengers!"

"Very irregular, sir, and not what I'm used to from the Quality—if you is Quality!" growled the coachman, eyeing Windon's many-caped greatcoat with disdain.

Awake on all suits, Windon withdrew half a crown and tossed it to the coachman. "Won't take a minute, word of honor."

The coachman caught the coin and bit it, then, satisfied, jerked his head in the direction of the coach door. Windon dismounted, handing Calliope's reins to the guard, and hastened to the door, wrenching it open and peering inside. There, wedged between a large woman with a chicken tucked on her lap and a youth with adenoids, was Miss Stowe. He nearly burst with relief.

She gaped at him. "My lord! What—"

"I've come to take you home, Miss Stowe."

"Home? But I have no home—did not you hear?"

"Heard some fustian about you being sacked, but that ain't what I mean." He reached over and took her hand. "Come out of there—can't talk with all these people gawping at us."

Miss Stowe, blinking in astonishment, said, "But they will go on without me. My trunk—"

"If it's filled with more of those frightful governess's gowns, think no more of it. Buy you whatever you like—only come out now. Coachman is giving me a look like murder."

She acceded to his request, but whispered fiercely, "I cannot go back to Randley, sir! My aunt is furious with me. There is nothing to be done with her—even Lord Tyndall did not stop her!"

"Don't intend to stop her," said Windon, drawing Calliope and Miss Stowe to the side of the road to allow the stage to move on. "Got another idea of where you'll reside."

She blinked at him. "You know of another position? Oh, Lord Windon! That—that is most kind. I am not very good at being a governess, but if you mean to help me, I must do my best. Heaven knows there is nothing else I am fit for."

"I've another idea altogether," he said, taking her hands and looking with some trepidation into her eyes. "Not sure how you'll take it, but got a notion you'll be pleased."

She was returning his gaze, her brown eyes warm and not without a hint of longing. "You are so very kind, sir. I will try to be pleased."

He huffed. "Dash it, Miss Stowe! Don't want you to try! Want to make you delirious with delight!"

"Very well, sir," she said, a trifle tartly, "but I warn you, taking charge of my horrid little cousins did not inspire such a feeling, and I doubt very much that being—what, a lady's companion?—would either!"

"Not a bit of it! Couldn't imagine anything more depressing! Thought—thought you could be something else. A—a gentleman's companion."

She wrenched her hands away. "Sir! Just what are you insinuating?"

"No! Beg pardon! Slip of the tongue—"

"It certainly was!" She turned from him, crossing her arms over her chest. "And now I cannot even get away from you, for the stage is gone and you did not bring a carriage. Just what were you proposing to do with me, sir? No, I do not wish to know."

She picked up her skirts and was about to march away from him down the hill, but he grasped her arm to stop her. "Prudence—Miss Stowe—all a mistake! Could cut out my tongue— usually have a way with words. Don't go."

She stopped but only cast a derisive glance over her shoulder.

Taking his hat in his hands, Windon turned it nervously. "Miss Stowe, what I meant to say—want you to be my companion. That is, want you to marry me." She turned completely to stare at him, and her incredulity nearly unmanned him. "Know it's not the thing—only really been acquainted a fortnight! But knew you were the woman for me when I came upon you in the stable—dashed brat caterwauling, you covered in dust and your hair skinned back—"

"As I recall, you chastised me for looking a fright!"

"Yes, but—must forgive that, Miss Stowe—quite a shock!" She began to turn away again but he rattled desperately on. "Fact is, haven't stopped thinking of you since! Not even another beauty put you from my mind, and every time I saw you, even in those horrid gowns, I wanted more and more to be with you. New experience to me." He shifted from side to side. "Never could think past a pretty face before you."

She was blinking at him, her brow furrowed, but at least she had not run off. He took courage and stepped nearer, gazing pleadingly into her eyes again. "Only wanted to take care of you after that. Cherish and protect, you know. Nothing much I could do, though. Dashed annoying you were held off from me, and obliged to run after those two brats. Well, Henry's not so bad, but that Anne!" He shuddered. "Hope none of our girls will be like her."

A surprised huff escaped Miss Stowe, and she said, "Lord Windon, I have not given my answer."

He colored. "Beg pardon—only, got it in my head you wasn't opposed to my company. Must have dreamed too vividly of the future—possibility of it, that is."

They stood a minute in silence on the side of the road, Calliope nibbling at stray grasses poking up from the snow that dusted the verge. Windon hardly dared look at Miss Stowe, for he fancied she could see into his soul—much like her ancestors in the gallery at Randley—and he dreaded that she would not like what she saw. He had been a frippery fellow all his life, after all, with no real goodness to recommend him. He did not like to think what he would do if she refused him.

At last, she said, "I must warn you, sir, that I do not always look pretty, even when I am not obliged to dress as a governess."

"Nothing I know better! That is—" He swallowed. "Don't signify. Always beautiful to me."

She colored and peeped up at him with her lovely brown eyes. "And you do not imagine Lord and Lady Dewsbury will object? I am hardly equal to your station—having been employed, you know."

"Equal to Miss Tyndall, aren't you, and she's a baron's daughter! Besides, Mama and Father won't object—been after me to form a lasting passion for years."

She blushed afresh and lowered her eyes, putting her hands behind her back. "Well, sir, I suppose I cannot—" She stopped, looking up and raising her chin. "No!"

Windon's heart was in his throat. "N-No?"

"You said, sir," she continued, "that you wished to make me delirious with delight, so I will not suppose. I will rejoice!" She clasped her hands and gave a little jump. "Yes! Yes, Lord Windon, I will marry you!"

He had only time for a sharp, relieved intake of breath before her arms were about his neck and she was hugging him and bouncing up and down, her bonnet falling to hang down her back. His arms closed about her waist and he lifted her up, her delight infusing him so that he swung her around twice before setting her down. Then he took her face in his hands and kissed her rosebud lips, finding them as delicious as he had suspected they were, and he could not bring himself to stop tasting them for quite some time.

When at last they drew apart, they looked with some amazement on each other before Windon remarked, "You look a fright, and dashed beautiful, too."

"You're mussed as well, but I own I do like it," she said with a mischievous smile, taking the hat from his hand and placing it on his head at a rakish angle. "What a pair we are."

He grinned, taking her gloved hands and kissing them. Feeling their coldness, he said, "Better get on our way. Expect you're half frozen."

She laughed and agreed, then paused at sight of Calliope huffing in the chilly air. "Why didn't you bring the carriage? Were you so diffident that you did not think I'd come back with you?"

"Not in the least—that is, couldn't be sure. But had to ride *ventre à terre*, you know. Faster, and Miss Tyndall thought it more romantic."

"To be sure," Prudence said happily. "You must put me across your saddle bow now, like a true hero."

He looked thoughtful. "Yes. Ought to carry you there, too, but the ground is so uneven I'd likely pitch us both into the snow."

She giggled and looped her arm through his as they walked down the hill to a stile where he could mount and pull Prudence up in front of him. He took advantage of her nearness to kiss her soundly again, then set Calliope off down the road toward Randley.

"Shall get a conveyance at the nearest inn, but I'm afraid we must go back to Randley for the night," he said. "Won't trouble you, though. Lady Tyndall can hardly toss my affianced wife out on her ear, can she?"

Prudence huffed. "She may still try, but I'm sure Honoria will aid me. She will have to lend me nightclothes, at any rate! How odious of you to have left my trunk on the stage."

"Full of your governess's gowns! Horrid drab things, the lot of them. Good riddance."

"And if I liked them?" she inquired with an imperious look.

He raised a brow but shrugged. "Buy you more. Lady Windon may wear what she likes. Sure I'll get used to it."

She laughed, putting her arms around him and briefly laying her head on his chest. "Never fear, my lord, I'll not put you to the trouble. Somehow, I do not believe I shall miss them at all."

The End

You can find out more about Lord Windon and his friends in *Piqued and Repiqued*, Book 5 of the *Branwell Chronicles* (may be read as a standalone).

Judith Hale Everett is one of seven sisters and grew up surrounded by romance novels. Georgette Heyer and Jane Austen were staples and formed the groundwork for her lifelong love affair with the Regency. Add to that her obsession with the English language and you've got one hopelessly literate romantic!

You can find her on Facebook and Instagram, or at judithhaleeverett. com, where you can join her email list and receive a free novella, *A Near Run Thing*, along with monthly announcements, Regency history tidbits, and other news. To learn more, scan the QR code.

The Viscount's Christmas Runaway

by Audrey Harrison

Prologue

London 1812

The feel of the crisp, white sheets slid over her body: the mattress so soft underneath, the blankets providing a cocoon, keeping her warm and secure. She snuggled deeper into the covers and smiled sleepily to herself. There was nothing quite like the feeling of real luxury on the skin. She had never truly appreciated it, but she did now.

"Hey, watch out! This blanket isn't big enough for the two of us as it is without you hogging it!" Rosie grumbled, disturbing her bedfellow's reverie.

Louisa opened her eyes. There were no crisp, white sheets, no comfortable mattress, no warm blankets. There was a cold and draughty doorway from which they would be forcefully removed if they dared to remain until the business owners arrived. There was also a hungry stomach, aching limbs, and more fear and danger than anyone at eighteen years old should have to deal with.

The memories of the dream faded into the deep recesses of Louisa's mind, where she forced them to stay every waking moment. There was no point longing for what had gone; pining would reduce her resilience and make her vulnerable to the elements and the people who threatened her every day. She left the tiny amount of comfort provided by half a blanket and Rosie's body heat and stood, disturbing Billy, their other bedfellow.

She was alive for another day and still determined to find work or shelter that would provide the three of them with some form of safety. Unprotected people didn't survive unscathed on the streets of London for very long. She was fully aware that, at some point, her luck would run out.

Grimacing to herself, she shook off her maudlin thoughts. The fact of the matter was that her luck had already run out. She was homeless, penniless, and terrified. She had never been as afraid in her life. Well, perhaps once, but to admit to her present fear was to give in. If she did that, all the risk would have been for naught, and she couldn't let it be so. She had to find a way of surviving and leaving the past behind where it could no longer hurt her.

He would not win. Not while she had breath in her body.

Chapter One

A day later.

Louisa hesitated when the gentleman indicated for her to approach him. She had not been on the streets all her life like Rosie or been forced to do some of the things Rosie had. The gentleman looked kind, but until she was even more desperate, Louisa was determined that her body would remain her own; it was the last portion of decency that she clung to, even if the odds were not in her favour.

He gestured again and smiled at her. He was probably in his fifties, slender and attractive for his age. His hair was greying but had obviously been deep brown in his youth. His chocolate-coloured eyes looked kindly at her wary stance. It was clear he understood she could bolt at any moment.

"Child, I will not hurt you," he said softly. "You have my word as a gentleman. My name is Lord Hindley, and you stood out when I drove past. You do not fit into this world, so let me help you."

Louisa flushed. She had tried so hard to blend in; it was the only way to remain safe. "This is where I belong."

"I would sound more convincing when telling a Banbury tale if I were you," came the gentle response. His sympathetic smile never faltered. "If I step towards you, do not run away. I want to talk to you, that is all. I promise you are under no threat from me."

"If you want to help, throw a few pennies, and that will be assistance enough," Louisa said, raising her chin a little. She hated begging, but it was necessary if the three of them were to eat.

"I do not think my conscience will allow me to throw a few pennies and then drive off. It is too cold for you to be out in this weather."

"There are too many of us for you to fix. The streets are littered with beggars. Your pennies will help us well enough. If we have food in our bellies, we can face the cold," Louisa replied matter-of-factly. It wasn't exactly true. Many urchins went to sleep during the cold winter months and never woke up.

Lord Hindley smiled at her response. "You have an excellent point, but please indulge an old man. Let me help you as much as I can. If nothing else, it will make me feel better."

Louisa wanted to be proud, but proud people died on the streets of London every day. She sighed and moved closer to him. She had vowed that she would return the kindness shown to her by Rosie and Billy when she had first found herself here. This man might be able to help them and enable her to repay her debt to them.

"Pennies will help. We are always hungry," she said less defensively. For some reason she did trust him, although she could never let her guard down completely. She had already learned the consequences of making that mistake, and that had been with family.

"Then you shall have all that I carry at the moment, although it isn't as much as I would like to give you," Lord Hindley said, reaching into his pocket and handing her more money than she had seen in a long time. "What else do you need?"

"Do you have blankets in your carriage?" Louisa asked. If he asked her to retrieve the blankets, she would take the coins and run.

"I do. Would you like one?" He directed his footman to retrieve a blanket.

Louisa blushed. "Do you have three? There are three of us, and we share everything, but Rosie says I hold onto the blanket when I sleep."

"I think we can manage three. Will the money buy you warmer clothes?"

Louisa laughed a little. Even she wasn't so naïve. "Probably, but we won't be allowed in any respectable shop, sir. We can barter with the less choosy businesses, but we will buy food first. I don't want to be forced to give up the money." She would be robbed by other street people if they saw it. There was no honour amongst thieves in the back streets of London.

"You mention there are three of you. Are you all girls?" he asked.

"No. One boy. Well, man really, he is eighteen." Louisa stiffened at why he would ask such a question. She wanted to give the impression that she had a little protection, although anyone meeting Billy would quickly realise he was the one who needed protecting.

"Your brother and sister?"

"No, not by blood in any case," Louisa replied. The footman

laid the blankets at her feet, and she stepped back from him, still wary.

"My child, no one will hurt you who is associated with me," Lord Hindley said reassuringly.

"Thank you," Louisa said. She was not convinced. So much money would come at a high cost; no one was this generous and wanted nothing in return. "What do you wish me to do in exchange for your kindness?" She was surprised at the flinch her words caused.

"I need you to make me a promise."

"What sort of promise?" Louisa asked, all suspicion.

"Meet me here at the same time, on the same day, next week. I will bring food, clothing, and more money. I want your word that you will be here," he insisted.

"Why would you do that?" Louisa asked disbelievingly.

"Because I can afford it, and you need it," he replied simply. "Do I have your promise?"

"I would be foolish to say no, would I not?" Louisa said with a small smile.

"You would," he replied, but his words were said so kindly, they held no sting.

"God willing, I will be here."

"Good. Until then, Miss?"

Louisa stiffened. She was grateful for his kindness but refused to supply him with any details about herself, but she did not want to lie to him either.

"Louisa. My name is Louisa."

He looked pleased that she had given him her name. "Well, Louisa, until next week. Take care, my child."

Louisa nodded. She would not reach down for the blankets until he had left. She still had some doubts about his motives. Just as he was climbing into the carriage, she was struck by something. "Sir!" she called out.

"Yes?" he replied, pausing mid-step.

"If I don't make it next week, would you still provide for Rosie and Billy?"

"Why wouldn't you be here? I thought I had your promise."

"I will stand by my promise," she responded proudly but then faltered slightly. "It is just that on the streets, you can never know..."

The sentence hung in the air between them. "I understand, my dear, and your words force me to extract another promise from you."

"What?" came the suspicious reply.

"I need you to promise that you and your friends will stay out of harm's way as much as possible. I cannot return sooner, I wish I could, but I need you to stay safe in the meantime. Avoid any situations that might lead to trouble."

Louisa smiled. "Your blankets and money will help and we will not put ourselves at risk as much as we can."

"Good. Until next week then. Take care, my child."

Chapter Two

Lord Hindley's money kept the three of them safe all week. They had avoided known trouble spots, were careful with the money, and stayed under the blankets each day as long as they could. Winter was fast approaching, and the luxury of the wool ensured that they were all warmer than they had been for a long time. They still had their original blankets, acknowledging that if their benefactor did not return and things worsened, they could trade the fine ones for food.

They discussed what the gentleman might want in return for his generosity. Rosie was of a similar mind to Louisa.

"You don't 'ave to do anything you don't want," Rosie insisted. "We were getting along fine."

Louisa smiled at her. Rosie was younger than Louisa's eighteen, but Rosie had lived through so much that a sixteen-year-old should not have experienced that she was older than her years. The other two very often turned to her for advice. "We were getting along thanks to you. Perhaps this way, I get to repay some of my debt."

Rosie rolled her eyes. "'Ow many times do we have to go over this? You'd 'ave done the same for me."

Louisa thought back to the time before she met her friends with a shudder. If she had not met Rosie almost as soon as she reached London, she would either be working as a lady of the night or dead, of that she was sure. "I will do whatever it takes to provide for us, for we need food for the winter," she said firmly.

As the time approached for the meeting, Louisa's apprehension increased. It was fine being brave and thinking that she was prepared to sacrifice her body to provide for her friends, but the reality of such an act galled her down to her soul. If she did give herself to the gentleman, she would have nothing left. She would be completely lost as a gentlewoman. She almost laughed out loud at the thought. There was no way back from the gutter now. If she attempted to return to society, she would have to face what she had escaped from in the first place. She had better make the best of this situation. If this was the only choice to survive the winter, then so be it, but she felt sick to the stomach as the evening approached.

Louisa was accompanied to the rendezvous by Billy and Rosie. They were determined to offer support, insisting she could walk away if what he asked in return was too much, which made Louisa yet more determined to do whatever it took to provide for them all. It did not prevent bile from rising in her throat when the carriage came to a halt at the roadside.

Lord Hindley got out and smiled at Louisa. "My child, I am extremely glad to see you."

"I gave my word," Louisa said, slightly offended that he had doubted her. Seeing him once more highlighted how different her life was now. Lord Hindley was dressed exquisitely, his dark frock coat clearly made by the finest tailors and boots that shone in the lamplight from his carriage.

"You did. And this is Rosie and Billy?" He turned to the two, who were hanging back.

"I'm Billy!" Billy was pleased he was being included and moved forward slightly before Rosie pulled him back with a hiss.

Lord Hindley smiled at the young man. It was clear he had immediately seen that Billy was still a child, mentally at least. "How do you do, Billy? I am delighted to make your acquaintance." He walked past Louisa, holding out his hand to Billy.

Billy beamed at him and shook his hand enthusiastically. Louisa groaned, Billy was so used to beatings that anyone showing even the smallest degree of kindness found they had a loyal puppy by their side, which is how Rosie had "adopted" him in the first place.

As Louisa watched, still on edge, Lord Hindley turned his attention to Rosie. "I am pleased to meet you, too, Rosie, and I hope that the blankets kept you completely covered this week. Louisa told me how she held onto the blanket you normally shared."

Rosie laughed despite being on high alert. "Yes, sir. I 'ave been warm, thank you." She turned to Louisa and said, "Did you tell him all of our secrets, you bumble 'ead?"

Louisa blushed, but Lord Hindley laughed a deep chuckle. "She did not. I promise you she was only explaining why she needed three blankets when I, in my ignorance, had offered only one."

"Oh," Rosie said, sending Louisa a pointed look.

"We all appreciated the blankets," she said quietly, knowing Rosie would lecture her later.

Lord Hindley returned his full attention to Louisa. "I hope to do even more for you this week," he said.

Louisa set her shoulders, but she made an involuntarily step back as Lord Hindley moved away from Billy and into her vicinity.

"There is no need to fear me," he said gently.

"I don't," Louisa said, but she could not meet his gaze.

They were distracted by the carriage door opening. They had presumed that the gentleman travelled alone, so Louisa was surprised when a fine lady alighted from the carriage with the help of a footman. She stepped out as if directly from a fashion plate. She was around the same age as the gentleman, tall and slender, with an open face that smiled at the group before her.

"Hindley, you are making a complete mess of this!" came a teasing reprimand. "Can you not see she is terrified and is acting as the lamb before the slaughter, waiting for you to devour her?"

"Devour her? But I have tried to be as careful as I can not to frighten her!" came the indignant response.

"Yes, and by not saying what you came to say, you are leaving her quaking in fear, waiting for goodness knows what!"

Louisa blushed. The woman could read minds, it seemed.

Lord Hindley turned back to Louisa. "Miss Louisa, please allow me to introduce my wife, Lady Florence Hindley."

Louisa was surprised into uttering, "Your wife? But I thought you wanted..."

"Oh, good grief!" Lord Hindley said loudly, his discomfort evident. "I am old enough to be your father! Nearly old enough to be your grandfather, I expect!"

"I am eighteen!" Louisa responded.

Lord Hindley laughed. "We shall settle on old enough to be your father then. My dear child, I am amazed and slightly shocked that you appeared today if you thought I was going to take advantage of you."

"We need to survive the winter, and you offered help," Louisa replied, scarlet in the face and hanging her head in shame. She could not bear the repulsion he must feel at her being prepared to offer herself to him.

Louisa did not see Lord Hindley exchange a look with his wife as he stepped closer to her. He lifted her chin until she could not avoid looking into his eyes. The expression held within them seemed to offer nothing but kindness, but she could not allow herself to believe it.

"Miss Louisa, you have haunted me this week, but for no reason other than to help you. I promise that none of you will come into harm when in my care, and like you, I keep my promises." He smiled slightly at her. "Will you trust me?"

Louisa nodded mutely. No one in her recent life had cared about her. He sounded so sincere and decent. Her throat constricted at his words, so she could not speak.

"Good," Lady Hindley said. "Now, let us get this business resolved so we can all go somewhere warmer."

"What do you mean?" Rosie asked, as suspicious as Louisa was.

"Nothing to worry you, I can assure you," Lady Hindley replied with an easy smile. "We would like to offer you a home with us until we can establish you in suitable employment." Lady Hindley had not expected that her offer would be received with cheers of joy, but she seemed astounded when the three huddled together the instant her words were uttered.

"Told you it was like dealing with a scared deer," her husband said smugly.

"Do not be afraid," she reassured them, shooting a glare at Lord Hindley. "Let me explain a little about our situation. We live in a large house on the edges of London. In fact, we have a few," she said a little apologetically. "We also have a son, who is off causing mayhem throughout society, and I long for the house to be filled with noise and bustle again. My husband explained how he had met you and that he wanted to help. So together we concluded that yes, we could offer you food and clothing, but to be a real help to you and us, we could offer you a home and support to become established in whatever work you wish to embark on."

"You 'ave only one child?" Rosie asked.

A look of sadness passed between the couple. "We only have one son," Lady Hindley said.

"You want company," Louisa's mind was whirling about the possibilities, but that she could not be seen in society was at the forefront of her thoughts.

"Yes, I suppose I do," came the quiet response. "But, if that company means I can help the three of you, is there any harm in it? We will all benefit from our scheme."

"Society would think you are harbouring thieves," Louisa said.

"We only deal with a few friends. My days of gadding about town are well and truly over."

Louisa sensed there was more to Lady Hindley's words than she was letting on, but Rosie interrupted before she could utter anything else.

"You are offering us a 'ome? We aren't refined," Rosie said bluntly. "Would we be 'idden from your friends?"

"You would be open to every part of our lives but only when you are comfortable with it," Lord Hindley assured them. "You can take whatever lessons you require, but you will not be hidden away."

"Lessons?" Rosie asked doubtfully.

"Dance lessons could be included?" Lady Hindley offered.

"Dance lessons? I could learn 'ow to dance proper?" Rosie asked. Her face changed from the hardened street child that she was to an excited girl of sixteen.

"You can do whatever you wish, but I do think a few other lessons may be useful too," Lady Hindley coaxed.

"I'm willin'!" Rosie smiled.

"What about you, Billy? Would you like to come and live with us and be warm and safe and able to eat whatever you wished?" Lord Hindley asked.

Billy's eyes brightened. "Anything I wished? Bread and jam and cake?"

Lady Hindley took Billy's hands into her own. "Bread and jam and cake, every hour of every day, if you should wish it. Our cook likes boys with hearty appetites, and I know she would love you."

Billy beamed at Lady Hindley. "Rosie, Louisa, can we go to Cook, please?"

Rosie looked at Louisa. "I want to."

Louisa sighed. She feared returning to a world that would bring back painful memories of the situation she had run away from, but she had promised to get her friends out of poverty, and this was the best chance they would ever have.

Lord Hindley touched her arm. "Louisa, let me speak with you alone for a moment." He led her a little away from the group. "What is troubling you, my child?"

"We do not belong to your world," she said simply.

"Do you trust that we have your best interests at heart?"

"I think so," Louisa replied, a little shamefacedly because such a lot was being offered, and she was questioning it.

"Well, that is a start," came the smiling response. "We won't force you into any situations that make you uncomfortable, but we can provide for you. We can give you security, respectability, and, hopefully, the chance for a more secure future. Do you not wish for that?"

Louisa closed her eyes. Yes, she wanted respectability; yes, she wanted security, but she was afraid. "Could you not take the others and be happy with that?" She knew the futility of the words even as she uttered them.

"Do you think I am the type of man who could walk away from you while taking with me the two people who have probably kept you focused and determined for however long you have been together? I accept that you might not wish to share your past, but I know refinement when I see it, and I am certain you were not brought up on these streets," Lord Hindley said gently.

Louisa sighed. "I think Lady Hindley and you have an uncanny ability to read people, my lord," she answered wryly.

"Let me help you smile again. I have a feeling you deserve to be happy, and no one should be alone with Christmas approaching."

Again, Louisa was left wanting to cry, a weakness in which she never indulged. She nodded her consent, and with a smile and a gentle squeeze on her arm, Lord Hindley led her to the carriage. Rosie and Billy were chattering excitedly to Lady Hind-ley, all hesitation and doubt removed. They clambered into the carriage and moved away, leaving blankets and a basket of food on the ground for someone else to find. Louisa knew it would not be long untouched, for there were too many desperate people about for such bounty to remain undiscovered.

Chapter Three

The first days in Lord and Lady Hindley's London town house felt to all three visitors as if they had been taken to another world, not just another part of the same city. They were fed until they could eat no more. They spent every morning in a bath, despite Billy's protestations, taking time to wash out the ingrained grime of the street, and they were fitted for new clothing, having been visited by a tailor and modiste.

They were not forced to leave the house, their hosts allowing them to become accustomed to their surroundings before venturing out. Lady Florence, as she said they should call her, had been correct in her assessment about the cook and Billy.

"I think Billy would happily live in your kitchen for the remainder of his days," Louisa said dryly on the fifth afternoon. She was alone with Lady Florence, Rosie chatting with Lord Hindley about what learning, if any, she wanted to undertake.

"I knew he would. Every young man loves Cook. Ours was the most popular house during Miles's school holidays, and although I would like to take the credit, it was Cook who was the bigger draw," Lady Florence said pleasantly.

Louisa smiled. She had never known someone more welcoming than Lady Florence and could imagine all the boys flocking to her. "Billy is perfectly happy here."

"I am glad you think so. He is a little special, isn't he?"

Louisa acknowledged the delicate way the question was formed. "Yes, I have not known him as long as Rosie has. She said that these last years he has been abused, beaten, or taken advantage of until he met Rosie. She shared a crust with him, and from that day on, she accepted that he needed her help to keep him out of trouble and protected as much as she could."

"He was lucky to have met her."

"We both were. Rosie discovered that Billy had been abandoned at a young age. When he was younger, people were kind to him, feeding him scraps and offering shelter, but when he grew, he became more of a target. It is strange how the older he became, the more vulnerable he was."

"People can be very cruel. How could anyone turn a child out, especially one that needed more care than usual?"

"Yes, but if he could not earn, he was worthless to them, wasn't he?"

"I suppose he was, but we are now his family too and will help look after him," Lady Florence said. "How long have you been with Rosie?"

Louisa was instantly wary. "Why do you need to know that?"

"I do not need to know," Lady Florence said gently. "I am interested in you, that is all. Anything you say will not leave these four walls, I assure you of that. Sometimes it is better to talk to someone who will not judge you, but do not feel forced into revealing anything you do not wish to."

"I must sound very ungrateful, and I am sorry for that, for I am deeply indebted to you," Louisa said with some embarrassment.

"I do not want your gratitude. I will be more than happy with your friendship. You are not obligated to us in any way," Lady Florence insisted.

"Thank you," Louisa said meekly. "I wonder, does your son agree with what you have done?"

"His father has advised him we have visitors. He is a troubled young man. I feel it is my turn to be more open with you," Lady Florence said, a cloud marring her features.

"Oh?"

"We spoke the truth when we said we have only one son, but we also have a daughter," Lady Florence started.

Louisa was silent. It was clear the words were costing her saviour a great deal.

"Two years ago, Melissa was foolish enough to form an attachment to one of our footmen. I suspected she liked him, but every young girl falls in love with someone unsuitable when they first start out. Mine was a groom." She smiled reminiscently. "I thought I would die of a broken heart if I was unable to marry him and live in a cosy cottage. When I returned home from school, I realised it was just the simple, uncomplicated infatuation of a young girl."

"Your daughter's was not so?" Louisa asked quietly.

"No. It seems they decided they could not live without the other, and two years, one month, and three days ago, they left this house, and we have not seen or heard from them since."

"That must be terrible," Louisa responded, reaching out to touch Lady Florence's clasped hands. "Did they get married?"

"We have no idea. We've done everything we can to trace them but to no avail. Lord Hindley goes out every night in his carriage to scour the streets to try to find her."

"And that is when he saw me," Louisa said.

"Yes. You see, my dear, he has been on the lookout for someone who did not quite fit into their surroundings, and you did not. Poor Hindley said that, for a moment, he thought he had found Melissa, but then he cursed himself because you are dark-haired, and she was— is blonde. But he could not leave you on the streets, whatever your story is. I hope it makes his motivation more understandable," Lady Florence explained.

"Not knowing must be so hard," Louisa said with sympathy. She ached that Lord Hindley and Lady Florence could be suffering so cruelly. She pushed aside that her parents might be worried about herself. They had forced the situation on her, and she could not feel guilty for reacting to something so galling.

"Yes. It has hit us all but Miles particularly hard. They were so close, and yet she did not confide in him. I know he blames himself for not guessing what Melissa was intending, and as a result, he is rampaging across London, trying to ignore his unjustified guilt and instead experiencing every form of excess a person could."

Louisa was shocked. "You know what he does?"

"My dear Louisa, problems begin when there are secrets, as we are now painfully aware. I refuse to have any secrets from those I care about. We do not know every detail, but we know enough not to expect a marriage or grandchildren just yet. The gossip papers love to report what Miles is doing in any case; they write article after article about his dissolute lifestyle."

Louisa wondered why a daughter could leave such a loving environment and such warm-hearted parents as Lord and Lady Hindley.

Her thoughts were interrupted by Rosie's entrance. "Louisa, 'is lordship would like to see you now. Let's see if you can avoid French classes like I just did!"

Louisa laughed. "What did you agree to?"

Rosie grimaced, flopping into a chair. "It isn't all good! I'm doing dancing, cooking, and needlework, which are all fine, but then I 'ave to take lessons, learning to read, write, and my sums! 'Orrible!" she finished with a shudder.

Lady Florence smiled. "My poor dear, you will soon know more than the teacher if I have guessed correctly. You do not survive on London's streets without being highly intelligent. Now come and tell me all about it."

Rosie beamed at the compliment and moved to sit comfortably next to Lady Florence. Louisa pondered how it was herself who was struggling to fit into this new world when, in reality, she should have found it the easiest. She approached the library door and knocked lightly, then entered on hearing the deep rumble of Lord Hindley's voice.

She had been in the study on her first day's tour of the house. It was a large square room, lined with books and decorated in blues and golds and looked rich and warm. It matched the man, who sat with his back to the window but facing the door. He smiled and stood when Louisa entered.

"Welcome. Please make yourself comfortable." He indicated a chair beside the fireplace and sat opposite her. "Has Rosie recovered from our chat?" he asked with a twinkle in his eyes.

Louisa laughed. "I am not sure she will ever get excited about learning how to read and write, but Lady Florence was doing an excellent job of soothing her with cakes when I left."

Lord Hindley chuckled. "Dear Florence, always the diplomat. Now it is your turn, my dear. What can I tempt you with to fill your days?"

Louisa looked down and fiddled with her fingers. What she said next would give away something of her background. "I do not need to be schooled, thank you, my lord," she replied quietly but firmly.

"I knew I had guessed correctly that you had probably completed your schooling." Lord Hindley seemed pleased to be right.

Louisa's eyes shot to Lord Hindley's face in panic. "How did you know?" she asked in a whisper.

"You can take a refined girl out of her environment, but she will still be a refined girl." Lord Hindley reached out and took her hand in his. "I am surprised you managed to survive on the streets for however long you did, and it makes me shudder to think what could have happened if the wrong type of person had found you."

Louisa's smile faltered. "I very nearly did end up with that type of person. Only I found Rosie, and it's not an exaggeration to say that she saved my life. I owe her so very much." She did not reveal that it was in society that her parents had found her an equally bad person.

"And because of you, I stopped, and so you have saved Rosie and Billy. Do not hold yourself back because you feel you owe them some sort of debt."

Louisa sighed. She was tired of being afraid and wary of everything. "I am not. They are my own restraints. I cannot go back to how I was before, and yet it feels like I will crumble if I let go and relax into this secure environment," she said, responding to the genuine man.

"You are safe here. Give it time, and the fear and insecurity will ease. I promise. Is there anything I can do for you?"

Louisa needed to be honest with him, and she trusted him more than she had anyone in a long time. Lady Florence, too, but with Lord Hindley it was different. He reminded her of her uncle who had been very dear to her.

She took a breath; it was time to reveal some of her background. "I was schooled, first at home and then at a boarding school. I can play the pianoforte, paint – badly – sew, speak French and Italian, and I can dance, although I have not been to a ball."

"Your parents?"

"Could we leave it at that? You could be forgiven for thinking I am just being missish, but I assure you I am not."

"Thank you for revealing what you have. When you are ready, I will be here to listen, and on the positive side, you will save me a fortune in lessons!"

Louisa smiled, relieved that he had not pushed her. How could she explain that she had left her parents as his own daughter had? She had good reason to leave, but he would hardly be sympathetic when he was suffering such pain. He was not to know that her parents would not have lost any sleep over her absence, only that they had lost face and, more than likely, money. She tried to lighten the mood and change the subject. "I shall spend it on clothes instead!"

"Are you sure you aren't related to my wife?" came the smiling response.

"Lady Florence has explained about your daughter." Louisa knew she was taking a risk by being so open.

A cloud passed over the handsome face. "Yes. Our dear Melissa. I will continue to search for her, but in the meantime, I am glad to assist you and your friends. I think your presence will help to fill some of the space that exists in this house since she left."

"I hope you find her one day. I am sure she regrets causing you so much trouble." Louisa wished there was something she could do to ease the pain of the lovely couple.

"Every member of every family causes trouble at some point in their lives. It is all part of being a family. Miles has the high spirits of a spoiled young man. He will grow to take over the title and heritage one day. For now, he can live the wild life."

Louisa was shocked. "You openly admit that your own son is spoiled?"

"It is the truth. Why should I lie? That would make me look ten times the fool. He has been over-indulged, but he is good underneath. We have all had the heart knocked out of us a little. He just has to realise that it was not his fault and let go of his guilt. He needs something else to fight for. Young men need a cause to champion, even without a family catastrophe," Lord Hindley said knowingly.

"From what Lady Florence says, you have many causes that you support."

"Yes, we had our causes prior to Melissa leaving, but more have benefited since."

"As have we," Louisa said.

"Yes. As long as there is good to come out of her disappearance, I can take a modicum of comfort from that," Lord Hindley admitted.

———— · ————

That night, Louisa could not sleep after the conversations with Lord and Lady Hindley. She climbed out of the bed she shared with Rosie and curled up on the chair in front of the fire, her mind full.

On hearing a sound from downstairs, she stiffened. It was late, so why would anyone be up at this time? She remained still until the fear that had made her escape from home drove her to her feet. She might only be in her nightclothes, but she could hide if needed.

Creeping out of the room, she peeped over the banister and was surprised to see a young man hugging a dishevelled footman. Her curiosity had her remaining in place rather than withdrawing.

"Stanley, you are a diamond," the young man said, releasing the footman but slapping him on the back. "Or can only women be diamonds? I'm sure I do not know, but whatever it is, you, my good man, are it."

"Thank you, my lord."

"I have to get to bed before Father realises I am here. Don't need a lecture to spoil tonight. I have been introduced to a new gaming hell, and even better, it is just round the corner! I can stay here and be the prodigal son."

"Let me help you upstairs, my lord."

"No, you are a ruby among men for opening the door, I am able to walk upstairs. Now shh, we don't want to wake the parents."

Louisa could only smile at the antics of the viscount. She should have been disgusted, knowing his reputation, but instead felt nothing but amusement. His actions were endearing; he was very handsome and well-dressed, but he was obviously in his cups and looked smilingly relaxed as a result. His words were slightly slurred, but he was very cheerful, and never having seen the good humour of a foxed individual, she could not help but see the funny side of the situation.

She watched him with the same concern as the footman who was following him upstairs. It was a case of one step forward and two back, but eventually he safely reached the top stair. Louisa suddenly recalled herself and moved to return to her bedchamber, but her action caught his attention.

"Hallo! Who is this?" Miles asked as he tried to bring her into focus. At Louisa's silence, he smiled. "You must be a nymph and a beautiful one at that."

Louisa was mortified that Miles's first sight of her was in her nightclothes, not to mention the footman, who still hovered in the background.

Miles took a couple of steps towards Louisa, who remained frozen to the spot. "You really are a sight to behold. Would you allow me to introduce myself?" He bowed deeply. "Oh dear, I seem to have forgotten who I am."

Louisa could not help giggling at the befuddled expression on his face, but at her reaction, he grinned at her.

"Ah, I have made you smile, my fair one. Please know that I am a wastrel and a cad, but I would very much like to kiss you."

Louisa took a step back, but thankfully the footman intervened. "My lord, your chamber is this way."

"Do you know Stanley?" Miles asked Louisa without waiting for a response. "He is an emerald among men. Right you are, Stanley, lead the way." Turning away from her, Miles looked back over his shoulder. "I will be dreaming of you, my sweet nymph."

The moment Miles had gone, Louisa dashed into her bedchamber, closing and locking the door. She should have retreated when she first saw that the late visitor was no threat to her, but she had been attracted to a handsome face and teasing nature. Now her cheeks burned to think what he would remember in the morning. Her mortification did not dampen the stirring she felt at being flirted with for the first time. It was a strange but enjoyable sensation. Climbing back into bed, she knew without doubt that she would fall asleep with a smile on her face.

Chapter Four

As the first few weeks passed, Louisa had never been happier and thanked God every day for her good fortune. She had not seen Miles since that night. He had risen late and spoken in private to his parents before leaving for his own accommodation. It had caused her both relief and disappointment in equal measure.

Her time was divided between helping Billy with his basic lessons, encouraging Rosie not to murder her various instructors and teachers, and spending time with Lady Florence.

Her most precious time, though, was spent with Lord Hindley. He would often seek her out and challenge her in some way, pull an opinion out of her over a book, give her instruction in gardening, a pastime he said kept him sane, or start a topical discussion that would get agreeably heated between them. Lady Florence would shake her head at the pair and then tease Louisa about bullying her husband.

Their love and acceptance relaxed Louisa and had an impact on her that she did not notice, but the others did. She blossomed.

The wary, nervous girl who had been brought to the house had gone to be replaced by a shiny-haired, elegant, well-spoken young lady. She laughed a lot and teased along with the others. Of the three children, Lord and Lady Hindley saw the biggest change in Louisa and wondered even more at her past.

Lady Florence encouraged Louisa to accompany her on visits and walks, and at first, Louisa resisted, but when it was pointed out that she would be visiting only Lady Florence's particular friends, she relaxed a little. Any socialising would be a trial for Louisa for reasons she dared not explain, but she was persuaded to join one or two excursions, though she was glad it was December. It was easier to hide with bonnets tied firmly to offset the chill of the frosty air.

After a chilly hour one afternoon in the garden with Lord Hindley, she returned to the house. They did not stay out for long, but work was still needed in the winter. He remained behind to speak to the gardener, but Louisa gratefully entered the warm house. As she entered the hallway, she was smiling and humming to herself and did not notice the young man watching her from the staircase.

"Someone sounds pleased with themselves, and who can blame you? It must feel like all your troubles are over," he said from above her head.

Louisa jumped in surprise at the voice. "I beg your pardon?"

"I was expecting someone a little more downtrodden than the society miss I see before me. Either you are not a very good actress, or you are playing a different game than I thought," he said, leaning arrogantly against the balustrade.

Louisa was mortified and confused at the difference in the man she had briefly met the night which still filled her dreams.

He was still as handsome as she remembered, the same tall, broad figure as his father. He had dark hair, slightly longer than was convention, and penetrating grey eyes. Louisa felt unnerved at his scrutiny, maybe because there were dark rings under his eyes, and he wore a stern frown, eyebrows low, making him appear handsome but threatening at the same time. Nothing at all like the teasing, jovial man she had already met.

Louisa raised her chin. "I am surprised you recognise a society miss. I had been led to believe your tastes leant more to a less respectable female."

Miles laughed, but it was a bitter sound. "Are you offering yourself? Is that the way you wheedle your way into the homes of unsuspecting fools? I thought my father would have more sense. But you are a tasty piece, I may have to try your delights myself."

"Do not bring your filthy suggestions into this house. Your mother and father deserve more respect than that; they are good people," Louisa said indignantly. She was mortified at his insult to her and the Hindleys. His tone was so unlike their first meeting, she could almost believe he was a different man.

Louisa's reprimand brought Miles down the stairs towards her. "Concerned about my mother and father, are you? Tell me, why I should not be alarmed about you under their roof? You could be planning to murder them in their beds."

"It has taken you three weeks to visit your parents, disregarding the occasion when you were too foxed to know your own name." She gained some satisfaction at the flicker of surprise caused by her words. "I feel that if you had any worries about their safety, even you would have exerted yourself to visit before now," Louisa snapped. She had resisted the urge to step back when he walked down the stairs. She had read about animals stalking their prey and suddenly knew how they felt, but she stood her ground despite being wary and intimidated.

"Do not let my absence fool you into a false sense of security. I am watching everything you do, and if you or your friends make a step out of place, I will not rest until you have paid dearly for abusing the trust of my parents, pretty nymph or not." The words were whispered close to her face.

She could feel his breath on her cheek, but she remained ramrod still. "Have you finished?" Louisa asked, impressed that her voice was calm.

"For now," Miles whispered. He used one finger to lift her chin so she looked into his eyes. "I hope we understand each other," he said as he turned away.

"Perfectly," Louisa said and ran up the stairs without looking back.

It took Louisa half an hour before she could return downstairs. Miles's reaction had shaken her. The encounter had brought back memories that she did not want to experience ever again. She clung to the thought that this was not the same. She was not unprotected even though it was Lord Hindley's own son. He would not allow her to be ill-treated. With that small grain of comfort, she returned to the drawing room to be formally introduced to the man who had just reminded her why she had to be so careful.

She strove to appear outwardly calm, although she knew she was a little pale; she was being closely watched. Lady Florence kept the conversation going until Billy burst into the room. "Cook said Master Miles was home!"

Lady Florence laughed. "And so he is, Billy, but he has not liked being regarded as Master Miles for many years now. You should just call him Miles if you are to be friends. Let me introduce you like gentlemen."

Louisa watched Miles closely as Lady Florence undertook the introductions. She saw the puzzled look the son had given to his mother before focusing his attention on Billy and going through the introduction slower than he normally would.

"Lord Hindley said you are a good shot," Billy gabbled.

Miles smiled. "I am. Are you?"

"Oh, I'm not allowed to touch guns. I'm not safe, you see," Billy explained innocently.

"Are you not?" Miles seemed a little bemused as to what response he should make.

"No, Cook said I would probably blow my own head off and said she would starve anyone who takes me shooting," Billy said proudly.

Miles grinned. "In that case, don't ever ask me for an outing. I would hate to be starved by Cook."

"Yes, she said you could eat two more potatoes than a pig," Billy responded proudly and looked around puzzled when everyone started to laugh.

"I expect I could," Miles said after he had control over himself once more. "But I shall have to speak to Cook about giving my secrets away."

"I've not got her in trouble, have I?" Billy asked, suddenly worried.

Louisa stood to comfort Billy. If he started to worry, he would become upset and need reassurance. She paused as Miles took hold of Billy's hand, an action that reminded Louisa of Lady Florence's mannerisms.

"You have not got her into any trouble at all," Miles said gently. "I love Cook, and the first thing I will do when I see her is give her a big hug. I won't tell her off. I was just teasing."

"Oh, I don't understand teasing. Louisa explains it to me," Billy said with a smile at his friend.

"That must help, and I will let you know if I ever tease you in future," Miles said. "Now tell me what you have been doing since you came here. Did Cook let you mix the Christmas puddings on Stir Up Sunday? I used to love that job."

Miles sat down with Billy and engaged him in conversation. Louisa had worried that he would openly ridicule Billy after her dealings with him, but he was more like the man from the first night, which was utterly confusing because he was clearly not foxed. He was devastatingly handsome when he smiled, and he did that a lot while talking to Billy. It was not the mocking look he had shot her, and it seemed a more natural expression.

Lady Florence murmured to Louisa, "I knew Billy would love Miles, and it looks as if he is taken with Billy too. It will do Billy good to have Miles around for a while. Hindley cannot spend enough time with him, so perhaps my son can help."

Louisa wondered if it would do *her* any good to have Miles around for any length of time. Their first meeting had been intriguing, but the second, well, the less said about that, the better. She was not sure which of the two personas was the real Miles. Thinking further, she was not sure that she wanted to know.

Chapter Five

Miles had bowed over Louisa's hand as his mother carried out the introductions. He had been surprised at the vision before him when she had walked through the hallway and was more than a little annoyed by his response to her. He was convinced that somehow his parents had fallen under the spell of a group of tricksters. Foolishly, when he was foxed, he had not identified the young woman as one of his parents' undesirable visitors. He could have kicked himself, for since that night, he had wanted to ask his mother to introduce him to the nymph-like vision he had been unable to stop thinking about.

He acknowledged that during their earlier conversation, she had reacted like a spirited girl rather than someone acting a part, but he would be speaking to his father about the folly of inviting street urchins into their home. Louisa must be hiding a lot more than he first imagined, as she was as far from a street urchin as she could be.

As the evening progressed, Miles observed her attentions to his mother and decided that a longer stay than he had intended was in order. He had his own lodgings, but it wasn't unknown for him to remain with his parents. Admittedly, it happened less often since Melissa had left, but that wasn't something to dwell on now. The protection of his parents was uppermost in his mind.

Miles spoke to his father at the first opportunity, but Lord Hindley laughed at his concerns. "Have you spent any time with them? Do you not see what I see?"

"Obviously not," Miles replied without the sneer he had aimed at Louisa. "Or I would not be doubting you now. What possessed you to bring them home? I can understand your wish to help. Of course I do. But to bring them here? That is madness."

"You would understand if you had seen Louisa that first night. She could have been Melissa."

"She's nothing like Melissa! Have you found out why she ended up on the streets of London? I agree with your assessment that she is refined, which makes it even more a havey-cavey business," Miles persisted. He was angry that his father was trying to project his beloved sister onto someone else. Louisa did not deserve such high regard, as much as she attracted him. He could not deny that she was pretty, very pretty, but that did not mean he had to like or trust her. His frustration at being so helplessly drawn to her was fuelling his anger further.

"She was like a frightened animal, ready to bolt. She still is, in many respects, so I am not going to push her too far. She will tell us her story when she is ready, although she has already told me a little about herself."

"Only a little? She really has got you charmed," Miles responded.

"That is a comment unworthy of you, my boy," Lord Hindley gently scolded. "If she were a member of your family, you would wish for the kindness of strangers to be bestowed on her, as you wish that for Melissa."

"It is different. Melissa is not on the streets."

"If you think that, why do you receive a report from Bow Street every week?" Lord Hindley asked gently.

Miles looked sharply at his father. "You know about that?"

"Yes. How many dead bodies have you viewed over these last two years, son?"

Miles rubbed a hand over his face. "Too many. And each time, it is horrific. Especially if they have been in the river for a few days," he admitted.

"I confess to being grateful I have not had to do that, but I would have if you had not taken it on yourself," Lord Hindley said.

"I keep thinking I should stop. But there is always the niggle that one of them could be her," Miles said. The fight had gone out of him, and the worry of the last two years was etched on his face.

Lord Hindley sighed. "Whether it is good news or bad, I hope that one day our searches will prove fruitful. None of us has lived a full life since she left."

"I find drinking oneself into oblivion helps."

"Be careful. I don't want to lose both my children. If that were the case, I would soon be one of the bodies dragged from the river," Lord Hindley said grimly.

Miles was taken aback at his father's words and tried to steer the conversation back to the three young people. "Is that why you have done what you have with these strays? To distract you?"

"I suppose so, to some extent. But I could not leave them there. Well, Louisa was the first one I met. The others were there the week after. It was one of the longest weeks since Melissa left, I can tell you. I could do little on the first night I first saw her, but the relief I felt when Louisa was there the following week was almost overwhelming."

"But surely bringing them here was foolish?"

"They are no threat to us," Lord Hindley insisted.

"Oh, I can see Billy is no harm, although I do not know what you intend for him long-term, but what about the other two?"

"Billy is a dear boy. I have appointed a special tutor who teaches him more slowly and patiently than normal. I hope he will acquire some skills," Lord Hindley replied.

"And then, will you send him out into the world?" Miles asked, surprised that his father would consider Billy suitable for work.

"No, I was hoping to speak to you about my plans. I would like, with your agreement, to set him up in a cottage on the Surrey estate. I think he would need only one manservant and a maid to tend to him, and I think with a small provision, he would spend the rest of his days content."

"You ask for my agreement, but it looks as if you have already decided," Miles said wryly.

"You will be Lord Hindley one day and able to throw him off the estate if you wish, but I would like to make a legal arrangement in case of accidents and the like."

"In case of angry husbands challenging me to duels, you mean?" Miles smirked.

"Your words, dear boy, not mine. Do you agree to my proposal?"

"Yes. It will not impact on me either way." Miles shrugged.

Lord Hindley smiled. "I thought that would be your opinion. Thank you. Rosie will be the trickiest of the three to sort out."

"Rosie will? Why?" Miles asked. In his opinion, Louisa was the tricky one, but for some reason, he did not like the thought of her being employed.

"Rosie has only ever known life in the slums and then on the streets. She is learning her lessons now and is a highly intelligent girl, but the reality is that she will not ever be able to join the gentry."

"Marry her off to some clergyman then."

"She would drive him mad within a sennight. She is being good for now, but I can see the restlessness below the surface. She's spending her time learning, soaking it up like a sponge, but once she catches up, there will be mischief from that one, believe me," Lord Hindley said.

"Rather you than me," Miles muttered. "What about the other one? What position will she be placed in?"

"If we can eventually find out her secrets, she will be able to rejoin society, and I have no worries about a good match for her."

"Society? You cannot wish to sponsor her, surely?" Miles asked, curious despite himself.

"She has spent most of her life in school, but something happened that separated her from the life she knew. Once she trusts us enough to tell us, we can return her to the position she would have been in," Lord Hindley explained, but he was clearly troubled about Louisa. "I have not yet found out as much as I would like from her, but she will confide in us once she feels safe enough."

"Is there no hint of what she is hiding from?" Miles asked.

"She is very reluctant to mix in society or meet new people. I can only think whatever it is must be serious, but there have been no requests for information about a young woman of her description in any of the newspapers, so I am not willing to approach Bow Street about her. I do not wish to stir up a hornet's nest before finding out what we are dealing with."

"Perhaps she is trying to fool you into believing she is something she is not," Miles offered, for some reason wanting to believe the worst of Louisa, as if trying to find a way to dislike her.

"No, she shows fear. She is the same frightened deer that we saw when we first met her, but she hides it better."

"Frightened deer?" Miles spluttered. "All I have ever seen is a hissing cat!"

"Does it come with an indignant tilt of the chin?" Lord Hindley chuckled.

Miles's lips twitched, despite himself, at the memory of a fiery Louisa. "Yes, it does."

Miles failed to notice that he was being assessed by his father. Nor did he guess that Lord Hindley had noticed the stiff way Louisa and Miles interacted. He would have been mortified to learn that Lord Hindley suspected there was some attachment there and had started to hope that Louisa would be in their lives for a long time to come. If Miles had known, he would have taken himself off to the safety of his lodgings as fast as his horse could be saddled, but thankfully he was too wrapped up in his confusing feelings about Louisa to notice.

Chapter Six

Lady Florence decided to hold a small dinner party to celebrate her wayward son's temporary return home. This sent
Louisa into a panic, and she questioned Lady Florence closely
on who would be attending and whether she could be excused
from the event.

After Lady Florence had insisted that Louisa was needed,
she left the room troubled. She did not recognise any of the
names mentioned, but all it took was one last minute change of
plan, and she would come face to face with someone she knew.
She did not notice Miles following her out of the room until he
grabbed her arm.

"If you would follow me, Louisa, I would like a word," he said
quietly, steering her to the dining room.

"Let go!" Louisa said angrily, shaking off his hold. "Why can
you never behave like a civilised human being?"

"When I am faced with other civilised beings, I can," Miles
responded insultingly.

"What do you want?" Louisa asked, but her concern increased

when he pushed the door until it was almost closed. "What are you doing? It is not appropriate to close the door."

"It is not fully closed, do not worry. I have no wish for anyone to think I had compromised you; this conversation is private," Miles replied. "Exactly what is your game?"

"For the last time, I have no game!" Louisa said, wanting to stamp her foot in frustration.

"Why are you so afraid of who you might meet? Who are you hiding from? What have you done?" Miles demanded of her.

He was far taller than she was, and although she tried to hold her nerve, she was intimidated by this version of him. "Why is it so important?" she asked, trying to feign confidence and stall for time. "If your father is happy with what I have told him, why are you dissatisfied?"

"That is the point. He is not happy. He does not understand why you do not trust him enough to tell him about your background. It is a fine way to repay his kindness, is it not? He offers nothing but welcome, and you repay him with secrets and dishonesty."

Miles had hit Louisa's weak spot, her affection for Lord Hindley. She went to bed every night wishing he could have been her father and woke up every morning thankful she would have another day with him. To hear that he was upset with her cut her to her core.

"Why did he not say something to me? I never wanted to upset him," she asked quietly.

Miles had gained the advantage and pressed on. "He is a gentleman and would not force you into doing something that would make you uncomfortable."

"Unlike you," Louisa muttered darkly.

Miles smiled, unabashed. "Yes, unlike me. I prefer to find out exactly what or who we are dealing with."

"I am trying to escape something I could not face." The fight had gone out of Louisa. She hated the thought that she had hurt her hosts.

"I know that," Miles interrupted.

"Do you want me to tell you or not?" Louisa glared at him. Only when Miles nodded in response did she continue. "I am not an heiress, and I had hardly any dowry. I thought I might be lucky enough to attract an eligible match, a farmer, or perhaps even a clergyman, but was under no illusion that any match would come with a large fortune."

Louisa paused, and Miles waited. She knew her eyes would reveal the pain and sadness of her past. He shifted as he stood before her, but his face did not soften. He clearly mistrusted her, and she could not stand the thought that Lord Hindley might feel the same way.

"Go on," Miles eventually said.

"My uncle paid for me to attend a good school, and my parents insisted that I stay there through the holidays. Probably to reduce the expense of my travels to and from school."

"Some of the richest children spend most of their time at school," Miles said.

Louisa nodded. "It was not a complaint on my part. I was happy there, and my uncle visited occasionally and took me out for the day; those are my treasured memories. Last year, I was summoned home, and my parents told me things I could not believe. I realised my situation was unbearable because of their actions; I was completely alone and could turn to no one. Perhaps I panicked, but I left that night and started walking to London." This was still vague, but it was more information than she had hitherto given. "It took me two weeks, walking mainly at night, but I managed it, though I was half-starved when I got there. I thought I could get work, but then I faced the reality of my situation. No references and looking like a beggar meant no job, so I ended up on the streets. There was a man one night, and he..."

Miles stilled. "Did he hurt you?"

"He was going to, and in some ways it was my own naïve fault, for I had answered him when he spoke to me. Rosie intervened and managed to chase him off. He had only ripped my dress. I was lucky it was not worse, and although I am older than her, she took me under her wing. Thanks to her, I managed to survive. It was terrifying. I did not know how the three of us would endure the winter. Billy could not do anything to help other than beg scraps, and I refused to make money the way Rosie had done in the past and did not wish her to be forced into that again. The harsh reality was, we would starve to death if we did not freeze first."

"And then my father came along," Miles said. For the first time, there was no condemnation in his voice, which surprised Louisa.

"Yes. The first time I met him, I thought he was like all the rest of the gentlemen who roam the streets at night, but when he returned, he brought Lady Florence, and they offered us so much. I had promised to repay Rosie and Billy's kindness, but your mother and father took the debt out of my hands and gave us much more than any of us could have hoped for. I can never thank them enough for what they have done."

"But you knew the society they keep could put you in touch with your parents again," Miles said. "If it was as bad as you said, why would you put yourself at risk of being discovered?"

"Your father insisted that it was the three of us or none. I asked him to take Rosie and Billy and leave me. I realised the risk I was taking by coming with him, but because I had not explained my situation, he could not know what I could be faced with here," Louisa admitted.

"So you thought to sacrifice yourself?"

Louisa reacted to the mockery in his voice. "Do you know what it is like to be desperate? No! Of course, you do not! You, who have had everything since the day you were born and will have it until his dying day. Little Lord-in-waiting, running around feeling he is hard done by if he loses at faro! Let me tell you about life on the streets. It is not the lice and rats that are scary, though those are plentiful. It is the women who would stab you for a single coin. And then there are the men. If they want you, they take you, as I nearly found out. Beatings are normal. They would force you to work for them, selling your body, or stealing for them until you are no longer any good for either. Then you would be abandoned. The survival rate for abandoned women is a matter of weeks, although death is probably a release. Through all of this, when we risked sleeping, I would dream of clean sheets and loaves of bread and wake up so bereft that I wanted to cry, but any sign of weakness and you have lost the fight. I could not allow myself to do that, or it would have all been for naught." Louisa took a breath. She had never spoken about her true feelings to anyone before, and yet here she was, shouting them at Miles.

He stared at her without uttering a word, and she could not tell if what she had revealed had any effect on him, so she continued, unable to stop now she had started.

"Your mother and father offered shelter, warmth, clothing, food, and safety. Condemn me for being weak, but I was tired of being scared. I just wanted peace. I want to hide away. I do not want to see anyone from my past again," Louisa said quietly. "I just want to feel safe."

Chapter Seven

Miles was shocked at her words. Her insult to him had stung, but he had listened and seen the emotions cross her face as if she were back on the streets, and he felt shame at having forced her into such an outburst. "Louisa, I..."

Miles's words were interrupted by Lord Hindley, who neither had noticed entering the room. "I think you have said enough, Miles," came the quiet but firm voice.

Both spun around to face him, clearly shocked that he was there.

"Your lordship, I-I am sorry I did not tell you," Louisa faltered.

"There is no need to apologise, my dear. I was frustrated that I could not help you more, but you would have told me in your own time, I was sure of it. Would you leave us now please, Louisa? I have a few words I wish to say to my son."

Lord Hindley did not say anything until Louisa had left the room and closed the door. He turned to his son, and with sadness more than anger, he asked, "What gave you the right to treat a guest in my house in such a way?"

Miles immediately became defensive. If his father had shouted at him, he would have taken his punishment and apologised, but the look of sadness on his father's face upset him more than anything else, and he reacted in anger. "One of us had to find out if there was some sort of fraudster in our midst."

"Do you not use your eyes, Miles, and see what is before you and your ears to listen to what is being said or hinted at? How on earth could you think she was such a devious person? Did our last conversation mean nothing to you?"

"She does not look as if she has spent the last months on the streets!" he spat, ignoring the fact that he believed Louisa's every word. His thoughts and feelings were in utter turmoil, and he wanted to follow her and beg her forgiveness, to tell her that he would be the one to keep her safe and provide her with somewhere she could find peace.

"Were you here when they arrived? Did you see the days of bathing it took to get them clean? Did you see the state of their clothing, their pallor or the haunted looks in their eyes, never mind that they were all skin and bone. Did you see any of that? No, you did not. It has been four weeks of hard work by everyone in this household to keep them warm, get them clean, replace the little they had, feed them regularly, and not frighten them into returning to the life they left behind. If they leave us, they will not survive. They will be condemned to a life of prostitution or, in Billy's case, crime, and it would be only hours before he was caught and hanged," Lord Hindley said angrily.

Miles's stomach knotted at the thought of Louisa being forced into prostitution. "I did not realise they had been so," he said quietly.

"No, and you decided to intimidate that poor child."

"I am sorry."

"It is not me you need to apologise to. You have ground to make up, and as a decent human being, I expect you to treat her with the respect she deserves. After you have begged her forgiveness, of course."

———— . ————

Miles was not seen for more than a week. Lady Florence explained to Louisa that he always ran away from them when he had upset his father. He could not cope with his disapproval. Louisa felt some shame for her part in his scolding. He was ultimately protecting his family, and she could not condemn him for that.

Preparations for the dinner party went ahead as planned. Lord Hindley had gone through the guest list thoroughly with Louisa, and she was reassured that no one with connections to her previous life was invited and there would be no last minute changes. She felt guilty when he explained that they only social-ised with a very few people since Melissa had left.

Rosie would be allowed to join the party after dinner for tea and entertainments in the drawing room. She was excited and almost bounced around Louisa's bedchamber while Louisa's hair was dressed.

"'Ow many guests are there?" she asked.

"Fourteen and then Lord and Lady Hindley, Miles, if he arrives, and myself. If he does not, it will upset Lady Florence as she's taken so much trouble over this evening, and it is in his honour," Louisa replied. She hoped that Miles would return but dreaded it at the same time. She was not sure how to react to him or if he would acknowledge her. That he filled her thoughts with longing both annoyed her and made her despair about herself. She was nothing to him; he had proved that time and again.

"Fourteen strangers. Do you think there will be any eligible men?" Rosie asked, fluttering her eyes.

"No! Lady Florence has invited her friends, so we will be the youngest by a long way."

"Oh." Rosie slumped.

"You are still in the school room. You are not allowed to flirt with men yet," Louisa reminded her.

"Pah! I was flirting before you were out of leading strings," Rosie scoffed.

Louisa acknowledged the truth of the statement but gently reminded her friend, "We are ladies tonight, Rosie. Everything we do will reflect on Lord and Lady Hindley."

"Oh, I know. I just want to dance and flirt and set my cap at someone, even if it is for one evening," she sighed.

"What on earth are you talking about?" Louisa laughed.

"It's what it says in the novels my tutor tells me about. She says the lending libraries have them, and when I am good enough, Lord Hindley will pay for my subscription," Rosie confessed.

"Ooh, I wonder if he would allow me to have a subscription now, and I could read them to you," Louisa responded.

"Ask him!" Rosie urged.

—— · ——

Louisa reached the bottom of the stairs and hesitated. The guests had not started to arrive, but she felt nervous walking into the drawing room alone. She felt more like a lady than she had ever done before in her life. The maid had artfully piled her hair up and left little wisps of curls framing her face. It made her look and feel delicate. She had been persuaded to add a touch of pink lipstick, just enough to bring out their natural colour. Her dress was cream, pale enough to fit in with convention for a girl not presented at court, but Lady Florence had insisted on a shimmering silk rather than plain muslin.

She took a deep breath and opened the door. Lady Florence came across to her, smiling and holding out her hands. "My darling girl, you look beautiful. It is a crime we cannot present you at court. You would be the hit of the season!"

Louisa smiled and blushed. "Thank you. You are very kind."

Each guest arrived, and although there was a second of panic each time a new name was announced, Louisa gradually relaxed. She flushed when Miles entered the room, but his greeting was cool rather than unfriendly, and he soon moved to speak to his parents' old friends.

At dinner, she was seated far from Miles, and although nervous at making small talk in case questions were asked about how she had met the Hindleys, she soon was able to laugh and enjoy the teasing from the gentlemen at either side of her. When the group rejoined in the drawing room, Lady Florence asked her to help distribute the tea and then join her on the sofa.

Louisa took a cup of tea to her hostess and sat next to her, smiling. "It has been a lovely evening."

"Good. I'm glad you have enjoyed it. I hope there is still more pleasure to be had. Would you mind playing for us?" Lady Florence asked.

Louisa paled. "I have never played to an audience before. I am not good enough."

"Nonsense! I have heard you practising. Your playing will give the group a lot of pleasure. It will also show Rosie what will be expected of her in the future," Lady Florence said in her usual no-nonsense way.

Louisa looked across at Rosie. She had entered with the tea, and once the gentlemen had returned, Miles had introduced her to everyone. They were currently talking to Lord Hindley and two of his friends. Rosie was giggling, flushed with pleasure. Louisa thought Rosie would fit into any situation she was faced with. She was fearless. Louisa wished she could be so, and tried not to acknowledge that the thought of being escorted around the room by Miles was the most appealing part of the situation.

Louisa could not refuse a request from Lady Florence, so she sat down at the pianoforte to play. If she pretended there was no one else in the room, she would relax. Hopefully.

After she had been persuaded to sing and continue playing, she finally managed to escape. She moved away to stand alone but was soon joined by Rosie. "I didn't know you could play like that," Rosie said in admiration.

"I made lots of mistakes, but it is a beautiful instrument."

"I 'ope they never expect me to play. I would probably cause injury to everyone's ears."

As Louisa had heard Rosie practising, she could only laugh at the comment. It was surprisingly accurate.

"'Opefully there'll be more entertainments while we're here. I am enjoying tonight," Rosie said. "I intend to make full use of meeting other people."

Louisa was filled with a sense of foreboding at her friend's words. "What do you mean?"

"Lady Florence has spoken to me about becoming a companion or a governess. If she thinks I will be someone's drudge, she's got it all wrong," Rosie whispered.

"We will both need to find positions at some point," Louisa responded. Lady Florence might be hoping to find her a suitable husband, but Louisa was more than happy with the thought of employment.

"Not me. I know some of these nobs used to visit the back-streets looking for girls like me. If they took a real fancy to you, they might set you up in a 'ome of your own. I'm going to be on the lookout for a man like that. I want to be kept in luxury. I deserve it," Rosie said.

"Rosie, no!" Louisa said, horrified. "You cannot wish for that to be your future."

Anger radiated off Rosie. "You can 'ave all your airs and graces and pretend that everything is right and tight, but be realistic. Who is going to be interested in us two? We've been on the streets. We are gutter rats, nothing more. Take what you can. I am going to take full advantage and make sure that no matter what 'appens, I won't be returning to what I've left behind."

Louisa was left alone. Rosie had turned her back on her friend as soon as she had said her piece. Blinking rapidly, Louisa realised that once more, Rosie had shown that she was the more astute of them both. She saw the reality of their situation, and although Louisa could never agree to her plan, she understood it.

For the first time since Louisa had joined the Hindleys, her future looked as bleak as it had before. There would be no happy ending for her type. She came from the streets. That is all people would ever see. She glanced at Miles, who looked elegant and relaxed in his perfectly fitted evening wear that enhanced the broad width of his shoulders. Here was a man who was secure in his place in the world, knew exactly where he fitted and never felt out of his element. He would continue the family name, just as his ancestors had, making a good match with a lady born to be at his side.

She was deeply saddened that he would, quite rightly, never think of her as anything more than a gutter rat.

Chapter Eight

Miles had turned at the first sound of the music. Louisa had hardly been out of his sight all night, although he had managed to refrain from approaching her apart from to say hello. He noticed her pale complexion, and something niggled deep within him. What was she still not telling them? What had happened to make her leave everything she had ever known behind? There was something still to add to the puzzle, but since she had told him a little of her background, he had struggled with unexpectedly strong feelings when thinking about her. He wanted to protect her, to be the one who made her feel safe.

That, more than the disappointment he had seen in his father's expression, had sent him scurrying away from the house. How could he want to protect a person he did not trust? His feelings were so intense, it seemed like he had been gripped by some form of madness. He watched her now, conscious of her fragile beauty, and felt drawn to her more than he had to any other woman.

When the piece came to an end, one of his father's friends

approached her and begged for a song. Her cheeks pinked, and she shook her head, but she conceded when he offered to accompany her on a duet. Miles was angered that the man could not see her discomfort and frustrated that her needs were being ignored.

"It is good that she is being encouraged to come out of her shell a little," Lord Hindley said quietly, approaching Miles.

"She is performing under duress."

Lord Hindley smiled. "She is, but I admit being glad of it. Listen to that voice; it is perfectly delightful."

Miles could not argue against his father. Her flushed cheeks and hesitant but perfect voice pulled on him like nothing ever had before. He tried to look away, but his eyes dismissed the commands from his brain and continued to take their fill of her.

By the end of the song, she glowed from the praise and the embarrassment of being the centre of attention. Beseeched to continue playing, this time she stood firm and begged to be released. Lady Florence took pity on her and invited another lady to take over.

Louisa stood to the side, against a wall, and it was not long before one of the male guests approached her. Miles's hand tightened on his cup as he watched the discomfiture flicker on Louisa's face. He struggled to restrain himself until the gentleman touched one of Louisa's curls. Placing his cup on a side table, he tried to appear nonchalant as he approached them, but his teeth were gritted so hard his cheeks ached.

"My dear, my father has asked that you show me the artwork you have been studying," Miles said smoothly, not even glancing at the man standing in front of Louisa. If he had, he was in danger of punching him.

"The artwork?" Louisa asked.

"She is busy."

"As you are a guest in my father's house, I would suggest that you watch your tongue, Mr Bleasdale," Miles snarled at the guest.

"Why, you young wastrel...."

"Of course I will accompany you. Please excuse me, Mr Bleasdale," Louisa said, dodging around the bulk of the man and taking Miles's offered arm.

Miles led Louisa out of the room and into the library. He did not close the door completely, but there was none of the animosity in the air there had been the last time they were in that room. He led Louisa to a chair in front of the fire and indicated she should sit.

"He had no right accosting you," he said gruffly. "Do you wish me to have him removed?"

"Oh no!" Louisa started to rise, but Miles put a gentle hand on her shoulder.

"He was in the wrong."

"I do not wish to cause a fuss. I know you have a low opinion of me, but please, the last thing I wish is to spoil this evening."

Miles closed his eyes for a moment. How had this woman got under his skin so quickly? Every time she spoke, more feelings came alive within him, and he did not know what to do about it. Deciding he needed to put some distance between them before he did something rash, he sat opposite her.

"You are not responsible for the actions of a man who should know better. If a fuss was caused, it would be because of him, not you."

Louisa shook her head. "But it would not be seen as that. I am the interloper; you have been clear about that."

"I am sorry."

"What for? Pointing out the truth?"

Rubbing his hands over his face, he looked at her, eyes serious. "I am sorry for how I treated you, for what I said. I am not usually so bullish."

Louisa smiled slightly. "I must bring it out in you."

Miles chuckled. "My own pig-headedness does that. I am truly sorry. I will admit there are still questions I wish to ask, but I will not. Father is correct about one thing, this house should provide the safety you long for."

"Your parents have been so kind."

He could tell she was wary, and he could not blame her. "My parents are good people, and I hope one day you will come to realise that I am not the nodcock I seem to be."

"I have seen so many different sides to you."

"Any of them good?" Miles needed to know that she did not think him completely obnoxious. His heart felt lighter when she smiled at his question.

"You were very kind to Billy and extremely amusing when you were foxed."

Grinning at her, he winked. "In that case, I should be constantly foxed around you."

"Your parents would not thank me for that. I appreciate that you rescued me, but why did you bring me here? Will our absence not be commented on?"

"I needed to apologise. I should have done it last week, but I was too cowardly to admit that I was in the wrong. I beg your forgiveness and hope that we can start again."

"I would like that."

Four little words that meant the world to him. How had he never realised that something so simple would make him feel whole for the first time in an age? "Thank you." Miles stood and offered her his arm. "Come, let us return to this party, but if you need rescuing, just glance my way, and I will immediately be at your side."

"That is very kind."

"It is the least I can do, and your comfort is very important to me." He was not surprised that she shot him a confused look, and he squeezed her hand. "I speak the truth, which probably surprises me just as much as it does you, my beautiful nymph."

For the remainder of the evening, Miles kept his eye on Louisa and Rosie. She was having a great time with the men in the party but was drawing a few disgusted glances from the women. He would need to speak to his mother about cautioning her. It seemed he cared about all the waifs his parents had taken in.

It was a relief when the party ended, and Miles could escape to his chamber. He was glad that he had cleared the air with Louisa, but every time she smiled at him, he wanted nothing more than to go to her and kiss her there and then. He could only hope he would not spend the whole night dreaming about her.

A thumping on his chamber door drew him out of his slumber, and he croaked a "Come in."

The butler, looking unusually dishevelled, entered the room. "I am sorry to disturb you, sir, but an express has been delivered."

Miles was immediately out of bed. He took the folded parchment, his hand shaking a little. Breaking the seal, he read and then looked at the butler. "Send word to the stables. I need my horse."

"Yes, sir."

He ran to his father's chamber and burst in, still in his night-shirt. "Father! They think they have found her!"

Lord Hindley sat up in bed, blinking himself awake. "What?"

"I have received an express. Bow Street thinks they have found Melissa."

Lord Hindley sank back against his pillows. "Thank God." Recollecting himself, he started to get out of bed. "I must go to her."

"No," Miles said. "Let me go first; we do not want to overwhelm her. I will send word as soon as I can."

Lord Hindley nodded. "You are right. As soon as you know anything..."

"I will send word, I promise."

"Godspeed, Miles, and thank you."

Miles was already on his way to his chamber. Dressed quicker than ever before, he was soon in the stables and mounting his horse. He tossed a coin to the sleepy stable hand, who was trying to suppress his yawns but reacted with lightning speed to catch the coin.

Within twenty minutes of receiving the note, Miles was on the way to what he hoped was his sister's address.

———— · ————

Louisa awoke and knew there was something amiss. There was no sign of Rosie, which was unusual since they had a safe place to sleep, as she was not an early riser. As Louisa pulled back the covers, a piece of paper fluttered to the floor.

"Oh no," Louisa muttered as she bent to pick up the note.

Louisa,

I have found the person who has promised to give me what I want. I did not want to go without saying goodbye, but he did not wish to cause a fuss. I will see you at the balls for I am to be a lady!

Take care of Billy,

Rosie

Louisa slumped after reading the scrawled note. The writing might be of the standard of a child, but the words were most certainly not. She was about to ring to get dressed when Lady Florence entered the bedchamber.

"Oh, thank goodness, I thought you had left us," Lady Florence said. "Where is Rosie?" Louisa handed her the note, and after reading it, Lady Florence looked at her. "Did you know?"

"No! I would have tried to stop her," Louisa said. "She was talking foolishly last night, but I just thought the attention had gone to her head. I never thought for a moment that she would act on her plans, especially not last night."

"She is an innocent fool," Lady Florence said without malice. "She will be turned out when they are sick of her, and she will be no better off than she was. Oh, Rosie, what have you done?"

"I think her innocence was lost a long time ago," Louisa said, blushing furiously.

"I do too, but that does not stop her being taken advantage of. Oh poor Rosie, I wanted her to have a comfortable life, and this will be such a precarious way to live. She could find herself back on the streets at any time. I know his lordship will want to track her down, but she knows where we are and, if she needs us, she will come back to us for help. There is no point in trying to force her to remain here."

Louisa agreed that chasing Rosie would only push her further away. "I am sorry for Billy; he will be upset."

"I will tell him, along with Cook," Lady Florence said. "We will make it right for him. There has been more excitement overnight." She went on to tell Louisa of Miles's departure.

"Oh, I hope it is her, and she can be returned to you," Louisa said, her heart aching for Miles. She hoped he would not be disappointed, and it was a shock to realise just how worried she was about him.

"As do I, but we must continue as normal until we hear further."

Louisa had a feeling that for the Hindleys, every minute would seem like an hour until they heard from Miles.

Chapter Nine

Louisa had never seen such joy expressed by two people when they eventually received Miles's letter about their daughter. Both had laughed and cried, embracing each other. She had given them privacy and sought Billy out in the kitchen.

"Hello, Louisa," Billy said as soon as he spotted her. He was eating a buttered slice of bread, and Louisa could not help the smile on her face. He never seemed to stop eating, yet he was as slim as he had been when they first arrived, although no longer gaunt and pale.

"Hello, Billy. How are you?"

"Rosie has gone."

"I know, but she hopes you know that she cares about you."

Billy nodded. "She told me she is going to be rich one day." Louisa did not know how to continue, but it seemed Billy did not notice her slight discomfort as he continued happily. "Cook said I am to live in a cottage, and I will have my own servants!"

"Really? That is wonderful." Louisa was aware of the Hindleys' plans for Billy but was surprised that they had told him so soon after Rosie had left.

"When Lady Florence stays at Hindley Hall, I will be able to see Cook. I like Cook and was sad that I was leaving her, but I will still see her, and someone else will cook for me. Does that mean I will be rich like Rosie?"

"I think it does," Louisa said, a lump in her throat. "When are you going?"

"Soon, but I can't go until after Christmas. Cook says there's to be boar head for dinner, and I don't want to miss that."

"I am not surprised; it sounds delicious." Louisa kissed Billy on his head, and he smiled up at her after stuffing the last of his bread in his mouth. He was so young and always would be, but he would be happy, of that Louisa was sure.

———— . ————

Two days after the news of Melissa being found, Lord Hindley came into the drawing room, a letter in his hand and a frown on his face. "Miles has sent me a note saying that we need to remain by your side at all times, Louisa. He will be returning on the morrow, but stresses that you are not to be left alone."

"What is amiss?" Lady Florence asked, looking between Louisa and her husband.

"We have to be on the alert in case a Mr Simmerton makes an appearance, either by knocking on the door or by more sinister methods."

Louisa felt the colour drain from her face. "He has found me?" She did not know whether to run or to hide, but panic was in danger of overwhelming her.

Lady Florence crossed to Louisa and took hold of her hands. "You are under our protection; nothing is going to happen to you."

Louisa turned fearful eyes to her. "I am not of age, and there was an agreement between him and my parents."

"That does not matter."

"How did he find me?"

"Rosie has been entertaining people with her escapades. She is quite a hit for the moment," Lord Hindley said with a hint of sadness. "Miles says that Simmerton was present at a party she was at. Miles only found out because he had sought Rosie out to try and persuade her to return home, but she refused and took great delight in telling him of the arrangement Simmerton claims to have with you."

"Not with me." Louisa shuddered. "My parents sent me away to school the moment my uncle offered to pay for me." It was time to explain everything. "They did not want me back until they had met Simmerton and arranged a marriage between us. There must have been something to their benefit, but I do not know what."

"Could you not seek the help of your uncle?" Lady Florence asked.

"He died," Louisa answered sadly. "He paid for my siblings to be schooled too. It is upsetting, but I have never met some of the younger ones."

"You never went home?"

"No. That was probably for the best, or I might have been married at sixteen. They sent for me once Uncle's money had run out, and by that time, I had turned eighteen. Within hours of arriving home, I was faced with Mr Simmerton and the information that the banns had already been read in church. I was to be married two days later."

"I presume he was not the eligible man you would have been willing to marry?" Lady Florence asked drily.

"No. I would have hated to marry a stranger, but this man was ancient and had children older than me. Everything about him repulsed me, and I just knew I had to get away. That was the start of my long walk into London."

"You poor child, that is a shocking state of affairs! He will not get to you while you are under our care."

"But can you really stop him?" Louisa asked, not daring to hope that they could prevent Simmerton from claiming her.

"There are ways and means of achieving success," Lord Hindley said to her with a wink. "You will not be alone until Miles returns. A footman will be assigned to follow you around and guard your chamber, and two maids will sleep in your room. Try not to worry. All will be sorted soon." He smiled at his wife before leaving the room.

"No visits for us today," Lady Florence said. "The weather is not very nice, so I think sitting before a roaring fire will be preferable."

"Please do not stay in because of me," Louisa said. "I hate that, yet again, I am causing you trouble."

"Rosie has caused this, the foolish chit, but it will be sorted to all our satisfaction. Have faith, my love."

Louisa knew it would be a very long day and did not really expect Miles to have a solution once he arrived. She cursed herself that she longed to see him when it was likely that Simmerton would claim her in some way, if not today, then soon. She had finally confessed to herself that despite a rocky start, she was attracted to Miles far more than she should be.

He was protective of his family, and she could not criticise him for that. In fact, it was one of the things she liked most about him. It also helped that he was very handsome, had a wonderful smile and treated Billy so kindly that it made her think he would be an excellent father when he eventually settled down. Those few minutes they had shared in the library had meant so much to her, even to the point of allowing herself to dream of a future she knew was unattainable.

He would inevitably marry a diamond of society, which left a bad taste in her mouth and a lump in her stomach. She wanted to be the one who made him smile, but she knew that even though she had been brought up as a gentlewoman on the lower edges of society, she was no longer respectable. If anyone learned about her background, she would be laughed out of society. With Rosie already telling their stories, it would soon spread; Louisa was aware of how fast gossip travelled.

She could dream of Miles, but that was as far as it could go. If she was very lucky, some decent, respectable man would take her on if Simmerton did not get his way. One thing was certain, she could never marry a man who would inherit an earldom.

284

Chapter Ten

Miles burst into the morning room where Louisa had been breakfasting, footmen on guard. Looking around, he nodded to the footmen. "You can leave."

"But, sir..."

"I will guard her. You can stand outside the door if you wish, but close it when you leave."

Louisa had patted her mouth with her napkin, her appetite lost, but she could not speak.

Eventually, Miles turned to her. "You are safe!"

"Yes, I am, thanks to your family. Your sister, is she here?"

"No, but she has written a long letter to my father. She will visit, but not just yet."

"She is well, though?"

"Yes, thank you. A foolish marriage to her footman has left her working her fingers to the bone and well on the way to having a houseful of children. It seems that she was with child when she left and has had twins since. She is embarrassed and needs to be in contact with our parents through letter before she feels able to meet them. I have ensured she is a little more comfortable and can afford what she needs for now at least. Hopefully, it will not be long before she is willing to return home."

"You are an uncle." Louisa knew they were avoiding the subject of Simmerton, but she did not wish to see the condemnation in his eyes.

"Yes." Miles smiled. "They are a handful, but I cannot wait to get to know them more."

"Your parents will be excellent grandparents."

"They will. This is not why I returned; I had to come back. Because of you."

"I am sorry. You must think the worst of me for not telling you everything."

"I could strangle Rosie for what she has done. She does not see that she is their darling now, but they will soon tire of her." Miles walked to the fire and held his hands towards the flames. "Why did you not trust us?" he said quietly, not looking at her.

Louisa felt the disappointment in his words as if he had struck her. "How could I say what I had done when your sister had done something similar? Your parents are two of the best people I have ever met, but they are also parents in distress; they would have empathised with my mother and father. I could not risk their contacting my parents, but I hated that I was deceitful when they were being so good."

"They would have understood the differences in the cases."

"I could not risk it, not until I got to know them."

"But you still did not say anything." Miles glanced at her, but Louisa had her head bowed.

"I did not wish this to end, not yet, which is completely selfish of me. Is Simmerton here?" Louisa was consumed with panic and desolation.

Miles came across to her, pulling her to her feet and keeping hold of her hands. "Not yet, but I know he intends to travel here today. It means we do not have a lot of time, so I hope you are ready to leave."

"I do not understand." Louisa savoured the feel of his hands, even now, when all was lost, wishing him to hold onto her forever.

"We have a dash to the border to undertake." He smiled at her, affection and a hint of mischief in his eyes.

"What? No!" Louisa pulled away in horror.

"You do not wish to marry me?" For the first time since meeting him, Miles seemed vulnerable, hurt at her rejection.

"It has nothing to do with my feelings! You cannot marry me!" Louisa cried.

"Of course I can. It is the perfect solution."

"You do not love me. You actively disliked me at the start of our acquaintance! How can you offer yourself up as some sort of sacrifice to protect me? It is too much." Louisa was in turmoil; her heart wanted to throw herself at him, not caring whether he loved her, beg him to marry her and take the risk that one day he would come to love her, even just a little, but she could not. It was her affection for him that made her wish to protect him, even against herself.

"You think I dislike you?"

"I know we cleared the air at the party, but we cannot be described as best of friends, can we?"

Miles crossed the distance between them and pulled her into his arms. She stiffened but did not resist him. "I think I fell in love the moment I saw you, my night-time nymph. I had never seen such a beautiful vision."

Louisa snorted. "You were foxed. I think you are coming it too brown."

Smiling at her, Miles kissed her nose. "When I realised who you were, I was furious with myself for being so attracted to you. I believed you were some sort of criminal, but my heart knew it could not be true. I had to suppress my need to declare myself to you until I was sure you were not trying to take advantage of my parents."

"You were very successful at hiding your feelings." Louisa wanted to believe him but would not let herself.

"I am sorry. I wanted to spend time with you after the party, allowing us the opportunity to get to know each other, but then I got the message about Melissa. Then Rosie, blast her, made everything more rushed than I hoped it would be. It felt like torture not being here to protect you and hoping that Mother and Father would understand the urgency. I was very candid in my letter to my father."

"They must think so ill of me. I am sorry to reject your kind offer, but no marriage can happen between us." As Louisa was still in his embrace, she knew she was being a tad hypocritical, but being with him felt so right, that it was where she was supposed to be. A pity it could not last.

"Why on earth would they think ill of you? They adore you, as do I."

"I will not allow society to ridicule you because you are

married to me."

"You put far too much emphasis on what society thinks and not enough on what I want to happen."

"Please, do not act the knight in shining armour; you do not have to." Louisa had to offer him a way out, but her resolve was weakening by the second.

Miles laid a warm palm against her blushing cheek. "I know I do not, but it is what I want. Fast, this all might appear to be, but the thought of not having you by my side for the rest of my days sends me into a blind panic. Please kiss me, Louisa, before I start to believe that you are indifferent to me, for I have a sensitive soul."

Louisa wanted to laugh at the comment and convince him that he was making a mistake. Instead, she wrapped her arms around his neck and lifted her face. With an appreciative groan, he bent his head and touched her lips with his. When she sighed, it was the only signal he needed to know her true feelings, and he pulled her close.

Louisa could not think; she just felt. The way he guided her, teasing her into opening her mouth and deepening the kiss. She had never been kissed but responded eagerly and with plea-sure. When he grasped her waist and pulled her to him, she did not resist. Feeling his strong, muscular body against hers made warmth rush through her and her heart rate increase. She clutched his hair, needing something to keep her grounded, or she was sure that she would lift off the floor.

A cough interrupted them, and although Louisa tried to pull away in mortification, Miles kept her close, smiling down at her flushed cheeks and rosy lips.

"There better be a good reason for your entrance," Miles said, not taking his eyes off Louisa.

"Just to tell you that the carriage is packed, and we are ready to leave when you are," Lord Hindley said, a smile in his voice.

"What?" Louisa was shocked enough to look around Miles at Lord Hindley.

Lady Florence was standing by her husband in the doorway, and they were both grinning at her. "You do not think that we would not attend the wedding of our only son, would you?"

"I— You want to join a dash to the border?" Louisa could barely utter the words; her mind was racing.

"Of course. If it is the only way of getting you out of a scrape, then we are more than happy to embark on this adventure with you." Lady Florence smiled.

"But my background, my history," Louisa said.

Lady Florence waved her hand. "You are perfect for Miles. You will not indulge him as we have, and we know you are already in love with each other."

"Mother!" Miles laughed at Louisa's embarrassment.

"But it is Christmas Eve tomorrow! How can you travel so far after all the trouble Cook has gone to!"

"I have spoken with Cook, and she is more than happy with our plans. She said that Billy will make sure there is no waste."

Louisa laughed. "She cannot have taken the news so calmly."

Miles took her hand. "Do not worry; Cook will already be planning a huge wedding breakfast for when we return."

"Which will be happening at Hindley Hall," Lord Hindley said. "It will be the first celebration of our family back together."

"This is all too much," Louisa said, eyes shining with tears.

Lord Hindley crossed to her and placed his hand on her shoulder. "We do not need to celebrate Christmas, as we have already received the best present we could hope for. Our daughter is alive and well and one day will return to the fold, and our son has chosen the best of brides. It will be a perfect Christmas, I assure you."

"You have been so kind to me. I do not deserve it."

"We think you do. Now come on," Lord Hindley urged. "We have a journey to undertake before that man arrives."

"Are you sure?" Louisa asked Miles. She wanted her future to be linked to his more than she could express. She could hardly believe that he felt the same.

"More than I have been sure of anything else in my life. I love you, Louisa, and I am sorry for being a fool at the start."

"I love you too," Louisa said. "I really do. This is the first Christmas present I have ever had."

"It will not be the last, I promise you that," Miles said, kissing her quickly.

"I am so happy."

"Thank goodness for that," Lord Hindley said. "Now, come on!"

Epilogue

The dash to the border was an easier journey than Louisa had expected. Lord Hindley assured her that Mr Simmerton would not follow them, especially as he had sent an announcement of the marriage to the Times. Over several days, Louisa came to know her husband-to-be further and love him even better, although the Hindleys did complain whenever Miles tried to kiss her in the carriage.

They travelled back to Hindley Hall in separate carriages, Miles and Louisa taking far longer than the Hindleys as they lingered in wedded bliss. When they eventually returned, Billy was settled into his new cottage, spending some of each day up at the big house with Cook.

Melissa was persuaded to leave her old life and bring her husband and children to Hindley Hall to reconnect with the family. It could have been uncomfortable, but the babies soon brought down any barriers that remained. Lord Hindley insisted on extending a wing of the house, and it became Melissa's home, with her husband accepted as a member of the family.

Mr Simmerton had arrived at the Hindleys' London home and was shown a copy of the Times by Lord Hindley's man of business. Apparently, he was furious and had cursed Louisa to the devil before being escorted off the premises; he was last heard of at the less salubrious parties in society, still on the lookout for a wife.

Rosie lived the life she wanted for many years. Her quick wit and intelligence stood her in good stead. The Hindleys had expected her to struggle, but they had not accounted for her resourcefulness. Rosie was careful with money and the presents she received over the years. When her looks were no longer sufficient to attract a man willing to keep her, she opened a faro house and became revered for giving the most splendid parties any young rake would appreciate. Louisa always kept in touch with Rosie, not liking the path her friend had taken but understanding that she could never have settled for life as a companion. Louisa never forgot what service Rosie had done for her, and there was always the promise that if she needed help, it would be given.

As for Louisa and Miles, their love blossomed without the pressures there were at the start. They were a couple who never seemed to tire of each other's company or of teasing the other. Very often, they would descend into peals of laughter while those around them shook their heads in bewilderment. When their children arrived, they moved to Hindley Hall permanently to join Melissa's growing family.

——— · ———

Ten years later

"Luke wishes his papa to teach him faro. Apparently, Billy has told him all about what Rosie does, and he wants to make his fortune at the faro tables," Louisa said as she climbed into bed and snuggled into Miles's open arms.

"If Billy was not so good with the children, I would strangle him, but I will need to speak to him. The last thing we need is for Luke to decide that he is going to visit our wayward Rosie."

Louisa laughed. "If he does, I am sure Rosie will send him back with a scolding he will not forget in a hurry."

"I am not so sure. Oof." Miles groaned at the elbow in his ribs.

"Do not be horrible. Rosie sends them all presents and always writes nice letters. She is not the monster you have her down as."

"I only do it because I know it angers you, and I love it when you are cross, especially that little tilt of your chin."

Louisa huffed out a laugh. "You are ridiculous."

"You are beautiful. When are we going to tell the children that they are to have another brother or sister?" Miles stroked the slight bulge in Louisa's stomach.

"Your parents will throw us out if we keep adding to our family. Melissa already has six."

"And with our ten."

"Ten? We only have four!"

"And this will be our fifth. I think ten is a lovely round number."

"I think you should start sleeping in your own room."

Miles rolled to look down at Louisa, her hair spread across the pillow, cheeks flushed, and eyes sparkling. "You are the loveliest woman I have ever seen. Why would you deprive me of your company and the opportunity to have little Louisas running all over the house?"

Louisa reached up and gave a lock of his hair a sharp tug in amused admonishment. "Luke and Richard are your double in looks as well as nature. They are the rakes of the future."

Miles grinned. "Glad that my own legacy will carry on. Now, what can I do to persuade you to agree to ten children?" He started to shower kisses on her face, neck and shoulders until her laughter turned into moans, and all thought of separate beds was forgotten.

———— · ————

"I do sometimes wonder why I ever wished for the house to be noisy," Lady Florence said to her husband one morning over breakfast. Whoops and shouts could be heard from the hallway as numerous feet thundered down the stairs and out of the front door.

"Shall I banish them all?" Lord Hindley asked, chuckling at a particularly loud screech.

"I suppose we would soon become bored, would we not?"

"I think we would." Lord Hindley clinked his teacup against his wife's. "We are very lucky, my love."

"We certainly are, except when it comes to winning the challenges our little darlings set. Do you think we shall win the rowing race today?"

"If not, I fear we will be turned out of our boat. For some reason, it is hilarious to see grandparents floundering in the lake."

"I believe you are right. I hope you are prepared to lose. Again." Lady Florence's eyes sparkled with laughter.

"You mean I cannot show them my prowess today or even a little of my talent?"

"It has been a while since we have had a swim in the lake."

"If you promise me a kiss under the weeping willow, then I can guarantee a loss."

"In that case, you have my word. For the children dislike that more than anything."

"Yes, their shouts of disgust are quite amusing. I cannot wait until they start to bring home their chosen ones."

"Oh, there will be endless opportunities for revenge. I have never been of the opinion that grandparents should be anything but menaces."

"Nor I."

The couple smiled at each other as the noise continued unabated.

The End

 Audrey Harrison was born in the wrong century. A shy child, she would lose herself in the worlds books created, and her first job was in a library (of course!). She can be found either with her head in a book, engrossed in writing, or visiting yet another museum. Her heroes and heroines always get a happy ever after, but she loves concocting unusual twists and turns along the way. In 2018, she was honored to be a finalist in the Amazon Kindle Storyteller Award.

To learn more, scan the QR code or go to her website at www.audrey-harrison.co.uk, where you can sign up to her email list and receive a free copy of *The Unwilling Earl*, along with early announcements of upcoming novels and other news.

The Viscount's Christmas Runaway ©2024 Audrey Harrison.
All rights reserved.

Epiphany Day

by Christina Dudley

Chapter One

She feared for William; by no means convinced...that
he was at all equal to the management of a high-fed
hunter in an English fox-chase.

—Austen, Mansfield Park (1814)

A group of huntsmen in scarlet coats crowded the yard of the Crest and Comb, their attendant grooms readying their mounts, as the Hampshire Tally Ho drew up.

"Rather a late start for them," observed Eliza to Kirby.

"You wouldn't catch Sir Miles dilly-dallying," replied the Ardens' sturdy maid. "And he hates when the master of the hunt invites strangers. Town swells who care for naught but riding hard."

"As if Sir Miles didn't ride hard himself," Eliza laughed. "He has been 'neck or nothing' since I was a child. Well, let us hope he remembered to send the Ardenmere carriage for us before he set off to spend the day thundering through gorse and woodland."

Heads turned to regard the young lady with the high color

and shining chestnut hair being handed down from the Tally Ho, heads which were averted the next moment when her hulking duenna descended after, throwing warning scowls about.

"You wait here, Miss Blinker," Kirby commanded, matter-of-factly guiding Eliza to stand near the inn door, "while I sort this out." "This" being the luggage and the whereabouts of the Ardenmere vehicle.

It was a cold December day which promised a hard frost, and Eliza drew her cloak closer about her. She had not, in truth, been looking forward to spending the vacation with the Ardens, though Lady Arden had been her mother's dear friend and never failed to extend regular invitations. Indeed, of all the teachers at Mrs. Turcotte's Seminary for Young Ladies in Winchester, Eliza Blinker was one of the few who never went anywhere between terms, having nowhere else to go. But this December, Mrs. Turcotte had been determined to repaint and repair the depredations wrought by two decades of pupils, and to this end she declared that absolutely everyone must find somewhere else to shelter for the month. With no alternative but to visit Ardenmere, if she did not want to share a narrow room in town with Madame Froissart the French teacher, Eliza yielded.

"Pardon me, miss," came a low voice, and with a start she retreated a step to let the gentleman by. He was a trim person—perhaps six inches taller than she and of pleasing proportions, and though not even the edge of his sleeve brushed her, she felt her face warm as if it had. Something about the hooded eyes which met her involuntary glance, eyes the shade of an amontillado sherry, set deeply in a finely cut face.

The moment was fleeting.

"Come on, then, Thornton!" someone hailed him. "We must ride hard to catch up."

Without a backward glance, this Thornton swung himself up, clicking his tongue to his mount and trotting away.

"What did I tell you?" grumbled Kirby, looming at Eliza's elbow. "Town swells."

———— · ————

Thankfully Sir Miles had not forgotten to send the coachman, and not twenty minutes after the huntsmen were gone the Ardenmere landau arrived, supplied thoughtfully by Lady Arden with hot bricks and blankets for the drive. Kirby had words for the coachman Molson and joined him on the seat, leaving Eliza to blissful solitude for the first time since leaving Winchester the day before. She was tired and creased and would need to gather her strength to meet Lady Arden.

Within the quarter hour they had turned up the gently winding gravel drive of Ardenmere which terminated in an old-fashioned manor house of red brick with contrasting stone trim and painted sash windows. A triangular pediment capped the center of the hipped roof, while a sweep of low steps led to the carved stone door-case.

"My dear, dear Eliza!" cried the good woman, rushing out on her tiny feet to meet the carriage and clapping mittened hands together while the crisp silver curls under her cap bounced. "How glad I am you have arrived, for the glass is falling and they say it will be icy tonight. Did you see the hunters as you came? I asked Sir Miles if he could miss just one hunt to await your arrival, but he declared it would likely be the last of the year, and therefore how could he? You will forgive him, won't you? I am so glad you have come at last. Since Frederica married I have been at sixes and sevens, hardly knowing how to occupy myself. And to think you will be with us until your school opens again in January!" Now she wrung her hands, even as Eliza gave her a kiss. "Oh, that Sir Miles! He should have been here. If only he didn't ride like such a madman! He will surely break something or fall into a ditch at his age, but he never listens to me."

"Well, you and I must manage as best we can without him," Eliza answered, when Lady Arden drew breath. "And thank you for sending Kirby for me."

"Certainly we could not let you travel alone, Eliza! Winchester might be only fifty miles as the crow flies, but who can say what mischief might befall a young lady alone in a coach with strangers?"

"Dear Lady Arden," laughed Eliza, as she led the plump and heavily shawled woman toward the house, "you speak as if I were still sixteen, instead of twice that."

But Lady Arden was not alone in thinking Eliza Blinker looked younger than her age. At Mrs. Turcotte's seminary it had happened more than once that a new parent mistook Miss Blinker, teacher of Italian and history and frequent dance-lesson accompanist, for one of the pupils.

"Two and thirty?" wondered Lady Arden. "Already? My, my. I had hoped you would marry one day. So many gentlemen pass through Winchester at one time or another for the Assizes or the races..."

Eliza would have sighed, except she had done her sighing in advance, knowing exactly the opinions Lady Arden would express. The same opinions she had been expressing since Eliza had been, in fact, sixteen. Therefore she wore her calmest smile—one her students would have recognized as suitable for a pupil being corrected for the fifteenth time: "No, Miss Price. It is '*per strada*' not '*in la strada.*' It simply must be memorized." With this hard-won, beatific expression in place, Eliza explained to her hostess, "There may indeed be plenty of gentlemen in Winchester, Lady Arden, but if I am ever in places where they may be found, it is usually in the role of chaperone. Becoming a schoolteacher is a way of becoming invisible."

"Perhaps, but not invisible to those who do not deserve the name of gentlemen." Lady Arden gave a mournful shake of her head over the ways of the world. "But at least you are safe from scoundrels here." She raised a hand to beckon her toward the staircase. "You will have your usual bedchamber, naturally, but I am afraid my maid Powell's tremor has worsened." Lowering her voice to a conspiratorial whisper she added, "I no longer trust her with the iron because her hand shakes so! She is as like to scorch herself or one's face, you understand. *These*—" pointing at the tight curls framing her forehead "—*are false.*"

"Oh?" asked Eliza brightly.

"Indeed. Therefore I hope you don't mind if Kirby serves as your maid. I know she doesn't look much like a lady's maid, but Powell has been instructing her..."

"I am sure Kirby will be fine," answered Eliza because, honestly, what else could she say? She cast a doubtful glance behind her to where Kirby followed them up the stairs with Eliza's trunk hoisted on her shoulder.

"We have a few suppers we have been invited to, and we must give one ourselves while you are here," went on Lady Arden, throwing open the door to Eliza's familiar room, unchanged not only from her childhood but indeed from the reign of Queen Anne: low ceiling, yellow curtains, walls painted leaf green to complement the walnut furniture. "It is the season, you know. But I'm afraid the only eligible gentleman you will meet is Mr. Marvin the curate."

"Oh, Lady Arden!" protested Eliza. "No matchmaking, if you please. I am happy to dine with your friends and neighbors, but please do not thrust me upon anyone!"

The well-intentioned Lady Arden pouted at this, and Eliza felt at once ashamed of her complaint, but not ashamed enough to retract it. With a grunt, Kirby lowered her trunk to the carpet and began unpacking Eliza's serviceable wardrobe, providing a welcome distraction. Eliza turned away to busy herself with arranging things.

"I will not insist," her hostess sighed. "Though you will see. He is a pleasant man, and Sir Miles likes him because he's a hunting parson."

"I quite believe that," Eliza replied, her humor reviving. "Is this Mr. Marvin out with Sir Miles today?"

"To be sure. Just like Sir Miles, Mr. Marvin never misses an opportunity to hunt if he can help it. The only time he could not avoid it was when old Mrs. Plimpsett was positively dying one morning, and poor Mr. Marvin could hardly leave her deathbed. But he felt it sorely, I can assure you."

"I hope Mrs. Plimpsett apologized for inconveniencing him," said Eliza with twitching lips.

"She *did*," Lady Arden replied innocently, "but he missed the hunt all the same."

Eliza put an arm about her companion's waist. "Well, we had better leave off discussing the parson now, Lady Arden, or I will fall in love with him despite myself. Shall we go down and have some tea? I would be happy to read to you or play for you. No need to wait for Sir Miles, for he likely will not return for hours."

———— · ————

Eliza was mistaken, however, for no sooner was the tea served and the Ardens' sheet music sorted through, than a loud confusion of voices was heard.

Before Lady Arden could remark, the drawing room doors flung open, admitting a cluster of men led by Sir Miles Arden and accompanied by an influx of chill air. But it was not the draught which elicited his wife's shrieks. Rather it was the burden laid out upon a door and carried by two of the huntsmen: a muddied and mangled and bloodied fourth party. Unconscious, mercifully. Eliza's heart gave a little jump. She could not say how she recognized the man in his present condition, but recognize him she did.

"Stop that fearful caterwauling, Mary, and get off the sofa!" shouted Sir Miles to his lady. "We're going to roll him onto it."

"You'll do nothing of the kind," Eliza declared, springing up with raised hand to stop them. "If he's broken anything, jostling and tumbling him will only make it worse. Better let the surgeon see him first."

"Oh—how now, Eliza," said Sir Miles. "You've come, have you? A hearty welcome, but what would a little miss like you know of broken bones?"

"I may teach at a girls' seminary, sir," she answered, "but we are no strangers to such injuries, having a few very tomboyish pupils. And our doctor Mr. Beckford entreated us never to move the patient if we could help it, for ten to one moving her would only add to the damage."

"Well, well, if you say so," he relented. "Ponsonby will be along shortly, and he knows a fair bit of doctoring, too. Gently, there!" The others left off at once, sparing the victim further mishap. Though from the looks exchanged, Eliza suspected the unconscious man had already experienced his share of rough handling.

"We could hardly leave him where he lay, miss," spoke up one of them, a bluff, ruddy-faced fellow who was the only one wearing a black coat rather than scarlet. "The hounds were running fast, and the fox took a line through the bushes—"

"You know the spot, Eliza," took up Sir Miles eagerly. "A ten-minute walk to the northeast. There's a bank with a rail at the top of it, after which it drops far down into the field. Makeless has taken that rail a dozen times and knew just the trick of it, but after we were over, I stopped to watch the others. It was your fault, Marvin. Thornton might have managed it, even on a borrowed horse, if he turned and rode hard at the jump, but when he saw you pressing on him, he had to make the attempt when he was too close. Sure enough, his horse caught a foot against the bar, and over they tumbled. Then you come along on Hautboy and come right down on them. What a tangle! It's a mercy you weren't carried out on a door yourself."

This was the clergyman Mr. Marvin, then, and scarcely were makeshift introductions performed than the door opened to admit the hunt's attending surgeon.

Tossing aside his hat and peeling off his gloves, Mr. Ponsonby took one look at Mr. Thornton and called for scissors. "He will have to be cut out of that handsome coat. Have you a spare shirt he can wear, Sir Miles? And better bring some brandy, in case he regains consciousness." When his orders were obeyed, the ladies retreated modestly to the far side of the room, leaving the surgeon to make his examination. Only once did the patient give a faint groan.

"Let's hope he remains insensible," said Ponsonby. "I'll have to reset the collarbone, and he's cracked two ribs, but the ankle is only sprained. The worst of it looks to be the mighty blow he took to the forehead. The eyes are still in there, but time will tell if he'll ever be able to see out of 'em again, what with the swelling and the blood. And when he comes to himself, he may not even know his own name." The surgeon passed a hand over his pate. "Here—pass me my bag and I'll bandage his head before we try anything. On no account is he to use his eyes for at least a few weeks, if there's been trauma to the optic nerves. You hear that, Sir Miles? Have the servants shut the curtains in here. Candlelight and firelight only."

"Certainly," agreed the baronet, pointing at the hovering footmen who scrambled to obey. "But shouldn't you be giving these instructions to the Crest and Comb, Ponsonby? Looks like this Thornton will be staying there a long time."

"The Crest and Comb?" snapped the surgeon, swabbing Thornton's wounds. "The man is not returning to the inn. He is not going *anywhere* for some weeks. I'm sorry to tell you, Sir Miles, but this Thornton must not be moved. When I'm done with him we will transfer him gingerly to the sofa, and there he must stay until I give him leave."

"In my drawing room?" the baronet blustered. "But we use this room! Cannot we remove him upstairs, at the very least?"

"Not upstairs, not one foot!" insisted Ponsonby. "Haven't you a partition or—or some sort of screen, Lady Arden? If you do, you may hide him behind it and still use the room when he is not sleeping. He hasn't lost his hearing, I imagine, and he might appreciate the company after a time."

United in dismay, Sir Miles and his lady gawped at each other. To be saddled with an invalid for weeks on end, in their very own drawing room? One who might turn out to be blind and possibly not right in the head?

Again it was Eliza who interposed. She had silently been assisting the footmen with the curtains and directing them where they might place Lady Arden's prized calamander lacquer screen. "Mr. Ponsonby, do you suppose when the poor man's bones have recovered somewhat, he might be moved at that time?"

"Possibly, possibly. It depends, frankly, on the extent of damage to his brains and eyes. I will look in on him regularly, to be sure, and a nurse can be sent up from the village, but for now here he is, and here he must remain."

"Very well," she said after a pause, seeing the Ardens still dumbfounded. "Leave your instructions with us. And we will send someone to the Crest and Comb to fetch his belongings and his manservant."

Mr. Ponsonby regarded her with dawning respect. "Exactly, Miss—"

"Blinker," she supplied. "Miss Blinker. I will be here at Arden-mere through Epiphany Day."

"Miss Blinker." He bowed his head and finished tying off Thornton's bandages. "And now, Marvin, Sir Miles—if you would each take hold of one of his arms, in case he wakens and tries to move—let me see about this collarbone."

Chapter Two

At ev'ry Word a Reputation dies.
—Pope, *"The Rape of the Lock"* (1712)

"No one could find his manservant," announced Kirby upon her return from the inn, "so a message was left. And then the nurse Mr. Ponsonby wanted was unavailable, so here's Mrs. Chop." With her thumb she pointed over her shoulder at the woman descending from the cart, one nearly Kirby's equal in size, though a deal older and rougher. Eliza's keen nose caught a whiff of gin, and she looked toward Lady Arden in alarm. Poor Lady Arden was already shrinking with unease, taken aback by the nurse's proportions and dishevelment. How things were going from bad to worse! First to be saddled with the blind, broken, insensible Mr. Thornton, and now to add this unkempt Amazon?

"Oh, Eliza," she whispered helplessly, wringing her hands, "it is too much."

"I will speak with her, madam," Eliza replied under her breath.

"Perhaps it will only be for a day or two, until the valet turns up and the nurse Mr. Ponsonby recommended is again at liberty."

Mrs. Chop did not improve on acquaintance, unfortunately. When Eliza took her aside to review the surgeon's instructions—how often Mr. Thornton should have water dripped into his mouth if he remained unconscious, what should be done when he did awaken, the care of his bandages, and so forth, Mrs. Chop listened with head cocked and jaw working as if she were chewing something. Perhaps she was.

Well, at least the woman would be strong enough to shift or to turn Mr. Thornton when necessary, Eliza thought. There was nothing more to be done at the moment in any event, so she showed Mrs. Chop her post beside the patient. They had chosen the most comfortable wing chair—Sir Miles' favorite—to set beside the sofa, along with a washstand from one of the bedchambers. Nearby stood a round table holding a tray of biscuits and sandwiches covered by a cloth.

"And where am I to sleep or ease myself?" Mrs. Chop asked, hardly glancing at her patient.

Eliza blushed. "There is a room prepared for you. The footmen or Kirby will show you presently. Mr. Ponsonby did say it would be better to sleep in the same room if Mr. Thornton does not come to himself before nightfall, in which case we will fetch a chaise longue and blankets for you."

The reply must have satisfied, for Mrs. Chop grunted and dropped into Sir Miles' chair without another word, and Eliza left her there. Heavens! If his hunting accident didn't kill Mr. Thornton, Eliza certainly hoped the man possessed a constitution iron enough to survive Mrs. Chop's tender nursing.

When she slipped from the room, Lady Arden hissed to her from across the passage. "Eliza! Come in here."

"What is it?" she asked when the door was shut behind her. "I know Mrs. Chop is not what we would wish, but I don't see what alternative we have."

"Never mind that woman. I am sure she will be good enough for the likes of him! Come and sit beside me, for I must tell you what more Kirby learned at the Crest and Comb."

Eliza's breath caught. She had not mentioned having seen Mr. Thornton outside the coaching inn, but perhaps Kirby had? Which would only draw attention to her own omission.

"Goodness, but you seem wound up," she murmured.

"As well I should be! Oh, Eliza, suppose we are nourishing a viper in our bosom?"

"What?"

"Kirby says the inn was in a ferment with talk of Mr. Thornton because of his accident—"

"Lady Arden, surely you needn't whisper. The doors are closed, and the poor man is unconscious, to boot."

"'Poor man,' indeed," sniffed her companion. "Eliza, you must be on your guard with that person in there. Indeed, you must avoid being in the drawing room by yourself for as long as he is here. For your dear departed mother's sake I will keep you safe."

Eliza could not help laughing. "Gracious me! What *did* Kirby hear? Is he a madman? A malefactor?"

"This is a serious matter, Eliza. That—person—lying in my drawing room is a man with no honor. He was engaged to a young lady of good family in Sussex, it seems, but then he refused to go through with the match! They even sued him for breach of promise—scandalous enough—but he had no shame, and rather than do the proper thing, he simply paid over the money. Can you imagine?"

"Dear me," breathed Eliza, genuinely struck. She remembered again the man's voice and disconcerting gaze. Yes, it might all be gossip, but even based on so fleeting an encounter with him, she could not deny it was plausible gossip. "What became of the young lady?"

"Why—who knows? It hardly matters. The point is, here is this dreadful scoundrel sheltered under Sir Miles' roof for heaven knows how long. Oh, Eliza! I would send you back to Winchester if I could, for your own protection."

"Lady Arden, do calm yourself," urged Eliza, amusement reviving. "I do not defend his conduct, but, if true, his roguery was of a specific nature, for jilting one particular young lady endangers no others."

"How can you say that? The unfortunate creature might simply be the one known victim in a long career of misconduct."

Eliza grinned. "A rather expensive career that would prove, I daresay."

"He can afford it! Kirby learned the recreant has a tidy fortune to his name."

"In any event, I will avoid being in the drawing room alone," Eliza soothed. "Though I do wonder what danger even a hardened scoundrel could pose, if he were unconscious, blindfolded, and immobile as Mr. Thornton is?"

"Mr. Thornton will not always be those things," Lady Arden insisted. "And if you have no sense of danger for yourself, I do, on your behalf."

Still shaking her head, Eliza took Lady Arden's hand. "Thank you. But I persist in thinking that my age, as well as my lack of fortune and family, will shield me like a cloak from unwanted attentions."

"From honorable gentlemen such things might," answered the older lady grimly. "From rogues, however...I am sorry to say your state only makes you easier to prey upon."

——— . ———

With the drawing room placed out of bounds and Lady Arden taking refuge in an afternoon nap, Eliza retreated to her bedchamber to inform Mrs. Turcotte of her safe arrival. But she had scratched no more than the salutation when a knock sounded and Kirby entered.

"I think you'd better come, miss," said the strapping maid, "for there's a groaning coming from the drawing room."

"A...groaning? But what does Mrs. Chop say?"

"She isn't there."

Eliza stared. "Of course she must be there! Where else can she be? Unless—did you look in the room we assigned her?" *The room intended for her to sleep in,* only *if her patient could be left alone!* Eliza added indignantly in her head.

"Not there either. And Sir Miles is a gone out again, miss," Kirby anticipated her next question. "He said there weren't any use in him missing the hunt supper at Cosworthy Park."

Of course he did.

Eliza sighed and laid down her pen. "Very well. Then I suppose we had better send for Mr. Ponsonby again."

The maid trailed her to the bottom of the stairs like a faithful mastiff and hovered while Eliza gave instructions to the footman

Hoskins. Then, when she glanced toward the drawing room doors, Kirby said, "Lady Arden says I am always to accompany you, if you are a–going in there. 'Don't you let her be alone with him, Kirby,' she told me."

"Well then, together it is. But perhaps we need not go in. I don't hear anything now."

As if to spite her, a protracted moan struck their ears, one ending in a sudden *whuff*.

Oh, dear. Suppose he had rolled from the sofa and could not right himself? Or that he had pulled off his bandages and was dragging himself across the room in search of light? Eliza found herself regretting her earlier bravado about broken bones. What precisely had she imagined she knew about injuries? Especially injuries the magnitude of Mr. Thornton's!

Taking a deep breath and nodding at Kirby, she opened the doors quietly and crept around the side of the lacquered screen. To her great relief, the man still lay upon the sofa, his bandages intact, though one hand fumbled at them.

"No, no," said Eliza, hurrying forward. "You mustn't. Your eyes must not be exposed."

Though she had not touched him, his hand froze in its exploration.

"Can you hear me, sir?" she asked. "Do you understand me?"

There was a long, long pause. Was he too muddled to speak? But no.

His hand fell back. "Have I...died?" was his unexpected question, the thrilling voice she remembered thick but recognizable.

"Died!"

"Am I...in the infernal place?"

That made Eliza grin. "You are at Ardenmere, sir, and very much alive by the grace of God, though considerably impaired after your accident."

"Accident?"

"A hunting accident. Your horse caught a foot on a rail, I believe, and there was a drop into a field, and you were somehow entangled with—" Eliza broke off when she saw his nails dig into the upholstery. Better not to mention Mr. Marvin's part in it, then. Quickly she tacked about. "—With another rider," she resumed. "The surgeon Mr. Ponsonby has made inventory of the damage. He reset your collarbone, but you still have a sprained ankle, two cracked ribs, and a—blow—to your head. It is a very promising sign that you have regained consciousness, sir, and that you seem lucid. Mr. Ponsonby does fear—possible damage to your eyes, however, which he hopes to forestall or mend by keeping you quiet and in the dark for some weeks."

Now the patient's hand clenched in a fist and struck the back of the sofa, but if the action relieved his feelings any, it exacted its own cost. A string of muffled oaths followed, which Eliza could not interpret, though her eyes widened at both its length and variety of emphasis. Kirby's more worldly ears caught enough that she clicked her tongue and advanced a step, as if she would—what? Press a pillow to the man's face to silence him? A shake of the head from Eliza stopped her. He was in a great deal of pain and confusion, she imagined, and therefore allowance must be made.

"Is it that bad, sir? Because Mr. Ponsonby left laudanum drops, and he said he would come again to see how you were doing." Even as she spoke misgiving filled her, because what did she know about administering laudanum? And where had that thrice-blasted Mrs. Chop gone?

The muscle along his jaw stood out, and Mr. Thornton's finely-cut mouth twisted in a grimace. He might have read her thoughts, for he bit out, "Are you the nurse? Or Lady Arden? Who are you?"

"I'm neither. I'm—nobody," she uttered, caught off guard. Given Lady Arden's warnings, Eliza hardly wanted to confess to being the unmarried female houseguest.

The vagueness of her reply only served to anger him. "Then you may take yourself off, Miss Nobody! I want no one with me. I suppose I must suffer Ponsonby's fussings and fiddlings, but I need not suffer yours."

"Fussings and fiddlings" indeed! When she had not laid so much as a finger on him!

Had Eliza been ten years younger she might have made tart reply, but as it was she managed to swallow it. *He is in pain*, she reminded herself, *and likely confused*. Without another word she withdrew, crooking a finger for Kirby to follow and then holding that same finger to her lips to enjoin silence.

Nevertheless, when they were safely shut in the morning room, the maid burst out with, "Miss Blinker, the face of that fellow, speaking to you like that! Why, he's every particle the rogue they said he was at the inn!"

"Now, now," Eliza pacified her, "if he were healthy and whole, I daresay he could be as courteous as the next person, but as it is I fear a certain amount of crossness is to be expected. We will do as he says and leave him in peace. The question is, where has that tiresome Mrs. Chop gone?"

"I'll sort her out when I find her," vowed the maid with lowered brow. "In the meantime, miss, remember Lady Arden doesn't want you going in there by yourself."

Eliza laughed. "Did I not just say I would stay away? Why does everyone think my heart's desire is to seek the company of a bad-tempered man of evil reputation? *You're* the one who summoned me, Kirby—not that it wasn't right to do so, Mr. Thornton being in the condition he is. No, no, rest easy. Lady Arden made me promise, and I will not venture into the lion's den without you or her by my side, lest the blind cripple spring up from the sofa and seduce me before I have time to run away."

The maid's frown deepened, and Eliza laid a hand on her arm. "Pardon me. I am being flippant, when you all have my best interests at heart. But let us see if we can find Mrs. Chop. If Sir Miles is paying her wages, the least she can do is stay at her post."

———— . ————

It was Mr. Ponsonby who discovered the whereabouts of Mrs. Chop, however, by virtue of stopping at the lodge and calling for the gate to be opened, only to glimpse the nurse slumped on a bench within when Simmons emerged.

"Dead drunk, I'm sorry to say," the surgeon reported when he was admitted to the morning room, now lit by candles for evening use.

Lady Arden gasped. "Drunk? But—has she returned with you?"

"I dismissed her. She would have been no use in her condition. She was not the nurse I hoped to send in any case, but Mrs. Plummer is already attending at least three people in the village through a positive outbreak of lumbago, and lumbago is the last thing Thornton needs, with his two cracked ribs."

This evoked a shudder from Lady Arden. "No, indeed. But—what shall we do with Mr. Thornton, then? Could Mrs. Chop return when she is...sober?"

"I would not recommend it," he answered crisply. "See here—there is good news and bad news. The good news is how quickly Thornton regained his senses and, as far as I can tell, his brains seem in decent order. Moreover he must have the strength of an ox, for I had hard work to convince him he must lie still for some time."

"What is the bad news, then?" prompted Eliza. "His eyesight?"

Ponsonby looked at her measuringly. "As I said earlier, we will not know about his eyesight for several weeks, and I repeat that he must not test it with any exposure to light. This I have also impressed on him, followed by a dose a laudanum, with what success remains to be seen." His thin lips quirked ruefully. "No, Miss Blinker, Lady Arden. It turns out the bad news is the same as the good: he has regained his senses, and he has the strength of an ox. Meaning, he will likely prove an impatient patient. That is, as a patient he will require nursing, but he will resent requiring it. He will resent lying there unoccupied. He will resent having to wait to learn the damage to his eyes."

"But—what do you recommend we do, Mr. Ponsonby?" fretted Lady Arden once more. "If Mrs. Plummer cannot come and Mrs. Chop will not do, who will nurse Mr. Thornton? Our maid requested that his man come to Ardenmere, whenever he should be found, but there has been no sign of him. Have you anyone else to suggest?"

"I have not," he admitted. "I hoped one of your servants might have experience. He would likely need a manservant to assist him from time to time in sitting or standing up to—er—attend to daily needs, but a woman might handle the rest, the administration of food and drink and the changing of the bandages."

Both Eliza and Kirby regarded Lady Arden, whose crisp curls trembled. Ardenmere's strapping footmen would surely be affronted to be asked to take on such duties.

"Oh, oh," moaned Lady Arden. "If it is only for a little while, I suppose Hoskins and Bigelow might manage it, but they will not like it. How burdensome it will be, and it is all Mr. Marvin's fault!"

"Excellent," said Mr. Ponsonby, interested in neither the difficulties of managing servants' self-consequence nor in assigning shares of blame. "And who might handle the other duties?"

"Kirby, dear," Lady Arden ventured timidly. "Might you?"

But to their surprise, Kirby had gone a little green and she backed away a step, swallowing convulsively. "Lady Arden, I could see helping with the food and such, but—but—I couldn't do bandages! If I so much as see blood or crust or pus or scabs—" There was no need to describe the consequences, for she was even now gagging with her hand to her mouth.

"Good gracious! A great big girl like you, shrinking from such things?" her mistress scolded. "I don't suppose you would have to change his bandages more than once a day, and if he will have to shut his eyes when you do so in any case, there will be nothing to turn your stomach. What will be the harm?"

But Kirby looked so miserable that Eliza spoke up. "Lady Arden, let Kirby and me work together, then. I think I might manage the bandages, and we could take the duties in turn."

"You, Eliza? Absolutely not! An unmarried gentlewoman?

Never, never, never. We already discussed what was said about Mr. Thornton."

With difficulty Eliza managed not to roll her eyes. "Yes, madam. Mr. Thornton's spotty reputation has been nothing short of drummed into me, but with Kirby beside me there will be no danger. And if Mr. Ponsonby thinks Mr. Thornton so quick to recover from his other injuries, perhaps there will not be so very much bandaging necessary...?"

The surgeon shrugged. "Nothing is certain, but if Thornton can be convinced to endure quietly, he might dispense with bandages within a week or two and merely wear patches over his eyes."

Knowing she was losing ground, Lady Arden's chin began to tremble. "But—but—it cannot only be you and Kirby, even if I permitted it. It is Christmastime! We have social engagements, Eliza."

"Let Kirby and me form one team, then," Eliza suggested, "and perhaps the chambermaid Shillbeer and—I don't know—the gatekeeper's wife Mrs. Simmons might be the other? They might do half the dinners and the late suppers, so that I may join you and Sir Miles."

Poor Lady Arden sputtered another moment, wishing the baronet were on hand to make her decision for her. But then Mr. Ponsonby delivered the death blow to her scruples. "I'm afraid, short of abandoning Ardenmere yourself, Lady Arden, there will be no avoiding caring for your unexpected guest. And the better he is cared for, the sooner he will be off your hands. Therefore I suggest you heed Miss Blinker's idea of taking the duties in turn. It will lighten the burden of care, especially if, as I suspect, he proves difficult.

Chapter Three

No light, but rather darkness visible
Serv'd only to discover sights of woe.
—Milton, Paradise Lost, i.63 (1667)

Whatever Mr. Ponsonby had done to Mr. Thornton, the patient gave them no further trouble that night, and slept much of the next, giving Eliza time to organize who should be responsible for what and when. Though Shillbeer the chamber-maid agreed with an impassive face and Mrs. Simmons (who had raised several children) with alacrity, there was grumbling among the footmen as Lady Arden had foretold.

"One would think Hoskins and Bigelow had been raised as princesses in Kew Palace!" Eliza muttered under her breath, but their grudging help would be better than having to wheedle Sir Miles into bestirring himself.

On the third day, when the laudanum wore off, the two foot-men crept into the drawing room like victims marked for slaugh-ter while Eliza, Lady Arden and the serving-women waited in the passage. Resisting the urge to press their ears to the door, they could not make out more than unintelligible voices and a thump or two, perhaps someone knocking into a piece of furniture.

"I hope that was not my screen," whispered Lady Arden.

"Or them dropping Mr. Thornton," Eliza whispered back. "But then I suppose we would have heard him roar."

When Hoskins and Bigelow finally emerged, their mistress prodded, "Well?"

Hoskins nodded and brushed off his handsome livery. "He's sorted out for the present, my lady, and a cross old bear he was to manage, but maybe a little breakfast will do him good."

"I see. Thank you. And how is he this morning? Is he confused? Still foggy from the laudanum?"

"Right addled," replied Bigelow, the larger and more taciturn of the two. Unmoved by Lady Arden's squeak of horror, he added, "Demanding that we send in a 'Miss Nobody.'"

Lady Arden gasped and seized Eliza's arm. "Heavens—asking for a—a—a female person to be sent to him! What can he mean?"

"Oh, I suspect he means me," said Eliza. Briefly she described Mr. Thornton's fit of temper the day before.

The baronet's wife shut her eyes, curls trembling. "Dear me! It is as Mr. Ponsonby fears. Mr. Thornton will find it tedious to lie blind and bedridden, and he will seek any means of amusement, whether it be to rail at you or—or to flirt with you in an attempt at seduction!"

Both Kirby and Shillbeer gasped at this, but Eliza held up a hand. "I have given the whole matter some thought, Lady Arden, and have a little scheme in mind which I hope will reassure you." Turning her eyes on the servants, she said, "Now, Mr. Thornton's reputation has doubtless been discussed below stairs, so you understand Lady Arden's uneasiness. Whether I believe myself in any danger or not, I would like to ask all of you to participate in a mild deception." She had their whole attention by this point and went a faint pink, for wasn't it all a little ridiculous, Lady Arden's fear? As if Mr. Thorton were some unbridled lecher and Eliza the temptation which could not be resisted!

"What sort of deception?" breathed Lady Arden, agog.

"Only this," continued Eliza. "We will add a few years to my age as insurance. I will be Miss Blinker, a genteel lady of middling age, and—*plain* features. If opportunity presents, you all might even make reference to what a pity it is, I should be so plain and old. Such a description will protect me as well as a suit of armor, I daresay."

"Only, what will happen if Mr. Thornton recovers the use of his eyes, miss?" asked Kirby. "And finds you not so old and not a bit plain?"

Eliza smiled at the sweet compliment. "I suppose then everyone can say something about me looking youthful for my age, and that 'beauty is in the eye of the beholder' or some such."

"Yes, good," agreed Lady Arden. "Let that be trouble for another day. Oh, Eliza, how this will set my mind at ease."

"I thought so, madam. And now that we have settled it, I daresay Mr. Thornton is beginning to wonder if this Miss Nobody will ever bring him his breakfast."

———— · ————

Coming from the passage, the drawing room seemed darkness itself. Apart from the glow of the fire and the wall sconces on the far side of the room, all was shadows.

"Surely, if he has bandages covering his eyes and Mr. Ponsonby has counseled him not to remove them, we might admit a little more light," Lady Arden hissed in her ear.

"Let us confirm that it is so, first," Eliza murmured.

"Who's there?" bellowed the patient. "Stop that confounded whispering and speak out."

The dishes on the breakfast tray rattled, and Kirby tightened her grip on it.

"Good morning, Mr. Thornton, we have your breakfast," announced Eliza, sweeping around the lacquer screen. She noted at once that the footmen had moved him to the armchair, with several of Lady Arden's cross-stitch cushions shoved in a wedge behind him and his sprained ankle supported by an ottoman. "Are you more comfortable sitting up?"

"If by 'comfort' you mean 'less subject to blinding bolts of agony when I move,'" he threw back. "Else why would I have permitted those oafs to arrange me thus? And you have not answered my question. Who addresses me?"

"Who else but Miss Nobody?" answered Eliza lightly. "I understand you called for me."

His lips parted as if he would retort, but then they unexpectedly curved into a grin, and Eliza could see his teeth shine in the gloom. Her breath hitched, not only from surprise, but because of the unsettling tug she felt in response to so small a gesture. The languor of it. The awareness of its possible effects.

Before she could recover, Lady Arden hurried forward. Perhaps she too sensed the latent charm of the smile and feared its effects. "Miss Nobody, nonsense!" she cried. "Mr. Thornton, I am Lady Arden who addresses you now, wife of Sir Miles

Arden of Ardenmere. And this youn—er—this *younger* lady is my houseguest Miss Blinker."

Mr. Thornton's head tilted, listening, and his grin faded. He gave one short nod. "Lady Arden. Miss...Blinker. James Thornton, at your service, which is less of a boast than I could wish. Forgive me for not rising to make my bows. Forgive me, moreover, for this imposition, which promises to be both lengthy and tiresome to many. Whatever costs you incur, I will of course repay."

Eliza drew two conclusions from this speech: first, that Mr. Thornton was not a man in the habit of having to beg people's pardons, for he did not sound particularly remorseful; and second, that Mr. Thornton included himself among those who would find his stay at Ardenmere tiresome. Nevertheless Lady Arden was all courtesy. "Of course you must not think of that now, sir. We are only too glad to be of some use while you recover. I'm afraid—as I am certain Mr. Ponsonby must have told you—no suitable nurse could be found, so you will be reliant on some of the servants and—and Miss Blinker for your care."

Hidden by the bandages, his eyes gave no clue to how he received this, but Eliza began to think he hardly needed eyes. She could picture his mocking brow, for his head turned a degree to where she still stood and said, "Indeed? Servants are all too used to having additional, unpleasant duties thrust upon them, but what has Miss Blinker done to deserve such treatment?"

"I volunteered," she rejoined quickly. Then, with a glance at Lady Arden, she began her program. "Because I have been a schoolteacher in Winchester for years and years, you see—"

"I don't, as a matter of fact," he interrupted blandly, tapping the bandage over his eyes. "And how cruel of you to remind me."

When Eliza colored and began to apologize for her choice of words, he waved it away, now contrarily annoyed by her fluster and sinking back into himself. "Never mind. It was a feeble joke. Go on," he said now, sounding weary and impatient. "You were saying? You have been teaching for years and years..."

"Er—yes. And—in all that time I have witnessed and tended many scrapes and sprains and broken bones."

"And now you consider yourself an expert. I understand." When Eliza could think of no reply he made a restless movement. "Well? Now that the niceties have been dealt with—"

"You would like your breakfast," Lady Arden supplied, biting her lip. "Of course. Just one more thing..."

"Yes?" It was almost a snarl. Eliza wondered if his injuries were paining him again. Would he require another dose of laudanum?

"Mr. Ponsonby is afraid you will find isolation tedious," Lady Arden ventured.

"And so I shall."

"It might not be so bad, if the family continued to use the drawing room," suggested Eliza. "We have placed a screen around you for privacy—"

His mouth twisted. "A pen for the bear, eh? Yes, Lady Arden. It is your house and your drawing room to do with as you will." He turned his head again in Eliza's direction. "I suppose this is the primary place where Miss Blinker makes herself useful to you, what with reading to you and writing for you and playing the instrument which no doubt features prominently somewhere hereabout?"

"I indeed do those things for Lady Arden," said Eliza, "and would like to continue. But all of those activities would require a little more light. If we were to open the curtains at the farthest window, would that—"

"Open away," he anticipated her, his voice sharp. "I might stand on the surface of the sun, and it wouldn't make a shred of difference. All is dark as Hades."

And then she understood. It was not the pain which made him such an ogre, though it might add to his ill-temper. He knew pain would pass.

No. Rather it was the darkness which frightened him. The fear of his blindness being utter and permanent. How could it not? An active, good-looking man in his prime, to be so stricken, with no guarantee of restoration. It would terrify at any age.

Sympathy gentled her reply. "Well, Mr. Thornton, we will open some curtains and light a few more candles, then. But not too many, as Mr. Ponsonby insisted your...optic nerve would heal the faster if not pressed into service."

But the softness of her voice provoked him anew. "Spare me your pity, Miss Blinker. You know nothing of the matter, nor much at all of nursing, despite your boasts, unless Ponsonby also recommended that I be starved to death. For why must I ask a third time for my breakfast?"

From the other side of the room, where she was opening the curtains to admit bars of light, Lady Arden whimpered at this rudeness, but Eliza merely nodded at Kirby and the other serving-women, saying, "We will set your breakfast tray on your right, sir. There is toast, egg, and boiled ham. If you would like butter or raspberry jam, you need only say so, and if you would prefer to feed yourself, the fork may be placed in your hand, as may your teacup."

With alacrity, Kirby obeyed Eliza's implied instruction, setting the tray down and buttering and pouring and spreading as commanded. Mr. Thornton did indeed prefer to feed himself, so Eliza wordlessly demonstrated to the others how to load his fork and place it in his hand. This degree of autonomy seemed to pacify him somewhat, for his brow above the bandages smoothed after a few minutes and his voice lost its sharp edge.

"Lady Arden—are you still somewhere about? My compliments to your cook."

"She seems to have gone, sir," Eliza told him. *Escaped, more like.*

"Seems to have? What—have you gone blind as well, Miss Blinker?" he asked dryly. "I thought I approved the allowance of more light."

"You did, and there is indeed more light now, but you remember the screen."

"I remember. To keep the bear hidden and to prevent Lady Arden's undoubtedly tasteful drawing room from smacking too strongly of hospital."

"Precisely," she replied, unruffled, drawing from him an unwilling chuckle.

He held out his hands to form a circle, and Kirby placed a teacup in them. Taking a careful sip, followed by another, he held the cup out again. Gingerly Kirby removed it, but not before his fingers brushed hers. The maid gasped at the contact, and Mr. Thornton paused, his head tilting and the corners of his finely cut lips curving.

Between the two of them Eliza and Kirby might have little experience with roguish young men, but that did not mean they did not instinctively recognize that here sat the very epitome.

He might be bandaged, rumpled and unshaven; he might have grumbled and snapped and lashed at them; but nevertheless the maid's little sound seemed to remind him that here lay possible amusement. After all, what was left to him for distraction in his passive condition but the exercise of his charm?

His considerable charm.

To Eliza's mortification, the thought streaked through her head before she could prevent it, *I wish I had said I would feed him.* She went as scarlet as if she had spoken aloud, but thankfully Kirby was buttering another triangle of toast and Mr. Thornton was—well—blind.

"Miss Blinker," he began, drawing out her name in a way which made the hair on the back of her neck stand. "As we will be much in each other's company, do tell me about yourself."

It was her turn for curtness: "I already have."

"Oh, yes." He accepted the buttered toast, this time with pincer fingers. "Let me see...you have been a schoolteacher in Winchester, you say, from time immemorial."

"Yes."

"And this in spite of the youthful limberness of your voice."

She made no answer to this. Had he already guessed she was not so old as she claimed? Had she done it too brown? Perhaps she should try to sound older now—but how exactly did one go about that?

Another little smile to himself. "What do you teach, Miss Blinker, or has it changed over the decades?"

She would not rise to this bait. "Italian and the history of England."

"Hmm. Would you say then that you are still *nel mezzo del*

cammin di nostra vita, or that you were approaching *la fine*?"

"You seem unduly interested in my age, sir," Eliza said with some asperity. "And quoting Dante hardly makes it less discourteous."

"How could I not be interested in age, when I have so recently stared my own mortality in the face?"

She supposed that might be a sincere statement, though she doubted it.

"It is pleasant to see, however," he continued, "that you are telling no fibs about your Italian."

"There!" said Eliza, sitting up straighter. "You called me cruel for reminding you of your present—blindness—but these last two times have been your own doing. Metaphorical references to sight are unavoidable, it seems."

That hint of a grin again. "Ah. So they are. I salute you, Miss Blinker, and will refrain from reproaching you there in the future. But to return to the subject of fibbing..."

"What fibbing?" she croaked.

"The ham, if you please," requested Mr. Thornton.

Kirby dutifully speared a bite of it with the fork and then turned the fork to place it in his hand, only to have that same hand flash out to swipe at her, striking her on the wrist. The maid shrieked from sheer surprise, to be joined in chorus by Mr. Thornton, who shrieked from pain at his unwise movement.

"Good heavens, sir," Eliza blurted, retrieving the fork from the carpet. "What was that about? If it caused you discomfort, you have only yourself to blame."

He was breathing heavily through gritted teeth. "You are not alone here, are you Miss Blinker? There are at least two of you here, are there not? An omission is as much a fib as an untruth. I demand to know who else is here."

"My maid is here, for one," she snapped, indignation humming in her voice. "It would hardly do for me to be alone."

"What is your name, maid?" Thornton demanded to the air.

"K–K–D–Derwent, sir," Kirby babbled.

"*Derwent*"? Eliza held up her hands in perplexity, and Kirby pulled a face, shrugging helplessly.

"It's Derwent," the maid repeated, committing herself. As an afterthought she added, "Kitty Derwent."

With difficulty Eliza stifled a groan. This was what happened when one began to lie, she supposed—things soon got out of hand.

Mr. Thornton must have thought much the same thing, for he shoved the breakfast tray away (his face going white with another wave of pain) and barked, "Go on. Get out. The both of you—Miss Blinker and K–K–Derwent. I don't know what you're playing at, but it's a rotten joke."

"Have you had enough breakfast, Mr. Thornton?" asked Eliza. "I'm sorry about not mentioning—Derwent—but I hardly thought you required a census of everyone in the room."

"Are there still others present?"

"There is another maid Shillbeer and a Mrs. Simmons as well," she admitted. "They were—observing—so they might serve you other meals."

"Then get out. All of you. If you please."

Eliza nodded at Kirby, who began to stack the tableware on the tray. "Should I send Hoskins and Bigelow in again to make you comfortable?"

He only grunted and made a shooing motion.

"Very well. We will go for now. Unless you would like another dose of laudanum...?"

"No, I don't want another dose of laudanum," he snapped. "I didn't want the one I received, for that matter. Makes me nauseous. If you're so very old, Miss Blinker, shouldn't you go take a nap instead of hovering over me like a hen with one chick?"

Eliza stood, still hesitating. "Yes, but perhaps I ought to take a look at the bandages over your eyes before I go," she ventured. "Mr. Ponsonby instructed me to inspect them once per day to determine whether they should be changed."

But this only drew a roar which sent Kirby scurrying out with the tray rattling in her grip and the others not far behind.

Chapter Four

He will not always chide: neither will he keep his anger for ever.

—Psalm 103:9, The Authorized Version (1611)

Two more days passed in much the same manner. Mr. Ponsonby dropped in morning and evening; the footmen assisted Mr. Thornton with dressing, arrangement, and basic needs (earning themselves the nicknames Hoghands and Bumblelow); Eliza and Kirby shared duties with Shillbeer and Mrs. Simmons to provide his meals. But in the last instance, the women's ministrations took place in virtual silence. Though both Eliza and Mrs. Simmons made attempts at conversation with Mr. Thornton, he answered with a minimum of words and emotion.

Eliza ought to have been relieved, but she was not, and Kirby said to her at one point, "Miss, somehow he is even scarier when he holds his tongue than when he bellows." Not scarier, perhaps, in Eliza's mind, but more *in the right*, if that made sense.

He was at their mercy, and whatever his reputation and whether or not young women required protection from him, the fact remained that they had begun by deceiving him, and he knew it. Were in fact still deceiving him, apart from the admission worked from them that Eliza was not alone when she tended him.

She pleaded with Lady Arden that the lie about her age be dropped. "It was clear I was not convincing," she explained, "or why would he accuse me of fibbing? Short of confessing that I'm only *oldish*, might we at least never make reference again to my age?"

Lady Arden tried to hold her ground. "No confessions!" But seeing Eliza's shoulders droop, she sighed. "You should have spoken in a low voice or affected a rasp. But what is done is done. Perhaps we might leave off talking about your age and only emphasize your supposed plainness."

Chuckling, Eliza shook her head. "I will leave that to the rest of you. What person, whether beautiful, plain, or anywhere in between, introduces her own looks as a subject for discussion?" Even Lady Arden had to laugh at this, and the two were still giggling when Mr. Ponsonby entered.

"How do you find your patient?" asked Lady Arden.

"Physically as well as I would hope," replied the doctor.

Her brow rose inquiringly. "Physically? Do you draw a distinction, Mr. Ponsonby?"

"I do. For it seems to me that he is depressed. Natural, under the circumstances, you will likely say, but I asked a few pointed questions and learned he has been left alone much of the time when his immediate physical needs are not being seen to."

"Ohh...well," said Lady Arden, "so he has, but we thought

he preferred solitude. He is so very cross with us. And we had a supper at the Frances' last night and a card party at Heathstone the day before."

"Of course he is cross," the doctor countered, "and so would we be if we were broken in places and possibly blind. And of course you must keep your engagements, but I think a little company and amusement would take his mind off of his woes. Have you been using your drawing room at all?"

The wringing of her hands was answer enough, and the doctor nodded. "Lady Arden, the inconvenience of Thornton's presence in your home will be that much shorter and that much less burdensome if you participate in his recuperation, whether he be cross or cheerful as a day in May. *Spend time* in your drawing room unless he expressly asks you to leave. This is my prescription."

"Yes, Mr. Ponsonby," said Lady Arden meekly.

"I bid you good day."

——— · ———

Lady Arden could not be expected to sit in the drawing room in the morning, of course, else why would Ardenmere have a morning room? But both she and Eliza felt guilty at their needle-work and letter-writing nonetheless. At the dinner table Lady Arden attempted to coax her husband into spending the afternoon within doors, but he begged off. "Whatever for? Now that the weather has improved, I intend to ride out."

"Come, madam," Eliza braced her. "We will manage it." Still, she could not help but think this must be what Shadrach, Meshach, and Abednego felt, when Nebuchadnezzar ordered them tossed in the fiery furnace.

"What is it?" Mr. Thornton growled from behind the screen, the moment Eliza led the way in. "Who's there?"

"It's Lady Arden and Miss Blinker, Mr. Thornton," she answered, waiting for her eyes to adjust to the dimness.

"Just the two of you? What about the other one?"

Eliza hardly wanted to say that she required only one chaperone at a time, so she made light answer. "Kirby was wanted elsewhere."

He leaped on this at once. "Kirby? Who is Kirby?"

Eliza winced. Mistake Number One. "I meant Kitty. Derwent. The maid. We usually call her Kirby."

"Because Sir Miles can never be bothered to learn new servants' names," Lady Arden interjected. "We had a maid named Kirby once, and now Derwent must be Kirby, as will be her successor, I imagine."

Thornton gave a grunt, and Eliza smiled her approval at Lady Arden's quick thinking.

"Well, what do you want?" he resumed. "The other two already fed me."

"Lady Arden would like the use of her drawing room," Eliza announced, "unless you were going to nap, sir."

He was silent a moment, and the two women half hoped he would order them out. But at last he replied, "What would Lady Arden propose instead? That we roll back the carpet and dance? Host the vicar and his wife for tea?"

"Nothing so ambitious," replied Eliza evenly. "But as you will be subject to whatever is chosen, it is only fair that you have a vote. I might read to Lady Arden or play the pianoforte for her."

"Please yourself."

"Perhaps you might read to me, Eliza," said her companion. "That will be less...boisterous for a start. The book by Mrs. Hunter."

"Eliza..." repeated the patient under his breath.

She set her chair near the window, through which the grey December light filtered, and Lady Arden took up her needlework. Because they were not many pages in, Eliza momentarily considered asking Mr. Thornton if he would prefer them to begin at the beginning, but refrained, thinking it would only earn her a sarcastic reply. As a compromise, she said, "If you recall, Lady Arden, the book began with the narrator's account of his various forbears."

"I do recall. There were too many to remember, so I hope they will not turn out to be important."

"I think we need only pay attention to the narrator's mother," said Eliza, "the Miss Fairfax of the story, who was in love with her friend's older brother..."

Much as Lady Arden relished novels and love stories in particular, Eliza had not read more than half a chapter of *The History of the Grubthorpe Family* before she saw her auditor's head drooping, the needlework fallen to the floor. The habit of an afternoon nap proved too powerful to resist.

She paused, uncertain. Should she wait until Lady Arden awakened? But when might that possibly be? When Lady Arden usually retired after dinner, she sometimes did not reappear until nearly supper. Perhaps if Mr. Thornton had fallen asleep as well, Eliza might tiptoe from the room.

As if in answer to her thought, his voice broke the silence. "Did everyone sneak out of the room?"

"No—we are here. But Lady Arden has fallen asleep."

"After a sentence such as 'The fever which menaced her life with loss of reason, has left her mind too feeble for any surprise'? Astonishing."

Clearly there was nothing wrong with the man's mind, if he could repeat that! "You were listening, then?"

"Short of stopping my ears, I could hardly fail to do so." Then, almost unwillingly, he added, "You read well, Miss Blinker. A consequence, I suppose, of the eons you have spent teaching school."

"Thank you," she murmured, glad that both the screen and his blindness prevented him seeing her surprise at the compliment. "Would you prefer that I continue, then?"

"What, and have Lady Arden miss more touching scenes of character after character bursting into tears? I would not dream of depriving her. But I do wonder if you might choose another book and venture closer. Then I might understand your words more clearly."

It was like being invited into the den of the wolf, and Eliza hesitated.

"Come now," he prompted. "What other books has good Lady Arden? I say Lady Arden, for I would be astonished if Sir Miles has opened a book since he left university."

An un-elderly giggle escaped her. It was absolutely true that Sir Miles never read anything apart from the occasional newspaper. Even the letters he received were read to him by his steward or Lady Arden. And if ever the baronet touched a book, it was merely to pass it to his wife at her request.

She took up the other volume on the table. "There is *Rimualdo: or, The Castle of Badajos* by W. H. Ireland, author of *The Abbess*."

"Dear heaven. Well, we must take what we can get, I suppose. Let's have it, Miss Blinker."

With a little shrug she complied, moving her seat to the end of the lacquer screen dividing the room, so that Lady Arden could see her if she happened to wake. In the gloom the man sat still propped on bolsters in the armchair, but Eliza knew from the footmen's reports that their duties included assisting him to limp about for twenty minutes at a time for exercise.

If Mr. Thornton objected to the floods of tears in the previous novel, *Rimualdo* began on an unpromising note, for within the first page both the titular character and his mother subjected the readers to one "agony of distress," one "overcharged bosom," and a deal of "anguish vented in audible sobs."

"We seem to go from bad to worse," commented Mr. Thornton, when Eliza paused for a sip of water.

"It cannot continue much longer," she answered. "Rimualdo is taking his leave, after all."

And so it proved. But when Rimualdo's father bade his son to "support the dignity of his honored house" and conduct himself in a manner "worthy his noble race," Mr. Thornton shifted restlessly.

Glancing at him, Eliza saw the furrow of his brow above the bandages. He said nothing, however, leaving her to resume. "'Then,' cried Rimualdo,'" she read, "'throwing himself at this father's feet, "I shall henceforth merit your esteem; for never will I act derogatory to the name I bear, nor sully the hitherto untainted lustre of our family—'"

"That will do," interrupted Mr. Thornton with a wave of his hand. "Better to go back to the waterpot Miss Fairfax than endure this noble milksop."

"But he has finally stopped crying."

"Only to spout inanities of another sort."

Eliza shut the book with a snap. "Mr. Thornton, I am perfectly willing to leave *Rimualdo* for another day, but I must observe that, in your present condition, it will be very easy for you to find fault with *whatever* is read to you."

"Undoubtedly, Miss Blinker. You speak plain, good sense, as a woman of your years ought. But if, instead of being a humdrum, schoolteacherly, middle-aged woman, you were born a man who had been subject from his earliest years to speeches such as Rimualdo's father delivered, you would understand how my impatience is redoubled in this instance."

"If you have indeed been subject to such speeches," Eliza rejoined sharply (smarting at his description of her), "should you not be the more interested in how Rimualdo fares?"

"He will prevail of course," said Thornton. "Don't they always, in novels like these? After a number of mishaps over which he triumphs and irresistible temptations which he alone resists, Rimualdo will emerge unscathed and spotless."

"I suppose such stories are meant to encourage as well as entertain. Do you think it so hard for you young men to avoid 'acting derogatory to the name you bear,' as Rimualdo put it?" As soon as she spoke her fingers flew to her lips, for she remembered the story about the jilted girl and Mr. Thornton's breach of promise.

He could not have seen her motion, of course, but again Eliza had the unsettling sensation of having her thoughts guessed.

"I *do* think it hard," he answered slowly. "Were my father still living, he would certainly accuse me of having behaved in a manner 'unworthy my noble race.'"

"Oh?" asked Eliza. It was scarcely more than a breath.

His beautiful mouth twisted in derision, but whether the mockery was aimed at her or himself she could not tell.

"If you are accustomed to reading such stories as these, Miss Blinker, rife as they are with kidnappings, seductions, and every manner of devilment, you can surely listen to a true tale."

"Have you...one to tell me?"

"Ah...though I cannot see you, I hear the trepidation in your voice. Trepidation not unmixed with eagerness. You schoolteachers must live for gossip."

She scowled at him. While she could excuse some crossness caused by his injuries, she suspected the desire to nettle others characterized him at all times, cracked ribs or no cracked ribs. "The love of gossip is universal, I daresay," she replied, "and not confined to schoolteachers. But keep your true tale to yourself, if you would rather."

"Oddly, I would *not* rather. It is too tempting. Because, Miss Blinker, unlike the wailing Miss Fairfax or the blubbering Rimualdo, you strike me as a discreet person. Confidential. Quiet."

She made no response. To say that the girls at Mrs. Turcotte's Seminary for Young Ladies frequently confided in Eliza was true, but to declare as much would sound both boastful and overeager.

He cocked his head, listening, but then went on. "Exactly. Now, whether this quality stems from your retired existence or from your many and ever-increasing years—"

"Which you do seem to harp upon," Eliza interjected.

How much he could express without his eyes! For now he feigned surprise. "I? Harp? I meant only respect, Miss Blinker, for you were the one to insist upon your ancientness, and I did not want you to think I forgot it."

"Hmm."

"Where was I? Oh, yes. Your retired existence and vast age, combined with our seclusion in this darkened drawing room, the winter storms blowing without—"

"On the contrary," she interrupted again, "it is overcast today but dry."

"Miss Blinker, I must insist you be a good counsel-keeper and hold your tongue." Catching the chuckle she tried to smother, his lips curved in a grin. "To resume: trapped in a darkened drawing room, overcast as the sky without, my sole companion an aged and retiring nurse, I could not forbear revealing my deepest secrets. Indeed, having nothing to contemplate beyond my own vulnerable state, hovering between life and death..."

"You ought to write novels yourself, sir," she said dryly.

"Considering the ones we have been listening to this after-noon, that is hardly a compliment, though I thank you all the same for your intent. But Miss Blinker, if you are quite ready to be serious, I have a tale to tell which will curdle your blood and possibly send you screaming from the room."

"Good gracious! Now I freely admit I would very much like to hear what you have to say."

"Are you so brave, Miss Blinker?"

"I claim only the usual allotment of courage, nothing remarkable."

"And are you beautiful?"

She inhaled so sharply she coughed. What a sly one he was, catching her unprepared like that! "I—I—surely you cannot expect me to answer such a question! Such an impudent question, at that."

He sighed. "It was, I confess, but I was lulled by the circumstances I have just described to you. May I humbly work myself back into your good opinion by saying you *sound* beautiful?"

"For my age," croaked Eliza, fighting a ripple of panic.

He attempted a half-bow which ended in a wince and a groan. "That went without saying. Beautiful, for your age." Touching his ribs gingerly he added. "You see what my curiosity cost me. Will you not from pity indulge me with an answer?"

"It is a question a person cannot answer for himself, sir," she said. "I have...never thought much of my looks, and—neither has anyone else." It was true enough. There had been one young curate who seemed to like her, years and years ago, but he had little to live on, and nothing ever came of it. Shaking off this memory, she added, "Mr. Thornton, you have wandered from your purpose. Have you changed your mind about telling me a story?"

"I have not." He shrugged, causing another wince. "It's a short story, at any rate, and do stop me if you've already heard it. I find that, though the years pass, the story lives on and often precedes or accompanies me wherever I go."

"Is it—the history of your broken engagement?" Eliza asked suddenly. "Because Lady Arden did mention it." For whatever reason—perhaps the accumulation of little lies she was telling him (or trying not to tell him)—she wanted to be honest about something.

"There." He lifted a finger and then let his hand drop back against the chair arm. "That is what I mean about my story going everywhere with me, like a species of portmanteau. Do tell me the version you heard. It's like different varieties of portmanteaux, some leather, some brocade."

"That you were engaged to a young lady and then...broke the engagement. They then sued you for breach of promise, and you paid the damages."

"Rather than do what a gentleman should have done in the first place, is your implication," he finished. "Yes, that version is true in the main, leaving out only why on earth I would be such a scoundrel."

A mumble came from Lady Arden at this point, and Eliza sprang up guiltily, though she had been doing nothing wrong. But seeing the older woman's head roll against the back of the sofa, she resumed her seat.

"There was a time when I was as spotless and well-meaning as our hero Rimualdo," said Thornton. "I too ventured forth into the world, though in my case it was to London rather than the road to Madrid, and in the capital I proved as foolish as any young man, I suppose, doing my share of gaming and carousing and such. But it soon palled because I had dreams of marrying a beautiful young lady I met there. She refused me the first time, but when she returned home after the season, I followed and tried again, and this time she accepted. Imagine, if you will, Miss Blinker, this young man's joy. A joy only increased when I saw with what urgency she and her family wished the ceremony to take place. We set the date, only to have my father fall ill. My intended bride wept. I wept, but I departed, promising to return when I could, to make her my own. My father lingered some months, months in which my beloved's letters grew more infrequent and distant. By the time he died, I was frantic with grief and anxiety. I rushed back to her side, without even writing to announce my return. And when I returned—"

"Yes?" said Eliza, hanging on his words in spite of herself. "What then?"

Thornton expelled a slow breath, and she knew he was seeing the scene again in his mind's eye. "When I returned I found her some months with child. Not mine, I need hardly say, since I was at that time as pure as Rimualdo. Then I at last understood her acceptance of my second proposal and her family's insistence on an early date."

"I see. Oh, dear. Dear, dear. But you refused to marry her."

Another shrug. Another wince. "I did. Some men would have stuck to it, I know. She told me if I truly loved her I would throw my cloak of honor about her. That was how she put it, my 'cloak of honor.' But my love had turned to ashes, and so had my honor, I'm afraid. For I thought I would rather be infamous than marry a woman I did not love and who had never loved me. A woman whose every word to me had been a lie. Her father raged; I stood firm. Her family sued; I paid up. And now I carry my little port-manteau wherever I go. Or it carries me. That, Miss Blinker, is the long and short of it."

"What—became of the girl?"

"A cousin was found to marry her," he said simply.

That must have been costly for her parents, Eliza thought. Aloud she said, "Have you ever regretted your decision, sir?"

"Ah, there are some houses I am still not received in. Arden-mere might have been one of them, if not for my accident. But altogether it's enough to make one lose faith in humanity, to see what a little money and time will do for a disgraced man. It's been ten years now, and even the dowagers are coming around and suffer me in company with their daughters."

"Why not choose one of those daughters, then?" she heard herself ask. "By doing so you might be redeemed and respectable once more."

"Is it that easy, Miss Blinker?"

"I think so," she answered. "For gentlemen of means and—and—"

"And—?"

"And other qualities," she concluded lamely. "A man of means may be out in the world, making what he will of it. But—if that cousin had not stepped forward to marry your young lady, all would have been lost for her."

"You blame me for jilting her?"

"Mr. Thornton, I hardly know you to blame you. No, indeed. I was thinking of the young lady, rather, because I—well—I know what it is like to think yourself without option."

"Surely not, Miss Blinker," he said in tones of mock horror.

Feeling herself color and glad he could not see it, she amended, "I did not mean I faced the situation of your young lady, to be sure. Rather, I meant that too many women, including myself, must…struggle to make their way in the world, if they are not fortunate enough to marry. Though you have not done so, Mr. Thornton, that was your choice to make. You are a man of means and, as you have observed, the world is willing once more to embrace you. But for women—singleness is too often a result of *not* having a choice. Because only to men has been given the right of choosing."

"Miss Blinker the firebrand," he said softly. "You must explain to me how you came to have no choice but teaching school, for you have certainly awakened my curiosity."

The warmth of his low voice sent a thrill along her, as if he were not several feet distant but right at her ear, and though Eliza felt her danger she could have cried in frustration when—

"Dear me!" came the voice of Lady Arden, yawning. "I must have dozed. Could you go back a page or two, Eliza?"

Chapter Five

Fine Doings at my House! A rare Kettle of Fish I have discovered at last.

—Fielding, *Tom Jones* (1749)

There was no further opportunity for private conversation for the next few days, and Eliza told herself she was glad of it. It was one thing to sympathize when she heard Mr. Thornton's controversial history, and quite another to feel her growing liking for him. A liking she was certain he intended her to feel.

Sitting there, hour after hour, afflicted by pain and ennui—*of course he must do something,* Eliza thought. What was there besides flirtation to fill the time? Even Mr. Thornton's abuse of "Hoghands" and "Bumblelow" occupied perhaps a cumulative hour and a half over the course of the day, and as the two footmen grew more adept with maneuvering him, they did not try his temper so sorely.

Moreover, Eliza had noted that, when Lady Arden awoke from her nap, Mr. Thornton retreated into cool, flawless courtesy, so much so that Lady Arden whispered to her later, "That was not so very bad. He must be feeling better, for he was not at all cross by the end. And I am heartened to see that our plan has worked—he is most proper with you, Eliza."

Whether or not the continual presence of others played any part, Mr. Thornton's model conduct continued. On succeeding days he listened to further installments of the Grubthorpes or Rimualdo without controversy and said nothing to Eliza to arouse comment, and she found herself almost disappointed.

It was not until Sunday after they returned from church that anything particular happened.

"Cook thought you might manage some thick soup," Eliza said when she and Kirby entered with his dinner. "Would you like to try to serve yourself, as you do with the fork, or would you prefer us to serve you?"

"Better bundle me in a napkin and let me have a go," he answered. While Kirby draped him, Eliza filled the spoon halfway and placed it in his outstretched hand. In this fashion, three sips were managed successfully before the drawing room doors flew open and Sir Miles was heard to say, "...Coming right along, and Ponsonby recommends amusement, diversion."

The identity of his guest was not long a mystery, for the baronet led Mr. Marvin the clergyman straight to the lacquered screen. "And here he is. Thornton, I've got the parson Marvin here. He's come to dine before his second service."

"Miss Blinker—you here!" exclaimed the curate, his brows high to see her seated beside the patient.

"Mr. Marvin."

"Sir Miles said you offered to assist with Mr. Thornton—good day, sir—but I did not expect...this!"

Without even glancing at the man in question, Eliza was aware of him stiffening, and fearing a tempest, she said hastily, "It is nothing. We have two teams. Kirby and I work together."

"Seeing I could not attend church, have you come to sermonize, Marvin?" asked Thornton. "More of the soup, if you please. And if you would help me this time...?"

With an apologetic look to the maid, and ashamed of her own cowardliness in the face of Mr. Marvin's disapproval, Eliza passed Kirby the spoon. But Kirby was awkwardly placed, leaning over Eliza, and the many eyes fixed on her made her clumsy. Carrying the spoon to Thornton's mouth, her hand shook so that his mouth closed on air.

"Steady there, Miss Blinker," he chuckled, his own hand rising to guide Kirby's. His touch addled the poor servant further, increasing her trembles until drops of soup sprinkled the napkin tied about him.

"Erm—" began Eliza. Should she correct his misapprehension? She would have steadied the maid, but Mr. Thornton anticipated her. With both hands, he lightly took hold of Kirby at wrist and fingers and guided the spoon to his lips.

The maid's eyes grew round as guineas, and she thrust the spoon back at Eliza the instant Thornton released her.

"How—how an audience does make things more difficult," Eliza fumbled.

"We will go, then," said Sir Miles, "but you must come too, Eliza. We dine early. Let Kirby manage the rest or send in that whatshername to assist her. Thornton, we'll come back later, if you've no objection."

Eliza rose to follow them, giving Kirby's arm a reassuring

squeeze. "I'll send Shillbeer straight away." But why, oh why, did she envy the maid getting to stay behind with Mr. Thornton? And—worse yet—why did she envy that brief moment when Mr. Thornton took Kirby's hand between both his own?

If there was any consolation, Eliza must find it in the realization that at least the curate did not appear to have any designs upon her. Apart from (or perhaps because of) his initial disapprobation on finding her beside Mr. Thornton, Mr. Marvin hardly spoke to her throughout the dinner, and when they returned to the drawing room he even carried on a conversation with Sir Miles during her performance on the pianoforte.

In contrast, Mr. Thornton asked for the screen to be folded and put aside, that he might hear better, and he proceeded to listen intently, head bent and silent.

When Eliza finished, Sir Miles applauded, loud in his praise, Mr. Marvin joining in with more moderation, but it was Mr. Thornton's small smile which flooded her with delight—delight followed rapidly by chagrin. *Oh, dear. Was she really, despite Lady Arden's precautions and her own good sense and maturity, developing a tendre for the man? Thank heavens he was blind. Now if only everyone else might remain as blind metaphorically, until she had mastered herself!*

Was it that he had confided in her, teased her, listened to her? So did others in her life, but Eliza had to concede that those who did were all of them female—and she could count them on one hand and not even require all her fingers.

He has nothing else to do and no one else to talk to, and he fears being blind for life, she reminded herself ruthlessly as she lay in bed that night. *Had he met you of an evening in company* at Ardenmere, he would have paid you scarcely more heed than Mr. Marvin did.

But it was one thing to talk firmly and sensibly to herself and quite another to experience any change of heart.

———— · ————

The following morning, Lady Arden decided Shillbeer and Mrs. Simmons might handle breakfast as well, leaving Eliza free for other activities. Activities such as weaving a wreath of the greenery the gardeners collected while Lady Arden oversaw the making of mince pies for the Christmas boxes. Eliza should have been relieved, even grateful, at the temporary reprieve from danger, but she was not. In fact, as she sat in the kitchen, braiding and twisting, ignominious tears threatened, as if she were a girl denied staying up for her first ball.

A commotion at the kitchen door interrupted the women at their work, and the next moment Cook opened to the gardener having words with a tall, slender man whom Eliza would have described as elegant if he were not red-faced and furious. "Where is Mr. Thornton? He will vouch for me! Admitted at the kitchen door, what rubbish!"

Seeing Lady Arden frozen with amazement, Eliza set down her completed wreath and hurried forward.

"Miss Blinker, this fellow wants to see Mr. Thornton," explained the gardener. "Said his name is Kettle."

"We sent for you at the Crest and Comb the day of Mr. Thornton's accident," said Eliza, "and had long since given you up for lost. But come, I will take you to him."

The drawing room waited in its usual gloom, and as the maids had finished serving Thornton his breakfast, he was alone, mouth grim and hands clenching the arms of the chair.

"Good morning, Mr. Thornton," she said quickly. "I have—"

"Oh, there you are, are you?" he growled, sounding quite as surly as he had the very first day. "Has tending to a cross, infirm, blind man begun to pall on you, that you now pass off the whole business to a pair of butter-fingered excuses for maids?"

She smiled in response before she could prevent it. He had missed her? And though Thornton could not see it, the smile transformed her. "Lady Arden asked me to help her make a wreath. It is nearly Christmas, you know, and there is much to be done on a great estate like Ardenmere. As I am here almost as much by sufferance as you, sir, I must do what I am bid."

His resentment faded upon hearing this explanation in her warm, happy voice, though he tried to cling to the appearance of it. "Is that so, Miss Blinker? Then I will have our hostess number me among your duties. It's dangerous to leave me at Mrs. Simmons' mercy. She talks so unceasingly of her children that I fear I will injure my eyes further from rolling them so often."

Laughing, Eliza turned to Kettle. "I have another attendant you might like better, Mr. Thornton. Your own man."

"What? Kettle? Where?"

"Here, sir."

"I will leave you two to talk," she said, backing away.

"But you are to bring my dinner, Miss Blinker," he commanded, "and to read to me the further adventures of the weeping Miss Fairfax or the virtuous Rimualdo. I'm not particular. Lady Arden may come and doze if she likes, but *you* must come."

"I had better not promise," she answered, still retreating, "but I will pass on your request."

When she opened the door, light from the passage brightened the room briefly, giving Kettle a clear view of Eliza glancing back and Thornton's own lifted head and parted lips. After the door shut behind her, Thornton heaved a barely audible sigh. Then he turned to the unpleasantness at hand.

"Where have you been all this time, Kettle?"

"Around and about," replied his valet carelessly. "I heard about your accident, sir, and that you were fetched away here, where I knew you would be well cared for. So I thought it a good time to keep clear."

"Take care, Kettle. I repeat: where have you *been*?"

His man waved a hand before the bandages and appeared satisfied with the result. Noiselessly he took a seat on the sofa, stretching his legs along it. "I think you'll understand, sir, when I say there was a pretty barmaid at the Crest and Comb who invited me on holiday, in a manner of speaking. And as you were laid up, and as I knew you yourself had an eye for a charming face and form—"

"You thought you might shirk both your duties and your employer's company?" Thornton finished for him. "You have my pocketbook, I trust."

"I do, to be sure."

"And if I were to ask Sir Miles or Lady Arden to count what it contains, they would find the amount I carried down with me?"

"There was the inn bill to be discharged," said Kettle sullenly.

"Naturally." Thornton tried to sit up straighter, only to be rewarded with a stab of pain. He gave it up, panting, furious that he must sit blindfolded and impotent when he would gladly have loomed over the criminal servant to throttle him. "Well, I invite you to empty the pocketbook of all but the smallest banknote and the coins."

Kettle stared, swinging his legs back to the floor. "Why would I do such a thing?"

"Because I am dismissing you. No—hear me. While you are far superior at shaving and dressing me than the makeshift dolts the Ardens have enlisted in your absence, in every other respect I am better off without you. I have overlooked the occasional disappearance of money or shining gimcrack—I knew you had your vices, as I have had mine—but that is all behind me now."

"The blindness is permanent, then?" asked Kettle, when he recovered from his astonishment at this treatment. His fists were clenched as if he would gladly have taken a swing at his erstwhile master. "Or the crippling?"

"The 'crippling' will pass. The blindness remains to be seen. No, Kettle. I meant I am leaving behind company such as yours and even the general pursuits with which I have whiled away the past decade. I am starting a new chapter of my life, *Deo volente*. Thank you for your past service, and perhaps the less said about your lapses, the better."

Kettle kicked out at the sofa. "This is the thanks I get for, what, seven years? A few notes from your pocketbook and a fare-thee-well?"

"That and, again, what you have helped yourself to, all along." The words were calm, but there was a rising note in Thornton's voice which, had he been his usual self, would have Kettle turning tail while he still could.

"All right, then," the manservant snapped, cowed in spite of himself. Withdrawing the pocketbook in question from his coat and rifling through it, he snatched a sheaf of notes and tucked them in his waistcoat. Then he slung the depleted item back on the sofa—let Thornton grope for it! "I'm going. Far be it from me to stand in the way of your sudden reformation."

A parting thought struck the manservant, and his lip curled with sudden malice. "But I'll say, if this idea of amendment has anything to do with that Miss Blinker person who was just in here, well, you might want to pray you never get your vision back. What you don't know—or don't *see* can't hurt you. Unless to be made a laughingstock for blindly marrying a dumpy, plain pudding of a dowd hurts."

Thornton gave a roar, his hand groping just as Kettle had imagined, but in this instance for something he might hurl at the villain's head. "Get out!" he bellowed. "Out! And pray I never find you again!"

When the drawing room doors slammed open and Kettle sprinted forth as if demons pursued, Thornton's curses rang out, extensive and colorful. In the morning room Lady Arden squeaked in horror, her hands flying to her ears. "Gracious heavens! What can it mean, Eliza?"

Eliza gripped her tambour frame so tightly it nearly snapped. "I suppose he is not very happy that Kettle disappeared for so many days. Should we—send in Sir Miles to see if Mr. Thornton requires anything?"

"Tut, send in Sir Miles! On such a fine day he will not be seen until dinner."

"Then we must do it, Lady Arden."

"But how can we? The Trentons and the Halletts both declared they would call. They will be here any moment."

"We must! Or *I* must. What if he and Kettle came to blows, and Mr. Thornton is even now lying on the carpet with his ribs truly broken? Or suppose he should roar like that when they are here? They would think you keep a menagerie at Ardenmere."

That drew a giggle from the baronet's wife. "I daresay they are calling in hopes of seeing our beast. Very well. You steal in and peep around the screen and see if he is in any state to receive callers. If not we will just have to keep the drawing room doors shut tightly and swear he is asleep."

Her heart thumping half in anticipation and half in wariness, Eliza slipped into the drawing room.

"Who's there?" he snarled at once.

"It's not Kettle, at any rate," she replied, "so you needn't bite my head off."

"Ah. It's you, Miss Blinker. You heard that outburst, I take it."

"I did. You nearly frightened Lady Arden to death."

"My apologies. In my rage I forgot greater care must be taken around old ladies. Which includes you, does it not, my dear Miss Blinker? Do stop creeping like that and come over here! I took the measure of your hand and wrist the other day and know you're no frail, withering crone. If anything, your wrist was thicker than mine, and if the rest of your form matches it, I would wager you come within a stone of my own size."

It was on the tip of Eliza's tongue to retort, "That wasn't *my* hand you measured, Mr. Know-All!" but she caught herself in time. If he did not believe the ruse about her age, he had better continue in this new mistake. He was right about one thing: Kirby was indeed a tall and sturdy young woman and probably within a size with him.

Instead she said, "I am glad to find you in your usual place, Mr. Thornton. From the sound of it, I thought you might have tried to struggle up, the better to murder your man Kettle."

"Don't think I didn't consider it. And he's no longer my man Kettle."

"What—have you dismissed him?"

"I have. You might not credit it in my present condition, but I am ordinarily a natty fellow, and Kettle kept me spruce. But he had his faults as well, which I am no longer inclined to tolerate."

Her gaze slid to the open pocketbook on the sofa. "Was it... dishonesty, sir?"

"From time to time. Has he left my pocketbook somewhere about? He flung it down after taking his wages. Thank you," he added, when she placed it in his lap. "No, his twitching fingers were not what broke me. Say rather that he reminds me of how idly and emptily I have spent my years since my unfortunate broken engagement. And even then I would not have lost my temper so, if not for—" He broke off.

"If not for the fact that your hold on it might generally be described as 'feeble,'" teased Eliza.

"Minx," he muttered, but he smiled, turning his head toward her. "Where have you gone? Come closer. Why should I have to shout?"

"You can hear me perfectly where I am. In any event, apart from ensuring that you are not in the throes of apoplexy, Lady Arden sent me to ask if you would be willing to entertain visitors. Just some neighbors, purportedly paying calls of the season, but more likely curious as to how you fare. Now, don't growl so. We would merely open the curtains a little wider and fold back the screen, and, after greeting them, you might sit there and be as misanthropic as you please."

To her surprise, he nodded. "Certainly. For how does the carol go?" He began to sing in a pleasant tenor, "'Tis ill for a mind to anger inclined, to think of small injuries now...'"

"'If wrath be to seek, do not lend her thy cheek, nor let her inhabit thy brow,'" Eliza joined him.

"They sing that one in Winchester, then?"

"I have heard it. And now I hear the callers arriving. Let me welcome them."

Chapter Six

Have you never heard, my good Ladies! of the Redemption of Time?
—*Edward Young, The centaur not fabulous (1755)*

Mr. Thornton kept his word. When the Trentons and Hallets were admitted, two mothers and a bevy of assorted daughters, he was all courtesy. "You must pardon me not rising to make my bow," he told them. "Though I improve hourly, the surgeon Mr. Ponsonby says it is all due to my docility as a patient, sitting here day after day."

This drew titters from the younger girls, as if he had said something witty, and Eliza saw them whisper to each other.

"We rejoice to hear of your recovery," intoned Mrs. Hallet, running an appraising eye up and down him which, to do her credit, she would have done even if he could see her. She turned this acuteness on Eliza next. "Lady Arden tells me what a help you have been, Miss Blinker, and I do admire what you have done with your dress. You had that one the last time you came, I believe, but you have trimmed it new. Well. This adventure will give you something to tell those pupils at your school, will it not? How long before you return to Winchester?"

"I will take the late coach on Epiphany Day."

"What a shame," tutted Lady Trenton, "for then you will miss our supper and ball."

Eliza murmured something regretful, though she did not mourn missing what would have been an evening of watching the younger ladies dance while she wore another old dress to stand up once with Sir Miles and once with Mr. Marvin.

One of the bolder girls accosted Mr. Thornton. "Too bad as well that *you* will not be able to dance, sir. We have heard you make a graceful partner."

He bowed his head. "My loss as well, Miss Trenton."

"I am Miss Hallet who addresses you."

"I beg your pardon. You see how little use I would be in a ballroom, deaf, blind and lame as I am."

"Oh, Mr. Thornton," cried another, "allow me to say how much I pity your blindness and pray it will not be forever."

"Thank you." But Eliza saw his jaw harden.

"*Will* the loss be forever, Lady Arden?" asked Lady Trenton, turning to her. "What does Ponsonby say?"

Seeing Lady Arden's eyes widen and Mr. Thornton's mouth twist in a way which boded ill for Lady Trenton, Eliza intervened. "Mr. Thornton may joke about being deaf, Lady Trenton, but I assure you he can hear and answer such questions himself."

Lady Trenton frowned awfully at this perceived impertinence, but Eliza was rewarded with him visibly unclenching and drawing a slow breath. "Indeed I can repeat what Ponsonby says, Lady

Trenton, but we will only know in another week or ten days whether my sight has suffered irreparable damage or not."

The sympathetic miss wailed. "How dreadful! Never to dance or ride or drive again! Never to do all the things dashing young men love to do."

Eliza feared this would provoke him anew, but he had got hold of himself now and merely smiled. "I am not so young as I once was. And perhaps, if I am fortunate enough to find a permanent attendant with the patience and skills of Miss Blinker here, I might one day be trusted to be led about on a pony or broken-down nag."

Uncertain chuckles met this, but it was Eliza's genuine giggle that drew his attention. "Unless you are weary of teaching school, Miss Blinker," he added. "In which case I would simply hire *you*."

Before she could reply, Mrs. Hallett struck over her. "Lady Arden, I am glad Mr. Thornton's care has not prevented you and Sir Miles from participating in the festivities of the season."

A discussion of the engagements which had passed and those still to come followed, which was sustained until the guests rose to depart. Thornton said then everything courteous as they took their leave, but Eliza could hear a hint of impatience. Perhaps facing so many at once after his isolation had exhausted him.

"Miss Blinker? Lady Arden? Are you still here?"

They were not, but they returned shortly. "I think that went very well," the baronet's wife was saying, "and if you are willing, Mr. Thornton, I need not put off the supper I planned to host. Sir Miles is glad of an excuse to dispense with such things, but I tell him we must return everyone's hospitality—"

"Yes," he interrupted. "Do what you please, Lady Arden. But can you send at once for Mr. Ponsonby?"

Eliza drew a sharp breath. "Is something the matter?"

"Only that I am tired of waiting. He must take a look at my eyes and tell me what he can."

She could not blame him. The suspense must be unendurable and the pity and concern of others maddening. But would not removing his bandages too soon jeopardize his healing?

Pressing her lips together, she held her peace. He knew all these things already.

"We will send a note," she said.

"And one more thing, while we wait for Ponsonby," he rejoined. "If he can be found, I would speak with Sir Miles."

———— · ————

Lady Arden and Eliza had taken their seats in the dining room and begun on their soup when the baronet entered.

"We had given you up, my dear," cried Lady Arden.

Sir Miles snapped out his napkin and waved Hoskins over with the soup tureen. "Thornton called me when I came in. Said something I never dreamed of, but there it is."

"There *what* is?" she pressed. "Something good or something bad? He wants Ponsonby to inspect his eyes early, I fear."

"Eliza will answer your question soon enough." He raised a brow at their guest. "Eliza, if you would put off your own meal for a minute, Thornton will take his now."

"But that's ridiculous," protested his lady. "Eliza is not his servant, and she is eating. If he cannot wait, Shillbeer and Mrs. Simmons may do it."

"Mr. Thornton did reprove me for not serving his breakfast," answered Eliza, laying down her napkin, "and those two will have to serve his supper when we are out, so I had better go."

"Let her go, Mary," said Sir Miles, and, surprised by his insistence, Lady Arden reluctantly yielded.

Eliza had no intention of indulging Mr. Thornton's high-handedness, however, and she would tell him as much. Clearly he was the sort who, if you gave him an inch, would take an ell. Finding Kirby on a stool in the kitchen, she beckoned to her to take up the tray, and the two of them repaired to the drawing room.

"It's Miss Blinker and Kirby," she announced, to forestall his inevitable question.

"No sign of Ponsonby yet?"

"Not yet. Mr. Thornton, while I appreciate the frustration of your condition, I must nevertheless say that we cannot continue in this fashion, with you issuing peremptory orders."

"No, we can't. That's true enough. Where are you? Come nearer."

"This is exactly what I mean," she replied, even as she complied. "Did you want the sandwich first or the soup?"

"Neither. There are moments in a man's life which require dignity, and I'll be confounded if I say what I have to say with soup splattered all over me. Kirby? Are you there? Go away."

"Kirby, wait," Eliza commanded, though the maid had not stirred a step. "Mr. Thornton, I insist she remain. Lady Arden would like the proprieties observed. And I must also request that you make a greater effort to consider the feelings of others. You still retain shreds of courtesy when you exert yourself, and you must piece these together now as best you can because I will not be spoken to like a lackey."

"You won't, you say?" He sounded delighted with her sternness. "Shall I serve *you*, then?"

"What?"

"Softly…" he murmured under his breath. And then, more clearly, "Very well, let Kirby stay. I have plumbed the depths of self-abasement since my injuries—what is one more mortification?"

"Sir, Kirby has been here throughout," she pointed out, "so her presence should prove no more mortifying than mine."

"I'll be the judge of that. Come, come, Miss Blinker. You say you intend on returning to Winchester on Epiphany Day?"

"I do."

"And if I am not yet well enough to escape my personal dungeon of Ardenmere, you would leave me to shift as best I can?"

"I am certain Lady Arden and Sir Miles will ensure your comfort, and Mr. Ponsonby's chosen nurse would likely be available by that time."

"Are you paid well at this seminary of yours, Miss Blinker?" came his next unexpected question. "You are comfortable? You have all that you wish?"

Her puzzlement deepened. "I don't know if any person alive could say he has everything he wishes. It is not in human nature. But I would say I am treated well at Mrs. Turcotte's. I have food, clothing, and shelter. I have companionship. These are personal questions, Mr. Thornton, and again you prove I have been too indulgent of you."

"What if I asked you to leave this Mrs. Turcotte's? To exchange the care and companionship of dozens of girls for the care and companionship of one man—one admittedly difficult, demanding man?"

Eliza stared. "Are you asking me to be your nurse? I—er—thank you but refuse, Mr. Thornton. You will not require nursing much longer, even if your sight takes some time to be restored, and you would do far better to hire another manservant to replace the perfidious Kettle."

Beside her, Kirby was industriously removing the peel from an apple in a spiraling, continuous strip. For a moment Thornton cocked his head, listening hard, and then his hand flashed out to seize the maid's substantial one. She hiccuped in surprise, the knife clattering to the dish, and the next instant he had carried her hand to his lips. "My dearest Eliza, I am asking you to be my wife!"

With a shriek that drowned Eliza's gasp, Kirby wrenched her hand away, fleeing to hide behind her, despite being six inches taller and the same amount wider.

"Do be serious, Mr. Thornton," scolded Eliza, putting a bracing arm about the shocked servant.

"I have never been more so."

Only see the mischief the man could create! It was one thing to tend his medical needs and quite another to be made the source of his amusement.

Releasing Kirby with a pat, Eliza frowned at their patient. "The soup is growing cold."

"And I will do it justice when you have given me an answer," he replied. "Miss Blinker, will you be my wife?"

"But—surely you jest! Or you are out of your senses. It is a good thing Mr. Ponsonby is coming."

"What could be more sensible? Listen to me, Eliza. I know I'm no catch—blind, infirm, spotty of reputation—and that you've seen me at my worst in the last fortnight, but I promise you I'm not usually so cross as circumstances have made me. I have money and a house in town—"

She was shaking her head throughout this incredible speech. This *preposterous* speech. Could he possibly, possibly be in earnest? She thought of the giggling Trenton and Hallett daughters. Thornton might be blind, infirm, and disreputable, but clearly his charm still held, even when he could not bring his sherry-colored eyes to bear.

"But—but—" she floundered. She would give anything to take him at his word. She could admit that now. Not for the money or the house in town but because, no matter his mood, she loved his company, and the thought of parting from him wrenched her.

Did Mr. Thornton even know who he was asking, though? He had never seen her—knew only what he had been told of her, and still he made this offer.

Her throat tightened.

This offer to a penniless woman of uncertain age, uncertain looks, old dresses, and large build.

"But—you don't know me," she said at last.

"I know you are kind, calm, capable, compassionate. I know I like to listen to you as much as I like to talk to you. I strongly suspect I would like to kiss you."

Her hands flew to her burning cheeks. "But what of my age and—and size" (with an apologetic glance at Kirby) "and lack of family or fortune?"

"Does this mean you accept, Eliza, if I can only persuade you of my sincerity?"

"No! That is—I—I don't know."

"Won't you sit beside me, at least?"

"I had better not."

He gave a gusty sigh. "Let us begin at the end, then. I know you have no family, which is why I asked for and received Sir Miles' blessing. Fortune is nothing—let mine suffice. So much for those two objections. Now, as to your vaunted age, exactly how old are you, my love? Tell the truth."

She licked her lips. "Two and thirty."

That made him chuckle. "I knew the lady protested too much. Well, you were right to warn me, for I am a mere one and thirty until Epiphany Day. And as for your size, or indeed, your appearance taken altogether—I almost thank providence for my blindness. It left me no choice but to fall in love with your charming voice. Your comfortable companionship. Your pluck. And now, whatever you look like, I'm sure I will find it everything I desire."

"Oh," she said, tears welling. She pinched herself. "But...don't you still want to know what I look like?"

"Very much, if only to picture you in my mind's eye. What color is your hair?"

"Brown."

"What shade of brown?"

"Chestnut."

He smiled. "My favorite. And your eyes?"

"Hazel."

"It will do for now," he sighed again, "since I doubt you will let me run my hands over your person. So tell me, dearest Eliza, will you be mine? Shall I, despite all that has befallen me, count my fall a fortunate one?"

She still had no answer, but reprieve came in the form of the drawing room doors opening to admit Hoskins and Mr. Ponsonby.

Though Thornton grumbled at the interruption, he recovered

soon enough, remembering why he had summoned the doctor in the first place.

"Good afternoon, Thornton," Ponsonby said, with a nod at Eliza. He took a second glance at her when he saw her flushed face. "Are you feeling unwell, Miss Blinker?"

"There's nothing the matter with her," struck in Thornton impatiently. "Look here, Ponsonby, you've got to remove these bandages and examine my eyes. Just let me open them a minute and know the worst."

A lengthy debate followed, with the doctor reasoning and objecting and Mr. Thornton maintaining his ground. When it became obvious the latter would prevail, Ponsonby called for a basin of warm water.

"Please, miss," Kirby whispered, when she returned with it, "if I might wait in the passage until he is covered again...?"

In the dimness Eliza could only guess at her greenness, but she nodded as Mr. Ponsonby said, "Miss Blinker, if you could bring the light nearer."

Eliza took it up, her pulse beginning to fly until she thought she would have to join Kirby in the passage. But no, this was not the sort of fear assuaged by waiting out of sight. Even wanting to take Mr. Thornton's hand for the dread moment was impossible, for it would not be the hand he expected!

When the medical man had his warm water, fresh bandages, ointments, eye patches, and sufficient light at the ready, he began to unwind the old strips, talking more to himself than the others. "Swelling gone, cut on the eyelid healed...eyes appear the same size and degree of protrusion from the socket. No visible discoloration." Carefully he cleaned the eyelids and corners. Then:

"All right, Thornton, I want you to open your eyes a crack. Just a crack. Good. No exudation. Do you see anything? Any light?"

"Light in the left eye." Thornton's voice cracked with relief as he spoke, and Eliza pressed her lips together to stifle her exclamation.

The doctor had him shut each eye alternately, but light penetrated only the left. "Very well. Now I will have you open your eyes as far as is comfortable so that I may examine them. Look straight ahead without moving them, and if at any point you experience discomfort, close them immediately."

All three held their breath as Thornton obeyed. "There is some light in the right eye!" he declared. "Hazy, but perceptible."

"Mm. It's clouded, but that may continue to heal. The left is clear. Slowly now, try looking around."

At once Thornton's gaze rose to Eliza holding the candlestick. He drew a sharp breath. "Where has Miss Blinker gone?"

"You cannot see her?"

Thornton's eyes roamed to Eliza's left and right. "No. Call her back."

"She is just here," answered the doctor, laying a light hand on Eliza's shoulder. "Beyond the candles. Can you distinguish her shape at all?"

Thornton frowned, his eyes dropping to her hand encircling the silver stick, a hand distinctly smaller than the one he had held—twice. "I do more than distinguish a shape," he answered, "but I thought—that is, I was allowed to think—"

"You were allowed to...imagine somebody different," she whispered.

"*You*, then, are Miss Blinker?"

She nodded, swallowing. "I'm afraid so."

"You can see her, then, with your left eye?" persisted Ponsonby. "Excellent. Excellent progress, but that is enough for the day. I am going to bandage you again, and we will see what additional rest will accomplish."

Thornton submitted to this in silence, having much to ponder, but he thanked the doctor, adding, "Ponsonby, if you would send the maid Kirby back in as you go? And Miss Blinker, you may as well throw wide the curtains, for the doctor has me bound tightly as a drum here."

In contrast to the previous gloom, the faint winter sunshine seemed to flood the room with welcome brightness, but Eliza was too unsettled to draw comfort from it.

"Mr. Thornton," she began, "how very, very glad I am that you have already recovered so much of your sight."

"Yes. I was afraid, you know."

"I know." She twisted her skirts in her hands. "But this means you will soon be very much yourself again, active and independent."

"Yes."

Hearing her draw breath to speak on, he held up a finger. "A moment, Miss Blinker. Kirby, are you here?"

"Yes, sir."

"Kirby, I would like to beg your pardon for the impudence with which I have treated your hand, grasping it and kissing it and such. Disgraceful of me."

"Yes, sir, but I daresay you thought it was Miss Blinker you were palming and paddling."

"So I did. In any event, have I your pardon?"

"Yes, sir."

"Good. I wish I might have taken a gander at you as well, Kirby, but perhaps in a few more weeks. In the meantime, to continue my earlier conversation with the person I now know to be Miss Blinker..."

As Kirby withdrew some distance, Eliza hastened to say, "And I must beg your pardon, Mr. Thornton, for the deception played on you. As much as the Lady Trentons and Mrs. Halletts of the world are ready to overlook your...history, Lady Arden feared for me and wanted to...prevent me becoming an object for idle flirtation. Ridiculous, really, at my age and—and unmarriageable as I am."

"Oh, no, I beg to differ, Miss Blinker. Lady Arden was quite wise in her precautions, if mistaken in her estimation of me."

"In any event, it is never pleasant to feel oneself deceived, and I am sorry for the part I played in it. It goes without saying, of course, that now that you know you will recover much if not all of your sight, and now that you know of our...little ruse... you are by no means bound by the offer you made an hour ago."

"Thank you for your understanding," he replied, and Eliza felt her heart sink to her very toes. "But I have a confession to make as well. An hour earlier—was it so long?—when you supplied your hair and eye color, that I might picture you, an image appeared so readily to me that I wondered if it was not a form of premature infidelity. I knew—or thought I knew—you to be a woman of substantial, strong build and possibly as old as forty—I could not believe you any older, with your youthful voice and manners—but the person who leaped into my mind was a young lady I encountered the morning of my accident, outside the Crest and Comb. A very pretty, if slightly shabby, young lady with beautiful chestnut hair and clear, sweet hazel eyes—"

Eliza's hands flew to her mouth. He had remembered her?

"—And when Ponsonby unbandaged me, and I saw you, I thought, 'Good God, I was picturing the maid Kirby. I have fallen in love with Miss Blinker's voice and personality, and Kirby's person!' Therefore, any resentment I may have harbored at being made Lady Arden's dupe has been completely swallowed up in relief that I have not inadvertently proposed to one woman when I might actually be in love with two."

"You—do—still want to marry me, then?" she breathed.

"More with each passing moment. Come sit beside me, and I will prove it, to the extent my blasted ribs will allow. You had better do it, Eliza, or I will summon Hoghands and Bumblelow to haul me up, that I might chase you about the room."

She laughed at this, a tide of joy filling her to the very crown of her head. "I will not put them to the trouble," she said. Heedless of Kirby's witness, she skipped to drop in the chair nearest him and to take his hand between her own.

"More. More!" he ordered in his most peremptory manner, attempting to turn toward her and wincing with the movement. "Your lips, Eliza, or you will jeopardize my recovery by forcing me to do something rash."

"Here then, Mr. Thornton," was her blissful, lingering reply, as she pressed her lips to his. "And here. And here."

"Better call in Lady Arden, Kirby," he commanded some while later, when he remembered the maid's presence at last. "And tell her, like the angels of old, you come bringing 'glad tidings of great joy.'"

The End

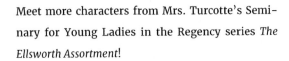

Meet more characters from Mrs. Turcotte's Seminary for Young Ladies in the Regency series *The Ellsworth Assortment*!

Whether writing sparkling Regency romances like *The Naturalist* and *Tempted by Folly*, or reimagining Austen in contemporary settings as she does in *Pride and Preston Lin* (Third State Books, 2024), Christina's books are all about that happy ending. Named to several Best Book lists by Austenprose and Austenesque Reviews, her stories have been called "a literary feast for any Jane Austen or Georgette Heyer fan," "swoon-worthy," and "ingenious and entertaining," while *Pride and Preston Lin* was chosen by Booklist as a Top Ten romance of 2024.

For more information and to subscribe to her newsletter, visit www.christinadudley.com or scan the QR code. Subscribers receive a bonus *Hapgoods of Bramleigh* short story.

'Twas the Night Before Christmas

by GL Robinson

In memory of my dear sister Francine, who loved Christmas.

Chapter One

"**W**atch out there, Guv'nor!" Wilf's voice came shrilly through the freezing night air. "That there's a sheet o' ice! You'll want ter pull back on the nags!"

But it was too late. The big back wheels of the high-perch phaeton swung wildly as they encountered the slippery surface and there was an ominous splintering crack. The vehicle immediately slumped to one side and the cantering horses, feeling the sudden check, reared up wildly.

"Damn and blast it!" The driver, who must have had wrists of iron, wrestled them to a stop.

Even before they were at a standstill, Wilf ran to the front and took hold of the horses' heads, speaking to them in a language only he and they could understand. Then he darted around and felt their legs.

"No 'arm done, far as Oi can feel, Guv'nor. Can't see a bloody thing, o'course."

"That's more than can be said for the phaeton," came a cultured voice from the back of the vehicle. "The left rear wheel's clean off. And the right looks as if it's cracked. Damn and blast it," he said again. "I blame it on the port. The one Aunt Florence left us with after that dreadful lunch. The prosy old fool of a rector must have thought he needed to pay for the multiple glasses he threw down his gullet by expounding on all the Old Testament prophesies foretelling the birth of Christ. And the squire encouraged him! I suppose he thought the longer he was at table, the more he could put away too. I have to admit, it was good port, but dammit, otherwise I would have been away an hour earlier."

"Yus, an' if yer weren't half cut yer might 'ave bin payin' more attention to the road an' all."

"That's enough commentary from you!"

The owner of the voice came round and stood beside his diminutive tiger. He was an imposing figure, made even broader and taller by his many-caped coat and the high, curly-brimmed hat on his head.

"Well, not much use standing about in this freezing weather. We'll have to unhitch the horses and walk into the village. I suppose there is a village somewhere down this godforsaken track. Come on, and bring our traps. We're going to have to rack up somewhere for the night. Perhaps it'll be in a manger." He laughed hollowly.

Leading the horses behind them, they walked in silence for about a mile until Wilf said suddenly, "There's a light up ahead Guv'nor. Not much of a one, though. Can't be a very big place. You want to take yer chance in there, or carry on?"

"Don't know about you, but I haven't felt my feet for the last half-mile. Let's see if we can warm up a bit, even if we have to carry on afterwards. At least they should be able to tell us if there's a wheelwright anywhere around."

Wilf grunted assent, though he didn't need to. His master knew he'd follow him through the gates of hell itself. He'd met him one day when the lad had fearlessly jumped on the back of one of a runaway pair harnessed to a curricle. They'd been frightened by a pair of cats who chased each other under the horses' hooves, fighting over a stolen herring. The groom who was supposed to be watching them had been distracted by a shapely ankle and was looking the other way.

Back then Wilf was even smaller: more than half-starved and dressed in rags. He had no idea how old he was or what his surname might be. He'd been left at the workhouse door as an infant and as soon as he could, he had run away to live in the London streets.

After the daring feat with the runaway horses, he was hired as tiger on the spot and now, several years later, well-fed and liveried, he was his master's self-appointed protector and guide. He would follow him into Hades, negotiate with Charon over the fare and argue with Satan himself if the conditions were unsuitable for the man he considered his Savior, despite what the Bible (which he couldn't read, anyway) might say.

Chapter Two

Following the direction of the light that twinkled, then disappeared, then twinkled again, they came at length to its source. It was a metal lantern swaying above the door of a cottage that stood a little back from the road, surrounded by a wooden fence. By the light of the moon that had now risen, it looked so much like an illustration of a cottage that one might find in a children's story book that to anyone of an imaginative turn of mind it must have been laughable. Since this was true of neither of the visitors, they saw but didn't appreciate either the thatched roof over the old stones or the rambling rose around the front door, now leafless and brown, that in the summer showered with scented petals those going in and out. They ignored both them and the neatly cut back flower beds that had surely been a riot of color a few months earlier.

Tethering the horses to the fence, the mis-matched pair walked up the garden path. The tall gentleman, whose head would certainly have been in the roses, knocked briskly at the old oak door with the head of his cane. He waited a few minutes, and receiving no response, knocked again. This time he was rewarded by the sound of the door being opened and a female voice saying, "It must be the carolers, Papa, though they are a little early. The mince pies are only just out of the pan. They'll be too hot to eat!"

The speaker now came fully into view. The lantern showed her to be a handsome young woman with a smudge of flour on her cheek and curls that were springing from a loose braid around her head. She was wearing a voluminous apron that she was now attempting to untie with one hand, while she held the door open with the other.

"Oh!" she said, looking up into the tall man's face. "You aren't the carolers!"

"No," he said. "I'm afraid not. I'm... I'm Fortescue." He executed a bow, almost knocking over Wilf, who was standing closely behind him. "And this is Wilf, my tiger."

"Your what?" the young woman looked puzzled. "He doesn't look very fierce, for a tiger. He's very small."

"He isn't usually fierce, except when he thinks he has to protect me," admitted the visitor. "But his sort of tiger is not hired for fierceness but for being good with horses and not weighing a lot. Rather like a jockey. Talking of which, we tethered our horses to your fence. I hope you don't mind."

"Oh, I see." She gurgled with laughter, "Though the idea of his protecting you seems idiotic. It should be the other way round. But why are you standing on the doorstep like that? Come in, for heaven's sake. Leave the horses, by all means, though the poor things shouldn't be outside long in this weather."

"Thank you. We will only disturb you for a moment." The visitor removed his hat and, bowing his head so as not to knock it against the lintel, stepped in, saying, "Wilf, wait with the horses."

"By no means!" cried the young woman. "It's freezing out there! And aren't tigers used to warmer climates?"

She laughed again, pulled Wilf into the cottage and closed the door. Taking off the apron had revealed a worn round gown in a brown and yellow windowpane check. It was in no way modish, or even flattering. She was still holding her apron, and now, catching sight of herself in the small mirror next to the door, she used it to scrub the flour from her cheek. The tall man found himself unaccountably disappointed. He had rather liked the smudge.

They were standing in a room that was somewhat larger than the outside of the cottage would have led one to expect. It was very cozy, softly glowing in fire and candlelight. A narrow staircase led off one side, disappearing quite quickly beyond the timbered ceiling that was so low, the tall man had to duck again to avoid hitting his head on a lantern hanging just inside the door. A wide hearth took up most of the far wall. The mantle above it held a two-branch candelabrum at each end. An elderly gentleman sat reading in a rocking chair on one side, oblivious to all around him. On the other side there was an armchair whose stuffing was showing an inclination to bolt for freedom. Opposite was a wooden settle whose cushioned seat was split down the middle. Against the wall just inside the door, where they were now standing, stood a wooden table and four chairs. This one room evidently served as both dining room and parlor.

"Papa," said their hostess, "this is Mr. Fortescue and Wilf his tiger." The visitor made as if to demur but evidently changed his mind. He bowed and muttered something that might have been *at your service*, as the elderly gentleman rose and returned his bow, still gripping his book. "This sort of tiger," continued the lady with a chuckle, "helps with the horses. He doesn't eat them."

She turned to the visitors and for the first time saw the tall man in the light. His many-caped coat was obviously from a very good tailor, for it fit perfectly across his broad shoulders and chest. Half open at the bottom, it revealed boots which, though now wet and soiled, were molded to a shapely calf, a far cry from the clumping footwear she was accustomed to on the feet of the local men. He was, she judged, in his early thirties and would have been very good-looking, except for a petulant expression that marred his countenance. Nevertheless, she was glad she'd removed the smudge from her cheek and self-consciously pushed at her curls as if to force them to behave.

"This is my father, Arnold Wilberforce," she said. "And I'm Elisabeth Wilberforce." She gave a small curtsey. "Won't you let me take your coats while you sit down and explain why you're here? I don't imagine this is a social call?" She chuckled again.

"Thank you." Mr. Fortescue shrugged off his heavy coat and handed it to her, together with his hat and cane. Wilf did the same with his gold-buttoned, blue-trimmed jacket and matching cap.

Elisabeth disappeared with the coats, saying "I'll just take these through to the kitchen and hang them by the fire. Our maid has gone home for Christmas and won't be back till Boxing Day, so things are even more than usually informal!"

The men sat down, Mr. Wilberforce into his rocker, Mr. Fortescue on the settle, which creaked ominously at his weight, and Wilf into one of the chairs next to the dining table. When their hostess came back minus the coats, she looked at their visitor perched a little nervously on the edge of the settle.

"Oh, Mr. Fortescue," she said. "You'd best sit in the armchair! That old settle isn't good for much, though I must say, it has its uses. When we have visitors we don't want to stay long, we put them on there, knowing it makes them too nervous to get comfortable." She laughed merrily.

"Well, I hope we won't outstay our welcome, even if I do take advantage of your kind offer," he replied, moving to the armchair by the fire. "The thing is, the icy road back there caused the back wheels of my phaeton to slip and end up in a ditch. One wheel is completely broken off and the other is cracked. I'm hoping you can tell me where a wheelwright may be found."

"Well, normally he may be found about half a mile down the road in his cottage, but tonight he's in church, ringing the bells. They always ring a full peal on Christmas Eve. It begins at about seven and takes three hours. After the midnight service they ring again, but only a quarter peal, which only takes about three-quarters of an hour. They need to get home to their beds, poor things! Listen! You can hear them starting now!"

Sure enough, the rhythmic sound of the bells ringing in descending order came clearly through the night air. They all sat and listened in silence for a few minutes. "Isn't it lovely?" said Elisabeth with enthusiasm. "When it's as cold and crisp as it is tonight, the sound is just wonderful."

"Hmm," said the visitor, who had never paid much attention to change ringing before, and was too preoccupied to think about it now. "I dare say." His petulant expression became more marked. "But I could wish the wheelwright weren't tied up all night. I was hoping he'd be able to fix my phaeton so I could be on my way."

"I'm sorry to say, I don't think that will be possible today or tomorrow. He won't get to bed until late. And no one works on Christmas Day!"

Mr. Fortescue sighed. "Then it looks as if I'm going to be stuck here for at least two days! Is there an inn in the village?"

"There is, but since it isn't a staging post and hardly anyone travels at this time of the year, the innkeeper Mr. Button and his wife have gone off to visit their married daughter. It's all closed up, I'm afraid."

Chapter Three

Mr. Fortescue looked around helplessly and asked the question to which there was seemingly no answer. "Then what in God's name are we to do?"

Elisabeth smiled at him. "Well, the Son of the God you just invoked found himself in much the same situation on Christmas Eve, or at least, his parents did, and people helped. We shall do likewise, though I won't offer you a manger! You can stay here. You shall sleep in my room and I'll sleep on the truckle bed in Father's. He won't mind. Will you, Papa?"

After the introductions, Mr. Wilberforce had returned to his reading material and had paid no attention to the discussion. Elisabeth repeated "Papa? You won't mind, will you?"

"What? Eh? Mind what?"

"If I sleep on the truckle bed in your room. Mr. Fortescue needs my room. Wilf can sleep down here on the settle."

"But I couldn't..." began Mr. Fortescue, but before he could say another word, the sound of voices raised in song could be heard outside, followed by a knocking at the door.

"The carolers!" cried Elisabeth and ran to let them in.

The room was soon filled with what seemed like a crowd but was in fact only eight people, bundled up to twice their size. Only their glowing red faces were visible between a mass of scarves and tippets and a variety of caps, bonnets and singular headwear it was impossible to name. They were all singing, not especially tunefully but at the top of their voices, *God Rest Ye Merry Gentlemen, Let Nothing You Dismay*, which dismayed Mr. Fortescue very much indeed.

He wasn't fond of carols. In fact, he wasn't fond of Christmas at all. For him it had always meant long dinners with relatives he preferred to avoid, like his aunt Florence, where he had just spent a boring duty visit of twenty-four hours. And look where it had got him. The petulant expression became even more marked.

Wilf came over and murmured in his ear, "If them's goin' to be makin' that God-awful noise all night, along of the bells, I think I'll take me chances and walk to Lunnon."

Mr. Fortescue scowled at him awfully and Wilf amended, "I'll just get me togs an' see to the 'orses." He slipped away in the direction their coats had been taken and was seen no more for quite a while.

After a rendition of *The First Nowell*, which is a long carol, Mr. Fortescue was hoping his suffering would soon be at an end, but he was subjected to a spirited *Here We Come A-Wassailing* before there was blessed silence. Into the calm Elisabeth called out gaily, "If someone will come and help, I'll bring out the wassail and the mince pies!"

Mr. Fortescue leaped immediately to his feet. In the kitchen he found his hostess, re-clad in her apron, stirring a big pot of liquid steaming over the fire with apples bobbing on top. On the deal table behind her lay platters of mince pies.

"I'm so silly," she said, stepping back. "I used the big pot and filled it over the fire. Now I can't lift it. Mary usually prepares it before she leaves but I told her I'd do it. I should have remembered she uses the smaller one."

Then, when the visitor made as if to pick up the vessel, she caught his arm, saying, "Careful! You'll need some cloths to protect your hands. It's very hot!" But no sooner had her hand touched his arm than she snatched it away, as if it too, were red hot. The feel of the muscles under his tweed riding coat made her heat leap. She thrust a folded cloth at him and turned away in her confusion. She picked up one of the platters of mince pies. "If you'll follow me," she said, trying to keep her voice normal.

They went back into the main room and placed the offerings on the dining table. Elisabeth stood next to the pot with a ladle at the ready. To Mr. Fortescue's surprise, the carolers each pulled a tin cup from his or her pocket and went for it to be filled. When everyone had been served, they raised their cups and chanted, somewhat raggedly:

> May joy and peace surround you, contentment latch
> your door,
> And happiness be with you now, and bless you
> ever more!

Then they fell upon the mince pies and rapidly demolished them. After which, they once more wished their hosts a Merry Christmas and a Happy New Year, and left, singing the wassail song.

"They are dear folk," said Elisabeth, closing the door behind them, "but I'm always glad we're one of the first houses they visit. They get quite inebriated and silly by the end. Then you can hear the snoring through the church service."

"But we saw no other houses before we got here," said Mr. Fortescue, whose upbringing had prevented him from sitting as long as the lady were standing, and who had remained standing to one side while the carolers were eating and drinking.

"Oh, they come to us first as we're furthest away. Then by the time they're in the village, they have no distance to go to the church. You'll see them later."

She seemed to assume he would be going to church with them, and for once in his life, Mr. Fortescue found he didn't dislike the idea.

"Now," Elisabeth continued. "Let us have some supper. It will be very simple, I'm afraid. We have our main meal in the middle of the day. But there are some mince pies left."

Thinking of the protracted lunch he'd consumed earlier in the day, their visitor could only be glad of the idea of something simpler. But first he said, "We have not yet settled where we are to stay the night. I find the idea of turning you out of your bed unacceptable. If you are truly kind enough to offer us shelter, I can sleep down here."

"On the settle?" she laughed. "We'd have to fold you in half! No, Mr. Fortescue, I shall be perfectly comfortable in the truckle bed. I've slept there before, when father has one of his bad nights. Wilf can stay down here. Where is he, by the way?"

"Seeing to the horses. He prefers their company to that of most people. Now the carolers have gone, he'll be back."

Sure enough, footsteps were heard in the kitchen, and Wilf's diminutive figure reappeared.

"There's a barn be'ind the 'ouse," he said. "I brung the 'orses in there out o' the cold. There was a bit o' 'ay in there too. I give it to them. 'Ope that's okay, Miss."

"Yes, of course, I should have thought of it myself," said Elisabeth. "We used to have a pony and trap but... well, we had to get rid of it."

"If we are to sit at table," said Mr. Fortescue, "I should like to wash my hands and change out of my riding attire, if I may."

"Of course! How silly of me not to have thought of that! Come this way." Elisabeth lit a candle on a small table next to the stairs and waited for him to follow.

The visitor took his bag from the corner where he had stowed it and climbed the narrow stairs to a landing, ducking his head as he reached the top.

"This house is really not built for someone your size," laughed Miss Wilberforce. "You are sure to bang your head at some point. I think you should wear a cap. I could loan you one of Papa's!"

"Wearing a cap indoors would make me much more uncomfortable than a bang on the head," he responded. "Anyway, perhaps it would knock some sense into me."

"Do you lack sense?"

"Since I rode us over ice without slowing down and ended up in a ditch with a broken wheel," he answered ruefully, "I should say the answer is yes."

"But then you would have missed the carolers, which I could tell you so enjoyed!"

392

He laughed. "Was it that obvious?" Then he said seriously, "But I would have missed meeting you, Miss Wilberforce, and that would most certainly have been a pity."

She raised her eyes to his. "Yes, it would," she said quietly. Then, shaking her head slightly, she added in a different tone, "We have so few visitors. It's nice to see someone different. Here we are."

She opened the door to a bedchamber, went in and put the candle on a table. "I'll send Wilf up with some hot water," she said briskly, and left him.

The visitor's initial reaction when entering his hostess's bedroom was to breathe in deeply. It smelled delightfully of her. He saw her nightgown hanging on the back of the door and had an urge, which he instantly quelled, to bury his head in it. Wilf arrived with a ewer of hot water that he poured into a basin on a washstand behind a screen in the corner of the room. Mr. Fortescue rapidly performed his ablutions and then opened his bag. That's when he remembered he'd packed in a hurry, anxious to be gone from his aunt's. Normally he would have had his valet with him, but the man had developed a putrid sore throat the day before he left home. He was going to be gone for only one night, and had thought he could manage without him. He'd changed into his riding apparel, and had all but thrown the clothes he'd been wearing that afternoon into his bag. Consequently, his only coat and waistcoat were creased. Luckily, his valet had given him an extra shirt and several neckcloths, knowing his master routinely went through two or three to get the folds just as he wanted. He dressed in the clean shirt and crumpled outer clothing, then did the best he could with his neckcloth and his hair in the small mirror over the washstand. But going down to supper, he was very dissatisfied with his appearance.

Miss Wilberforce's feelings were quite different. As he descended the stairs, she first saw shining Hessians with jaunty tassels. Above them came slim, buff-colored pantaloons. A super-fine, swallow-tailed coat in a deep navy blue was gradually revealed, then a grey pin-striped waistcoat. She didn't notice the creases. Last came glimpses of a spotless shirt with a moderately high collar, a neckcloth wrapped round it in complicated folds. When his neck and head came into view, his hair combed into a perfection of artistic disarray, Elisabeth almost caught her breath. In his riding apparel with his hair uncombed, he had been an attractive man. Now he looked very handsome indeed: an illustration for the best-dressed man about town.

She knew this because amongst the papers that arrived periodically from London, Elisabeth sometimes received copies of the *Mode Illustrée*. Although she was by no means a follower of fashion and laughed over the creations more than she pined for them, she had no difficulty in recognizing the very modish style of their visitor's dress. How he had been able to achieve such perfection in that small mirror she could not imagine. She herself usually glanced in it only enough to make sure her curls were not entirely wayward. Now, looking down at her serviceable gown, she wished had thought to change for dinner, too. She and her father had given up the habit of doing so, since in the country they didn't dine so much as sup in the evening.

Chapter Four

"There you are, Mr. Fortescue," she said as naturally as she could. "Now please won't you all sit down? You too, Papa!" She raised her voice to her father, who, once the carolers had gone, had returned to his book. He looked up and, gesturing to the table, she said, "Supper, dear," then went into the kitchen.

Wilf looked up at his master. "I don't got t' sit in 'ere, do I, Guv'nor? I'll be better off in the kitchen."

Mr. Fortescue nodded and followed him in that direction. "Miss Wilberforce," he said, ducking his head through the kitchen door, "Wilf would much rather eat out here, if you don't mind. He's, er, unaccustomed to society manners."

Elisabeth laughed. "So are we! I'm afraid you'll find the distinctions of class quite lacking here, but it's as he wishes. I want him to be comfortable." She smiled at Wilf, who blushed.

Supper turned out to be a soup of mostly vegetables, flavored with a little bacon, and served with bread and cheese, with mince tarts to follow. After the heavy and ill-cooked meal he'd been forced to consume earlier, Mr. Fortescue found it perfect. The conversation turned to politics, into which Mr. Wilberforce joined with an enthusiasm that surprised their visitor. There was a lively and often humorous exchange of views. It became clear that though they lived in a very retired way in the country, they were quite well informed; Mr. Wilberforce received regular letters from London. More than that they did not say, and their visitor was too well-mannered to ask.

Once the supper dishes were cleared away, Mr. Wilberforce returned to his seat, and his daughter announced she was going to bring in the holly and ivy to decorate the hearth.

"Let me help you," offered their guest. He was more and more fascinated by this woman who talked London politics one minute and washed dishes the next.

"Oh, the holly is frightfully fierce this year," she said, "It pulled my shawl all to bits when I approached it. I should hate for your fine clothes to be damaged. Or for your lovely boots to be scratched."

Mr. Fortescue, to whom an injured coat meant no more than a trip to his tailor to order a new one, and whose boots were as a rule tenderly polished every day by his valet, using a mixture of champagne and wax, laughed this off. "It's the least I can do," he said, "to repay your hospitality."

"I'm a-comin' too," pronounced Wilf, who had decided Miss Wilberforce was a bang-up mort for whom he was more than willing to receive a scratch or two.

Elizabeth took an ancient handsaw from the dark recesses of the kitchen, the three of them donned their coats, hats, and gloves and went out the back door of the cottage. Neat furrows of an extensive vegetable garden could be seen, the ice on them glistening in the moonlight. "Brr! It's so cold," said Elisabeth.

"I should have done this earlier, but I got caught up with baking the mince pies, then you arrived and…"

"All the more reason for us to help," replied Mr. Fortescue, taking the saw from her hands and attacking the holly with it. "Ouch, you brute! And through my gloves, too! But I shall prevail. Which branches do you want, Miss Wilberforce?"

"How lucky you're so tall!" she said. "The branches with the best berries are always above my head. Look! Those there."

In a few minutes, three or four branches with good loads of bright berries lay on the sacking Elisabeth had brought out for the purpose.

They then pulled strips of ivy from the side of the henhouse, causing a few disgruntled shufflings inside. Wilf carried the ivy cuttings into the kitchen, while his master wrapped up the holly in the sacking and did the same.

"What I usually do is make small loops of string on the holly to hang it on the mantle," said Miss Wilberforce. "There are hooks on it from years ago. Then I festoon it with the ivy. But the holly fights you all the way. No wonder it's always been considered the male plant. Did you know that? The smooth ivy leaves represent the female."

"That seems a little unfair," protested Mr. Fortescue. "I've known a number of women with very sharp tongues."

"Of course! But we women mostly hide our sharpness. Men are much more direct. Ivy climbs up things using tiny little claws you don't even notice. But holly, once you get past the thorns, is defenseless." She laughed.

It turned out that Wilf, with his small, strong hands, was especially adept at making the string loops on the holly, so it wasn't long before the shiny green leaves and red berries adorned the mantle. The ivy was then festooned over and under it. They all stood back, admiring their handiwork.

"Now we drink a cup of the mulled cider to toast the holly and the ivy," said Elisabeth. "It's supposed to ensure fertility, though that's hardly appropriate in this house."

"I don't know, daughter," said her father, speaking up suddenly. "Mr. Pounds has been showing you a marked attention these past months."

"Who's Mr. Pounds?" asked Mr. Fortescue, before he could stop himself.

"The curate," Elisabeth answered. "You'll see him in church tonight."

If her visitor had some lingering reluctance to go to the services that night, it immediately disappeared.

Suddenly, the bell ringing stopped. In fact, they had ceased to hear it, and the silence smote their ears more than the sound.

"Oh! They've come to the end of the peal!" said Elisabeth. "We'll need to get ready for church soon. It will take us about half an hour to walk there, so we need to leave around half past ten. I'll just run up and change my gown. I won't be long."

She wasn't long, but in any case, most of the time was taken up in changing the sheets on her bed. She replaced them with the best set they had: the only ones not sewn ends-to-middle to get a bit more wear out of them. Then she took her slippers from under her bed and her nightgown and robe from behind the door, blushing to think Mr. Fortescue must have seen them earlier. That done, she quickly changed her gown, ran her fingers through her braids and deftly brushed her curls up onto the top of her head. She fiercely secured them with pins, hoping they wouldn't work loose before they even left the house. Then she bundled up her old gown with her nightclothes, and took them and her sheets into her father's room.

As she came downstairs, Mr. Fortescue watched her as she had watched him. Her boots peeped out from under the hem of a green silk gown that he knew immediately was not of recent vintage. The skirts were fuller than the prevailing mode, but had the advantage, he observed with appreciation, of fitting into her trim waist. A fine shawl hung from the crooks of her elbows. The *décolleté* of the bodice revealed a tantalizing glimpse of the tops of her breasts, and her slim, white neck held a head crowned by a riot of red-brown curls. He, the darling of the *ton* for the past five seasons and object of innumerable attempts to engage his interest, thought he had never seen a more alluring woman.

Chapter Five

The heavy outwear necessary for the weather soon covered the finery of the two members of the company who had any to cover. Mr. Fortescue shrugged on his caped coat and took up his hat, gloves, and cane. Miss Wilberforce wrapped her shawl around her head and over her shoulders, then put on a heavy cloak that completely enveloped her. Her father donned an ancient woolen garment and hat that must have been purchased in the previous century. Wilf at first objected to going to church at all, and said he'd "stay wiv the 'orses." But after a frown from his master, he resignedly buttoned up his livery coat and put on his cap.

The four set out to walk to the church, Elisabeth at first urging her father to take her arm in case of ice patches. But when she herself slipped and had to be steadied by Mr. Fortescue, the pairing changed. Mr. Wilberforce walked with his hand on Wilf's shoulder, the diminutive tiger declaring he "'adn't never slipped on nuffin in 'is life," and Elisabeth took Mr. Fortescue's arm. She experienced the same thrill as she had before at holding onto an arm that felt as strong as iron, and for the first time in her life thought how nice it was to have someone to lean on.

"Have you lived here long?" ventured the gentleman once they had gone a little way. His curiosity was more powerful than his upbringing, which normally forbade personal questions. Elisabeth Wilberforce was by birth no country woman, he was sure.

"A little over ten years," she replied. "We came here when Papa had some difficulty... oh, I may as well tell you! It's ancient history now. Papa used to write articles for magazines and newspapers. Political and social commentary, that sort of thing. Then he made the mistake of saying something that an important man took exception to. He sued for libel and was able to prove that father's remarks were a personal attack. That was entirely false: Papa never had any such intention. But the barrister we hired to plead his case was incompetent and the opposing Counsel very good. We lost all our money and had to sell our house. We had to leave London. It killed my poor mama. She died the first year we were here."

She told him she was fourteen when they moved to the village. She'd been educated at home by her parents. Her mother was the daughter of a cleric, an intelligent woman who helped and fully supported her husband in his writing. She did not tell him that though they were not by any means members of the *ton*, she had until that point expected her life to be like that of the other young women she knew: introduction into society, marriage and children. But things had worked out very differently.

"We are not country folk," she said, "but on the whole, I'm happy here. What I really miss is someone to talk to. We socialize with very few people. We rely on letters from friends. Nowadays my father counts on me more and more. He's a dear, but becoming dreadfully vague."

"I see," was all Mr. Fortescue said, and changed the subject.

This was the first time Elisabeth had spoken to anyone so frankly about her family's misfortune, but she was glad to have done so now. Mr. Fortescue was easy to talk to and made no comment. She wanted no commiseration and certainly no pity. And her story was safe with him. He was only passing through. Once his phaeton was repaired, he'd be gone for good.

As they neared the village, Elisabeth suddenly said, "There's the wheelwright's house. I'll just run in and ask him to see to your vehicle as soon as he can." She ran off, but he caught up with her in a couple of long strides.

"I can take care of it, you know, Miss Wilberforce."

"Oh! I'm used to doing everything myself, and it never occurred to me I was being interfering! I'm so sorry!"

"And I'm used to having everything done for me, I'm afraid, but in this instance I insist on being allowed to rise to the occasion."

Elisabeth stayed where she was, thinking about his words. She had already guessed he was a man of means, but he wasn't so high in the instep that he wouldn't cut her holly for her. And his readiness to accept their humble hospitality confused her. She was still thinking about it when he returned.

"It's just as you said. He didn't want to work on Christmas day. But I was able to persuade him to at least haul the phaeton into his yard tomorrow afternoon so he can get to it at once on Boxing Day."

"Goodness! You must be very persuasive!"

Mr. Fortescue laughed. "I think my pocketbook was more persuasive than I, Miss Wilberforce!"

This response by no means lessened her confusion, and they resumed their walk in silence.

Soon they could hear snatches of carols, interspersed with loud good wishes in slurred voices that displayed the over-consumption of hot alcohol on a cold night.

"You see why I'm glad we're first on the list," remarked Elisabeth. "But I don't blame them. They have few opportunities to enjoy themselves. The lord of the manor stands them a meal at the end of the harvest, but that's about it."

"There's a lord of the manor?"

"Yes. Lord Brookstone. He has a big house a couple of miles up the road. But he spends most of his time in London. It's a pity you didn't break your wheel closer to them. They would have been able to put you up in much more suitable conditions, although, come to think of it, I don't think the family is here at the moment."

"I don't know why you think I need more suitable lodging." Her partner looked at her. "I'm very happy where I am. Though I can see it would have been better for you not to have to turn out of your room to accommodate me."

"That's not what I mean at all, Mr. Fortescue! I've told you I don't mind sleeping in my father's room on the little bed. I've done so often."

"Well, all I can do is thank you again. I wish I knew how I am to repay you."

"Cutting down the holly was payment enough. I should have scratched myself to ribbons! And we still have to bring in the Yule

Log. I shall need you for that. It's too big for me. In fact, I don't know what I should have done without you. I would have had to ask one of the carolers, and then ply him with more mulled cider and mince pies!" She smiled up at him and he thought he would gladly bring in a thousand Yule Logs, whatever they were, if she would smile at him again like that.

Chapter Six

They caused a stir when they entered the church, Elisabeth leading the way to empty pews near the front. Her father followed her, with Mr. Fortescue behind him. Wilf saw his opportunity and hung back, darting at the last moment into an empty place in the back row, where he proceeded to ogle the country maidens who giggled when he winked at them. They'd never seen anyone dressed like him and couldn't make out if he was a soldier or in costume for some sort of mummers' play. The church was bitterly cold and no one removed their outer garments.

They had just settled in when there was another stir and a group of well-dressed individuals walked in a stately fashion down to the boxed pews on the other side of the aisle. Many churches had private pews with high backs and (often locked) gates, purchased by wealthy families generations before, so that they could sit away from the prying eyes of the unwashed peasantry in the rest of the congregation. Mr. Fortescue had guessed when he saw the boxes that they belonged to the Brookstone family. He groaned silently when he saw the family coming in now.

An elderly lady with a cane, dressed in a fur-collared coat much too big for her, headed the line, accompanied by a female of indeterminate age, dressed far less richly in a plain brown cloak and uncompromising hat. Behind them came an equally elderly gentleman, leaning very heavily on the arm of an embarrassed boy, barely in his teens, who might have been his grandson. Then came a pair, obviously husband and wife, probably in their forties and both dressed in the latest style. The gentleman was carrying a curly beaver and wearing a coat with as many capes as that belonging to Mr. Fortescue, but since he was almost a foot shorter, he looked as wide as the church door. The lady was clad in a luxurious velvet cloak with a hood trimmed with swans' down. It released small feathers into the atmosphere as she moved. Lastly came a young woman who bore a marked resemblance to the lady with the swans' down, and must be her daughter. She was also dressed in high fashion, with a frivolous bonnet entirely unsuitable for the season, and carrying a huge white fur muff.

This lady stopped short when she saw Mr. Fortescue. "James!" she cried, oblivious to the ecclesiastical surroundings, "What are you doing here?

He stood and bowed. "Good evening, Anthea," he said in a low voice, "I'm visiting friends."

"I didn't know one *had* friends in this out-of-the-way place. Heaven knows, I come here as infrequently as possible for that very reason."

Her eyes fell coldly on Mr. Wilberforce and Elisabeth, who both shifted as if to stand, but she made no move to salute either of them so they subsided again.

"I'll see you after the service, darling," she said and followed the rest of her family into the boxed pew.

James, thought Elisabeth. *Darling*. And her heart fell.

Then she and everyone else in hearing were distracted by a scuffling from the boxed pew and the sound of a petulant voice saying, "No heated bricks? Why ever not? Didn't they know we were coming?" A low voice mumbled a reply and then the response, "Well, I do think it's too bad. It's absolutely freezing in here. If I'd known I wouldn't have come. I shall write to the bishop."

If this threat received a response, no one knew, for the organ struck up the opening hymn, the officiants processed down the aisle and the service began.

It was the same service they had all heard every year, but the ancient words fell on ready ears:

> And it came to pass in those days, that there went out a decree from Caesar Augustus, that all the world should be taxed. And this taxing was first made when Cyrenius was governor of Syria. And all went to be taxed, every one into his own city. And Joseph also went up from Galilee, out of the city of Nazareth, into Judaea, unto the city of David, which is called Bethlehem; because he was of the house and lineage of David, to be taxed with Mary his espoused wife, being great with child. And so it was, that, while they were there, the days were accomplished that she should be delivered. And she brought forth her firstborn son, and wrapped him in swaddling clothes, and laid him in a manger; because there was no room for them in the inn.

The service took its accustomed course and as soon as the vicar intoned the parting blessing, the bells started up again. Everyone waited for him and his entourage to leave, followed by the family in the box who swept out without looking to left or right. The vicar stood at the door, greeting those coming out. Next to him stood the man James Fortescue had judged to be the curate, the Mr. Pounds Elizabeth's father had spoken of as having been paying her marked attention. He was a man of average height with regular features and not unhandsome. But he had a doughy look that to James' eye denoted a sedentary, self-indulgent nature. He disliked him on sight.

Chapter Seven

The curate came forward eagerly as they came out of the church. He took both of Miss Wilberforce's hands and saying, "Elisabeth! A word with you, please, my dear. May I crave permission to come and see you tomorrow afternoon?"

Elisabeth? My dear? thought James. *How dare he!*

"Oh, Mr. Pounds! We have a visitor at the moment and..."

Mr. Pounds, thought James. *Good. Use his surname. Put him in his place.*

"You cannot be ignorant of the reason for my wishing to see you, my dear. I shall not keep you long. Afterwards I shall beg a few words with your father, of course."

A few words with your father? thought James. *Of course? He's certainly sure of himself!*

"But, I don't think..."

"Good, then. It's settled. Let's say two o'clock?"

It was as well for the curate that Anthea Brookstone chose that moment to run up to Mr. Fortescue and pull him away, for he was about to point out to the curate that Miss Wilberforce had clearly stated she was too busy with a visitor to see him and if he didn't understand when a woman says no she means no, he would be glad to take him behind the church and teach him some manners.

But as it was, his own manners made him go with Anthea, though not without casting a look behind him to see what Elisabeth was doing. She was watching him, but when she saw his eyes on her, she turned to help her father.

"James, darling! Who are those people you were sitting with?" cried Anthea. "They look like cits! Surely you can get away! Come home with me! Only Mama and Papa are there and my pip of a brother... well, Grandmother and Grandfather of course, but they don't count. So we will have lots of time to ourselves. Do come!"

"I'm sorry, Anthea, but I cannot change my plans. I, er... I owe Mr. and Miss Wilberforce a good deal."

"Wilberforce? Never heard of them! Who are they? What can you possibly owe them? Give them a few pounds and come to us! Nothing could be better!"

"No, Anthea. It's impossible."

The same complaining voice that had come from the box earlier now called, "Anthea! What are you doing? For heaven's sake, come along. We're all positively frozen!"

"I have to go, James, but I'll see you tomorrow. Bye!" And she ran off before he could say anything more.

James was walking back to Elisabeth and her father when Wilf trotted up.

"'Ello Gov'nor! I were just comin' to get yer away from that Anthea Whatever'ernameis. I remember she were after yer something terrible couple o' months ago."

"What do you know about it, you scoundrel? Anyway, where were you when you were supposed to be in church?"

"I were in church, God's truth, I were. In th' back. I can't go sitting up front with the toffs. Miss all the fun!"

"What fun? Church isn't supposed to be fun."

"If yer a toff, it ain't, but fer the likes o' me it's all right!"

"I hope you haven't been picking people's pockets."

This was a profession Wilf used to engage in when he was on the streets, and James had a hard time breaking him of it.

"On me honor, I ain't, Guv'nor! No, I were a-cuddlin' a female, that's what. She give me the eye in church and we met up out back after."

"Good God! I'd no idea you were in the petticoat line."

"I ain't a patch on you, but I gets about."

"Well, be careful. We don't want a lot of brats running around the place."

"Don't you worry 'bout me, Guv'nor. Look after yer own self. That Anthea, she'll get 'er 'ooks in if she can."

James remembered Elisabeth's laughing remarks about the ivy, how it was smooth on the outside but had little gripping claws underneath.

He gave a bark of laugher. "I'm a hard man to hook," he said, but then, catching up with Miss Elisabeth Wilberforce, he thought, *but it depends on the ivy.*

Chapter Eight

They walked back in the same configuration as they had come, Elisabeth taking James' arm and her father leaning on Wilf.

"I take it that young lady – I think you called her Anthea – is a friend from London?" began Elizabeth. "And I heard her call you James. You didn't give us your Christian name, and I wondered why. Then I thought perhaps it was something odd like Ezekial or Thor or Marmaduke."

James laughed. "I have a friend called Marmaduke. Is it an odd name? I've never thought about it. We all call him Duke. He isn't, though. A Duke, I mean." He hesitated and seemed to be about to add something, but then said, "But I like Thor. I wouldn't mind being called that."

"It would be hard if you were a dull, unprepossessing sort of boy, though."

Like the curate, thought James, and couldn't help asking, "What is the curate's name?"

"Oh, I see," she replied, smiling at him. "That's what you think of him."

"I think he's unworthy of you."

"His name is Ernest and it suits him. He has a very good opinion of himself. Won't that do?"

"No. You deserve better."

"The trouble is," she said softly, "In this village there is nobody better. I am a woman of twenty-four, moderately good-looking but with no money and a father I cannot leave by himself. Where do you think I'll find someone else to take me on?"

He tried to find a way to respond to that, but couldn't, so said nothing.

"Coming back to Anthea," said Elisabeth after a pause. "I take it you are good friends? She called you darling."

"I don't know what to say without sounding like a poltroon. Yes, I know her. Yes, she calls me darling but I do not call her the same. Does that answer the question?"

"You mean, she wants you but you don't want her?"

"If your father was as direct as you," said James Fortescue, "I can see how he got into trouble."

"Oh, when you live in the country amongst very literal-minded people, you get used to being direct. When we first moved here, before we had our own hens, we used to buy from a farmer's wife who invariably gave us cracked eggs. My mother said, 'Mrs. Jones, your eggs are excellent, but several I bought last week were somewhat damaged'. But the next time, it was just the same, and the time after. So when she came to deliver her eggs the time after that, I said, 'We will pay you after we've examined the eggs. If any are broken, we will refuse to take them all.' And they were, so we did. She never gave us broken eggs again."

"You drive a hard bargain, Miss Wilberforce," James smiled.

413

"I hope I never have to do business with you."

By now they were approaching the front door of the cottage. "The only business we have before us, Mr. James Fortescue," she said with a laugh, "is to bring in the Yule Log. You will not disappoint me, I hope."

"Not if I can help it," he replied, "but what is it?"

"It's a very big log we put on the fire on Christmas Eve and hope to keep burning till New Year's Day. The tradition is that it will bring luck and prosperity. I cannot say it's ever been visibly successful, but on the other hand, who knows if things would have been worse if we hadn't done it. That's the thing about traditions – we keep them up because we don't dare not to! One of the trees at the bottom of the garden was hit by lightning in September and a big branch fell down. I paid one of the farm lads to trim it, but now we have to drag it in. We'd best do it straight away, while we have our coats on."

"Show me the way to this magical log!"

It was not an easy job, not so much because the log was from an oak tree and very heavy, but because it was almost five feet long and unwieldy. But between them, Wilf and James pulled it through the kitchen and into the main room. Elisabeth had deliberately let the fire die down before they went to church, so they rolled it onto the now smoldering coals.

"Wilf, please watch it doesn't flame up," said Elisabeth. "We need it to just smolder and not be consumed. Mr. Fortescue and I are going to take the hot bricks up to the beds."

"He ain't rightly *Mister* Fortescue," said Wilf, but met such a quelling look from his master that he closed his mouth firmly.

"What did he mean?" asked Elisabeth busily wrapping up the

warm bricks she had placed in the kitchen hearth before leaving for church.

"I don't listen to him. He has odd fancies. Just ignore him like I do."

"But you gave him such a look!"

"Because I'm tired of his nonsense. He was flirting with one of the village maidens when he should have been paying attention in church."

Elisabeth laughed. "What fun! Better than listening to the vicar. I swear, he gives the same sermon every Christmas. Besides, everyone has the right to a little nonsense now and then! Can you carry two of these?" She gave him two bricks.

"All three, if you like."

"Now you're just showing off!"

Since Mr. Fortescue was a keen amateur boxer and regularly trained with heavy sandbags, he could have easily taken them all, but he just smiled. Elisabeth realized that the petulant look he'd had about the mouth when he arrived had disappeared. But, she reflected, the less he smiled at her like that, the better for her poor heart.

Chapter Nine

Elisabeth brought down some quilts for Wilf, who had been prepared to stay awake all night watching the Yule Log.

"You don't need to do that!" she said. "You need your sleep as much as the rest of us. How else will you have the energy to pursue the village maidens?"

"Me, persoo them? Not on yer life, Miss. They wants me, they'll 'ave to come and persoo me."

She laughed.

"For heaven's sake don't encourage him," said Mr. Fortescue. "The last thing I need is having to deal with his amatory adventures!"

You're busy enough with your own, it seems, thought Elisabeth, though that did not make her laugh.

They all went upstairs soon after. Mr. Fortescue sank with gratitude into his bed, his feet against the warm brick. He lay in the candlelight for a few minutes, looking around the low, timbered ceiling that sloped almost to the floor on the front side of the cottage. The nightgown behind the door was gone. He could hear muffled voices from the other bedroom and imagined Elisabeth wearing it, climbing into her narrow bed and wishing her father goodnight. Then, except for the occasional scratching from the small animals who made their home in the thatch, it was very quiet.

This was a peace Mr. Fortescue rarely experienced at home in London, where outside the streets were hardly ever silent, and inside the servants, who slept on the top floor of the house, seemed to be always on the move. It took an army of them to keep everything going. How did Miss Wilberforce – Elisabeth – manage? There was a maid, apparently, but her absence was hardly noticed. He was used to a host of helpers: people to prepare his food, wash and iron his clothes, brush his boots – even to help him dress – then make his bed, clean his rooms… dammit, he hadn't even been able to pack his bag properly! For the first time in his life, he realized he was almost as helpless as a babe. It was a sobering thought and one he pondered for some time before falling into a dreamless sleep.

Quiet it might be in the country at night, but morning was a different matter. He was woken by the cocks crowing as soon as day began to break, and not long after he heard someone descending the stairs. He guessed it must be Elisabeth, for her father did not seem the type to bestir himself. Soon after he heard Wilf's voice, and then Elisabeth's, though not clearly enough to understand the words. Then he heard her laugh. He lay in bed wondering what to do. He couldn't appear downstairs without getting dressed, and he couldn't get dressed without first shaving. But to shave he needed hot water. There was of course no bell rope to pull for service. Should he just shout for Wilf from his bedroom door? He decided no: Mr. Wilberforce might still be sleeping, and anyway, that seemed unmannerly. He would just stay where he was, though it confirmed the conclusion he had come to the night before: he was helpless.

He was just beginning to think he would have to ignore good manners and shout, when after a brief knock, Wilf appeared at the door with an enamel ewer in his hand.

"Miss 'Lizbeth said to bring yer 'ot water to shave an' says yer welcome t'stay in bed. Just call down when yer wants breakfast."

"Please thank her and say I'll be down in about forty minutes but please not to do anything that she would not normally do for breakfast."

"Don't know 'bout that, Guv'nor. She's cut some bacon off a flitch she's got in th' larder and she' a–mixin' up somethin' in the kitchen. I'm orf t' get some eggs from the 'en 'ouse."

Mr. Fortescue's stomach growled at the idea of bacon and eggs. He was hungry, he realized.

"Once you've got the eggs, see what you can do with these boots." He thrust his Hessians at Wilf. "But if Miss Wilberforce needs you, help her first. The boots can wait."

It was over forty minutes before Mr. Fortescue appeared downstairs. He sniffed appreciatively at the smell of bacon and coffee, though he felt he hardly deserved it. He had actually attempted to make his bed, something he had never done in his life. But nothing he did seemed to make the covers lie as smoothly as they had before he'd got into bed. He was also ashamed of the creases in his clothes and the imperfectly cleaned boots that Wilf had brought back.

His hostess seemed to notice nothing. She was once again enveloped in her large apron, and the same brown and yellow gown as the day before. Her curls were springing forth from loose braids and her face was pink from standing over the fire.

"Happy Christmas Day, Mr. Fortescue! I hope you slept well?" she said gaily. "Please sit down at the table. I'm just going to take a tray up to Papa. He likes to read in bed in the mornings and frankly, I find it easier to do the housework without him underfoot. Then I'll bring in your breakfast."

"My best wishes to you, Miss Wilberforce and yes, I was very comfortable. I hope the same can be said of you. I am more than ever conscious of your goodness in taking in strangers at this time of the year when you have no one to help you in the house. May I at least take that up for you?"

"But Christmas is the perfect time of year to welcome strangers! And thank you, that would be very kind. I'll fry your eggs while you take father's tray up. Assuming you'd like eggs?"

"I would. I'm unusually hungry this morning. But I hope you haven't gone to any special lengths for me. I would be happy with anything." This from a man who, when his eggs were not exactly as he required them, regularly told his butler to go to the devil and take that damned mess with him.

"But it's Christmas Day! If we don't go to special length today, then when?"

"I hope at least you will sit and eat with me. I could not be comfortable being waited on."

"I shall. Wilf has eaten and is very kindly bringing in wood for the fires. Look! The Yule Log did just as we hoped. It just smoldered and can now sit at the back of the hearth until we bring it forward again tonight. Wilf has been so helpful with the fires! He's not big, but he's strong! You must value his service."

Mr. Fortescue rarely thought about Wilf at all, except to give him orders about the horses, but he said, "Er, yes. He's very willing." And as he said it, he realized this was so. His tiger didn't, in fact, need to be told what to do. He was always one step ahead. His master now wondered why he hadn't noticed that before.

He followed his hostess into the kitchen, with its wonderful breakfast smells, and received the tray for Mr. Wilberforce. Apart from eggs and bacon, there was a roll, a dish of butter and another of jam, a jug of coffee, a smaller one of cream and a dish of sugar. Elisabeth saw him looking at the tray and said, "We don't have jam and coffee every day, but for Christmas morning, I'm afraid we do rather spoil ourselves."

"It all looks delicious," replied Mr. Fortescue. His hunger had now reached raging proportions, exacerbated by looking at the tray. He had never looked forward to a meal so much in his life.

Mr. Wilberforce was inclined to want to talk, but their visitor excused himself on the grounds that his own breakfast was on the table, so it was only a few minutes later that he was downstairs again. He walked into the kitchen. Wilf was stacking logs in the alcove next to the hearth and hailed him.

"'Ello Guv'nor! You're up early. I ain't never seen you about this time of the mornin' afore."

"What nonsense!" replied his master with some heat, annoyed at being shown up for the sluggard he in fact was, "I'm often up betimes. To go to Gentleman Jackson's, or exercise the horses, for example. Stop telling such tales and get on with your work."

Wilf muttered something under his breath and Elisabeth laughed as she carried plates of food into the main room.

"An interesting difference of opinion," she said.

Chapter Ten

The breakfast was as delicious as Mr. Fortescue had envisioned. The coffee was hot, the eggs perfect, the bacon crisp at the edges and the rolls warm. He ate two from the basket and had to restrain himself from taking another.

"These are wonderful," he said. "Did you make them?"

"Yes, or rather, Mary made the dough and put it in the larder before she left. I put it out to rise by the hearth overnight. All I had to do was punch it down, knead it again and let it rise a second time before baking. As I said, Wilf was a great help. He dealt with the fires while I did the rolls. There's nothing better than warm bread, is there? Please help yourself. There are more in the kitchen."

He broke down and took a third roll, noticing, however, that Elisabeth ate only sparingly: only one egg to his two and one rasher of bacon to his three. He wondered to what extent he and Wilf were literally eating into her budget. Should he offer her money? After all, if they had stayed at an inn, he would have paid his shot. But every feeling rebelled at the idea. He didn't know what to do.

They had finished breakfast and Mr. Fortescue was staring into the fire, still wondering what to do about paying Elisabeth, when a knock came at the door. It was the wheelwright. He was on his way to pick up the broken-down phaeton. He'd decided to get it early and hopefully work on it after dinner. The loss of his day off was well worth the price he'd been promised for an early completion of the job, and he wanted to demonstrate his keenness to his customer.

Mr. Fortescue declared he'd go with him. A good walk would help him mull over his knotty problem. He shrugged on his caped coat and with Wilf trying to keep up with his long strides, walked back to where they had left the mangled phaeton.

Elisabeth was glad of the opportunity to use her bedroom to wash and change. She smiled at Mr. Fortescue's attempts to make the bed, and was torn between re-making it and leaving it alone. In the end, she left it, not wanting her visitor to think his work unsatisfactory.

Persuading herself that one should look one's best on Christmas Day, and refusing to admit she was doing it for Mr. Fortescue's sake, she put on the best of her day dresses, or at least, the one of her mother's gowns she thought she had most successfully altered. Luckily, she and her mother were much of a size, and the gown fit her well. She was aware the current mode was for much narrower skirts falling from beneath the bosom, with no waist to speak of, but she was an indifferent seamstress and her work had been limited to taking some of the fullness out of the voluminous skirts that were in style when her mother had bought them. So the gown still fit to the waist and, with its full sleeves, it was quite unlike those in the *Mode Illustrées*. But any other modification was beyond her capacities.

She had no full-length mirror in the house, and could not see how well, in fact, the style became her. The gown showed her trim waist and shapely bosom and the fine deep red wool set off the russet tints of her brown curls. She was going to confine her hair in the braids she usually wore wrapped in bands around her head, but, once again using Christmas Day as an excuse, decided to tie it up with a ribbon. She had bought the ribbon in the summer from an itinerant peddler because it was precisely the same color as her gown, but she'd never before worn it. Knowing her heavy hair had a will of its own, she anchored the topknot with several pins and hoped it would hold.

She had just finished her *toilette* when a knock came at the door. She sighed in irritation. It must be the curate. He had said he would be coming at two o'clock but was evidently too eager to wait. She was glad her father was still in his room and would not be available for the *few words* Mr. Pounds had so confidently expected. She took another quick look in the mirror, tucked away an errant curl and went downstairs to answer the door.

To her astonishment, on the doorstep stood not Mr. Pounds, but the young woman who had called Mr. Fortescue *darling* the night before.

"Mi...Miss..." stammered Elisabeth, feeling the woman's eyes run up and down her body.

"Brookstone. Anthea Brookstone." The young woman didn't extend her hand or offer any greeting, but simply stood, obviously waiting to be invited in.

"Ah, yes. Please come in, Miss Brookstone." Elisabeth stood back and allowed the visitor to push past her.

She was wearing a very modish pink pelisse and matching bonnet. The fact that it was entirely unsuitable for the season and the country setting did not prevent her from looking very pretty. Elisabeth, who just a few moments before had been quite pleased with her appearance, suddenly felt unstylish and dowdy.

"Is Lord Northney here?" enquired the visitor haughtily.

"Who?" Elisabeth felt stupid. Who was Lord Northney and why should he be there?

"Lord Northney. He told me last night he was staying here."

"The only person staying here is Mr. Fortescue. Well, and his tiger, Wilf."

"Yes, exactly, James Fortescue, the Earl of Northney. Is he here?"

"Mr. Fortescue is the Earl of Northney?" The scales fell from Elisabeth's eyes. So that's why he seemed so very superior, so accustomed to command. He was a Lord! Suddenly, she was very angry. Why hadn't he told her? Did he think she was too inferior to even be told his title?

"Of course." Anthea Brookstone's voice cut through her tumbled thoughts. "Well? Is he here? Either he is or he isn't. The answer can't require so much thought!"

"No, he is not," replied Elisabeth curtly. "He went to supervise the loading of his broken-down phaeton. If you didn't pass him with the wheelwright on your way through the village, he must be still up there, or perhaps by now on his way back. If you walk up the road you will probably run into him."

She opened the door and all but pushed Anthea outside.

That lady stood looking with astonishment at the door closing behind her. Why, one could almost imagine that Miss Wilberforce, in her out-of-date gown and tumbling down hair, had wanted to get rid of her. What on earth had made James imagine he owed her and her father anything? She was nothing but an ill-bred, ignorant country girl. She hadn't even offered her any refreshment. Not that she would have taken it in a place like that – it looked as if they lived and dined all in one room – but it should have been offered. Really, the lower classes didn't know their place these days!

Anthea stalked back to her gig where she had told her maid to wait. She hadn't wanted her snooping on her imagined *tête à tête* with James. She climbed in without a word, took the up the reins and clicked the horse into a trot. They hadn't gone more than a few hundred yards when she saw them: the wheelwright leading a huge carthorse pulling a long, low trailer on which a high-perch phaeton lay on its side, and walking next to him, James Fortescue, Earl of Northney. A small person was trotting along behind him, giving shrill commands to the wheelwright to watch what he were a-doin' and not break 'is lordship's phae'on any more than it were broke already.

She drew the gig to a halt as they came abreast of her. "James!" she said, "The girl told me you were here. I've come to pick you up."

Chapter Eleven

Meanwhile, Elisabeth had angrily turned away from the door, ripping out the ribbon from her hair. She immediately went upstairs and brushed it out, redoing her habitual bands around her head. She considered changing her gown, but really couldn't waste any more time. She needed to start making dinner. Her father became confused if he didn't have his meals on time, and it was already gone eleven. They hadn't been able to afford a goose, and she had planned to make a pie with the small amount of beef left over from Christmas Eve. That would have to do, the Earl of Northney or no Earl of Northney. She'd bake it while she was getting the potatoes and cabbage ready. And the curate had said he'd be there at two! She'd forgotten about him. Well, if the dinner was still on the table when he got there, he'd just have to wait.

She ran downstairs, pulled on her big white apron and in a temper, began making the piecrust. She pummeled at the flour and lard on the wooden board until realizing, too late, that she had worked it too hard and too long. It was almost grey. That made her angrier; it would be heavy and unappetizing. *And it was all his fault! The Earl of Northney!* She whacked the ball of pastry onto the table and rolled it out with angry, heavy strokes. *Why hadn't he introduced himself properly from the start?* She plopped half of the pastry in the bottom of the pie plate. *Was she so far beneath him he didn't think her worthy?* She fiercely minced the beef and onion, threw it into the pie plate, doused it with gravy, slapped the top over it, and angrily pricked it with a fork. *Of course, he only let important people know his real name.* That must be it. She rammed the pie into the cast iron baker, slammed on the lid and kicked it into the coals.

"Get off there!" she said to the cat, who was sleeping on top of the sack of potatoes and who, unaccustomed to her tone, leaped off with a hiss. Never have potatoes been peeled with more speed and lack of attention. Eyes were left in and peel hacked off at different depths, resulting in a pile of misshapen, ill-favored objects that only vaguely resembled the familiar vegetable.

"Oh dammit!" she said, and was mortified to hear the astonished voice of her father say from the kitchen door, "What's that dear? What did you say?"

That brought her to her senses. "Oh! nothing, father," she said. "I said 'oh, the darning!' I was just remembering I'd forgotten to do it yesterday afternoon. With Mr. Fortescue arriving as he did, it went out of my head." She couldn't help the scorn in her voice when she said the name.

But her father, for all his vagueness, was sometimes very acute. He came into the kitchen. "Why did you say his name like that?" he asked. "I thought you liked him. He seems a nice enough fellow to me."

"Well, since you ask, Papa," she replied, allowing her wrath to build again, "allow me to inform you that he isn't Mr. Fortescue at all, but My Lord the Earl of Northney. So I have been reliably informed by that Anthea Brookstone who was in church last night. She came looking for him."

"I don't see why that's anything to get so cross about, Elisabeth. The fellow can't help his name."

"CAN'T HELP HIS NAME?" For the first time in her life, Elisabeth raised her voice to her father. "No, he can't, but he can at least tell people what it is, so people don't think he's just a well-mannered and rather attractive ordinary person. So people don't start liking him without even knowing who he is. So people don't begin having false hopes," she ended, dropping her voice to a whisper.

Her father looked at her oddly. "He must have had his reasons. He probably didn't want to puff off his consequence to strangers he met by chance in the country."

Elisabeth had thrown the misshapen potatoes into a pot of water and hung them over the fire. She now took a cabbage and cut it in half with one blow from her sharp kitchen knife. She then proceeded to hack it into small pieces, raising her voice with each movement.

"Because we're too far below him? *Thwack!* Is that it? *Smack!* He doesn't want us to become encroaching? *Chop! Chop! Chop!*"

"Don't be silly, Elisabeth! You are reading too much into it. What does it matter? If we know and like a man as James Fortescue, why should we not know and like him as Earl of Whatever you say he is?"

"Yes, why shouldn't you?" came a well-modulated voice from

behind them. There stood the Earl in his long, caped coat and curly-brimmed beaver. Elisabeth gave such a start, she almost cut off a finger, and the knife clattered to the flag-stoned floor.

Chapter Twelve

J ames had been forced to acknowledge Anthea when she drew up next to them. He wanted nothing more than to see his phaeton safely in the workshop and get back to Elisabeth, but manners obliged him to talk with her for a few moments, and find some convincing explanation why he didn't wish to be taken up in her gig.

"I, er, I want to make sure the wheelwright knows what he's doing," he said, "and I'm, er, expected for dinner with Miss Wilberforce and her father."

He had no idea if this were true, but it seemed plausible. Elisabeth had said they ate their main meal in the middle of the day.

"Oh, pish-posh," said Anthea, airily. "You'll get a much better meal with us. I know for a fact cook has a nice haunch of venison on the spit. Father always likes to keep one for Christmas Day. Ride with me to the wheelwright's and I'll wait for you. Amy can walk." She turned to her maid. "Get down, Amy, Lord Northney is getting up with me. You can walk home. It'll do you good."

Not wanting to cause any sort of scene with so many

interested observers, James reluctantly did as he was bid. It was probably just as well. Once they were out of earshot he could tell Anthea plainly what his intentions were towards her. He had had a flirtation with her a couple of months back but had avoided her recently. She was a lovely girl but, as he had found out, spoiled and unlikeable. He should have set her straight before but had been too lazy to do so. He thought she'd get the message. She hadn't. Evidently, she rated her charms too high.

"This is kind of you, Anthea," he said, turning to look at her, and in spite of what he knew about her, admiring her straight back and calm mastery over the horse, "but I shall have to leave you once we get to the wheelwright's."

"Why, darling? I don't mind waiting for you!" She smiled brilliantly at him.

"As I said, I'm expected back at the Wilberforces'. Besides, Anthea, I have to tell you..."

But before he could continue, Anthea interrupted. "Oh, for heaven's sake! I don't suppose they'll even notice you're not there! I spoke to that girl. She didn't even know who you were! When I asked for the Earl of Northney she looked all at sea. I believe she may be a little simple. And what a sight she presented! Her dress had to be twenty years old and her hair was in a positive shambles!"

The Earl could not let this pass. "They are not people of fortune," he said without the glimmer of a smile, "and Miss Wilberforce is not accustomed to going into society, but I assure you, she is as sensible as you or I. More so, in fact. If she did not know me by my title, the fault is mine. I'm afraid I did not inform her of it."

"I can understand why! People like that are bound to be so encroaching! Anyway, if they are not people of fortune, they will be glad not to have to have an extra mouth to feed. You would be doing them a favor by coming with me."

"Enough!" The Earl's patience was at an end. "Look, Anthea, whether they have no fortune or are as rich as Croesus, whether they go into society or not, whether Miss Wilberforce's gown is from the Ark and her hair like a bird's nest, I am going to have dinner with them. I am going because I want to. I am going because I admire Miss Wilberforce. I may even be in love with her. I'm sure she thinks I am a good-for-nothing, useless sort of a man. And she is right. But I hope to do better. With her help, perhaps I will."

There was complete silence. The Earl was astonished to have said what he did. He had only wanted to inform Anthea tactfully that he was not interested in her. He had no intention of baring his soul. He had no idea what had come over him.

Anthea looked as if someone had struck her in the face, but she was the first to recover. "If that is the case," she said coldly, "you had better descend now. We are just in front of her door." She drew the horse to a halt and waited, her face averted.

"Thank you, Anthea," said the Earl. "I hope we my continue to meet on friendly terms."

"I doubt it," said the lady, and, barely waiting for him to step down, whipped up her horse into a gallop.

Chapter Thirteen

Now, before his startled audience in the kitchen, the Earl came forward in two long strides and picked up the knife she had dropped.

"I collect that unfortunate cabbage was the stand-in for my head," he said, handing it to her. "You seem to have been quite ruthless."

Elisabeth looked at the vegetable that lay in shreds upon the board, then at him, and burst into laughter. "Yes," she said. "I was really very angry, but I'm better now."

"I'm glad," he said, smiling at her, "because I have just made what I think will be a lifelong enemy of another woman. It would be careless of me to lose the affection of two in one day. Anthea Brookstone invited me to their home for dinner, assuring me it would be much better than the one I would get here. But I refused, saying I was coming to dine with you. She was insistent, but I clung to my plan and made her quite cross. You see, my dear Elisabeth, as I told her, I admire you, and may, in fact, even be in love with you."

"Oh," said Elisabeth, her color rising, "I can see why she might have been quite cross. But you may change your mind after you taste the pie and the cabbage. Oh, and the potatoes. They look like misshapen pebbles."

"My absolute favorite sort."

The Earl of Northney put his arms around Elisabeth Wilberforce, still clad in her voluminous apron and her hair curling wildly in the steam from the potatoes. Then he thought again and broke away to take the knife from her hands and lay it on the table.

"Just to be sure," he said, and kissed her.

"Yes," he said, when they broke apart, "I was right. I am in love with you. You will marry me, won't you?"

"Only if Papa may live with us and I never have to chop cabbage again."

"I am delighted with the first and agree wholeheartedly with the second. I shall never be able to look at the vegetable again without feeling distinctly insecure. That is to say," he turned to Elisabeth's father, "if you permit my marrying your daughter, sir?"

"If you really need my permission, my lord," replied the old man, who once again was more acute than anyone realized, "you're not the man I thought you were."

Elisabeth ran and hugged her father, then turned to James.

"Yes, Lord Northney," she said, blushing a little, "I will marry you. But at this moment I must get the dinner on the table."

The men sat down and the wretched meal was served. Its poor preparation made no difference, however, since James and Elisabeth, smiling stupidly at each other, hardly tasted a mouthful.

They had just finished when a sharp knock came at the cottage door.

"Oh Lord!" said Elisabeth, coming to earth with a bump, "It's the curate! Now we are in the basket!"

"Not a bit of it," said the Earl. "Leave it to me. Stay where you are." He went to the door and flung it open.

"Come in, come in," he said to a bewildered Mr. Pounds, who had expected Elisabeth, but found himself facing the tall, commanding stranger he vaguely remembered from the night before. "How kind of you to be the first to congratulate us!" He extended his hand, which from force of habit, the curate took.

"C...congratulate you?" he stammered.

"Yes, Miss Wilberforce has just now agreed to become my wife, though how you knew about it so fast is beyond me. Divine intervention, no doubt."

"W...wife? B...but..."

"Of course! But you hoped to marry her! In the ecclesiastical sense, of course. That is to say, officiate at her wedding. But, my dear sir, you may still do so. At least, the Bishop will want to conduct the ceremony, but I hope you will agree to be co-officiant. This falls well, for I believe a nice living in my gift has just become available. In Richmond. A very pleasant place. I am Northney, you know. The Earl."

The curate, his head swimming from the swift passage of his ideas from marrying Elisabeth himself, to officiating at her wedding with a Bishop and taking up a post in one of the most desirable parishes in the kingdom, nodded dumbly.

"We can settle the details later, but thank you again for being the first to wish us joy."

He ushered the man inexorably to the door. The whole interview, if such it could be called, since one participant had scarcely spoken a word, had taken less than five minutes.

Elisabeth had brought her hand to her mouth, barely able to contain her giggles, and as the door closed behind the bewildered curate, she burst into laughter. "Oh, James! That was priceless." She imitated his voice, "'I am Northney, you know. The Earl.' You sounded so pompous!"

Then she sobered up. "Now I remember! When you arrived, you hesitated before saying your name. I thought it was a bit odd at the time, but I see now you were trying to decide what to call yourself."

"Yes, I was. You see, in London and at our places in the country I never have to tell anyone my name. They know me and I know them. Fortescue is the family name, but since my father died no one has called me that. My close friends call me James or Jim and the not so close call me Northney. Even when I go abroad I see the same people. I've never ventured outside the same group. It's idiotic. I didn't want to give you my title. As you say, it's unbearably pompous. When you first called me Mr. Fortescue it sounded odd to my ears, but by then it would have been even worse to tell you I'm not Mister anything. Wilf tried to say something, but I shut him up. I'm sorry. Just call me James and we can both be happy."

"So it wasn't because you thought we were so beneath you? I slaughtered the potatoes and cabbage for nothing?"

James laughed. "Of course not! I thought you adorable with the smudge on your face. Then I found you were amazingly kind and hospitable. You are lovely, you know, inside and out, especially wearing an apron and with your curls springing loose from their bands. Like now."

Elisabeth looked down at herself. "Oh, I forgot to take off my apron before sitting down!" she cried. "And I know my hair is a mess. I just can't manage it. How am I ever going to learn to be a Countess?"

"I don't want you to learn. I want you to be just as you are. Your curls can do what they like. The only thing you have to manage is me. And since I saw you with that knife, I know you can."

The Earl took his wife-to-be in his arms and was kissing her again when there was an eruption in the kitchen and Wilf appeared.

"Sorry to interrupt yer kissin' and cuddlin', me lord," he said "but I went to the wheelwright's like you said. But seein' as you wasn't there, I thought you'd a-gone wiv that Anthea, so I walks over there along o' Amy, 'er maid. I 'ung around a bit but then Amy come down and told me 'er mistress was mad as fire, throwin' 'er togs all over the place, she was. Yellin' that you was goin' t' marry 'er but changed yer mind."

"I was never going to marry her. I made her no promises and told her no lies. In fact, I'm going to marry Miss Wilberforce."

"Thank Gawd! She's a bang-up mort and no mistake."

"I'm glad she meets with your approval," said his lord-ship dryly.

"Yer not the only one lookin' to be under the cat's paw," said Wilf, ignoring him. "I don't say as 'ow I might not be joinin' yer. That Amy 'as caught me, right and proper, she 'as."

"Oh, Wilf!" cried Elisabeth. "Are we to wish you joy, too?"

437

"Not yet a while, Miss. I needs time to see. I'm not like 'is lordship, like a butterfly from one to t'other!"

"A butterfly, eh?" said Miss Wilberforce. "They are known to be attracted to cabbage. But I know how to deal with that."

The End

Glynis Louise Robinson is from Portsmouth in southern England but has lived in the USA for over forty years with her American husband. Her romances are written in memory of her dear sister Francine, who died unexpectedly in 2018. They were both in a convent boarding school as girls and used to giggle at romances under the covers after lights out. GL is retired after a career as a French professor. She likes gardening (except for weeding!), reading in bed, having tea parties with her grandchildren and boiled eggs for breakfast at the weekends!

Scan the QR code to go to her website at romancenovelsbyglrobinson. com, where you can sign up to her email list and find out how to receive a free copy of *The Earl and the Mud-Covered Maiden*.

If you enjoyed these stories, please take a moment to leave a review on Amazon or Goodreads, or anywhere else you'd like! Reviews are extremely important for authors, and we so appreciate your taking the time to leave one.

———— · ————

Thank you for spending time with us in our Regency world! We hope you have thoroughly enjoyed yourself in reading as we have in writing these stories. Please feel free to join us again in our other books and series!

Printed in Great Britain
by Amazon